PURPLE WINGS

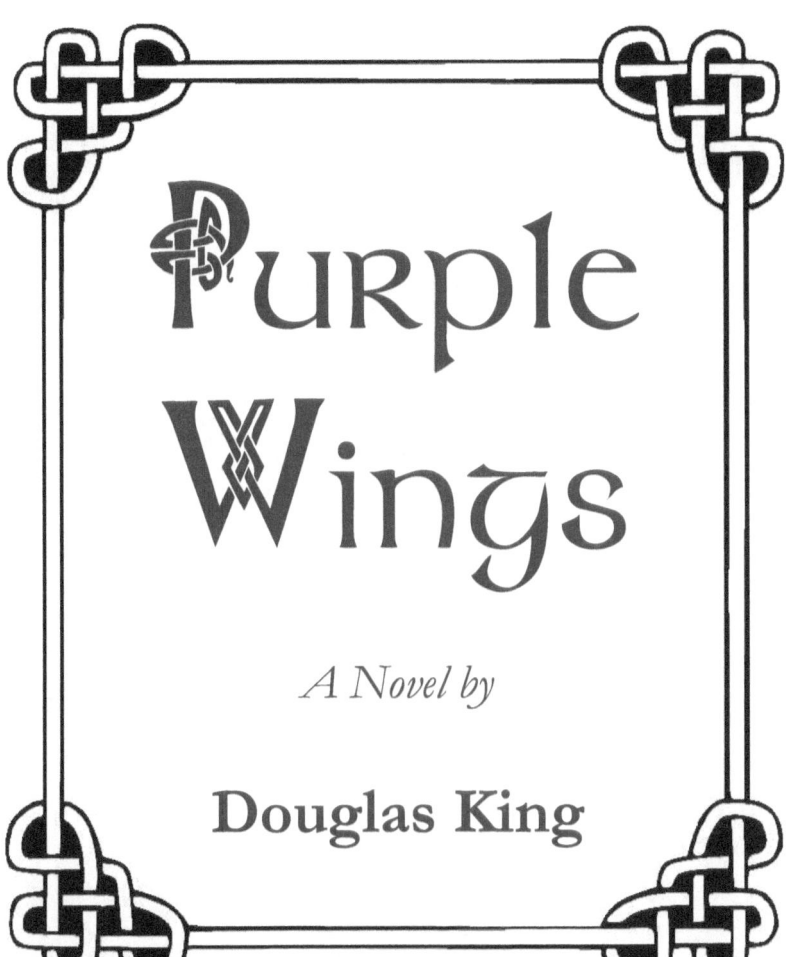

Purple Wings

A Novel by

Douglas King

E-PRIDE Books

Copyright © 2015 Douglas King

ISBN 978-0-9882671-4-5

First Edition
10 9 8 7 6 5 4 3 2

To Nolan
Bealtaine Grá fhaigheann tú

Come away, O human child!
To the waters and the wild
With a faery hand in hand,
For the world's more full of
   weeping than you can understand.

William Butler Yeats, *The Stolen Child*

A Word about Fairies and Gaelic

The author apologizes to fairy purists as he has taken many liberties with the received mythology. I do use the older convention of referring to this race of otherness as *Fey* in the noun and *Fei* in the adjective. However, any dive into the supernatural requires a suspension of belief to some extent, just as much as any religion requires some suspension of modern world view. Who's to say that my views on the *Fey* are any less true than anyone else's beliefs? Faith never requires scriptures. As for my samplings of the beautiful Irish Gaelic tongue, I make no apologies. I have tried diligently to imply the meanings of the Gaelic used when I thought it necessary. If you need someone to blame, blame the internet. Like any good modern author, that's where I turned for answers, and so should any of the literalists or just curious among you. If I got any of it wrong, well . . . *cac**!

* Irish Gaelic word which translates
to something approximating shit

Douglas King
is also the author of
The Q Factor, The High Range,
The Fabergé Conspiracy, **and**
The Sucession.
He works as a medical investigator
and lives in Beaumont, Texas.

Prologue

My name is Ron. Well, Oberon, actually. By the goddess, who would ever name a boy-child, Oberon? Some Shakespeare-obsessed actor wannabe, I guess. But what adolescent male can make it through high school being called . . . Oberon? The name is strange enough that at least one tech-nerd would Google it and . . . yeah . . . which of them could help—could resist the relishing responsibility to report to all the other males. Oberon was King of the Fairies . . . or in the old stories King of the *Fey*. Oberon was *Fey*. Rhymes with gay. OMG! Thanks mom and dad— whoever you . . . were. Thanks bunches!

No one really knows if I'm an orphan or not. It was enough that I was put up for adoption— well, to be honest, it was more like I was left on Mab Maguire's doorstep— literally—and she adopted me. Now, if you think being called Oberon, King of the . . . you know . . . Well, even that pales to being the adopted son of the *craziest* woman in Ennis. Herbalist, seer, fortune teller . . . let's be frank . . . witch—definitely someone who practiced the Old Religion, and much to the distress of Father Hugh. Roman Catholicism is the antithesis of religious tolerance. Still, the same ones who loyally attended weekly Mass at St. Brigid's, were the same ones who would go to Mab Maguire to stock up on herbal teas for potency, for pregnancy, or for contraception, as well as talismans, and spells for love, for materialism, for political gain, and for cursing an enemy. It wasn't that the citizens of Ennis decried the use of modern drugs and medical acumen, so much as an inherent duality of faith. Even Doc Curtis recommended Mab's chamomile and cinnamon tea for stomach ache.

Growing up with an honest-to-goddess practicing Wiccan was fun and daring for a child—dancing naked in the moonlight on Walpurgis Night, singing child-like chants around the goddess fire on Beltane, and gaining the reputation of psychic prodigy . . . but, puberty changes everything. What was once fun becomes . . . embarrassment. Let's not even talk about dancing naked in the moonlight—with your mom—your *old* mom—and her *old* coven sisters! Not to mention the shame of standing apart as *different* from everyone else—at a time when fitting in, being accepted by your peers, being *normal* was the goal— the obsession!

I didn't fit in. I didn't belong. I have not been able to find or accept my place in the archetypical scheme of life. The looks—the stares—the fears—it drives a late-blooming teen to withdraw—to separate himself even more. I had no control over what I was. I couldn't help that I could *see* what others couldn't even imagine.

My name is Oberon—but only my dog can call me that . . . and yes, I can understand what animals speak. Anyway, for now it's Ron to you . . . Ron Maguire.

So you want to see what I can see. You want to feel . . . to experience another wedge of the universe that I have come to call my other home. You want to understand things that cannot possibly be incorporated into your modern world view—a view devoid of true spirituality or any true sense of what reality is? You asked for it. Come on. I'm gonna rock your world! *Go maire tú!*

Chapter 1

Bolcán studied the position, shape, and pigmentation of the steaming entrails splayed before him on the obsidian-colored slab of ferrum that dominated the central dome of the temple, dedicated to the destroyer goddess, *Caillech*. The air teemed with acrid smoke and particulate billowing from the nearby sacred fire that consumed the annointed haruspex's previous eight attempts to divine the meaning of the rumors that had recently come to the *Tionál*, the ruling elven assembly. A *Fei* presence had entered the world of men—the one food that the Great Lord *Salach* craved. This rumored, rogue fairy meant that the long-thought extinct *Tuatha* lived, hidden among the worlds—those infinite places of being ordered by the ineffable father-god *Dagda* at the beginning of time.

Bolcán poked at the fetid guts and offal with his talon, annoyed that he might need to eviscerate yet another troll spawn, and then he saw it. The tell-tale markings, the mottled petechiae written by fate across the greying liver—a rune confirming Bolcán's worst suspicion. Lord Salach would reward his dark talents—even more so if Bolcán could speed up the retrieval process.

He threw his head back.

"*Phooka*!" Bolcán shouted, invoking the drove of

beast-like but obedient goblins into being. "*Teacht an seo!*"

The vaulting space erupted in a conflagration of chaotic wind and a wreath of dark, fathomless forms quickly surrounded him. Bolcán looked over his assembled pets with great pleasure. They would not fail him.

He waved his clawed hand above the entrails on the altar and a wee point of light was pulled up from out the once hidden signets. Frightened by this horror of brightness, the dark creatures about him retreated to the edges of the sanctuary.

"*Eistigi liom!*" Bolcán commanded and the creatures stopped their retreat from the paining light. "Find it!"

Bolcán's voice echoed off the surrounding stones.

"Bring it here! Alive!"

His great, skin-like wings unfolded, and as he gestured, the meager point of light drifted out to his goblins.

"Sense it! Learn it! Find it!"

The pinpoint of light floated out into the surrounding space. One by one, the black creatures took their turn approaching it, smelling it, absorbing its vibration and wavelength until it was no more.

"*Ar an dul!*" Bolcán ordered. "Go now!"

The circle of dark forms dissolved into the oppressing smoke and Bolcán smiled bearing his crooked fangs. He would have laughed if he had any concept of the emotion. It was enough that he was satisfied. The evil he had unleashed would enter the unbounded world of men and bring the *Fey* to his Lord. They would soon know where the *Tuatha* were hiding, and the feasting would be great!

Bolcán flexed his unfeathered wings and rose above the smoke. He must report his discovery. The Great Lord would be pleased—very pleased.

The narrow Rocky Mountain valley that harbored the hamlet of Ennis, British Columbia, accepted the benign fog that descended every night from the surrounding peaks, moistening the blades of emerald green grass that blanketed the yards of its citizens and its surrounding hills. The region's verdant shades were strikingly reminiscent of the ancestral Irish lands for which almost every soul in Ennis embraced a genealogical claim.

While the "old ways" were still remembered in the mythology of its inhabitants, Ennis had increasingly become arrayed in the trappings of modern life. Its antique cinema headlined the latest Hollywood offerings. Its radio station proffered the tuneless drone of Z-generation rap and the screaming scat-songs of the current R&B divas. The younger set donned whatever peer-approved grunge or butt-sagging pants fashion was the rage. The worst fact of life for the village teens was the complete lack of cellphone signal—except for the one "rich" kid who sported a satellite phone as the ultimate status symbol. Satellite television kept the teens connected to their zeitgeist and modern world view.

Still, the myths managed to persist. The old superstitions were still practiced, if not devoutly, then out of habit. Most every yard had its mountain ash and hawthorn trees, and the gardens their share of patches of clover, daisies, and St. John's wort. An iron gate was a prized possession, and the symbols of Celtic heritage were worn in gold and silver effigy about the necks of both sexes. While the pews of the old, stone Roman Church of St. Brigid's were sparsely populated at any given offering of Mass, God help the

Ennis child that would even consider marrying outside the Faith.

No confirmed history could explain how the small Irish settlement had come to be so far from the Atlantic Coast of Canada. It was thought to be one of the many results of the Great Potato Famine that drove so many from the motherland in the mid-eighteen hundreds. Still, an Irish presence was suspected, if not known, to pre-date that traumatic event. Parish baptismal records dated to a time a hundred and fifty years earlier, and the oral traditions offered little about Ennis' origins.

It was a May Day tradition at St. Brigid's Regional High School for senior boys to hike up into the mountains for an overnight of camping and retreat, which the participants usually interpreted to mean illicitly obtained beer and whiskey, junk food, and campfire tales of sexual prowess and soccer field bravery. And so it was on this May Day, that Ron Maguire (no one dared call him by his birth-name, Oberon), his Irish setter Rory, his best friend Collin O'Quinn, and the other four male seniors raced up the mountain trails, trying to get as far from Ennis as a day's trek could take them.

"Hurry up, ladies!" shouted the muscular giant in the lead. "I'd like to get there before we have to come back!"

Nolan Reid was a swarthy, brown-headed adolescent at six-foot-three. His stride was twice that of most of the other teens who clamored along behind him trying to keep up over the path of glacial rock that peppered the floor of the forested mountain side.

"Slow down, Nolan!" yelled Ron from the rear of the caravan. "The others can't keep up with you."

This was not a problem for Ron whose height and build in the past year had blossomed dramatically.

"We'll get there long before dark," said the fiery redhead, Collin O'Quinn.

He had been Ron's best friend since third grade. His white, freckled skin gleamed in the isolated rays of sunlight that penetrated the loblolly canopy overhead.

"O'Quinn, you little fag!" Nolan shouted back at him. "You should let Maguire carry you!"

Collin stopped, pulling himself up to his full height of five-feet-five.

"The only reason you can move so fast, Reid," Collin said, "is because there's nothing between your legs to get in the way."

The other boys laughed nervously, waiting to see what reaction would explode out of Nolan.

"Fuck you!" Nolan called back over his shoulder.

"Suck my man-dick, boy!" Collin shouted back.

He could get away with it. He was small in stature, but incredibly blessed by the goddess in the cock department. None of the soccer team felt secure showering anywhere near Collin O'Quinn—unless of course you wanted to leave with a heavy sense of emasculation and penis envy.

Nolan stopped. His hunched shoulders indicated Collin's last comment had struck a nerve.

Nolan spun around and bore down on the smaller man-boy. "Your smartass mouth is gonna—"

"Keep on climbing, Nolan," Ron said, stepping up in front of Collin.

Ron was an equal match to Nolan's musculature, but the growling, fang-bearing animal beside Ron made up for any difference there might have been.

Ron smiled down at his dog.

"*Ta athas fearg*," the dog's mind growled to no one in particular.

Ron understood the Gaelic, having spoken nothing but the ancient tongue at home for as long as he could remember.

"I know he's made you angry, Rory, but I think I can handle this."

Ron looked up at Nolan with a menacing smile. He ran a hand through his own, thick auburn hair, before planting himself, hands on hips, between Collin and the hot-tempered Nolan.

"You'd best keep your boyfriend's mouth in check, Maguire," Nolan said, not wanting to test the match of man and dog.

"Boyfriend?" Collin bristled like a bantam rooster. "I'll show you—"

"Sheath your sword, Collin." Ron punched his friend in the arm. "You both need to chill," he said, trying to lighten the situation, "or get laid or jerk-off more!"

"Collin'll win that match," said Dylan Higgins, shaking the sweat out of his long, ash blonde locks. "He was the Grand Circle Jerk champion in seventh grade!"

They all laughed.

"Well," said Ron, shaking his head at his friend, "I guess that's as good an explanation as any for how Little Collin got stretched into Big Collin."

"Hey!" Collin backed away, raising his hands into the air as if to accept applause. "Whatever works!" He gestured toward his groin, "and believe me—it works!"

"You should see Father Hugh when he comes out of the confessional with Collin," said Kane Casey, the last senior in the group. "He has that look that only bottomless shots of Bushmills can relieve."

Another chorus of laughter pushed them farther up the mountainside.

"How much farther?" Dylan asked, with a lazy groan.

"Almost there," Nolan called back, having reasserted his lead. "Keep your skirt up."

The rocks littering the steep incline became boulders, and in the final hundred feet to the mountain ridge, the boulders became house-sized blocks of weathered, rounded granite. A constricted path curled between two rocky monoliths up to a deceptively level section of densely forested land, bordered by giant walls of granite. The boys made their way to the one sunny spot, circled by a stand of aspen. In the center was a man-made circle of stones containing ashes of decades of senior camp-outs.

"Dibs on the hammock trees," Collin yelled as he pulled Ron along to their chosen campsite near two, low, thick-trunked aspens.

Their bark was permanently scarred in rings where a succession of boys had hung a sleeping hammock.

The other boys staked their own claims to campsites and began the work of unloading backpacks and erecting their tents. The three tents were conveniently sited at the vertices of an equilateral triangle about the center fire pit.

"Foley, you'd better have remembered the hotdogs," Nolan said, as he assembled a pile of dead sticks he had scavenged into the fire pit. "Otherwise you're going back for them."

"Don't worry," Kane Foley responded, rummaging through his back pack nervously. "They're in here." He pulled a small cold pack out of his bag. "Got 'em!"

"What about the buns?" Nolan asked, without looking up from the now crackling fire he had started.

"But . . ."

Kane froze, staring at the cold pack of wieners in his hand.

"Don't worry," Dylan said, laughing at his friend's distress. "I brought them." He slapped the semi-squashed packet of hotdog buns into Kane's free hand. "Saved your ass again!"

Kane laughed and shot him the bird.

"Collin and I'll get the skewers," Ron said, flipping open a pocket knife he had pulled from his bag. "You did bring a pocket knife, didn't you?"

"Hell, boy!" Collin reached down and pulled a hefty hunting knife from an ankle sheath. "As usual," he said, flashing the long-bladed dagger, "mine is bigger than yours."

"Yeah, yeah," responded Ron, grinning. "Just don't cut yourself playing with it."

The group went about their appointed tasks as Ron and Collin headed into the surrounding stand of aspen. The sun had already dropped behind the tree line, streaking the thin layer of clouds with pinks, blues and lavenders.

"This one looks pretty good," Ron said, stretching out a promising branch.

"This tree's got two good ones," Collin said, hacking away at a branch with his knife.

Rory panted impatiently at Ron's feet. Ron laughed down at him. Rory was obviously hungry.

"*An bhfuil ocras ort*?" Ron asked innocently in his mind.

Rory stopped panting. His eyes communicated a sarcasm only other dogs . . . and Ron could understand.

"*Hurry, or I will eat one of your friends*," Rory's mind said. The dog snorted at his own humor.

"Let's hurry, up Collin," Ron warned. "Rory's starving and he says he's gonna eat you if we don't get back and feed him."

"Ron," Collin said, rolling his eyes. "You and that dog

are just a little too . . . close, if you get my drift?"

Rory growled low in his throat.

"Shit!" Collin took a step back. "You'd almost think he understood me."

"Oh, he understood you all right."

"Right." Collin looked at the collection of sticks in his hand. "Okay, we've got enough."

They had an accumulation sufficient to last a week, much less the one night they were going to be in the mountains. The colors had left the sky, which was now a blackening grey. It was a new moon, and none of the usual reflected light streamed down—only starlight.

"We'd better get back." Ron tugged at Collin's collar.

"I'm right behind you," Collin responded, pushing his knife back into its nest at his ankle. "I'm hungry, too."

"You're always—" A fleeting movement in the dark foliage beyond caught Ron's peripheral attention. "Did you see that?"

Ron searched the leafy darkness for the source of the motion he had sensed more than seen.

"See what?" Collin asked, watching Ron's frantic head turns.

"I thought I saw something . . ." Ron stared back into deep underbrush. "I don't know . . . fly past or something."

"Could be an owl," Collin responded, trying in vain to see what Ron was staring at.

Rory had made a dash into the foliage. The boys could hear him racing to and fro, growling and barking.

"No, there wasn't any sound of wings flapping." Ron's eyes continued to dart from one dark recess in the trees to another. "I swear, I thought . . ." He look confused. "It was different from anything else I've ever sensed—" He regretted his words the instant he said them. "I mean seen."

"Dude," Collin responded, throwing his hands up. "Have you been smoking weed again?"

"Shut up!" Ron said, ignoring Collin as he continued to monitor the intensifying darkness for movement.

"Cause, man, if you have and you're not sharing—"

"For Christ's sake, Collin, I'm not doping," Ron said. "I saw . . . I felt something, and it felt big . . . and I think it's safe to say that Rory has sensed something as well."

"It *felt* big?" Collin's face scrunched into a sarcastic smirk. "Are you starting this again?"

Ron snorted with irritation and brushed past Collin in the direction of the camp.

"Now, don't get all pissy!" Collin chased after him. "If you say you . . . felt something, I'll believe you."

"Bullshit!" Ron pushed on through the low aspen branches. "Forget I said anything!"

"Okay." Collin chuckled to himself. "Suit yourself, witch-boy."

Ron stopped short and turned on his friend. "I told you not to call me that!"

"Okay, okay!" Collin's hands went up in surrender.

"I don't call you pixie-boy, so don't—"

"Who's been calling me, pixie-boy?" Collin said, holding his ground. "Who, cause I'll kick their—"

"Chill out!" Now it was Ron's turn to laugh. "No one's calling you *pixie*."

"Well, what the hell—"

"Not anymore, anyway." Ron threw his arm around the smaller teen's shoulders before the boy could respond. "Come on. Let's get back to camp. I'm hungry."

"Just tell me . . ."

"No. It's no big deal."

"No big deal?" Collin pushed Ron ahead of him. "A pixie's fairy folk. So someone's calling me a fairy! It's that prick, Nolan, isn't it?"

"Come on, Big C," Ron said, laughing."

"If anyone's queer around here, it's that—"

Ron spun around and grabbed his friend by the shoulders.

"Give it a rest, Collin!" Ron said slowly

Collin blinked at the hard stare Ron was giving him. "What's your—"

"Calling you a pixie is not the same as calling you queer, okay?" Ron's voice was low in his chest.

Collin shrugged. "Well, it's about as close as you can get."

"Pixie, sprite, gnome, *Fey* . . . those are mythological spirits."

"I know that. We all had the same history class on ancient Irish superstitions."

"Then you should know better," Ron said pointedly.

"That's not what people mean today when they call you a fairy, is it?"

"They didn't call you a fairy," Ron said. "They called you a pixie . . . probably more in reference to your height, not your sexual orientation"

Ron rapped his friend on top of the head for emphasis.

"Either way—" Collin began.

"I can see the camp fire," Ron interjected quickly. "Hurry up now before the other hungry trolls come looking for us."

"Troll . . . see there?" Collin said, pushing Ron out of the way for the firelight ahead. "That's a perfectly good insult!"

"Shut up, pixie-boy," Ron said, taking a swipe at his friend's head and missing.

The boys stumbled through the remaining vegetation out into the dome of light cast by the blazing fire pit. They continued taking half-hearted swings and kicks at each other.

"It's about time, you two got back!" Nolan looked up from the fire with a sneer. "The others were beginning to talk."

Collin paused in his sparring with Ron.

"I'm sorry to tell you this, big guy," Collin said, "but people have been talking about you for years."

Nolan lobbed a freshly fallen pinecone at Collin.

"Yeah, probably because I've been in the newspapers." Nolan flexed his muscles. "That's what being a sports star does for you, *little* guy." Nolan reached for one of the aspen spears that Ron was brandishing. "Now, for the love of God, let's eat!"

The other boys accepted one of the wooden skewers from Ron and Collin and impaled a hotdog, stretching it over the fire, vying for the best spots.

"What took you two so long?" Kane said, kneeling on the ground by Ron. "Get lost?"

"These sticks don't cut themselves," Ron responded, working his hotdog in and out of the fire.

"Ron got one of his feelings about something when we were out there," Collin said, without thinking.

"Collin!" Ron snapped.

"What was it this time?" asked Nolan, groaning. "Ghosts? Spook lights? Sasquatch?"

Ron narrowed his eyes at Nolan. "Don't start with me."

"I mean," Nolan continued. "Really, I think you're

doing too much acid again."

"I've never . . ." Ron glared at Collin. "Nothing. Let it be."

"Yeah," said Nolan. "But let's face it, Ron, you did psych-out when Jamie Jones went missing."

The boys silently recalled the incident from the previous year when the young girl had disappeared. The police came to Ron because he had an established reputation since early adolescence of *seeing* what no one else could. He had on more than one occasion given the police crucial clues that pointed the way to answering questions about what happened and to whom. There was a shallow attempt to keep Ron's involvement on an investigation quiet, but as is always the case in an otherwise closed community, word gets out.

"Look," Ron said finally, wrapping a bun about his hotdog. "I don't know what I . . . saw, or if I saw anything. It's dark and it could have been anything . . . an owl, a—"

"But," interrupted Collin, "you said—"

Ron cut him off with a sharp look.

"O come on, Ron," Collin said, slapping his own burnt wiener into a bun. "What's the big deal? You're psychic. Everyone knows you're the psychic dude. Even the police use you. Get over it!"

"You try living with that," Ron responded. He glanced at Rory who ignored him in favor of his own hotdog which he chomped on happily.

"Hell, boy!" Collin persisted. "Do you have any idea how much any one of us would love to have that kind of gift?"

"Gift?" Ron almost choked.

"Collin's right," Dylan interrupted. "It's like being a super hero."

"Yeah, right." Ron shook his head. "And what do all super heroes have to do? Hide their true identities so they don't get burned at the stake."

Something like a sharp wind exploded from the aspens. Two of the tents collapsed without warning. The encapsulated wind blew across the fire pit, enveloping the circle of teens in dense, acrid smoke.

"What the fuck!" shouted Nolan, jumping to his feet.

The wind seemed to have a discrete source, betrayed by the smoke which encircled it and followed it, outlining its anthropomorphic semblance.

"What is it?" shouted Kane, who sat frozen by the fire pit, grasping his knees.

"Whatever you do stay back from it," Ron shouted above the din.

The fine hairs on the back of his neck and arms straightened and tingled.

Rory had sprung to his four feet, annoyed at the interruption to his meal.

"*Go dtachta an diabhal tu!*" the dog's mind barked, calling on the devil to choke the thing. He chased the ball of smoke about the campsite, snapping at its unseen feet.

Ron grabbed a handful of cold ash from the perimeter of the fire pit. He stood his ground, throwing the ash into the center of the swirling wind.

"*Imeacht gan teacht ort!*" Ron commanded, his strong baritone rising above the confused shouts of his friends.

The wind exploded into drifts of cold ash that settled slowly onto the grassy, forest floor.

Ron stood straight, but shaking, his fists clenched at his sides. He stared blankly at the now empty air, lit only by the recovering flames of the fire pit.

"What the fuck?" Nolan reiterated, stammering from

behind. He turned slowly, brandishing a large rock yanked from the ground at his feet.

"Is it gone?" Collin piped up. He held his hunting knife at the ready. "What the hell was that?"

Ron shook his head, still staring into the darkness.

"I don't know," Ron said, "some sort of freak tornado?"

"Tornado, my ass," said Nolan, slamming his rock back into the ground.

"Really?" Ron turned to face Nolan. "Then what's your explanation?"

"You tell me," Nolan threw back at him. "You're the one that got rid of . . . it—you and that . . . that witch spell you used."

"Witch spell?" Dylan said from where he was checking for any damage to the tents.

"Yeah," Kane said softly. He still sat on the ground by the fire, not having budged. "What was that language you were speaking?"

"It was Gaelic, you idiots!" Collin said. "Not witch-craft. Ron's spoken Gaelic since he was a kid—Mab's doing. Sometimes he lapses into it when he's not thinking."

"It was just a few cuss words," Ron said, giving Collin a grateful look.

"Cool," Kane said, laughing. "Wish I could cuss in two languages."

Rory came bounding out of the darkness into the fire-light.

"*Ta me go hiontah*," the barked to his master.

"*Buchaill maith*! Good boy!" Ron laughed. "Yes, you are wonderful," he agreed dropping to his knees to scratch the dog's ears.

"That dog is just as weird as you are," Nolan said,

spitting into the fire.

Ron ignored him and looked into Rory's eyes.

"*Why were you in the trees?*" Ron asked with his mind.

"*To chase the Phooka,*" Rory responded, panting excitedly.

Ron sat back. *Phooka.* He remembered the word from Mab's stories—an elven goblin with a variety of beast-like forms. He decided it best to keep this to himself.

"Dammit!" Kane said suddenly. "That . . . wind made me drop my wiener in the fire."

"Dylan, Nolan said, laughing, "give the kid another wiener to play with."

Ron relaxed as the others laughed, now distracted from the earlier events.

"Okay, okay," Kane said, rolling his eyes. "Enough with the wiener jokes."

"Any serious problems with the tents?" Ron asked, to bring everyone back to the present.

"Nah," Dylan said. He had already pulled one of the tents back into shape. "The ground is soft here and the stakes didn't hold."

"Okay, everyone," ordered Nolan. "Let's get those tents secured."

"Ours wasn't blown down," Collin announced. "It's all in knowing how to properly stake a tent."

"Screw you, O'Quinn," the other boys said in unison.

They set about straightening their tents.

Collin turned to Ron and found him staring off into the darkness again.

"What are you looking at?" Collin asked nervously.

"Nothing," Ron responded flatly.

"Don't give me that shit!" Collin said. "You see something."

"No." The hairs on Ron's neck were tingling again,

but with a different vibration. "Just thinking."

"In English or in Gaelic?"

"Yeah," Ron said, squinting at the darkness. "Thanks for that earlier."

"Whatever," Collin said, and then whispered, "but that was no cussing you were doing."

Ron could just make out the curvature in the darkness about some transparent shape—a figure hiding behind the aspen branches—almost human looking, slight, almost frail.

"Oh," Ron whispered back. "You speak Gaelic, now?"

"Let's just say I know most of the cuss words," Collin responded. He stared into the trees, following Ron's sight line. Nothing.

Without looking away, Ron's mind reached out to Rory. "*What is that?*"

"*What is what?*" Rory cocked his head toward the aspens.

"*You don't see it?*"

"*I see the darkness.*"

Ron caught his breath. Why could Rory not see it?

"Ron?" Collin whispered.

Ron swore he could sense movement around the almost invisible figure not twenty yards away—an undulation bending the space about the figure—like the beating of wings.

"Ron?" Collin said again. He nudged Ron's arm.

"What?" Startled Ron turned his attention to Collin.

"Don't *what* me. What are you looking at?"

"Nothing. I was just thinking."

"Okay, don't tell me." Collin glared at his friend. "I'm only you're best friend."

"If I see anything, I'll tell you," Ron said, giving Collin

a slap on the back. "Quit making something out of nothing."

"Screw you!" Collin turned away and headed back to the fire pit, mumbling under his breath.

Ron turned back to the darkness. It was gone. The tingling at the base of his skull had stopped. With a sigh, he followed Collin to the fire.

"Who's got the goddamn whiskey?" Collin asked, taking a seat by the fire.

"Got it!" Dylan called back. "I swiped a big bottle from my Dad's stash." He proffered the bottle to Collin.

"Who else is getting drunk?" Collin asked, opening the bottle to take a swig.

"Let's have it," said Nolan, reaching for the bottle.

Ron took a seat next to Collin and waited his turn at the bottle. He was already seeing things. What harm would a little whiskey do? He took the bottle from Kane and took a short drought from the liquor bottle, swallowing the fiery alcohol with a grimace. He looked back at the dark recesses of the trees. Nothing. He took another long swig of the whiskey. It would be one way to get some sleep.

"Quit hogging the bottle," Collin said jerking it out of Ron's grasp.

Ron laughed and popped his friend on the back of the head.

"*Sláinte*, you little shit!" Ron said.

"*Sláinte!*" the other teens sang out in unison.

"What?" Collin asked, almost choking on the liquor.

Ron grabbed the bottle from him. "It means *cheers*, dumbass!"

Chapter 2

Ron sat at the rough-hewn, oak table watching his mom scurry about extracting various herbs and other unidentifiable substances from her cabinets and toss them purposefully into her mortar. While one could never accuse Mab Maguire of having the slightest domestic inclination, nothing got her juices flowing like a medical emergency. While Ron had expected a strong reaction from her when he came home that morning still nursing a bad hangover from the camping trip, he had not expected her to be particularly happy about it. Of course, it wasn't the hangover that elated her but rather the need—her skills were needed—she was needed—and by the boy she had watched over since finding him on her front stoop almost eighteen years before. She crushed the collection of vegetable matter with her pestle and dumped it all into a blender containing an equally unidentifiable, grey liquid.

"Geez, Mab, please say you're not going to make me drink that!"

When a baby, Ron had found *Mab* easier to say than mom, and it stuck.

"Look here, love," Mab said, revving up the blender. "If you're gonna start going off and getting pissed on too much whiskey, you need to learn the cure for a hangover.

Ron's mom had never been particularly learned in the traditional sense, but she certainly was a proponent of education. Of course, her idea of education often clashed with the established institutions otherwise responsible for it.

"What good is history without your cultural roots," Mab would preach. "What use is their science if you can't account for a thing's spiritual essence? What good is a cosmology without an understanding of the divine forces that hold it all together?"

Mab took no prisoners in her disdain for materialism and technology.

Ron watched her as she pulsed the contents of her blender. "Mab, that's more than I drank to get the hangover!"

"And you'll be drinking every drop of it," Mab said, her eyes twinkling. "It'll set you right for sure."

"Are you sure this is a cure," Ron asked with undisguised sarcasm, "or a punishment?"

Mab's hands went to her over-abundant hips.

"I've nothing against a good brew, boy," she said. "But this is what happens when you abuse a natural force."

Ron laughed much to the detriment of his throbbing head.

"Mab, you've been brewing your own mash out in the woods for as long as I can remember," Ron teased, "and you're the only one I know with the stomach to drink it."

Mab grunted dismissively.

"What good is that watered-down, tainted, horse piss they sell?" Mab said. "The natural way's the best."

"For gettin' a good buzz on?" Ron asked with doubtful innocence.

"For me potions, me cures, me—"

"Hell's bells!" Ron was laughing uncontrollably, holding his head. "Mab, you haven't doled out enough *cures* in your life to account for the barrels of hooch you've got stowed in the cellar."

Mab smiled, unashamed. She poured the thick, putty-colored *cure* into a highball glass.

"Well, my beautiful little stag," Mab said, "so long as the *cure* works, neither one of us has anything to worry about."

"Whatever." Ron begrudgingly accepted the unappetizing glass of goop and stared at it unconvinced. "I think I'd rather keep my hangover."

"Drink!" May commanded.

"Aw, Mab!" Ron shuddered.

"Drink, or you'll be welcoming the moon's power with the rest of us tonight!"

That was a threat that secured Ron's compliance. Mab never understood her adopted son's hardcore sense of modesty. When her son hi puberty, he seemed to lose his previous, delighted participation in the ritual and *au naturale* dancing in the light of the goddess. Still, Mab was always one to turn a negative into a positive—meaning that what once was a welcoming invitation, was now useful as a technique of behavior modification that could bend her son's willful rebellion into almost instant obedience in other areas.

True to form, Ron lifted the glass to his lips, closed his eyes, held his breath, and sipped.

"All of it!" Mab persisted.

"It's awfully thick," Ron protested.

"The thicker, the better." Mab reached out to tilt the bottom of the glass upward.

Ron knew it was better to get it over with and quickly

gulped down the licorice-flavored concoction.

"Good." Mab took Ron's head in her rough, beefy hands. "*Beannacht leat*," she intoned.

Ron smiled at her deep concentration. "How long before I'm cured?" he asked with a hint of sarcasm.

"A spell doesn't happen within the constraints of time, lad," Mab said, shaking herself from the trance.

"Yeah, but . . ." Ron stopped.

His headache was a distant memory.

"It worked," Ron said, trying to hide his surprise.

"Well, what were you expecting," Mab asked, laughing. "Lightning bolts?"

"Thanks Mab." Ron relaxed back into his chair, much relieved.

"*Ta grá agam duit!*" Mab said softly, patting her son's cheek.

"I love you, too," Ron responded genuinely. "Gotta go!"

"But what about the *Bealtaine* new moon?" Mab said, pleading. "The girls will be over later. It'll be a real celebration."

"Mab . . ."

"You used to love it so!"

"I also used to play with toy cars, Mab, but I'm not a little kid anymore."

Mab didn't look convinced. "The girls will be disappointed," she said, pouting.

"The *girls* are a median age of sixty-six," Ron said, heading for the door, "and a median weight of about two seventy-five!"

"You don't have to be naked," Mab insisted. "You can—"

"Mab!" Ron shook his head. "Whether or not I'm

dressed doesn't matter as much as the fact that the *girls* will not be dressed."

"Are you saying that the female nude is not beautiful to you?"

"No," Ron tried not to laugh. "Just those *particular* female nudes."

Mab shrugged. "I guess that Margaret Maddison *has* lost her figure."

"And gained about a hundred pounds."

Mab chuckled and threw a twig of sarsaparilla at him.

"Get on with you, you and your insults," Mab said. "Will you be home for supper?"

"No ma'am," Ron replied pulling open the door. "I'm going back up—"

"Whoa, whoa, whoa!" Mab gestured for Ron to stop. "Get back here!"

"What?"

"Back *here*!" Mab insisted, pointing to the chair he had just vacated.

Ron sighed and rolled his eyes. Silently he returned to his chair. He stared at his mom like a mute.

"Well?" Mab asked.

Ron shrugged. "Well?"

"Boy, you are skating on thin ice." Mab's visage darkened ominously. "I caught a word leaping out of your mind just now."

Ron's heart sank. Sometimes it wasn't just Rory who could hear his mind-voice.

"I don't know what you're talking about, Mab," Ron responded.

"Really?" Mab circled the table and stood over him. "You say you're going back up into the mountain and I hear the word *sídhe* scream out of you." The ancient Gaelic, catch-all word for a supernatural being hung in the air.

"Mab, I was just—"

"Bullshit!" Mab got in his face. "Don't try to hide something like this from me—don't think for one minute I don't know what's going on here. What did you see? What did you sense?" She rapped him on the head with her big wooden spoon. "What is up there that you have to trek by yourself up into that mountain wilderness—"

"I'm not going by myself," Ron quickly assured his mom. "Rory's going with me. I'm gonna take my bow in case I run into a bear and I—"

"Bear?" Mab's voice hit a new octave. "That is not what you're hunting!"

"It's nothing, Mab." Ron met his mother's eyes and knew he needed to give her a small fact for distraction.

"Something disturbed our campsite last night," Ron said, "and I want to see if I can find some tracks or anything that will identify what it was."

"More bullshit!" Mab turned away and slammed her spoon onto the table. "Fine." She said, turning back at him sharply. "Just tell me one thing. Was it friendly or malevolent?"

"Mab, it was an animal . . ." Ron wanted to allay her fear, but how? "Who knows?" He pulled his mind away from the evil that had first visited and focused his mind on the second apparition he had seen hiding in the trees.

"I didn't feel anything evil," Ron added quickly.

This was the truth. The second visitation seemed to just be watching. Ron let his mind pour that impression into his aura.

Mab studied him. The vibration of his aura seemed to back up what her son was saying.

"Fine," May said. She had no choice but to believe

him. "I'll drop it."

"Thank God!" Ron said, reaching out to hug her neck.

"Thank the goddess, you mean," Mab said with a chuckle. "Before you go . . ."

She circled the table to her cabinets and rummaged through the drawers.

"Dammit! I know it's in here somewhere." Mab rifled each drawer in vain. "I know I . . . oh, wait . . ."

The agitated witch zeroed in on the sideboard and the breadbox-sized chest that dominated it.

"Now I remember." Mab lifted the little chest's lid and studied the contents. "There you are!" She pulled out a small, leather pouch and held it up reverently. With an inscrutable smile, she offered it to Ron.

"What is it?" he asked, accepting what was clearly a very old, deteriorating leather receptacle.

"Open it," was all Mab would say.

Ron obeyed, loosening the leather tie and upending the pouch into his other hand. A large but unadorned silver ring fell into his palm.

"It's a ring." Ron said flatly. He turned it over, looking for some hint as to its meaning. "Okay," he said with a shrug. "What do I do with it?"

"Wear it, boy!" Mab said, impatient. "What do you think?"

"Thanks, Mab." Ron rolled his eyes again. "I would never have figured that out."

Ron tried the over-sized ring on, but it just hung on his ring finger. It had a concave curvature, a wave to its exterior surface that raised five equidistant points about its circumference.

"It's way too big." Ron held up his hand as proof.

"It was made for a man," Mab said, seizing the ring

from him. "Here." She pushed the ring onto his thumb. "As long as it fits on one of your fingers," Mab said, "it's time for you to wear it—it'll do its job."

"Which is?" Ron admired the ring's highly polished surface.

Mab looked at him silently.

"Come on, Mab," Ron tried again. "Is it glamoured or something?"

"You tell me." Mab's expression told him nothing.

Ron shook his head and focused his concentration on the light reflecting off the ring. He waited for some impression, but there was nothing. Still it fit comfortably on his thumb, and there was nothing malevolent about it.

"I can't seem to sense anything, Mab," Ron said, closing his eyes. "You've got to give me a clue or something."

Mab sighed. "It's got to be telling you something," she said, unconvinced that her son was really trying. "You're not listening to it. What do you feel?"

"Like this is a waste of time."

Mab grabbed up her wooden spoon threateningly.

"Okay, okay," Ron said, holding up a defensive hand. "I'll give it—"

Mab swung the spoon at Ron as if it were a hammer. Ron ducked just in time, wincing at the stream of air that followed the heavy spoon's trajectory, just missing his left ear.

"Mab!" Ron cried out.

"Damn!" Mab sat the spoon back on the table. "Well, it's obviously not a defensive charm."

"What?" Ron straightened. "You don't know what it's for, do you?" he said, eyes wide. "You almost creamed me!"

"Don't be silly," Mab said with a dismissive wave. "Still, I *did* miss you."

"I've been ducking that spoon for years, Mab." Ron's arms crossed. "I think your missing me was due to my hard-earned skill and not magic."

"Well, wear it anyway," Mab responded, plopping back into a table chair, appearing exhausted. "It *is* for something."

"What?"

"And it's for you!" Mab shook her head, annoyed with herself.

"What do you mean it's for me?" Ron asked. "What are you talking about?"

Mab stared at the table for a few moments before finally meeting her son's gaze. She tried to smile, but found it hard to be positive about anything that reminded her of her artificial motherhood.

"What is it, Mab?" Ron reached out to take her hand. Rare it was to see his mom misty-eyed.

"Just rememberin'," Mab responded softly, "back when I found your wee self on my front steps."

"Okay." Ron said, trying to hide his surprise and wondering what had brought this on "Does this have something to do with the ring, or are you just trying to distract me?"

Mab sat up in the chair sharply. "It has everything to do with the ring, boy!"

Ron grabbed up her wooden spoon before Mab could.

"I'll just put this in the sink," Ron said, trying not to laugh. He tossed the spoon over Mab's head and it dropped into the sink with a splash.

Mab didn't protest. She was deep in her thoughts.

Ron leaned in and took Mab's face in his hands.

"What about when you found me?" Ron asked softly. "What about the ring, mom?"

Mab blinked at the unaccustomed title. "I'm not really your mom, you know."

"Yes you are," Ron said, smiling at her. "It's too late to get out of it!"

That made Mab's eyes twinkle. "You've got a right puckish tongue," she said.

Ron caught her eyes with his and held them.

"I'm Mab Maguire's son. Everyone says so. I say so," Ron said, pinching her cheeks. "So, tough!"

Mab laughed and reached out to pinch her son's cheeks in response.

"Now, what about the ring?" Ron continued.

"I found you in a small basket woven out of pine straw," Mab said with a shrugged. "You were wrapped up in a wide ribbon of tatted lace. Inside the wrapping was that little leather pouch, monogramed with a name."

"Oberon," Ron said, frowning.

Mab nodded. "The moment I saw it," she said "I knew it was a charm. I thank the poor soul who put you there—"

"You mean abandoned me there!"

"No!" Mab insisted, shaking her head. "I think that person knew that I, of all people, would understand the ring's significance—that I would take you in and protect you—and I have, too."

"That's for sure!" Ron said. "I had so many spells and charms decorating my room that you couldn't even see the wall-paper."

"Kept you safe, didn't it?"

"From what?"

"From whatever it was that caused someone to leave you in my care," Mab responded, slamming a her table.

"You're assuming an awful lot, Mab."

"You were not abandoned here, boy," Mab insisted. "You were gifted to me. I fell in love with you the second I saw you. It was meant to be."

"But—"

"But nothing. I don't believe in coincidences. You know better than that."

"Okay, okay!" Ron said, standing. "There's no arguing the randomness of the universe with the likes of you."

"Damn right!" Mab said, swatting Ron on the leg. "You were a gift in a straw package and you've been givin' me grief ever since!"

"Whatever." Ron escaped to the door, laughing. "I'm out of here!"

"You'll keep the ring on?" Mab asked, almost pleading.

"I'll keep the ring on."

"You'll be back for the celebration?"

Ron paused at the door. "Actually, Rory and I will be backpacking it. I want to camp out again tonight!"

"Alone?"

"No, not alone," Ron responded. "Remember, I'll have Rory."

He could tell Mab wasn't happy about that. "But I'll keep the ring on." He hoped that would ease her mind.

"Be careful, then," Mab said, relenting. "Will you at least welcome the new moon tonight and keep the *Bealtaine* rituals?"

Ron couldn't help grinning. "Rory and I will dance naked about our campfire."

"Blessed be!" Mab cried out, a smile finally breaking on her face.

"*Oíche in haith!*" Ron said slipping out the door.

"A good night to you, too, lad!" Mab called after him.

Mab sat very still for a moment, eyes closed. Focusing her concentration, she reached out with her mind.

"Rory?" Mab whispered. She waited until a sense of connection enveloped her, and then sent out her message. "Do you understand," she whispered. "*An dtuigeann tú*?" Mab repeated in the ancient tongue.

Three sharp barks echoed into the house from the outside.

Mab smiled. She turned her thoughts to the many preparations needed for the new moon celebration. Mab grabbed up her basket. There were herbs and other elementals to gather . . . she pulled the door to with a smile . . . and she would definitely need a few pints of fresh brew from her hidden still.

Chapter 3

Even in the bright light of day, the mountain floor was a world of dim, misty shadows. Below the towers of pine, several additional layers and levels of understory plants sheltered the mostly unseen, hidden denizens that crept about attending to their habitual and instinctive activities of daily life. Only a few hardy specimens would brave the daylight and forage out in the open. The mountain wilds were like any untamed habitat—the rules of biological evolution reigned and all but the rare and solitary grizzly were in the food chain line for some other wild species.

The possibility of being on a lower rung of the food chain was never a concern to the likes of Rory. He had outrun bears before and even intimidated a few as well. Besides, he was a danger junkie. He never hesitated to confront any creature, regardless of size. If things turned from his favor, his four lean and muscled legs could move him out of harm's way like a beam of light. So it was that the forest floor was one big amusement park for him. No skink, squirrel, or beetle escaped his scrutiny or his loud, barking challenge.

While Rory darted to and fro, Ron had focused on the climb. The backpack he had carried kept him bent over, concentrating on the path, his feet, and on what he might discover about the previous night. After setting up his small, domed tent, he had spent the better part of the afternoon studying every leaf, limb, and root within the aspen grove where he had seen . . . whatever it was he had seen. Nothing even gave him a hint—no tracks, no broken branches, no evidence of anything out of the ordinary.

By the time he had gotten a fire going in the fire pit, Rory had returned from his explorations, panting, hungry, and anxious to fill Ron's head with the sounds, scents, images, and emotions of his day's adventures.

"*Tóg bog é,*" Ron said aloud, trying to separate his thoughts from Rory's litany of the senses, "and while you're settling down, think about what you'll have for supper."

Supper. Now that was a possibility Rory could obsess on.

"*Ba mhaith lion feoil,*" the canine's mind shouted.

Ron laughed at him. "If you want meat, then go hunting for it."

Rory plopped down in the grass and rested his head on his forepaws.

"*Tuirseach,*" Rory said with a weak bark.

"And if you're tired, it's not my fault," Ron said, rummaging in the bottom of his backpack. "There!" He extracted a wad of aluminum foil. "What's this?"

Ron tossed the large, oddly-shaped object in his hand, trying to get Rory's attention.

Rory would not be budged from his disappointment.

Ron opened the foil package.

"You could at least show a little interest," Ron said. "Guess you don't want this hambone Mab sent for you."

Rory's ears went up. "*Cad é sin?*" his eyes said widely.

"I said, it's a hambone." Ron said, pulling the large,

meat-encrusted bone from the foil. "Guess I'll eat it."

Rory launched himself into the air, landing atop Ron, toppling him onto the ground. Gone was the dog's semblance of communication—replaced by hunger and the smell of something good to eat.

"Okay, okay!" Ron wrestled with the dog, finally giving up the bone to his sharp-toothed companion. "Try eating the bone and not my hand!"

Rory put the bone in an oral death grip and carted it to the other side of the fire. He loved his master, but this . . . this was a very superior bone—of no use to a dull-toothed, small-mouthed human.

Ron left Rory to his bone. Twilight had captured the horizon and Ron was surprised to see hints of an aurora twinkling above the open dome of the small clearing where his fire offering was brightly burning and crackling, filling the cooling air with the scent of burning pine. Remembering his promise to Mab, Ron pulled out a zip-lock bag of crushed herbs that he knew without looking, would be there. Mab would not be denied. He cast a handful of the potpourri into the fire and a haze of sweet smoke billowed upwards.

"Blessed be," Ron whispered, smiling at his own inward joke.

For once, obedient to his mother's wishes, he slipped off his shirt and jeans, tossing them into his tent. After a moment's hesitation, he stripped off his boxer shorts, and stood shivering in the slight but brisk evening breeze. He laughed out loud, enjoying the exhilarations of standing completely naked, except for his sneakers, out in the open—isolated as he was.

"Alright!" Ron shouted at the sky.

The dog, sensing excitement in his master, raised his

head up from his tormented bone, making sure he wasn't missing anything. Unimpressed by his furless lord's exhibitionism, he plopped back down to his gnawing.

"Come on, dog!" Ron called out.

He shuffled over to the fire pit, bending closely—but carefully—over the warming flames.

"You heard, Mab. We have to welcome in the new moon."

He glanced up at the now star-laden sky above the clearing, searching. There, inching above the tree line was the thin, luminescent crescent that signaled the vigilance and power of the mother goddess.

"There she is, Rory," Ron whispered.

He stretched out his arms and slowly spun round and round, following the circle of the fire pit. He kept his eyes focused on the arch of the waxing moon which staved off any motion dizziness.

Rory ignored him, preferring the meaty pig tibia to the lure of the moon.

After a few turns around the fire pit, Ron stopped. Hands on hips, he stared up at the now fully exposed moon.

"There," Ron said. "If she doesn't feel welcome, it's not my fault." He squatted by the fire to pet his oblivious pet. "You better back me up and tell Mab I was a good boy."

Rory seemed to shrug and gnaw ever harder at his bone.

"Okay, be that way." Ron stood and stretched.

He braved the cold once more and returned to his tent to extract the goat cheese and roasted red pepper sandwich Mab had packed for him. Ron took a large bite out of it and quickly returned to the fire.

"Forget about it," Ron said to the now interested,

Rory. "You don't share your bone, I don't share my sandwich."

Ron knelt by the fire. It felt so good to be in the mountains—naked—just one of the forest creatures. He watched Rory gnawing on his bone and sensed the strong connection they had—not master and pet, but more a bond of family. A stronger gust of wind rushed through the aspens. Ron turned to watch the understory tree leaves shimmering like glitter in the dim crescent moonlight. The fine hairs on the back of his neck and forearms rose, tingling. Ron became instantly alert.

Sensing his boy's urgency of mood, Rory's head and ears went up.

Ron stood slowly, circling the tree line with his physical eyes, focusing his mind into the darkness beyond. Something was there—something watching—something . . . other! He grabbed his right hand. His thumb was aching. Ron looked down at the five-pointed circle of silver that embraced his digit. He was aware of a vibration in the silver—a vibration that seemed to engage his own internal harmony—a vibration that took hold of his very bones and traveled like an electric current through his entire skeleton. He could hear the low hum in his ears.

Ron felt the need to leave the fire and enter the darkness beyond. He was not being controlled, but he was drawn—not compelled—but attracted. He let his spirit eyes seize the moment, looking for any sign of evil in the ether, or as his physics teacher would say, the black matter that encompassed everything in an energy field that connected those who could experience it with all other things. No sense of danger followed.

Ron followed his instincts into the aspen grove. He walked ever so slowly through the branches extending his mind's eye ahead, still vigilant. While Ron was aware that the air was cold, he felt no discomfort. He forgot his nakedness and continued his forage in the center of the dense aspen grove. A sense of motion pulled his eyes sharply to the right. Ron froze. A figure—a human-like figure seemed to hover in the branches not fifteen feet from him. It glowed like a dim light bulb—transparent—almost invisible in the foliage. Ron stared, concentrating. His thumb ached all the more.

The gauzy creature's eyes blinked, suddenly aware that it was no longer hidden. It was seen! Suddenly it raised a hand. A flash of light engulfed Ron and pushed him backwards onto the leafy forest floor.

"Who are you?" Ron cried out, shielding his eyes with his hand.

The thumb ring quivered and seemed to absorb the light, clearing Ron's vision. He blinked, not able to trust his eyes. An almost imperceptible rippling in the space about the creature was evident. Ron shielded his eyes closer. Wings?

"What the fuck are you?" Ron shouted, pushing against the force that still held him. "Let go of me!"

Another flash of blinding light.

Suddenly the air was still. Ron's ears were still ringing, but he could pull himself to his feet at last. His eyes re-accustomed to the dark and he stood face to face with . . . a boy—a boy as naked as he.

"What the hell . . ." Ron stared, shocked.

The hair on his neck and arms had returned to their natural, smooth state. The aching in his thumb was nonexistent. The boy stood staring back at him, wide-eyed, slightly smaller than Ron, with short, straight blonde, almost white hair. He was pale, slightly built . . . the most beautiful . . .

"Wait!" Ron interrupted his own thoughts. "Who are you? What are you doing out here?"

The beautiful boy stood mute, staring.

"Where are your clothes?" Ron stepped toward the boy, slowly. "What happened—"

"Where are your clothes?" The young man's voice was light and airy. He cocked his head to one side, eyeing Ron up and down.

"Hey!" Ron covered his private parts. "Stop that!"

"Stop that!" repeated the boy.

"Stop what?"

"Stop what?"

"Dammit, stop repeating what I say!" Ron threw his head back in exasperation.

The youth looked down at his hairless privates and covered them like Ron. He smiled up at Ron.

"What are you?" the fascinated boy asked with wide-eyed innocence.

"What do you mean, what am I?" Ron reached out to touch the boy's chest. "Well, you're real anyway."

"I am real." The boy reached out and touched Ron's chest. "You see me?" he asked.

"Of course I can see you."

"I mean . . ." The boy shrugged. "You saw me?"

"Yeah, well, you weren't very well hidden were you?" Ron looked behind the boy. "How were you . . ." No wings. "What, were you sitting up in the tree or something?"

"I," the boy said, pointing behind him, "was over there."

"No shit!" Ron said, rolling his eyes. "One more time. Where are your clothes?"

"Where are your clothes?"

This was starting to piss Ron off.

"Look," Ron said, turning back toward his campsite, pointing. "I'm camped back there." He turned back to the boy. "But that doesn't explain . . ."

The boy stood fully clothed in jeans, sneakers, and polo shirt.

"Jesus-H-Christ!" Ron's hands went to his hips. "How the hell—where the—how did you get dressed so fast?"

"I am dressed okay, am I not?" the boy asked in hopeful innocence.

"You're . . .*am I not?* . . . What the hell is that?" Ron rolled his eyes. "We're not doing Shakespeare—where are you from?

"From here." The boy gestured up the mountain.

"There's nothing up *here* but . . ." Ron sighed heavily. "Look, just come with me."

Ron took the boy's arm and pulled him toward the campsite. He noticed the boy staring inquisitively at his nakedness.

"And stop staring at me!" Ron insisted.

"And stop staring at me!" the boy said, following.

"I'm not . . ." Ron stopped. "Goddamn it!" He tugged at the boy's arm. "Just come with me."

"I am," the boy replied.

Ron hauled his find toward the fire.

"Rory!" Ron yelled at the still gnawing dog. "We have company!"

Rory looked up. He barked instinctively and jumped back from his bone.

"*Stad!*" the dog barked. "*Cade e sin?*"

"What do you mean, what is that?" Ron asked. "It's some guy I found back in the trees." He eyed his dog, surprised.

Rory circled the fire and approached the blonde youth slowly, sniffing the air.

"*Cad is ainm duit?*" Rory growled low, asking the boy his name.

Before Ron could speak, the blonde boy bent over Rory smiling.

"*Finn is ainm dom,*" the boy responded in perfect Gaelic.

"Finn?" Ron's mouth dropped.

"Finn," the boy said with a nod.

"Well, Finn," Ron said, eyeing the boy with heightened suspicion. "How the hell is it you can understand my dog?"

Finn looked at him, not understanding.

"You understand your dog." Finn replied.

"Of course I understand my dog, he's my goddamn dog!" Ron tried to push the anger back. "The question is, how is it that you can understand my dog? No one understands him but me!"

"But, he speaks well." Finn said, still not understanding.

"And you speak Gaelic?" Ron persisted. "*An dtuigeann tú?*"

"*Tuigim,*" Finn replied with a shrug, "I understand."

"Yeah," Ron said, shaking his head. "Clearly you do."

"This feels very warm." Finn moved closer to the fire.

"Of course it does! It's a fire. And while we're on the—"

"Did you make it?" Finn asked, kneeling at the fire. He cocked his head at Ron's naked groin, blinking.

"Just a minute!" Ron said, holding up a hand.

He left the fire pit for his tent and retrieved his

clothes. He pulled on his boxers and jeans and turned to the fire pulling a sweater over his head.

"Okay. Now we can talk," Ron said, pulling up his sleeves.

"Weren't we talking?"

"Yeah," Ron said with a smirk. "But you had a slight advantage. You were dressed and I wasn't."

"You are very well made," Finn said, unselfconsciously.

"Yeah, well . . . you're . . . pretty well made, too."

The conversation made Ron nervous.

"But that's beside the point," Ron said. "Now, I'm just trying to find where you came from. There's no other town around here but—"

"I came from here," Finn said, apparently annoyed at Ron's failure to understand him.

"Yes," Ron said with growing annoyance of his own. "But where is *here*?"

Finn tried another approach. "Where are you from?"

"I'm . . ." Ron sighed. "Okay, me first. I'm from Ennis . . . down below in the valley."

"You are a human people?" Finn's glistening, pale blue eyes widened.

"What, I . . ." Ron wanted to scream. "Of course I'm people. What the hell do I look like, a *Taibhse*?"

"No." Finn laughed. "You don't look like a ghost. A ghost is—"

"I know what a fickin' ghost looks like!" Ron said in exasperation.

"Then why did you ask if—"

Ron shut him up with a look. He turned his attention back to Rory who was ignoring both the boys for the remains of his bone.

"Goddamn it, Rory," Ron said, "say something!"

Rory looked up, unconcerned.

"What am I dealing with here?" Ron asked with his spirit voice.

Rory blinked at his boy. "*Fey*," he responded to Ron's mind.

"What?"

"Yes," Finn said clapping at the dog. "That is me. *Finn na Fey*."

"*Fey*?" For a moment, Ron was frozen. "You're of the *Fey*?"

Finn nodded and smiled up at the moon, now directly overhead.

"Let me get this straight." Ron sat on the ground beside Finn. "Just so we're on the same page. When you say *Fey*, are we talking . . . I mean, are you saying you're *Fey*, or . . . you know . . ."

"I am . . . *Fey*." Finn looked at Ron as if concerned about the other's sanity.

"Okay, let's try this another way." Ron swallowed hard. "You say you're a fairy. Now do you mean . . . fairy . . . or, you know . . . *a fairy*."

"I am Finn. I am Fairy Folk." Finn looked at Rory as if seeking a translator. "You are . . ."

"Oh shit!" Ron realized he had never introduced himself. "Okay. Sorry. I'm Ron . . . Ron Maguire . . . from Ennis . . . down at the bottom of the mountain," he said, pointing. "That way."

"Where people live?"

"Yes where people . . ." The conversation was making Ron dizzy. "Are you high?"

"I am high," Finn replied, nodding. "I am atop a mountain. You are high."

"Fuck this!" Ron said, standing. "You must've been

smoking some magic mushrooms."

"You found magic mushrooms?" Finn sat up excitedly.

"I found . . ." Ron threw his hands up. "That's it, I'm going to bed." He headed for his tent. "I don't know who you are, what you are, where you're from, or what the hell you're doing up here, and right now, I don't care!"

Ron ducked into his tent.

"If you're still here in the morning," Ron said, peeking his head out, "we'll try this again—maybe!" Ron pulled the tent flap shut, stripped off his jeans, and fell back onto his sleeping bag, muttering. "I would find some sorta goddamn wacko up . . ."

He stopped himself. What if this was some runaway from a care facility? There was an annex to the church where the nuns looked after . . . special kids, who couldn't make it in the main school. What if . . .

"Shit!" Ron slapped himself on the side of the head. He reached for the tent flap, just as Finn's head popped through.

"What the . . ." Ron caught himself.

"Are you going to sleep?" Finn asked, crawling into the small tent next to Ron's sleeping bag.

"Yeah, I'm going to bed, and . . ." Ron stared at Finn.

The boy was once more without clothing.

"What the hell are you doing?" Ron said, pulling the sleeping bag up to his chin.

"I'm going to bed, too." Finn said. He stretched out on the floor of the tent beside Ron. "Can we bring the fire here?"

"No we . . . you can't just . . ." Ron couldn't corral his thoughts. "Look. You need to get on home. It's gettin' colder and you're gonna freeze to death. Now get your clothes back on and—"

"I'm not too cold," Finn said, getting comfortable. "I sleep up here all the time and I like your little nest. How did you make it?"

"My . . .What the hell did Mab put in that sandwich?" Ron shook his head. "Suit yourself!" he said, pulling the sleeping bag over his head.

Ron waited a minute before peeking out.

The nude boy was still there.

Ron stared at him. What was going on? He glanced up and saw that Finn was staring right back at him. For some reason, Ron was unable to avert his eyes.

Finn huddled in a fetal position, his arms wrapped about himself.

Ron became keenly aware of the cold. He could sense a slight shiver pass through Finn.

"Look," Ron said finally. "You're gonna freeze to death. I can sleep in my clothes and you can have the sleeping bag."

"You are not making sense," Finn said, sitting up. He grabbed the sleeping bag cover and slid in beside Ron pushing him over.

"There's room for both of us," the slender youth said.

"Yeah, but . . ." Ron forgot the cold and was keenly aware that another boy . . . a naked boy, was suddenly pressed up against him.

Finn showed no similar concerns. He snuggled against Ron, pulling the sleeping bag tightly over him. He fussed with the open side.

"Can we tie this shut?" Finn asked. "It will keep the heat in."

Ron squirmed uncomfortably at the rising heat inside the sleeping bag.

"No," Ron responded, nervously. "I mean . . . we can zip it shut."

"Zip?"

"Yeah."

Ron reached over Finn, brushing his arm over the blonde *Fey's* silky, hairless skin.

"Um . . . like this." Ron pulled the zipper up, closing them both in the quilted bag.

"Much better." Finn said, pressing himself under Ron's arm. "You are very clever, making such a bed as this."

"Well, I didn't . . ." Ron stopped short.

"I'll sleep well tonight." Finn draped an arm across Ron's chest and pressed his strangely warm skin against Ron's. "*Siochan leaat*," he purred, closing his eyes.

"Yeah," Ron stuttered. "Peace . . . be with you, too." He knew he would not be sleeping well.

Rory, having tired of his bone, slouched through the tent flap and stretched out beside the sleeping bag.

Ron listened to the two of them breathing as they quietly slumbered. Finn fit the space beside him like a puzzle piece. Ron tried to relax—tried to be natural—but the circum-stance was completely foreign to him. He had never held another person this closely, this intimately, and certainly not this . . . nakedly. Ron stared at the perfect profile of the sleeping *Fey* . . . if that's what he was . . .well, it's what he said he was. He let his fingers rest on the boy's shoulder. He listened. Something passed between them— something too new to comprehend. This was uncharted territory. Mab had not prepared him for this.

He closed his eyes, trying to calm his inner self. But, as his thoughts quieted, he could smell the boy's honey-like scent, and before he realized it, found his face nestled in the boy's fine, silken blonde hair, sniffing. He thought about pulling away, but his action didn't seem to disturb Finn, who snored lightly in his arms.

Ron took a deep breath and willed himself to be still. What the hell was going on?

Chapter 4

The chirping of birds that always accompanied the dawn woke Ron from his hard-earned, but fitful sleep. Rory still occupied his place next to Ron, stretched out like a sphinx on the tent floor. There was no sign of Finn.

Ron sat up, trying to clear the cobwebs of sleep.

"Finn?" Ron called out.

No answer.

"Rory, where's Finn?"

The dog blinked his eyes open. He cocked his head, questioning.

"Where's Finn?" Ron repeated, throwing off the sleeping bag cover.

Rory just stared at Ron, not answering.

"Fine, be a shit!"

Ron pulled on his jeans and began to lace up his sneakers.

"What's your problem today?" Ron asked sharply.

The dog sat up, panting, but silent.

"What's going on?" Ron tugged his shirt over his head. "Rory?"

Ron grabbed the dog's head. Nothing. He focused his mind, listening. He could always hear what Rory was up to . . . but there was only empty silence.

Ron crawled out of the tent and stood scanning the site. There was no one in sight.

"Finn?" Ron called out again, his breath condensing in the cool morning air. "Anybody?"

The only response was the bird songs.

"Dammit!" Ron paced in front of the tent. "Rory, get out here!"

The beautiful, golden setter came bounding out of the tent.

"Which way did Finn go?" Ron asked.

The dog sat at his feet, looked up at Ron, panting.

"Well?" Ron's level of annoyance was rising. "Is your nose broken? Which way did the *Fey* go? *Ca bhfuil, Finn?*"

The dog blinked at him, showing no signs of comprehension.

"Say something, goddamn it!"

Reacting to Ron's exclamatory tone, the dog jumped up and ran in a circle around his human charge, barking excitedly.

Try as he might, Ron could not discern any intelligible communication in the barking.

"Something's not right here." Ron dropped to his knees and reached out for the dog.

Rory came to him obediently. Ron took the dog's head in his hands and stared with his mind into Rory's expressive eyes.

"What's wrong, boy?" Ron asked gently. "What's happened?"

Ron began to accept the possibility that Rory didn't understand him, and vice versa.

"It's okay, boy," Ron said, scratching Rory behind the ears, "We'll figure this out."

Ron stood again. He headed for the aspen grove,

entering it slowly. In the ensuing hours, he scrutinized every leaf and twig, looking for some evidence of the blonde youth. He found the niche where he had first spied the boy . . . or as Ron was beginning to believe . . . the *Fey*. There was nothing evident—no footprints, no broken tree limbs—nothing. For the rest of the day, he scoured the granite rock face searching for a hidden doorway, a cave, or even a simple fissure in the monolithic rock surface, all to no avail.

Ron returned to the camp. Rory had returned to what remained of his ham bone and sat gnawing contentedly. Ron pulled up his tent and stuffed everything back into his pack. He tossed some dirt into the dead fire pit for safety's sake and pulled the heavy pack onto his shoulders.

"Come on, Rory," Ron called to his dog. "We need to get home." He started for the trail.

"Ron?" A distant voice echoed from the trail below, causing Rory to bark excitedly.

"Who the hell . . ." Ron stopped in his tracks.

"Ron Maguire!" the voice yelled again.

"Collin?" Ron hollered in response.

A mop of red hair appeared around the turn in the trail down the mountain.

"There you are," Collin said, relieved. "Down, boy!" He wrestled with Rory who was demanding a pet. "Mab said you were up here."

"What are you doing up here?" Ron asked, closing the space between them. "What's wrong?"

"What's wrong?" Collin's voice rose. "Are you kidding me?"

"What?" Ron shrugged.

"You weren't at Mass this morning, that's what?"

"Oh, shit!"

"Father Hugh was in a mood. What's going on?"

Ron shook his head. "What time is it?"

"Almost ten," Collin responded, checking his watch.

"I lost track of the time."

"More like, what day of the week is it? What are you doing up here?"

"Just looking around," Ron said, adjusting his back pack.

"Aha!" Collin poked a finger in Ron's chest. "I thought so. I knew you wouldn't let it alone. Why didn't you ask me to come with you, for Christ's sake?"

Ron sighed heavily. "'Cause I really didn't think you'd come . . ."

Collin started to object.

". . . and you already think I'm loony."

"I don't think you're loony," Collin replied. "And I would've come with you. Did you find out what all that was?"

"No." Ron hesitated for a second. "It's been a pretty uneventful night."

"Speaking of that," Collin said. "You also apparently forgot that we—you, me, Briana and Claire—were supposed to go to the movies this afternoon."

"Crap!" Ron's hands went to his face.

"Yeah," Collin said with a smirk. "You remember Claire, don't you—your girlfriend?"

"I forgot."

"You forgot?"

"Well, jeez, Collin," Ron said, "I had some things on my mind. I had to see if I could figure out what it was I saw—what it was that disturbed our campout so."

"Look," Collin said. "I understand. Believe me . . . but Claire—that's another story."

"She's really mad?"

"Well, let's just say I've seen her . . . Nah. I don't think I've ever seen her this pissed before. You should've called."

"Let's get back to town." Ron sighed again.

"You're sure in a hurry to face the music." Collin grinned.

"Maybe we can get back in time."

"That's a big maybe."

"Look," Ron said. "You know that Claire and I are just good friends."

"Sure." Collin slapped his friend on the back. "I'm just not so sure that she knows that."

"Well . . ." Ron looked at his feet.

"Well?" Collin folded his arms.

"Shut up and let's get off this mountain," Ron said, moving briskly ahead on the trail.

Collin watched his friend scurry ahead. Something else was up.

They headed down the mountain at a pace that caused Collin to slip and fall more than once. By the time they reached the bottom of the trail, Collin was in a foul mood with his friend.

"Dammit, Ron, I'm bleeding back here!" Collin yelled.

Ron stopped. He had forgotten Collin was behind him.

"Sorry, dude," Ron said, turning back to his friend. "I just wanted to get back in time."

"Great." Collin stumbled up to him. "Well, you have fun!" He wiped at the trail of blood from his contused knee. "I'll be at the hospital."

"Good grief, Collin." Ron said, dropping to his knees. He pulled a towelette from his backpack and daubed at Collin's knee scrapes.

"Ow!" Collin jerked his knee back. "Dude!"

"Don't be such a baby!" Ron said, grabbing for the injured leg. "Let me clean the dirt out of that cut."

Collin allowed Ron to continue, sucking in air off and on, depending on the sensitivity of the spot Ron was doctoring.

"Okay," Ron said, rising. "You'll live. Let me get home and change. How much time do I have?"

"We're supposed to meet the girls in," Collin checked his watch, "thirty minutes."

"Shit!" Ron started running. "You're closer than I am!" he yelled over his shoulder. "Stall for me!"

"Just get there before the feature starts!" Collin yelled back.

Ron dashed through the mountain path gate and leapt off the curb onto the narrow, paved street. He had a ways to go as the house was well out of the town limits. He took advantage of his long stride, and like an Olympic runner, almost flew across the pavement, block after block, street after street. Rory trotted happily alongside his master, occasionally peeling off to investigate some scent or sound.

Ron's pace slowed as he turned onto the gravely, dirt road that led out to Mab's homestead at the farthermost edge of the valley proper. He all but jumped the iron gate that anchored the stone path through the front garden up to the door. He hoped that Mab was out weeding her herbs or something. He had no time to answer questions—no time and no desire. He burst into the house and headed toward the bathroom at the back hall, shedding shirt, shoes, and socks on the way.

"Whoa, boy!" Mab said, stepping out of her kitchen. "You got a bear chasing your ass or something?"

"No time, Mab!" Ron said, diving through the

bathroom door. "I'm late."

He slammed the door shut, stripping off his remaining clothes and jumping into the tub. As he turned on the shower, the initial surge of cold water caught him by surprise, but warmed quickly.

"Collin stopped by," Mab yelled through the door. She could hear Rory barking at something outside.

"I saw him," Ron yelled back.

"You forgot a date with that . . . that Buckley girl."

"It's not a date, Mab," Ron responded. "It's just a movie."

"Well," Mab said, leaning against the bathroom door. "Movie with a pretty girl sounds like a date to me." She heard the water cut off. "Hope she's understanding."

Mab almost fell through as Ron yanked open the door.

"I'll make it," Ron said, barreling out the door wrapped in a towel. "I've got to get dressed!" He raced down the hall to his bedroom and slammed the door behind him.

"Boy!" Mab eyed the pile of dirty clothes on the bathroom floor.

She gathered them up in her arms and carried them down the hall where she dropped them in an unruly mound in front of Ron's bedroom door.

"Ron Maguire!" Mab called in a volume that rattled the door.

The bedroom door swung open and Ron hopped out on one foot, trying to pull a tennis shoe over the other foot.

"I've got to hurr . . ." Ron tripped on the clothes pile and tumbled into a heap on top of them. "What the hell!"

"Oh good," Mab said, leaning back against the opposite wall, arms folded. "You found them. I was afraid you had lost dirty laundry somewhere other than the laundry basket where it belongs!"

Ron kicked the clothes pile through his bedroom door and jerked his shoe on.

"Thanks a lot, Mab," Ron said, jumping to his feet. "You're a real pal!" He started down the hall.

"I'm not your pal, boy!" Mab shouted after him. "I'm your—hold it right there!"

Ron froze in his tracks. "I'm gonna be late, Mab."

"Did you find anything up the mountain last night?"

"Mab—"

"Yes or no!"

"Yes and no," Ron responded, making a dash for the door.

"What the hell—"

"I'll explain when I get back," Ron said, exploding out the door. "Love you!"

Mab watched the back of him disappear out the door. She spun round in a huff and returned to her kitchen.

"Stay, Rory!" Ron yelled over his shoulder.

The setter headed round the house for his water bowl.

Ron closed the distance to the downtown square in no time. He saw the flashing neon marquee of the small movie theater and zeroed in on its double glass doors, pushing through them and into the brightly lit foyer next to the ticket booth. A shapely girl with long auburn hair stood by the ticket window.

"There you are," the girl said, releasing a pent-up sigh.

"Sorry," Ron said genuinely, pausing to catch his breath.

"Movie's already started." The girl brushed the thigh of her sequined denims. "I sent Briana and Collin on in."

"Has the movie itself started or just the previews?" Ron asked, hoping against hope.

"No, the movie's already started," the girl responded.

She eyed Ron up and down. "Should I just go home?"

"No!" Ron assumed his most apologetic mask. "I really am sorry, Claire, I thought I'd be home in time. It just took a little longer than planned."

"What took a little longer?" Claire had already mastered a school teacher's disapproving look in anticipation of her career choice.

"We had some problems up on the mountain the other night and I wanted to check out . . ." Ron could see that explanations were a waste of time at that point. "Well, there's really no good excuse," Ron added quickly. "I should've been here when I said and that's that. I really am sorry."

"That's a better answer," Claire said, unfolding her arms. "So, what's the plan?"

Ron thought quickly. "Have you eaten yet?"

"Not this early," Claire said. "I was just gonna grab something here during the movie."

Ron made a quick mental inventory of his wallet's resources.

"Let's walk down to the Dairy Barn," Ron suggested, "and have something decent to eat—my treat!"

"You rob a bank on the way here?" Claire smirked at him.

"Of course," Ron responded, flashing a smile. "That, and my lawn business has picked up since the spring thaw."

"Okay, let's do it." Claire returned the smile. "But you know this is gonna cost you?"

"Yes, ma'am! Understood!" Ron took Claire's arm and ushered her back out into the approaching night air.

"It still gets dark so early." Claire adjusted her purse strap over her shoulder. "I thought the days would be lengthening by now."

"They will," Ron assured her. "It's a little chilly." He pulled off his letter jacket and draped it over her.

"Thanks." Claire looked up at him. "You're lucky you showed up when you did," she said. "I've never been stood-up on a date before." Her eyes twinkled at Ron.

"I hope I'm never found guilty of that," Ron said. "You know." He looked up at the roof tops. "In case we're ever out on a date or something."

"What do you mean, *in case?*" Claire hit him on the shoulder playfully. "What do you call this?"

"This?" Ron pursed his lips. "Good friends getting together . . ."

"Really?"

Ron started to respond in what he thought was a playful mood, but the look he got stopped him.

"I'm serious," Claire said, stopping.

"What's wrong, Claire?"

Ron hoped the conversation wasn't going where it seemed to be.

"Ron Maguire!"

Ron had heard that tone once this evening already.

Claire waited till Ron was appropriately facing her. "Let's figure something out here."

"Okay." Ron responded, hoping innocent acquiescence was the best approach.

"Am I your girlfriend, or not?"

"Well, gee, Claire. . ." Ron stared at his feet. "I mean . . . you're a girl and we've been friends since junior high. I think—"

"Don't give me that crap!" Claire's glare strafed Ron. "Now let's be honest about this. I know I'm your friend and you're mine. I hope that never changes . . . but I need to know. Are we past that and on to something more, or not?"

"Claire, what's brought this on? I mean, I'm really sorry I was late and all—"

"To hell with being late! I didn't want to see that stupid movie anyway."

"Okay." Ron shuffled his feet.

"And I'm not mad at you, Ron, honestly. I just want some clarification. Briana and Collin are clearly more than just friends. Everyone thinks we are too . . . that we're a couple. I just want to know where your mind—your heart is right now."

Ron looked at her sadly. "Okay, you're right." He took her arm again. "Let's go in and sit down so we can talk."

He escorted Claire into the Dairy Barn and found an empty booth for the two of them.

"You wanna burger?" Ron asked, before he sat down.

"Sure," Claire responded, "and an unsweetened tea."

"Fries?"

"I'll just eat some of yours."

"No prob."

Ron went to the counter and placed their order. He watched Claire out of the corner of his eye, trying to discern the best way to handle the situation. He carried their drinks over to the table.

"One unsweetened ice tea," Ron said, trying to sound upbeat.

"Sit down," Claire said, accepting her drink. "Let's not make a big deal out of this. We just need to talk."

"You're right."

Ron sat across from her, his level of apprehension at an all-time high. He'd rather face a blood-thirsty banshee than this discussion any day.

"Okay." Claire took a sip of her tea. "Let's talk about

us."

"Okay." Ron reached out and took her hand. "You first?"

"No, I think you first." Claire cocked her head at him and smiled.

Ron took a deep breath and stared at Claire's hand a moment.

"You're one of my best friends," Ron began, trying to find the words that would honestly, but benignly say how he felt. "I love spending time with you—going places with you, talking to you . . ."

"Of course, you feel the same way about Collin."

Ron couldn't deny this. "You're right." He took another deep breath. "And what Briana and Collin have is more than that."

"Well," Claire offered, "at least different from that."

"Yeah." Ron nodded. "I . . . I've just . . ." He considered his words carefully. "I don't want to say anything to hurt you, Claire. He looked across the table at her, wishing he could divine her feelings at that moment. "I love you, Claire, but . . ."

"But you're not *in love* with me, are you . . . right?" Claire squeezed his hand.

Ron nodded. "I don't even know what that means," he said honestly. "I've never had that feeling for someone before. I don't know, maybe . . ."

"I think we can safely say, Ron, that if you're not *in love* with me now . . ." Claire paused, studying his reaction. "You're probably never going to be *in love* with me."

"I'm sorry, Claire." Ron looked down at the table.

"There's nothing to be sorry about," Claire said, straightening. "We don't have much control over who we fall in love with."

Ron looked at her silently, unable to think of anything more to say.

"Besides, I love you, too." Claire pulled his hand to her cheek. "We are good friends, and I want to keep that, too."

"You're the best, Claire," Ron said, dizzy with relief.

"That's true."

They laughed to relieve more of the pent-up tension.

"Of course," Claire added, "you know what this means."

Ron raised an eyebrow.

"We'll have to learn to handle one or both of us dating other people," Claire added.

"I . . ." Ron sat, back caught off guard. "I hadn't thought about that."

"Will it be a problem?"

"Well . . ." Ron shrugged. "I can't honestly say I won't be jealous. Sharing you with some other bozo won't be easy."

"Ditto."

"Things are gonna change no matter what we may think."

"Yeah," Claire said, "but . . ."

Their order number was called from the counter and Ron scooted out to retrieve their food.

"Sorry," Ron said, doling out their portions.

"I was just saying," Claire continued, "that while things are bound to change, we control how we let those changes affect our friendship."

Ron nodded. "I agree. We can still hang out."

"Of course."

"Well, at least until the other bozo gets jealous."

"Or," Claire said, laughing, "the other bozette!"

"Bozette?"

"Don't make me hit you!"

"I guess," Ron said, laughing, "that this is where the conversation gets painful."

"No," Claire took a few of Ron's French fries. "that'll come from trying to figure out how to break this to Briana and Collin."

"Ouch!"

"Yeah," Claire said with a sigh. "I'll take Briana. Collin's your responsibility."

Ron choked down the last bite of his burger. He grabbed for his soda.

"Here's hoping neither of them make a big deal out of this." Ron held up his soda to her.

"Here's hoping your hoping is effective." Claire met his toast with her tea.

They finished off their sodas and slid out of the booth.

"It's still early," Ron said, opening the door for Claire. "Wanna do the town?"

"Oh, yeah!" Claire's laughter was infectious. "Let's see . . . we could probably walk all four blocks of it in about twenty minutes, especially with everything being closed since five."

"That's true," Ron said, making a wide, sweeping gesture with his arm. "But it's really all about the journey, isn't it?"

"All twenty minutes of it?" Claire giggled.

"Plus, a spin in the park so I can push you on the swing."

"Deal." Claire slid her arm around Ron's waist and he reciprocated in kind.

"You sure I can't fall in love with you?" Ron smiled down at her.

"Positive," Claire said, resting her head against his shoulder.

"To hell with the town," Ron said suddenly. "Let's just do the park."

"To the park!"

They crossed the narrow lane to an expanse of grass and playground equipment that fronted the collection of small public buildings comprising City Hall and the one-man police station. The lone police car was, as usual, absent . . . on its routine rounds by the school and the outlying farms. The park was lit by two Victorian lamp posts on opposite corners of the park at the diagonal.

"Oh," Claire said, pointing. "They've got the fountain working."

"I think Old Lady Murphy got fed up waiting for the mayor to allocate the funds and took it upon herself to pay for the repairs."

"Can't blame her," Claire said, nodding. "She gave the fountain as a memorial to her husband."

They strolled over to the small fountain that splashed out of a circular marble encased pond.

"Throw a nickel in," Claire urged. "We need to make a wish."

"What are you gonna wish for," Ron asked, digging in his jean's pocket.

Claire took his arm. "That you find a truly remarkable person to fall in love with."

Ron held the nickel up. Claire's declaration filled him with a quiet discomfort—a realization that maybe she knew him better than he knew himself. He forced himself to look at her, relieved at the acceptance and affection he could see in her eyes.

"And I'll wish the same for you," Ron said, lobbing

the coin into the air.

It arced over the water and splashed down at the base of the fountain. Before either could speak, a pulse of cold wind struck them like a runaway car, almost toppling the two of them into the pond. Instinctively, Ron grabbed hold of Claire and pulled her to the edge of the fountain.

Claire's hand went to her hair. "What the hell was that?" she screamed.

Except for several whirling eddies of fallen leaves, the wind had stopped as quickly as it had hit.

"Sit down, Claire," Ron said, standing slowly. He scanned the dark corners of the park.

"Whatever it was has stopped," Claire said. She tried to smooth her windblown hair.

"Let's not be so sure," Ron responded.

The circumstances were all too familiar. The hairs on his arms and neck rose in a tingling reminder of the recent events at the campsite.

"Let me check things out," Ron said, venturing away from the fountain, alert for any movement.

Ron focused his awareness into that special spectrum of sight that was his gift since childhood and searched for any alien shift in the auras of the natural world about him. A billowing abstraction—an aphotic roiling sphere of darkness hovered above the swing sets not twenty feet from him. Ron froze, staring.

"What is it?" Claire called out. "What do you see?"

"Stay down!" Ron ordered.

This time he had no little bags of Mab's special tea in his pocket—the fennel and sage to ward off evil.

"Who are you?" The strength in Ron's voice was forced. "What do you want?"

The tingling sensation spread through Ron's body.

Something was about to happen.

"Goddammit!" Ron knew he had to protect Claire. "Piss off!"

Taking the offensive, he broke into a run toward the malignant, unnatural thing that seemed to dare Ron to act. The dark hole in space seemed to swell momentarily. If darkness has shades, the entity appeared to ripple, then it shot forward—straight for Ron.

Instinctively Ron clenched his fists and raised his arms like crash bars on a truck and lowered his upper body. He dropped like an offensive lineman in his charge, bracing himself for the impact, or whatever was going to happen. When the thing hit, Ron was overcome with a wave of nausea. Just as quickly, the dark effluvium seemed to melt into and through him in an instant. In the absence of any real impact, Ron fell forward bound by the laws of inertia and, hitting the ground, rolled over into a sitting position facing back the way he had come from. He saw the thing swirl about a screaming Claire and lift her off the ground.

In a panic, Ron scrambled to his feet. "No!" he shouted, stumbling forward.

In a subtle twinkle of light, Ron became aware that another figure was standing on the other side of the fountain.

"Finn!" Ron whispered in recognition.

The incredibly pale boy seemed to glow in the lamplight like a phosphorescent lightening bug. Finn raised his hand, palm out facing the thing that held the struggling Claire in its tendrils of dark matter.

"*Imeacht gan teacht ort!*" Finn cried out, condemning the thing using the exact same curse Ron had used at the campsite.

A pulse of light flashed from his palm in a discrete ball

that struck and enveloped Claire and the darkness about her.

Ron froze, hoping the thing would now weaken and release its hold on his friend, but the dark form pulsed as if in laughter and increased its pressure about Claire's oxygen deprived, spasming body.

"Fuck!" Ron shouted.

Without knowing why, he raised his own hand, aware of the tingling heat in his ring finger. His legs seemed to root into the ground and a wave of supernatural strength leeched in a stream up through his body as if he were a tree pulling water from the soil. The ring heated to a bright glow in an instant, releasing its potential energy in a throbbing pulse of amethyst light. The lasering light impacted and enveloped the darkness along with its captive in a blinding flash. The entity itself imploded to a point and then dissolved. Claire dropped to the grassy ground and lay speechless and in shock.

Ron scrambled over to her. "Claire! Claire!" He dropped to his knees beside her. "Claire, are you okay?"

Claire tried to sit up, slowly pulling herself into Ron's arms.

"Wha . . ." Claire looked up at Ron, stunned. "What's going on?"

"Just sit here a minute and catch your breath, Claire." Ron expelled a sigh of relief. "Whatever it was is over with now."

A shadow crossed between them and the lamplight. Ron found Finn standing over them, wearing the same white shirt and jeans he had sported at the campsite.

"Finn!" Ron stood. "Where did you come from?"

"I was here," Finn said in his soft, melodic voice that seemed puzzled at Ron's question.

"No, I mean . . ." Ron reached out to touch Finn's arm just to be sure the boy was real. "What just happened?"

"I was just wondering that myself," Finn responded, raising an eyebrow.

"You . . ." Ron shook his head. "What was that thing?"

"Ah," Finn responded. "One of the dark *sidhe tuatha*."

"The dark . . . what?"

"One of the *Phooka* demons."

"Okay." Ron rubbed his temples. "What was it doing here? Why did it attack Claire?"

"That is a good question," Finn said, cocking his head at the strange, long-haired and oddly-shaped creature holding onto Ron's leg.

"Hello?" Claire grabbed for Ron's arm and pulled herself up from the ground. "What does he mean, *Phooka*?"

"Claire." Ron held her steadily. "Are you alright?"

"I'm fine," Claire said, brushing his hands away. She stared at Finn. "And who are you?"

Finn eyed Claire suspiciously. "I am Finn of the—"

"Maguire," Ron said quickly over him. "Finn Maguire. My cousin . . . from . . ."

"*Murias*," Finn replied, trying to help.

"From Ireland," Ron added quickly, trying to down-play Finn's reference to one of the mythical four cities of the Gaelic Otherworld. "He's visiting a few days. They get out of school earlier than we do."

"Really?" Claire eyed Finn with equal suspicion. "You didn't mention anything about this. Hello, Finn" she said, extending a hand to strange boy before Ron could reply. "My name is Claire . . . Claire Buckley."

Finn looked at her hand.

"Shake her hand," Ron said with a tight smile. "It's a

sign of greeting over here."

Finn shrugged and accepted Claire's hand. "How do you do?" he said, giving Claire's hand a quick side-to-side shake.

"Cousin, huh?" Claire found it difficult to take her eyes off the exotic looking boy.

"You are Ron's . . . bond-mate?" Finn's sky-blue eyes narrowed at her.

Claire dissolved into laughter.

"No, dude," Ron said quickly. "No. Claire is a good friend of mine."

"Friends are good." Finn brightened.

"Anyway." Claire brushed off her jeans. "I'd still like to know what that was. I feel like I've been gassed."

"That's probably it," Ron said, seizing on the idea. "I'll bet there's a gas leak somewhere nearby and you got caught up in it—some sort of gas bubble."

"Whatever." Claire did not look convinced. "It was like I couldn't move, or see, or—"

"It was a dimensional shift," Finn explained evenly. "It was trying to take you—"

"What Finn means," Ron interjected quickly, "is that the gas deprived you of oxygen, causing you to almost lose consciousness." He gave Finn a pleading look. "That's as good an explanation as anything, right, Finn?"

Finn blinked at him.

"The important thing," Ron continued, "is that you're okay now. I'd better get you home."

"Home!" Claire said, "but . . ."

"You still look a little pale," Ron said, giving her his most concerned expression.

"But I feel fine." Claire insisted.

"Let me see," Finn said, turning Claire to face him.

Claire's eyes widened as Finn captured her gaze with his own.

"You look tired," Finn said in his low, musical voice.

Claire nodded absently.

"You need to rest," Finn stepped around her to Ron. "She'll want to go home now," he said.

Claire continued to stare off into the space Finn had just vacated.

"What did you do to her?" Ron asked, concerned.

"I have helped her to see your point of view," Finn responded.

"See my . . ." Ron put a hand on Claire's shoulder. "Claire?"

Claire blinked and shook her head. "I probably should get home," she said in a voice strangely free of inflection. "I am so tired." She put her hand on Ron's. "Is that okay?"

"Of course it is." Ron caught Finn's smile out of the corner of his eyes. "We'll take you home."

"Ron?" a familiar voice called out. "Claire? There you are."

Ron spotted the two shadowy figures across the street from the park.

"Collin?" he called out, checking his watch. "The movie can't be over this soon."

Collin and his companion crossed the intersection hurriedly.

"It sucked!" Collin said. "We both wanted it to be over with."

"Well," said the petite, short-haired girl holding his hand. "I'm not the one who wanted to see it in the first place."

"No, baby," Collin began, "I heard it was supposed to be pretty good. Anyway . . ."

"That's not what I heard," Briana replied, dropping his hand and hurrying over to Claire. "Claire, are you okay? You look peaked."

"I'm just tired," Claire replied, a little more animated. "I got in some sort of gas leak nearby and thought I wasn't gonna make it out."

"Oh, for God's sake!" Briana looked at Ron accusingly.

"Don't look at me like that," Ron said defensively. "It was a freak accident. We came over to throw a nickel in the fountain."

"Whatever." Briana put an arm about Claire. "Girl, we need to get you home, and . . ." She caught sight of Finn. "Oh," Briana said, surprised. "I don't think we've met." She smiled seductively. "I'm Briana." She held out her hand.

"I am Finn," the alluring, pale boy replied, taking her hand to shake it.

"And I'm her *boyfriend*," Collin interposed, stepping up beside Briana. "Name's Collin." He also shook Finn's hand. "Don't think I've met you before."

"He's just visiting," Ron said. "My cousin . . . from Ireland."

"Cousin?" Collin gave Finn the once over. He turned to Ron. "I thought you were adopted."

"Oh, really, Collin!" Briana fumed.

"Well . . ."

"Yes, he's adopted," Briana said, glaring at the now contrite redhead. "Which means, Mr. Know-It-All, that Mab Maguire's extended family is his as well."

"Sure, I was just . . ."

"God, Collin!" Briana's hands went to her hips. "You can be so insensitive sometimes."

"But . . ."

"It's okay," Ron said, laughing. "But Claire really does need to get home."

Claire nodded with a sigh.

"We go by her house on the way," Briana said, taking Claire's hand. "We'll get her home."

"But, Briana," Collin pled. "I thought . . ."

"We're taking Claire home," Briana said, glaring at Collin, "and that's that!"

"No, no!" Collin rolled his eyes. "That's fine."

"Gee, Briana, that would be great," Ron said. "I need to show Finn where the house is and we're on the other side of town." He gave Claire a buss on the cheek. "I'll call you tomorrow." Thanks for being so understanding."

Claire smiled warmly at him.

"Leave it to us." Briana pulled Claire toward the sidewalk. "Come on, Claire. It was nice to meet you, Finn."

"Night, Ron," Collin said dejectedly as he followed the girls across the street.

"Thanks, Collin," Ron called after him. "I owe you, man."

"Yes, you do, boy!" Collin turned and shot Ron the bird.

Ron laughed and waved at him. He stood silently next to Finn, waiting for his friends to get out of earshot.

"You have nice friends," Finn said. "The funny shaped ones . . . they are . . . female people?"

"Are you for real?" Ron said, laughing.

"Don't I look real?"

Ron wondered. Could anything that beautiful be real?

"Here." Finn took Ron's hand in his. "You can feel my touch. Yes?"

"Yeah," Ron said, looking around to be sure no one was watching. "Around here, this can get you in a lot of trouble."

Finn shrugged. "But we are friends," he said. "Like Claire and Briana."

"That's different," Ron responded, trying to hide his discomfort. "Girls are different."

"Girls?" Finn said. "How?"

"We have a lot to talk about," Ron said with a sigh.

"I can sleep with you again tonight?"

"Well . . ." Ron caught himself. He knew Finn meant sleep, but Ron had . . . "Sure," he said quickly. "You're going home with me."

"I am curious about your home," Finn said.

"Yeah, and I'm curiouser about yours."

Finn laughed and put his head on Ron's shoulder.

"You'll get to meet my Mom," Ron added.

"Mom?"

"Yeah, you know, my mother."

"Mother?" Finn pressed against Ron's side. "What is . . . *mother*?"

"Well," Ron responded, keenly aware of Finn's closeness and its unexpected effect on him. "That's a little complicated in my case."

"I will meet your . . . mother." Finn curled his arm through Ron's.

"And more, importantly," Ron said, nervously, hoping the boy's effect on him was not too noticeable. "My mom will meet you."

Chapter 5

Mab shoved the dusty notebooks away with a frustrated grunt. She had searched and researched the ancient tomes for the past two hours in vain. Now, she wondered if she would be able to get their mildew smell out of the wood of her kitchen table. These hand-scribed notebooks were her greatest legacy—the collected learning, spells, visions, and apothecary of ten maternal generations. Her own contribution lay open to a blank page that she had hoped to fill with some understanding of recent events. She knew in her deepest soul marrow that her adopted son was her mission, but she could find nothing to hint at that mission's higher purpose.

Ron's clairvoyant fits had been evident from an early age. What were the chances that such a child would be given over to her care without a connected purpose? She—a spinster, loner, pagan—not the usual choice for a baby's guardian. From the moment she had found that dark-haired, dark-eyed cherub on her stoop, swaddled in a leafy blanket, she had loved him, accepting the sure knowledge that her binding to him was an act of some powerful magic—a supernatural contract—but, why her? Why Ron? Eighteen years of uneventful child rearing, and now this . . . this magical attack in the mountains. Why now?

She sipped her soothing, chamomile tea. Perhaps it was just an isolated visitation—some momentary rip in the fabric of reality—a fluke. She shook her head. Mab Maguire did not believe in coincidence. The interconnecting of all things, all events, all universes, was a credo of absolute faith on her part. A life's experience enriched and reinforced this pagan world view every moment that she breathed.

A heavy sigh escaped her lips, expelling her frustration into the world outside her. This, too, was an act of magic. Abandoning the search, Mab pulled up from her chair, resolved to check on the solidarity of the various charms, amulets, and spells that encircled her small cottage, protecting it and its inhabitants from . . . whatever malevolence that might seek her out.

Without warning a wave of intense dizziness hit her. She grabbed the edges of the table to steady herself. She knew this feeling, and the dyspnea was quickly replaced by a panicked fear. Her gauntlet of charms was warning her. Something was coming . . . something not natural . . . something that didn't belong.

Mab staggered to her cabinet and pulled it open, scanning the contents there. She pulled a small canister down, popped open the lid and grabbed a handful of the moon-blessed cocktail of essential herbs and crushed minerals. She muttered the appropriate incantations and bindings, tightening her fist about the powdery potion, filling it with her own life force. She straightened, her face a stony and invincible mask, letting her unfailing intuition guide her to the front of the house.

It was coming . . . and she was ready.

Ron was thankful it was dark. Even in the dim lamp light along the sidewalk, he found himself nervous and uneasy walking arm-in-arm with the slight, platinum blonde *Fey*. He wasn't sure if it was his own inability to take his eyes off the creature's unearthly beauty, or if it was the boy's penchant for almost dancing along the sidewalk, rather than simply walking—and his habit of hugging tightly to Ron's arm, occasionally resting his head on Ron's shoulder—and the melodic laughter. The dim environment offered little camouflage as Finn literally seemed to glow in a halo . . . an aura that Ron hoped he was the only one who could see.

It was a mix of conflicting emotions that filled Ron as they came to the country lane that wound through the stands of pine to the Maguire homestead. Ron stopped at the entrance to the property. The cottage sat back from the road at the end of a stone path.

"Here we are," Ron said, not sure if he was relieved or disappointed that the short trek was at an end.

"This is your home?" Finn asked, taking Ron's hand in his.

"Yeah," Ron answered, forcing himself to not look away from Finn's gleaming, ice-blue eyes. "For the last eighteen years." Ron felt Finn squeeze his hand.

"You lived in a box for eighteen years?" Finn looked horrified.

"Well, we call it a home." Ron laughed. "It keeps the rain out."

"You are afraid of rain?"

"No, we just don't . . ." Ron got the impression that

Finn was not up on modern architecture. "You don't need to worry. It's a nice house . . . very comfortable . . . warm and dry."

Finn accepted that information tentatively. "People are very strange," he commented.

Ron laughed again. "Yes they are." He tugged at Finn's hand. "Come on. This is a lot better than my tent."

They walked up the path toward the low, decorative iron fence that remained one of the more popular, old-world influences in Ennis. As he got closer, Finn seemed to hug tighter to Ron's arm. As Ron reached out to open the gate, Finn jerked him back in a panic.

"Don't touch it!" Finn cried out, obviously frightened.

"It's okay!" Ron put an arm about the smaller Finn. "It's just a gate."

"It is iron," Finn said, his voice almost a whimper.

"You don't like iron?"

"It hurts."

"You're hurt?" Ron turned the *Fey* to face him.

"No," Finn said, reaching up to touch Ron's cheek lightly.

"How is it hurting you?"

"It hurts if it touches."

"It's supposed to ward off evil spirits," Ron said. "I guess it doesn't discriminate between the good and the bad.

"I am good," Finn said. His eyes stared up into Ron's, pleading.

"I know you are," Ron replied. Their closeness excited him in ways he wasn't expecting . . . some sort of sexual tension pulsed in the space between them.

It didn't seem to bother Finn, but Ron was taken completely by surprise—well . . . not completely.

"It's okay," Ron repeated, stepping backward. "I'll . . .

okay, just watch." He reached down and touched the gate. "See? It doesn't hurt me. I'll open it so you can pass through safely."

Ron swung the gate open.

The action caused Finn to gasp in alarm. He grabbed for the hand Ron had touched to the gate and pulled it up to his face, scrutinizing Ron's hand with eyes and fingers, looking for some sign of injury.

"No pain?" Finn asked, looking to Ron for reassurance.

"No pain," Ron replied. "I'm fine."

Finn smiled up at him again, lifting Ron's palm to press against his own cheek. Ron marveled at the glass-like smoothness of the *Fey*'s skin.

"Well . . ." Ron coughed and stepped through the gate, breaking his contact with Finn. "We'd better go in. Mab's probably already in bed." He held out a hand to Finn. "Come on through . . . careful."

Finn took Ron's extended hand and sidled through the gate, taking great pains to not brush against any part of it.

"Okay?" Ron asked.

"Okay," Finn replied, looking back at the iron fencing nervously. "Will there be more iron?"

Ron considered this.

"Nothing I know of that is strictly iron," Ron said. "There will be some steel, but that's a hybrid. Does anything with iron in it hurt you?"

"No," Finn said, shaking his platinum locks. "All things in this world have some evil in them, but it is pure evil that burns."

"Iron is evil?"

"Iron is bound by the dark ones," Finn said. "It has fed on their blood and is a pathway for their dark force. It has invaded many things, even people . . . your blood!"

"Okay." Ron wasn't quite sure what to make of that. "Does it hurt you to be near me?"

"No, no," Finn replied, smiling up at Ron. "In you it is bound by other, living things."

"We . . . you ought to be okay then, from here on in." Ron guided Finn to the door and turned the knob. "Well, let's get this over with," he said with a heavy sigh. "Mab's gonna have a cow!"

Before Finn could respond to the literal implications of Ron's unfamiliar metaphor, the door bolted open as if kicked. Mab sprang onto the stoop like an avenging angel, causing Ron to fall backward.

"*Téigh I dtigh diabhail!*" Mab shouted.

She let loose with the potion she held in her hand, pointing at whatever was in front of her with the other hand gripping her athame blade.

"*Damnú ort!*" she shouted for good measure, waving the small dagger in the air, making pentagrams in the haze of dust and herbs.

"Mab!" Ron shouted from the porch floor where he had landed. "What the hell?"

Mab froze, staring wide-eyed at the two boys she had just cursed and banished. She could not speak.

"Mab!" Ron said again, scrambling up from the porch. "Are you crazy?"

"But . . ." Mab stuttered.

"Finn!" Ron turned to his companion. "Did she hurt you?" He knew the power Mab's spells could unleash.

Finn looked about him at the falling herbs and mineral dust smiling. "It's very pretty," he said, holding out his hands to catch some of the sparkling cloud. "It smells like the wildflowers up on the mountain."

Ron sighed with relief to find Finn relatively unscathed. He turned back to Mab.

"Hello?" Ron stepped up to face her. "Anybody there? Have you been smoking your herbs again?"

Mab shook herself.

"But . . ." Mab looked from Ron to Finn. "Something was coming! Something not of this world." She looked out into the yard beyond them. "I felt the signs. My charms were warning me." She looked down at her empty hands. "I don't understand." She grabbed Ron by the shoulders. "Did you see anything? Feel anything?"

"Well, I feel a little dirty covered in all this mess you threw at us. "

"I've never misread a warning before," Mab continued, beside herself. Something's not right. I . . ." She noticed Finn for the first time. "Oh . . . I'm sorry, young man, I . . ."

Something caught Mab's eye and her gaze narrowed on the peculiar boy. She looked at him, calling upon her inner vision . . . then she looked at Ron.

"Well?" She pointed at Finn. "What's going on here?"

Ron shrugged. "Finn, I'd like you to meet my mom, Mab Maguire. Mab . . . meet Finn. He says he's one of the *Fey*."

The word hung in the air.

"F . . ." Mag was struck speechless.

"I hope that *f* was the *Fei* word," Ron said, trying to lighten the moment.

Mab straightened.

"Well. I'll be a monkey's uncle," Mab stuttered. "So . . . one of the *Tuatha*." She smiled at Finn. "Welcome, Finn," she said. "*Fáilte go hÉireann*," repeating the greeting in the old tongue.

"*Saol fada chugat*!" Finn responded, making a circular gesture through the air with both hands.

"I've already lived a long life, child of the goddess!" Mag giggled. "Listen to that accent. Flawless. Born to it." She clapped her hands. "Come in, both of you. What a night. The goddess has come through in spades!" Mab ushered the boys into the house.

As he passed, Ron grinned at his mom and bobbed his eyebrows.

"He looks like a china doll," Mab whispered in Ron's ear.

"Make sure nothing of pure iron touches him," Ron whispered back. "That part of the myth is apparently true."

Mab's eyes widened and she nodded.

"You both come in and get comfortable," Mab said, back to her usual boisterous volume. "I want to know everything that's happened."

Finn stood in the middle of the parlor, looking about intently, taking in the jumbled hodgepodge of colored pottery, glass, and carved wood.

"Come sit on the sofa," Ron said, taking the *Fey's* arm. "Unless," he added with a sly smile, "you'd rather float around nearer the ceiling."

"What?" Mab croaked.

"Float?" Finn asked. "How would I do that?"

"But I saw you," Ron protested. "Up on the mountain. When I first saw you, you were hovering up in the aspen branches."

Finn laughed. "I was not floating. I was sitting on a branch."

"Impossible!" Ron looked at Mab for support. "Those branches could barely hold a blue jay, much less a full-sized person."

"What's a blue jay?" Finn asked.

"Oh, for God's sake, you . . ."

"If he is *Fey*, as you say," Mab countered, "then he could have sat on an aspen branch. He isn't made the same as you and me."

"What?" Ron looked back at Finn, confused.

"You're made of elemental matter," Mab continued. "Minerals, metals, living tissue, water—things with a great deal of weight . . . mass," she explained.

"But . . ."

"Finn's composition would be different, wouldn't it," Mab continued, always the teacher of the arcane. "The *Fey* are creatures of light . . . and . . . well, only the gods know what else."

"That's ridiculous!" Ron wrinkled his brow. "He looks just as substantial as you or me . . . well . . ." Ron grinned again. "Maybe not as substantial as yourself."

"Oh, you, boy!" Mab brought a hand back.

Joking!" Ron raised his hands in submission. "Just joking, Mab."

Instead, Mab's hands went to her very substantial hips. "If ye don't believe me, test the theory," she said.

Ron looked at Finn. The young *Fey*, smiled at him—a smile that was quickly proving to be very addicting for Ron.

"Okay, Finnster Man," Ron said.

"Finn," the *Fey* corrected.

"Whatever." Ron slid his hands under Finn's arm pits. "Let's just see how . . ." He lifted the smaller boy into the air.

Unfortunately, Ron used a level of strength that his eyes told him would be needed to lift someone of Finn's size. Finn sailed up into the air like a launched rocket. Ron reversed his lift quickly, grabbing hold of Finn's waist before the Fey's head crashed into the ceiling. Ron was suddenly very grateful for the cottages Victorian ceiling heights.

"Jeez, Finn," Ron said, setting the feather light *Fey* back on his feet. "I'm so sorry. I had no idea . . ."

Finn was laughing uncontrollably. He slid his arms about Ron's neck as he was lowered back to the floor.

"You are very strong," Finn managed to get out amidst the laughter.

"Yeah, well . . ." Ron blushed. "I had no idea you were that light."

"I *am* light," Finn replied, still laughing.

"You need some protein powder in your diet or something."

"No, Ron," Mab said with a knowing smirk. "He means, he *is* light . . . well, that bound with a few more substantial elements."

Ron stared at Finn, unsure at that point.

"Well, in any case," he said, "I'll be more careful. You almost smashed into the ceiling!"

Finn put a hand on Ron's shoulder. "Throw me up again," he said excitedly.

"Are you crazy?" Ron shook his head. "You could've had a concussion—or worse!"

Finn put both of his hands on Ron's shoulders.

"You will see," Finn said, a strange look in his eyes— a sense of worry about Ron's reaction. "You need to see me more clearly if we are really to be friends."

"Finn," Ron said, his voice low and full of emotion. "I don't want to hurt you."

"Don't worry." Finn pulled both of Ron's hands to his own waist. "Throw me up!"

Ron looked at Mab.

"Go ahead," Mab said. "Trust what he says."

Ron sighed. He looked at Finn. "If I hurt you . . ."

"You will not."

Finn's smile melted Ron's reluctance. He gripped Finn's waist.

"Okay," Ron said reluctantly. "Here goes."

He lifted Finn from the floor. His biceps flexed as he flung the ephemeral *Fey* upward.

"Shit!" Ron cried out as Finn's head shot to the ceiling.

Then it happened. Finn didn't stop at the ceiling, but passed through the wood and plaster like a phantom till only his feet were visible below the unaffected ceiling. Ron could hear the *Fey*'s laughter echoing in the attic above. Slowly . . . very slowly, Finn's body began to float downward, defying the usually strong pull of gravity, until he alit on the floor below, directly in front of a stunned Ron Maguire.

"I am *Fey* . . ." Finn took Ron's face in his hands, his eyes beaming into Ron's. "Of the *Murias* tribe of the *Tuatha Dé Dannan* . . . what the people . . . you, call *tire sídhe* . . . Fairy Folk."

For the first time, Ron could find no room for equivocation. It was true. It had to be true. There was no other explanation.

Putting his hands to Finn's, he said, "You're not what I was expecting." He realized how lame that was the moment it came out.

"And you are not what I was expecting," responded Finn, cocking his head to one side.

"Now you two boys settle down and stop all this horseplay!" Mab ordered, pushing the boys toward the kitchen. She did not miss the coy looks the *Fey* was giving her son, or her son's infatuated response. "Now come in my kitchen, sit down, and tell me what's been going on!"

"We'd better do as she says." Ron pulled Finn along into the kitchen.

"This female is your lord?" Finn asked.

"Lord? No," Ron responded, looking back at Mab.

Mab bobbed her eyebrows at him, having overheard.

"She's my mom," Ron explained.

"Mom?" Finn didn't appear to understand.

"Yeah . . . you know . . . parent?"

"Parent?"

It was going to be complicated.

"I am her child," Ron said.

"Ah!" This seemed to register with Finn. "She is your birther."

"Well, if I understand that word, you're getting close." Ron smiled back at Mab who was offering him no help in his attempts to explain. "Let's just say," Ron continued, "that she has taken care of me and raised me since my birth as if she were my . . . birther."

"He is raised well," Finn said, nodding to Mab.

"Not bad, if I do say so meself," Mab said, slapping Ron on the back. "But he has gotten a little head strong recently."

"Mab!" Ron rolled his eyes.

"I am the same way," Finn said. There was that smile again. "I'm not supposed to be here, you know."

"Now we're gettin' somewhere." Mab circled her table as the boys took a seat. "Let's start with that. Why are you here?"

Ron started to protest, but Mab gave him a look that made him change his mind.

"I have left the World," Finn said.

"The world?" Ron shook his head.

"My world," Finn replied.

"What, are you from outer space?"

"Outer space?" This did not seem to register with Finn. "I am from the *Fei* World, the world of my kin."

"How far away is it?" Ron asked, trying to understand.

"There is no distance," Finn explained. "It is other."

Ron looked at Mab blankly.

"I think," Mab offered, "that we're talking . . . something like another dimension rather than somewhere in this universe."

"Okay." Ron accepted that. "Why did you leave?" he asked, returning his attention to Finn.

"I was unhappy." Finn's brow knit into a frown.

Ron nodded an invitation for Finn to continue.

"There was no love there for me."

Ron sat back in his chair. "That's hard to believe, Finn. Who couldn't love . . ." He paused suddenly self-conscious about Mab's presence. "I mean . . . why was there no love for you? Did you do something bad?"

"I have no . . ." Finn shrugged. "*Clann?*"

"No family?" Ron said. "How awful! What happened to them?"

"Happened?" Finn looked away. "*Tá mé* . . . I am . . . *faoi chrann smola!*"

"Cursed? You're cursed?" Ron looked to Mab again, but she busied herself making tea, listening. "How are you cursed, Finn?" Ron asked.

Finn was visibly upset at the admission. He had begun to tremble. "*Tá mé* . . ." He searched Ron's mind for the English. "I am . . ." Finn lowered his head in shame. "*Corcra!*"

"Purple? You're purple? I don't understand. What do

you mean, you're purple?"

"It doesn't disgust you?" Finn asked, not looking up.

"How can it disgust me? I don't know what it means."
Ron reached out and tugged on Finn's hand, trying to get
the young *Fey* to look up. "What does being *corcra* mean . . .
exactly?"

"When I was birthed, the ancient ones divined my
purpose . . ." Finn sighed. "The goddess chose me to mate
the great *Sciathán Corcra*, the Purple Wing . . . the Cursed
One!"

"Okay." Ron tried to suppress the strange feeling
welling up in him . . . disappointment . . . or . . . jealousy.
"Who is this Purple Wing you're supposed to mate?"

Crystalline tears cascaded down Finn's cheeks.

"He was . . ." Finn stifled a sob. "Greatest among the
Greats. Our tribe's defender. The Sword Bearer."

"Doesn't sound very cursed to me," Ron said, unimpressed.

"But he is no more." Finn would still not look up.
"Not for over two hundred cycles of life. He was killed in
the Great Uprising—the war between the forces of the
Leanan-sidhe and the Trooping Tribes . . . the *Falias*, the
Finias, the *Glorias*, and my tribe, the *Murias*."

"So he was shamed in defeat?"

"No, no!" Finn's eyes met Ron's for a split second.
"He was poisoned with iron . . . a traitor among our own."

"But how does all this curse you?"

"He and his consort, the *Sciathán Bán*, the White Wing,
birthed before they were killed . . . but, the cocoon was
lost."

"The cocoon?"

Finn looked up, confused, and tried to search Ron's
mind for a likely synonym.

"Never mind," Ron said. "Let me get this straight. The . . . child was lost, but you're . . . I don't know . . . promised to this missing . . . Purple Wing?"

"There have been others before me," Finn said softly. "But the Purple Wing's betrothed are all shunned. No one can risk bonding with the Purple Wing's betrothed—so the ones promised to him are kept cloistered—shut away. They all eventually . . . destroyed themselves."

Ron couldn't believe his ears. "And you're one of these . . . promised ones?" he asked.

Finn nodded.

They sat in silence for a moment. Without a word Mab set out cups and poured the tea.

"So you escaped," Ron said, finally. "You left."

Finn tried to meet Ron's gaze. He could only nod.

"Well, I'll tell you this right now!" Ron's voice and volume went up, making Finn cringe in his chair. Ron reached out to Finn, taking both the *Fey*'s hands in his own. "You don't disgust me!"

Finn slowly looked up.

When he had Finn's eyes, Ron said, "They disgust me! What they've done to you is wrong!"

"But it is my destiny." Finn stifled another sob. "Why I was made. I have shamed my *Clann*."

"Bullshit!" Ron turned angrily to Mab. "Have you ever heard such crap?"

"The *Fey* are not like us," Mab said, gently. "They have different ways—different moral imperatives . . . reasoning." She looked at Finn. "But that's not everything is it?"

Finn sat silently, looking at his hands in Ron's.

"No," Finn said, taking a deep breath. He looked at Ron. "I am also doomed!"

"What?" Ron managed to say. "What do you mean

doomed?"

"The *Phooka* of the *Leanan-sidhe* will kill me," Finn responded hopelessly. "They have already tried."

"You mean that black thing in the park?" Ron let out his breath. "The same thing that happened up on the mountain?"

Finn nodded.

"But . . ." Ron caught himself. "But those things attacked me—attacked Claire!"

"You were attacked!" Mab turned from her tea brewing. "How?"

"This dark . . . thing," Ron stuttered. "I don't know what it was. We . . ."

Mab turned on Finn. "You said these demons were after you," she said, standing over Finn like an angry lioness. "Why did they attack my son?"

"Take it easy, Mab," Ron said. "Give Finn a chance to explain."

"When I left the World . . ." Finn shifted in his chair, his look pleading. "The *Leanan-sidhe* was able to sense my presence in this world. Somehow he knows who and what I am. He is the sworn enemy of the Purple Wing."

"That doesn't answer the question," Mab muttered.

"Mab?" Ron glared at his mom. "Go on, Finn."

"I have tried to stay hidden," Finn continued, "far away from the Gateway."

"Gateway?"

"The passage between this world and mine. It was forbidden, but . . ." Finn smiled slightly. "I found it."

"Go on." Ron glared at Mab again. She only shrugged at her son.

"I heard you and your friends in the mountain," Finn continued. "I was cold and you had . . . fire." Finn seemed to shrink into his chair. "I watched you all from the trees. When the *Phooka* came for me, I bound myself to the trees where it could not see me. It must have sensed my interest in your group, and . . . he attacked you to draw me out."

"Apparently that didn't work."

"Yes." Finn grew excited. "Because of you. You have a powerful magic!"

"Well . . ."

Mab intervened. "What does he mean by that?"

"He cursed the *Phooka*!" Finn said. "He cast his magic on the creature and it was no more."

"Well?" Mab raised an eyebrow at her son.

"Jeez, Mab," Ron said with a shrug. "It wasn't anything like that. I just grabbed up some of the ash from the fire like you do when you're sanctifying the Coven's holy ground. I used your spell and threw the ash. The thing went away. Go figure!"

Mab said nothing. She nodded to herself, thanking the training she had given the boy in the past.

"But tonight was different," Ron said before he could stop himself.

"How?" Mab shot forward in her chair, holding on to the edges of the table. "What happened tonight?"

"Crap!" Ron mumbled.

"The goddess has given him *Fei* power," Finn said, his excitement growing. "Great power. His is stronger than mine. I sent the light at the demon, but it did not affect him. I am too newborn . . . but, Ron's light was more powerful. Again the *Phooka* was banished to *hIfreann*."

"Banishing something to hell may be an overstatement." Ron said, laughing. He sensed Mab was about to explode. "Okay, justa minute!" He tried a different approach. "I don't know what happened. It . . ." He looked down at the cool, silver encircling his thumb. "It was something to do with this ring. It gets hot and . . . things happen!"

"So. It is charmed!" Mab stared at the ring. "Made to protect you."

"Show me!" Finn demanded.

Finn grabbed for Ron's hand and studied the oddly shaped ring intently. His eyes lost their usual sky-blue color, matching the silver hue of the ring as he looked for a deeper sense in the object.

"Ooo!" Finn sat back from it. "This is *Fei* magic. *Danu* is in it. It has been wrought by the *Trí Dé Dána*!"

"The what of what?" Ron looked at the ring, comfortably wrapping his thumb.

"The *Trí Dé Dána*," Mab replied. "The three gods of *Fei* craftsmanship—creators of the Four Hallows of the fairies—the *Tuatha Dé Danann*."

"Hallows?" Ron sighed. "You people are talking a foreign, foreign language."

"The Four Hallows," Mab repeated, impatiently. "The four treasures."

Ron stared at her blankly.

"Where is your brain, boy?" Mab threw up her hands. "You've studied the mythology—the Cauldron of Renewal, the Stone of Destiny, The Spear of Victory, and the Sword of light!"

"Whatever!" Ron shook his head. "All this could have a perfectly natural explanation. Let's not go all *Harry Potter* over circumstances that could just be group hysteria and—"

"Group hysteria!" Mab said, slamming her hands on the oaken table, rattling the array of teacups. "For someone who lives with a witch and has the gifts you were obviously born with, you are just a dense eighteen-year-old boy!" The last word she spat like a bad taste.

"But, Mab—"

"But Mab nothing!" Mab pushed off from the table to get her teapot. "And while you're fishing around for . . . natural explanations, I can't wait for your scientific assessment of . . ." She hovered over Finn with the steaming pot of tea. "This!" She tapped Finn on the head.

Ron bit his lip. That was a hard one to explain away.

Finn smiled up at him, fascinated by the contest between Ron and the woman.

"And," Mab thundered. "While you're plodding about in denial, you've got elf demons coming for you to get at . . . him!" She tapped Finn on the head again for emphasis.

Finn's expression dropped. "The witch is right," he said above a quivering chin. "I have put you in danger."

Ron shook his head. "Don't be—"

"I have!" Finn insisted, wringing his hands. "I must go. I must—"

"The hell you will!" Ron jumped up. "You're not going anywhere!" He turned on Mab. "I don't know about *Fei* moral imperatives, but I do know about human ones. We cannot turn out someone in need. Where's the hospitality in that? It's against everything you stand for—everything you taught me!"

"Now . . ." Mab said. "No one said anything—"

"I won't do it!" Ron looked down at Finn. "You are not leaving!"

Finn started to speak.

"No!" Ron interjected. "You promise me. Promise me you won't leave!"

"They will come for me," Finn said, weakly. "They will come."

"Let 'em!" Ron said. "You'll be safe here, right, Mab?

This house is magically sealed-up tighter than the Pentagon."

"The Pentagon is not invincible," Mab said, pouring tea into everyone's cups.

"I'm not worried." Ron tried to sound convincing. "The house will give us time to think and plan."

Finn looked at Mab and she at him.

"Mab?" Ron said, regaining his chair. He put his hands on hers. "There are no coincidences, right? Everything happens for a reason. That's what you say. We," he gestured to Mab and Finn, "are together here for a reason. Surely the goddess expects us to . . . to do whatever it is we're expected to do!" He threw his hands up, unable to articulate his thoughts any better.

"You're a real little shit, boy," Mab said, fondling her teapot's snout, "turning me own words against me."

"Yep." Ron grinned at her. "You also taught me how to do that."

"Right." Mab turned to Finn. "You are welcome here, *Fey*. The *Tuatha Dé Dannan*, the children of the goddess, are great spirits in my faith." Her eyes veiled as she looked at the boy with her spirit eyes. "You are light . . . a pure light. *Mo shecht mbeanacht ort!*" she said, in blessing.

Mab's words affected Finn visibly. At first, he could only nod. "*Slán leat!*" he said, returning the blessing to her.

"That's that." Mab sat back. "Let's drink our tea."

Mab and Ron sipped at their steaming teacups.

"Have you any honey?" Finn asked with a sly smile.

"Sure," Ron said, pointing to the counter behind Mab. "Mab keeps a few hives at the wood's edge."

Mab put her teacup down slowly.

Are you sure that's wise?" Mab asked, giving Finn a knowing look.

"It would renew my life force," Finn replied. "Don't

worry, I'm used to it," he added with a coy shrug. "It's expected of the White Wing."

Mab looked from Finn to Ron and back again. "This ought to be interesting," she said with her own shrug and reached behind her for the honey pot.

"What's the big deal about the honey?" Ron asked. "I think I'll have a little too."

"All right. Honey for everyone," Mab said with a chuckle. She slid the honey pot to the center of the table between Finn and Ron.

Ron offered it to Finn first.

The young *Fey* hugged himself with excitement.

"I love honey," Finn said, mewing with pleasure. He loaded the honey dipper and held it over his cup until its contents fully drained into his tea. He returned the dipper to the honey pot, but before Ron could pull the container over to himself, Finn spoke up. "Once more, please?"

"Sure." Ron let go of the honey pot. "You've been at your stash in the cellar, haven't you?" he asked Mab, annoyed by her incessant chuckling.

"Okay," Mab said, standing and picking up her cup and saucer. "I'm done here and I'm going to bed. I've got a lot of craft to study in the morning to keep our butts out of the fire." Something that she said made her giggle again as she retreated for the hallway.

"What's with you, Mab?" Ron asked with unbridled sarcasm. "What's so funny?"

Mab turned and assumed her most serious expression.

"Nothin' my wee son, nothing," Mab said, the edges of her lips quivering. "Just a little concern about the honey."

"The honey?" Ron looked at her like she had truly gone off the deep end. "What does he do?" Ron continued smugly. "Turn into a giant bumble bee or something?"

"Don't be silly, son!" Mab could not contain her laughter as she held onto her cup and saucer for dear life until she could finally recapture some semblance of composure. "Funny thing about honey, though . . ." She started back down the hall. "It's rumored to be one super-duper aphrodisiac for fairies!"

Mab laughed her way down the hall.

Ron looked at Finn. The *Fey* smacked his lips, slurping his tea with great relish.

"Oh." Ron sipped his own tea nervously.

Ron soaped himself, letting the hot water drench over him. He had finally gotten Finn settled in a sleeping bag on the floor by his bed and was relieved to have a few minutes to himself to sort out the evening's events. After three cups of honey laced with tea, Finn had not changed into a raving maniac leaving Ron to wonder at Mab's bad joke. Did she suspect something about . . . He lifted his face into the shower stream. He didn't even know what he was feeling, so there was no way his mom . . .

In any case, his plan was to take things very slow with the *Fey* and figure things out. *Fey* rhymes with gay. Collin's words were a constant, haunting—no, nagging meme stuck in his head. He had never thought of himself as . . . He soaked his hair, massaging his scalp vigorously. He liked girls. That was the problem, though. *Like* was never enough.

Ron propped his hands against the tile behind the showerhead and leaned into the stream of water. What would Mab think? Hell's bells, what would Collin, Claire—goddess forbid—Nolan, and the others think?

Ron heard the shower door shut behind him and

turned sharply, finding Finn standing pale, naked, almost shimmering as the water droplets covered him.

"Finn!" was all Ron could get out.

Finn said nothing in reply. He had a look in his eyes— one Ron had not seen before, except maybe when he had offered him the honey.

"Finn?" Ron said again as the young *Fey* moved in closer. Ron could feel a warmth—an intense heat radiating off the smaller boy's skin.

Finn slid his hands around Ron, and pulled their bodies together. He rested his head against Ron's chest, sighing heavily, digging his fingernails into the skin of Ron's back.

Ron couldn't speak . . . couldn't move . . . couldn't . . . well, parts of him were obviously unaffected by the paralysis. He wasn't sure if it was fear, panic, or something new he battled as he felt his own erection rising up between them.

"Finn," Ron tried again. "I . . . maybe we . . . shouldn't . . ."

"You are right," Finn said in a hoarse whisper, turning his face up to Ron's. "A White Wing is not permitted to bond with anyone but the Purple Wing." His eyes swam in their silvery orbs like shiny, clear marbles. "And we are expressly forbidden to bond with human people."

Ron was at once relieved and . . . oddly disappointed at Finn's revelation.

"That's good," Ron said, unable to pull his eyes away from Finn or his attention from the heated excitement that seemed to hold their bodies together with an almost magical force. "I thought . . . why can't you bond with a human?" Ron asked, biting his lip as the words escaped his mouth— only because Finn seemed to have the same physical equip- ment . . . working equipment as a human male.

Finn's exotic, comely features shone through the

building shower steam.

"Human people have not always survived the effort," Finn said. His face seemed to float up out of the steam, closer to Ron's like a perigee moon. "But you are exceptionally strong," Finn added, pulling Ron to him in his own display of strength. "And you command a *Fei* power not unlike my own."

Finn brushed his forehead against Ron's lips.

"I . . ." Ron thought he might explode. "We . . ." His whole body throbbed with the same pulsing heartbeat that engorged his exquisitely pained cock-head. "Jesus!" he almost croaked.

Finn's finger nails dug into Ron's buttocks, burying human's throbbing member against the *Fey's* silken belly.

"I think you will survive," Finn said, as he slowly slid down Ron's wet body to his knees.

"But . . ." Ron's eyes followed Finn on the journey down, but clenched shut as he felt the *Fey's* hot breath envelope his excruciatingly ripe manhood. "I . . . thought . . ." Ron shook with the rhythmic stroking of Finn's feverish lips over his shaft. ". . . this was . . . forbidden!"

Finn stopped his oral pleasuring and gracefully rose to bring his face up to Ron's.

"It won't be the first rule I've broken," Finn whispered, touching his lips to Ron's.

"But . . ." Ron began

Finn pressed his lips hungrily to Ron's, forcing his tongue into the human's consenting mouth. When he finally pulled away, Ron was panting heavily, but not from lack of oxygen.

"Your bed looks comfortable," Finn said. He ran his fingers up into Ron's black curls.

He pulled Ron to the shower door.

"But . . ." Ron continued to protest weakly. "What if Mab hears . . ."

Finn smiled and everything else disappeared from Ron's vision.

"Tonight," Finn said, his supernatural desire radiating from his every pore, "even the goddess will hear your pleasure screams!"

"Oh . . . my . . ." Ron allowed . . . or stopped resisting as Finn led him out of the shower, the *Fey's* long, pale fingers wrapped tightly about Ron's hardness.

Chapter 6

Ron woke with a start, gasping in air as if he had just surfaced from a long, deep-water dive. He relaxed as the large, bohemian star chandelier above, brought him back to his familiar surroundings. A light weight pressed across his left side, and he looked down to find Finn stretched out over him, entwined in a sheet that barely covered the milky skin of his buttocks. A mixture of shock and contentment filled Ron as he felt Finn stir slightly in his arms. Finn's face was buried under Ron's chin and Ron listened to the *Fey's* rhythmic breathing.

It was true! He had actually done . . . it . . .with a guy . . . well, a *Fei* guy . . . but a guy nonetheless. He waited for some expected tinge of shame to ruin the exhilaration that the memory of the previous night seemed to envelope him in, but no rapprochement dared intrude. A blushing heat rose in his cheeks as he relived the pleasure he had endured—acts he had committed—the idea of which before, he refused to even face. Now as he let his eyes feed hungrily over the flawless, delicious beauty that was Finn, he did not deny the overwhelming desire to repeat the previous night's revelry.

He remembered, too, the aching desperation he felt at the end of the first two hours of lovemaking as he tried to satisfy an insatiable Finn, who, thankfully, receded into the unconsciousness of sleep, leaving Ron in a state bordering on laughter and tears—completeness and fracturing—exhilaration and exhaustion. Ron knew he would do it all again—in a heartbeat—and that was the most satisfying thought of all.

"Boys!" A light rapping knock shook the bedroom door. "You decent?"

Ron hesitated. "No, ma'am," he called out, smiling at the honesty of his answer.

There was a momentary silence.

"Breakfast is ready if anyone's interested." Mab's voice receded with her down the hall.

Ron extracted Finn's head from under his chin and slid down in the bed to lay face to face next to him. He stroked the *Fey's* fair cheek with his fingers.

"Finn?" Ron said softly. He leaned in and brushed his lips over Finn's eyes. "Finn?"

Finn stirred awake, inhaling deeply.

"Are you awake?" Ron waited for the *Fey's* eyes to slowly open, revealing their bright, sky blue irises. "Hi," Ron greeted their waking.

Finn smiled, blinking his eyes against the bright sunlight streaming in through the sheer curtains, next to the twin bed they were both squeezed into. He shut his eyes again and pressed his forehead against Ron's cheek.

"My head hurts," Finn said, humming deeply in his throat.

"Maybe you'd better lay off the honey for a while," Ron responded, suppressing the desire to laugh.

"Honey?" Finn sat up, his eyes fully open.

"No more honey!" Ron replied through his laughter. "At least, no more today or I'll need emergency medical care!" He kissed Finn's nose. "We'll have to find a safer way to feed your sweet tooth."

Finn sighed and collapsed against Ron, resting his head on Ron's chest.

"I like honey," Finn said wistfully.

"I do to," Ron said, stroking the *Fey's* back. "But when you eat honey, I think I'd better smoke crack or something."

"Crack!"

"Never mind." Ron smiled down at Finn's now amethyst eyes. "Wait," Ron said, surprised. "I thought your eyes were . . ." He lay back into his pillow. "Whatever. You've got me major screwed up!" He chuckled. "Major!"

"I've hurt you?" Finn sat up. "I did not mean to." His face registered his worry.

"No, no," Ron replied quickly. "You didn't hurt me . . . actually . . . quite the opposite."

"I healed you?" Now Finn's eyebrows knitted in confusion.

Ron looked at him in silence for a moment.

"Yeah," Ron said softly, stroking Finn's cheek. "Yeah, I guess you have."

"That's good." Finn snuggled into Ron's embrace.

Ron's arms tightened about the slight *Fey.* He breathed in the florid scent of Finn's platinum locks. Finally he sat up, still holding Finn cradled in his arms.

"Let's eat something," Ron said. "Something other than honey," he added quickly, smiling down at Finn. "You'll like Mab's cooking."

"Cooking?"

"Okay." Ron thought a minute. "Guys are from Mars and *Fey* are definitely from . . . somewhere else altogether." He laughed at his own joke. "Come on. Let's get up and get dressed."

Ron spun around on the bed to grab his gym shorts that usually served as his pajamas.

"We . . ." Ron stopped short. When he turned back, Finn was standing on the opposite side of the bed, fully dressed.

"How the hell do you do that?' Ron shook his head. "Never mind." He pulled on his shorts and grabbed a tee shirt out of the nearby chest of drawers. "You get in and out of clothes like . . . well, I don't know like what."

"I am not really wearing clothing like you," Finn said, stretching his lithe frame.

Ron pulled his head through his tee shirt and froze. Finn stood stark naked. He waved coyly to Ron.

"But . . ." Ron stammered.

Now Finn was fully dressed again.

Ron rolled his eyes. "Best stay like that when other people are about," he said, motioning Finn around to the foot of the bed. "People are a little funny about nudity."

"And when others are not around?" Finn took Ron's hand.

"Oh." Ron grinned at him. "Just be yourself."

"You are people," Finn responded with a shrug. "Does . . . nudity not bother you?"

"Yours doesn't."

"No?"

"I think you're very beautiful to look at." Ron felt himself blush.

"I am beautiful?" Finn threw his arms about Ron and hugged him.

"Yes," Ron said, kissing the top of Finn's head. "You are beautiful . . . more beautiful than any people I've met."

"I will be your bond-mate," Finn said, looking up at

Ron, his eyes wide and full of emotion, "if you like."

"I'm not sure what that means," Ron said truthfully, "but if that means a repeat of last night, I'm all for it!"

"It does!" Finn tried to pull Ron back to the bed.

"Whoa, whoa!" Ron could not contain his laughter. "I need some recovery time!" He pulled Finn back into his arms. "A good breakfast will be the start of that recovery."

Finn shrugged again. "Then we must eat."

As the boys started out into the hall, Finn grabbed for Ron's arm and attached himself to Ron's side.

Ron stopped, and nervously assessed the situation.

"Finn," Ron said, trying to sound matter-of-fact. "If it's okay, I'd kinda like to keep our . . . our feelings for each other private. I'm not sure Mab would approve of people and *Fey* being . . . bond-mates."

"Not approve?" Finn looked up at Ron, puzzled. "The witch does not like me?"

"No, no, no!" Ron put an arm over Finn's shoulders. "It has nothing to do with that." He turned Finn to face him. "Remember when I said people here are funny about nudity?"

Finn nodded.

"Well," Ron said with a shrug, "they're even funnier about sex."

"Sex?"

"Bond-mating."

"People think . . . sex . . . is funny?"

"When I say people are funny about sex," Ron said, sighing, "I mean that sex makes them very nervous, especially . . . especially when it's two . . . guys."

"Guys?" Finn frowned. "We are not . . . guys. You are a people and I am *Fey*."

"That's true," Ron said, chuckling, "and that will

probably make people even more nervous."

Finn thought about this. "What should I do?" he asked.

"Well, just pretend that we . . . you and I are friends."

"We *are* friends."

"Yeah, but . . . we're more than friends."

"So . . . no bond-mating?" Finn's disappointment was evident.

"Well, not in front of other people."

"I don't understand."

"Okay," Ron said, hearing Mab rustling in the kitchen. "Just do what *Fei* friends do."

"I am."

"This is how *Fei* friends act?" Ron nodded to Finn's tight grasp of his hand.

"We are very . . . tactile."

"And that's a good thing when we are alone," Ron responded. "But, too much touching is interpreted by many people as . . . well, as bond-mating."

"Really?" Finn's eyes widened. "People are very strange indeed."

"Now you get it."

"I am not happy about this." Finn released Ron's hand.

"I know," Ron responded, realizing he felt the same way. He pulled Finn to him and kissed him lightly on the lips. "But, it gives me something to really look forward to when we're alone."

That made Finn smile. "You have much to look forward to." He pressed his body against Ron's.

"Food!" Ron jumped back, laughing. "Man does not live by bond-mating alone!"

Finn gave a dismissive wave and pushed ahead into

the kitchen.

Mab looked up from her omelet construction. "Well," she said, returning to her work. "It's about time you two showed up."

"Give us a break, Mab," Ron said. "We had to get dressed."

"Indeed," Finn said, giving Ron a meaningful look. "*Sonas ort!*" he said, nodding to Mab.

"*Dia duit ar maidin,*" Mab responded, bringing two full plates over to the table. "I'm glad to see the two of you are okay."

"What's that supposed to mean?" Ron sniffed appreciatively at his plate.

"Oh, nothing," Mab replied, sighing dramatically and returning to the counter for her own plate. "I thought the Pentecostals had you in their thrall, what with the number of times you screamed out to the Christian god."

"We . . ." Ron's face went crimson. "We were just fooling around . . . wrestling . . ." He glanced at Finn. "Finn's stronger than he looks." That excuse wasn't even convincing him.

"Really?" Mab gestured theatrically. "I thought you were being tortured or something." She took a bite of her eggs, and looked at Finn. "You didn't hurt my little boy, did you?"

"I do not think pain was a problem." Finn added, looking her straight in the eye.

Ron choked on his food. "Try the bacon," he said, recovering. "Mab cooks it thick and crispy."

"This is animal flesh and fowl ova." Finn stared at his plate.

"Well . . . yes . . . I guess it is." Ron swallowed hard and looked at his own food. "You don't like bacon?"

"This was sentient life. How can you consume it like a rabid *Phooka*?"

"It's what we eat!" Ron's stomach roiled as he swallowed a bite. "But, now . . ." He jumped up from the table and fled toward the bathroom.

Mab watched her son barrel out of the room. "Interesting," she said. "Well, my young *Fei* friend. You seem to have put my boy off his food."

"Have you anything . . . non-sentient in your cupboard?" Finn asked.

"Oh, I think I can find you something." Mab stood with a smile. "Will you consume milk?"

"Oh," Finn said with a big smile. "Milk is very good."

Mab pulled a bowl from the cabinet and a crockery jar from the counter.

"You'll like this granola I make. It's all grains and nuts . . ." She smiled to herself. "Flavored with honey."

"Honey!" Finn shook with excitement. "I will love your . . . granola!"

The bemused witch filled Finn's bowl with the crunchy cereal and doused it with milk.

"*Bain suit as an bia*," Mab said with a chuckle.

Finn set upon his cereal with great gusto, shoveling large spoonful's of the honey-sweetened granola into his mouth.

"Oh, man!" Ron hung onto the counter by the kitchen door. "Jeez, Mab!" he said, fighting back a dry heave. "Do you think there was something wrong with the bacon?"

"There's nothing wrong with my bacon, boy," Mab retorted. "It's all in your head."

"Actually . . ." Ron stumbled back to his place at the table. "It's all in my stomach . . . well, at least it was."

Finn swallowed to make room for speech. "You

should have some granola."

"I think I'll wait on it," Ron responded, holding his stomach.

"It has honey!" Finn added, spooning another heap of the cereal into his mouth.

Ron gave Mab a look.

"What?" Mab sipped her coffee. "Honey's good for you."

Ron ignored her. "We talked about the honey, Finn."

Finn paused in his chewing. He blinked at Ron and swallowed hard.

"But . . ." Finn pointed at Mab. "Honey is good for you."

Mab dissolved into laughter.

"Mab, you're not helping," Ron said, rolling his eyes.

"But the boy likes honey," Mab said, wiping her eyes.

"Yes . . . but . . ."

"But what?" Mab raised an eyebrow at Ron.

"Nothing," Ron said with a sheepish smile to Finn. "Eat your cereal."

Obediently and with undisguised pleasure, Finn shoveled another large spoonful of the hearty cereal into his mouth.

"What about you? Mab asked. "Has your stomach settled?"

"Yeah." Ron pushed the plate away. "I'd better have cereal too. Can't seem to handle the bacon this morning."

"Hmmmm," Mab intoned, eyeing her son intently. "Hope you're not coming down with something. Graduation's only a week away." She reached for a bowl for Ron.

"Graduation?" Finn swallowed. "What is graduation?"

"From high school," Ron said, pouring milk over his granola. "Education."

"Ahh!" Finn filled another spoon with cereal. "I, too, am done with that."

"You graduated high school."

"I do not know this . . . high school, " Finn said with a shrug, "but I attended my last lessons with my elder mentor before I escaped. He was tiresome."

"Aren't they all?" Ron laughed. "So . . . I've been meaning to ask . . . I guess that's where you learned to speak English so well."

"English?"

"Yeah, English."

"What is English?"

Ron sat back. "You know," he said, "the language we're speaking?"

"The . . ." Finn blinked at Ron. "Oh, yes, I see. No, we do not learn English."

"But, how do you know how to speak it?"

"I . . ." Finn thought a moment. "It just is. Your . . . thoughts . . . your communication is inherent in your aura . . . your physical vibration. I . . . join it. It is how *Fey* communicate with all manner of beings. But you do the same. You speak *Fey*. You both do."

"We speak Gaelic," Ron said, shaking his head in amazement. "We learned to speak it. I'm still learning."

"So much effort." Finn looked from his spoon to Ron. "People are very strange." He maneuvered the heaping spoon into his mouth.

"Oh, yeah," Ron said, grinning at Mab. "People are *very* strange."

"Hmmm," Finn managed through a mouthful of granola. He chewed fiercely. "Especially about bond-mating."

"Bond-mating?" Mab's eyebrows went up.

Ron shook his head at Finn to no avail.

"Yes," Finn continued with a mouthful. "Sex."

"Indeed?" Mab watched the cascade of crimson flood through Ron's face and neck. "It would seem you and I had the wrong birds and bees lecture."

"Mab!" Ron choked on the word.

Mab narrowed her eyes at Ron. "I guess all that . . . noise I heard last night wasn't just a wrestling match, now was it?"

"Oh, no!" Finn laughed. "Ron makes a lot of noise when I—"

"Finn!" Ron managed, gasping for air. He fought for control. "This is not a conversation we're going to have with my mom!"

Finn looked from one to the other, puzzled.

"The details are unimportant," Mab said chuckling to herself. She cut her eyes at Finn. "You don't have any strange diseases you could give my son, do you?"

"Mab!"

"No, no." Finn said, shaking his head. "I only give him—"

"Finn!" Ron wished for a spell that would shrink himself into the floor boards. "Both of you . . . let's change the subject."

"We can talk about the grandchildren later." Mab patted her son's hand.

"Mab?"

Mab laughed uproariously. Finn joined her, not really understanding the joke, but he loved to laugh.

"What are you laughing at?" Ron asked, fully aware that Finn was in the dark.

"This is fun," Finn responded, scraping the bottom of his bowl with his spoon.

Ron rolled his eyes again. "What we should be talking about," he said, cutting his eyes at Mab, "is what we're going to do about these *Phooka*!"

"Yes." Mab pushed up from the table. "Already ahead of you." She returned to the counter and retrieved her notebook. "While you two were . . . sleeping last night . . ." She winked at Finn. "I was looking through the family archives." She plopped back into her chair and flipped the notebook open. "*Phooka* are elven in nature. They've been purposefully bred . . . devolved into single-minded, obedient slaves who obey one master."

"They are evil and smell like dung!" Finn interrupted with a nod.

Mab continued. "The elven clans tend to stay clear of this plane as they have a weakness to a lot of our environment . . . light, pollen, silver, ashwood . . . to name a few."

"That makes things easier," Ron said.

"Don't bet on it!" Mab warned. They are very powerful. They can absorb weak light and be almost invisible in the dark. They are far stronger than we mortals. They can harness and fire off huge amounts of dark matter that can annihilate the positive matter that binds this world together, and . . . because of their photovoric nature . . ." She eyed Finn. "They eat fairies!"

"What?" Ron shot up.

"It is true," Finn said in a whisper, shivering in his chair. "They are ravenous, deadly foes of the *Fey*!"

Ron regained his seat. "Shit!" He almost spat. "We'll just have to try and stay in a protected area at night."

"Sure," Mab replied. "That'll work for a while, but how long do you plan on . . . hiding out at night? Graduation's at night. You have to go to the movies at night . . . a lot of life takes place at night."

"You're right, of course." Ron pushed back from the table. "We'll have to have a face-off eventually. We'll have to find a way to stack the cards in our favor."

"I'll work on that," Mab said, glancing up at the wall clock. "Meanwhile, you have a fitting for cap and gown in an hour."

"Oh, man!" Ron almost fell out of his chair. "I forgot." He gave Finn a pleading look. "I have to be at the school this morning. Will you be all right here?"

"Yes," Finn said, pushing his empty bowl away. "But I will not be here. I will be with you."

Ron caught his breath, not expecting this possibility.

"Of course, he'll be with you," Mab said. "Why would you go off and leave the boy here with me?"

"Well . . . I . . ."

"Is there a problem with him going with you? Something you're concerned about?"

"No! I mean . . ."

"Claire, perhaps?" Mab asked with feigned innocence.

"Mab!" Ron rolled his eyes. "It's not a problem." He smiled at Finn. "Of course you're going with me. Besides, I don't think the *Phooka* will bother us in the bright light of day."

"Will there be other peoples at this school?" Finn asked, clasping his hands excitedly.

"Sure."

"More of your girlfriends and boyfriends?"

"Well . . . no," Ron said, uncomfortable at Finn's choice of words.

"No?" Mab said with a low chuckle.

"What I mean," Ron said, cutting Mab a sharp look, "is, yes . . . there will be lots of my school friends there . . . both male and female." He prodded Finn under the table with his foot. "The words *girlfriend* and *boyfriend* mean more than the words imply."

Finn's eyebrows went up, questioning.

"They imply," Ron said, "something more than friends."

"Oh!" Finn ran his hands up through his platinum hair. "Bond-mates?"

"Not necessarily," Ron responded quickly. "More like . . . pre-bond-mates."

"Hmmm." Finn pursed his lips. "People relationships can be very confusing."

"Ha!" Mab clamped a hand over her mouth.

"Come on," Ron said getting up from the table. "Let's get out of here while my mom is speechless."

Finn stood to follow. "Thank you for the honey," he said, grinning widely at Mab.

Mab could only nod, her eyes tearing from suppressed laughter.

Chapter 7

The closer they came to the school, the more on edge Ron became. Finn had held Ron's hand the entire trek down the dirt road to the main street into town. Ron had extricated himself from the new intimacy under the pretext of sending Rory on ahead as the scout for any potential preternatural encounters. He could tell that Finn was unhappy about the withdrawing his hand—even a little hurt by it. Ron struggled with his competing feelings and hated himself for not doing what his heart demanded.

"That's the school," Ron pointed to the only piece of modern architecture in Ennis. "We're almost there."

"Finn?" Ron turned.

Finn had slowed and lagged ten to fifteen feet behind him.

"Perhaps you should go on alone." Finn wouldn't look at him.

"Come on!" Ron tried to smile. "We're almost there."

"No!" Finn said emphatically. "You don't want me here! I can see it in your aura."

"My aura lies then." Ron closed the distance between them. "Either that or you're misunderstanding what it means."

Finn looked down at the asphalt, silent.

"Finn?" Ron reached to put a hand on Finn's shoulder. "Please come on."

Finn shook his head.

"No!" Finn took a step back. "Those people there . . ." He pointed to the school. "Humans. They are your priority." Golden tears leaked out of the side of one of his azure eyes. "You need to be with them." Finn turned to leave.

"No, you don't understand!" Ron grabbed the small *Fey* and pulled him into his arms. "It's not what you think, Finn. You mean more to me. I'm just . . ." The truth caught in his throat. "I'm worried what they may think. What . . ."

"You're afraid of what they think?"

"Well . . ." Ron sighed heavily. "Humans don't all agree on what . . . relationships are good and which are . . . not so good."

"Our bond-mating is bad?" Finn's brow wrinkled.

"No, no, no!" Ron took the boy by the shoulders and looked him in the eye. "Humans are afraid of what is different—of what they aren't used to. Hell, most don't even believe that *Fey* are real."

"Well," Finn responded, unconvinced by Ron's argument. "There is no need for them to know that I am *Fey*. I appear perfectly human."

"Yes, you do, but . . ." Ron tried not to stutter. "But then there's the other thing."

"What other thing?" Finn's hands waved in the air dramatically.

"You're a boy!" Ron exclaimed. "Some places it's okay, but most people here . . . I mean it's a freakin' Catholic— a religious thing. It's not acceptable to most for boys to . . . bond-mate with boys!"

"But I am not a boy!" Finn almost shouted. "I am

Fey!"

"Believe me, Finn." Ron smiled in spite of his confusion. "I've seen you naked . . . you're definitely a boy—at least you are to people around here."

"Humans!" Finn's grabbed his head in frustration.

"I know, I know," Ron said, looking about. "Let's settle down some. People are starting to look at us."

Ron's eyes went to the sidewalk across the street where a group of women gathered about the fruit bin outside McGregor's Grocery.

"It's gonna be fine," Ron said, guiding Finn on toward the school. "Let's just get through this morning."

Finn remained quiet. He went where he was led, but his stony silence made a definite impression on Ron. By the time they came to the brick steps of the high school, Ron's nerves were exhausted. He steeled himself at the door.

"Finn." Ron put a hand on Finn's back, but Finn stared at the door. "Please help me get through this and we'll have a long talk this afternoon."

Finn nodded stiffly.

"This . . ." Ron slid his hand about Finn's waist. "This is very new for me. I . . .I've never acted on . . . or even had this type of . . . attraction before. I'm a little off balance. I just need a little time."

"I should probably just wait outside," Finn said, pulling away. "Let you do what you need to do."

Ron considered this, but only for a second.

"No," Ron said decisively "That's not necessary. I need my friends to know that you're with me." Against his better judgment he opened the door.

Ron led Finn into the vaulting hallway of the old school. They walked silently along the intricate, marble parquet toward a din of voices that crescendoed from the cafeteria at the rear.

"Here we go," Ron said, forcing a smile. He pushed open the double doors and guided Finn into the brightly lit and densely overcrowded lunch room.

"Maquire!" a high pitched male voice boomed. "It's about time you got your sorry ass up!"

Ron felt Finn tense beside him.

"He's only joking," Ron whispered. "Hey, Collin! Does this mean you actually passed—they're going to let you graduate?"

Collin waved his middle finger in the air.

"Okay, okay," Claire said, breaking out of the crowd of teens trying on caps and gowns. "Ron, Ms. Carry has your regalia by the coke machines."

Claire brushed past Collin and hugged Ron tightly.

"Hi, Finn," Claire said, turning to the frowning *Fey*. "I can't believe Ron dragged you to this chaos."

"He *asked* me to come," Finn responded, looking her up and down.

"Okay." Claire gave Ron a bemused look.

"I wanted him to meet the guys," Ron said quickly.

"Well, they're all here," Claire said with a sigh. "Acting the fools, as usual."

"There you are!" Nolan Reid shoved through the teeming teens. "I can't get this damn beanie cap to say on!" He eyed Ron, sheepishly. "Oh . . . shit! Maguire. I didn't see you earlier."

"I just got here," Ron said. "Cap too small for your big head?"

"Big ha, dumbass!" Nolan said. He looked at Finn. "Who's your boyfriend?"

"What do you . . ." Ron almost swallowed his tongue.

"That's Finn," Claire interrupted. "And he's Ron's cousin and new in town. The least you could do is save your childish insults for someone who already knows what an ass you are."

"Jeez, Claire," Nolan said, visibly chastened. "I was just joking." He quickly extended a hand to Finn. "I'm Nolan. Please to meet you."

Finn stared at the proffered hand.

"Shake his hand," Ron said.

Finn took Nolan's hand and shook it side to side.

"Where's he from?" Nolan asked no one in particular. "Neverland?"

"Ireland," Ron answered. "So try to be a little culturally sensitive."

"Whatever," Nolan said, putting an arm about Claire.

Ron stiffened visibly.

"Oh," Nolan said, cheerily. "You don't mind, do you? I mean, I heard that you and Claire had broken up and—"

"Nolan Reid!" Claire shook the boy's arm off her shoulder. "We did not break up. I told you that. There was nothing to break up. Ron's my best friend and he will always be my friend. What about that—"

"Okay, okay." Nolan held up his hands in surrender. "I got it." He looked at Ron, suppressing a smirk. "So, you won't mind if I ask Claire out on a date."

"No." Ron tried to maintain his composure. He turned to Claire. "Nolan?" he asked, shaking his head at her. "Really?"

"Well," Claire responded with a shrug. "He asked."

Ron gave her an apologetic look.

"It's a quantum leap for him," Ron said, "but you can . . . and will do better. I have faith in you."

"Good answer!" Claire laughed.

"Blah, blah, blah!" Nolan picked at his nose. "Seems to me, Maguire, you had your chance and blew it!"

"Had his chance?" Claire glanced up at Nolan. "And just what is that supposed to mean?"

"Nothing, nothing," Nolan said, hands up again. "Just sayin . . ."

"Say less!" Claire ordered, hands on hips. "Before I rethink going out with you."

"Ron!" The familiar high-pitched male voice piped above the din. "Ms. Carry is looking for you!" Collin stopped short. "Oh, hey Finn. How's Ron treating you?"

"He treats me well," Finn said with a weak smile.

"He's not used to our big breakfasts around here," Ron said quickly.

"Man's got to eat!" Collin said. "Hopefully more than the sausage biscuit I had to pick up in order to be here on time."

"You'll live," Briana said, coming up to take Collin's hand.

"Come on, Finn," Claire said. "Let's get Ron fitted for his cap and gown." She grabbed Ron's arm to pull him along.

Finn quickly grabbed Ron's other arm and pulled him forward as well.

"Take it easy, guys!" Ron said. "I've got two good legs of my own."

"Then use them," Claire said, giving Finn a wink.

Finn tried not to smile at her, but he couldn't help himself.

"Maguire!" boomed a large and buxom woman with short white hair. "It's about time!" She jerked a pair of plastic pouches off the table beside her. "Here! Try these on and be quick about it!"

"Yes, Ms. Carry," Ron said, accepting the large plastic envelopes containing his cap and gown. "Sorry I'm late."

"Why should today be any different than any other day?" responded the overly proportioned woman, glaring up at him.

"Yes, ma'am." Ron grinned back at Claire.

"Ron had a houseguest this weekend," Claire offered in way of explanation and diversion. "This is Finn," she said, taking the *Fey's* hand and pulling him forward. "Finn—"

"Maguire!" Ron piped up from under the billowing rayon robe. "Same as mine."

Finn cocked an eyebrow. "We are family," he said, offering a hand to Ms. Carry.

"He's from the Old Country," Ron added.

The large woman ignored them. "Try it on quickly," she almost growled at Ron. "I'd like to get out of here by lunch."

"Yes, ma'am," Ron said. He ripped open the second plastic pouch and pulled out the flattened cap, handing it to Finn. "Can you hold this for a sec?"

Finn took the strange object, turning it over in his hands. Ron tucked his arms through the sleeves of the robe and shook the folds out of it. It fit.

"So far, so good," Ron said, reaching for the cap Finn held. He adjusted the tassel and propped it on his crown. "Well?" He made a turn for Claire and Finn. "How do I look?"

"Who cares how you look," Ms. Carry announced. "It fits and that's what matters. Here!" She thrust a clip board into Ron's hands. "Sign by your name."

"Now what?" said Ron, doing as he was told.

"Hang it on the hanger and clip the cap to it with the clothes pin." Ms. Carry slapped the two items into Ron's hands. "Give it to me when you're done and I'll label it!"

"Yes, ma'am." Ron struggled out of the gown.

Claire took over the duty of hanging everything up. She handed it over to Ms. Carry.

"You're done!" Ms. Curry boomed. "Now go home and tell all this other rabble to go home too." She breathed heavily. "Go home!" Ms. Curry yelled out into the room.

"Okay. That's over with." Ron escaping back to his friends.

"We can go now?" Finn asked quietly.

"Yep!" Ron looked out at the press of teen grads who seemed to have gathered in an arc about them.

Ron felt all their stares. He looked about for the source of their open-mouthed, stunned attention.

"What's everyone . . ." He looked to Claire. "What's happening?"

Claire smiled up at him—almost grinning. She nodded to Ron's side.

Ron's eyes cut downward. He froze. Finn's hand was in his. They were holding hands. A flushing heat flooded through his body from head to foot. With an involuntary gasp, Ron jerked his hand out of Finn's. He turned to Claire again, his eyes pleading. Claire's smile never broke. She only raised an eyebrow.

Finn, on the other hand, looked at Ron, at first hurt, but just as quickly his face quivered with anger. He turned and ran from the room.

"Shit!" Ron breathed to himself.

"Ron?" Claire said sharply.

Ron could sense Claire's disapproval—but not for the reasons he might have thought.

"For Christ's sake, Ron!" Claire punched Ron's arm. "The cat's out of the bag. Don't you dare just stand there!

You go after him!"

Ron continued to stand frozen amidst the cutting stares.

"Go after him!" Claire shoved him hard.

Ron's feet responded. He ran toward the door. As he broke into the hall he heard the din of voices, all speaking incoherently at once, filling the cafeteria behind him. He bolted out the door and down the mountain of steps to the long sidewalk below.

"Finn!" Ron called out, searching for some sign of the *Fey*. He spotted the youth turning the corner into downtown. "Finn!"

Ron sprinted down the road and in seconds turned the corner where he had spotted Finn. The young *Fey* was also running—fast—very fast.

"Finn!"

Ron broke into a run, but Finn was moving at a preternatural speed.

"Dammit!" Ron willed his legs to their limits. "Finn!"

The buildings on both sides of Ron disappeared into a blur. He felt a shock of energy fill him, drawn from the earth below. His speed matched and then exceeded Finn's own. He caught up to the *Fey* at the base of the mountain.

"Finn! Stop!" Ron grabbed Finn's arm and pulled him to a stop.

Finn stumbled backwards into Ron. His face registered shock at being overtaken.

"How!" Finn exclaimed, trying to wrestle free from Ron's grip.

"Come on, Finn!" Ron held the boy's arm tightly. "Settle down!"

"I will not!" Finn faced him defiantly. "Let me go!"

"Not until you listen to me!"

"No!" Finn pulled free. "You have nothing to say to me! We . . ." Finn brushed the tears from his face in anger. "We have nothing!"

"Finn, I was just—"

"No!" Finn backed away. "I was a fool to think I would find love and life away from my tribe!"

"You don't understand!" Ron said, pleading. "Let's talk—"

"No!" Finn held up a hand. "You will not see me again. You are not real. This place is not real. Humans are not real!"

"Finn, I understand why you're angry, but—"

"I'm going home!" Finn broke away and headed up the mountain.

"Wait!" Ron watched the Fey disappear up the trail. "Finn!"

Ron stood for a moment paralyzed by doubt and indecision. He fought to clear his thoughts. It was the heart-empty pain of loss that spoke loudest to him. Part of him was being ripped away. The wholeness he had tasted over the past twenty-four hours was slipping away.

"You can't go!" Ron shouted and bounded up the trail in pursuit.

Ron kept calling the *Fey's* name, willing his legs to a pace that should have been impossible. The nimble *Fey* was more adept at negotiating the dips and turns at such a break-neck speed, but Ron was about to close the distance enough to see glimpses of the platinum-topped blur as it disappeared around tree trunks and boulders on the path above. He breached the clearing in time to see Finn melt into the aspen grove beyond the campsite.

"Finn!" Ron gasped, fighting for air in his aching lungs. "Finn!"

Ron bolted into the aspen grove and then into another small open space at the base of a granite outcropping that towered above.

Ron stood breathless, listening. Silence. "Finn!" he called out again. "Finn!"

Ron sank to his knees in despair. "Finn!" he wailed into his own echo.

Chapter 8

The first shower of spring was uncommonly cold—the chilling drops within seconds of congealing into hail. Ron trudged slowly through the constant icy shower that called up a fog of condensation from the earth that had earlier been warmed in bright sunlight. He had paced the length and breadth of the granite outcropping on the mountain for several hours, hoping for some sign of Finn. His self-hatred had blossomed like a thorn bush and he was now exhausted from regret, painful self-recrimination and shame. His unrestrained response to Finn's act of public intimacy, Ron now knew, was an act of cowardice. That alone was enough to keep him on his knees, sobbing into the unresponsive granite aloofness of the mountain.

As he stepped off the mountain path onto the road-side, the hot tears retraced muddy streaks down his cheeks. He stumbled over potholes at the edge of the road, losing one of his sneakers in the last, watery hole.

"Fuck!" Ron yelled hoarsely, slamming the side of his head with his fists. He kicked the other shoe off angrily and watched it arc over the roadway into the dense brush beneath the grey-hued stands of pine.

The loss of his favorite pair of Van's was not what

collapsed his body down into the wet asphalt in a heap of numb despair.

"Finn," Ron croaked weakly, succumbing to a spate of reinvigorated sobs.

"Ron!" The girl's voice yelled at him from beyond the adjacent pasture.

Ron could not hear it. He was lost to his surroundings.

"Maguire!" Another, lower voice yelled out.

Claire and Collin sprinted across the field toward the lonely, ragged boy on the road. They each wore a green plastic poncho and Claire struggled with a large golf umbrella against gusts of wind that randomly broke across the open field.

"Ron!" Claire stopped abruptly at the edge of the road, shocked by what she found. "My God! Ron!"

Claire stomped the mud off her green, paisley-patterned galoshes and thrust the umbrella into Collin's hands before crouching down beside her disheveled friend.

"What happened to you, Ron?" Claire put a hand on his shoulder.

"Is he hurt?" Collin asked from the roadside.

"I don't think so." Claire squeezed Ron's shoulder. "Look at me!"

Slowly Ron looked up at her blankly. He had begun to shiver from the wet and cold.

"Ron!" Claire shook him.

"Claire?" Ron managed through chattering teeth.

"What happened, baby?" Claire took his face in her hands. "What are you doing out here on the road?"

Ron's face contorted and he collapsed into Claire's arms.

"I fucked up, Claire! I screwed it all up!" Ron wailed. "I'm a fucking coward!"

"Where's Finn?" Claire held him tightly. "Collin," she called out. "See if you can find Finn!"

"He's gone!" Ron wailed again.

"What do you mean *he's gone?*"

"Home!" Ron reached behind, pointing to the mountain. "He went back home. I'll never see him again."

"Home?" Claire took his face in her hands again. "Honey, there's no train out this afternoon. Did he have a car?"

"We can get my truck," Collin offered, trying to help. "He can't have gotten far. We can catch him."

"No!" Ron slapped his hands into the puddled pavement. "You don't understand. He's *Fey*—not human. He went back to his own dimension. I've lost him forever!"

Claire and Collin exchanged glances.

"Sweetie . . ." Claire struggled to her feet. "We need to get you home. Stand up now. Collin, help me get him to his feet."

Collin did as he was told, helping to pull Ron up from the roadway with one hand, and balancing the large umbrella over head in the other.

"I can't!" Ron cried. "The *Phooka* will find him. It's all my fault?"

"*Phooka!*" Collin held Ron by the armpits. "Dude! Man, are you drunk?"

Ron's whole body tensed. He threw his head back and screamed. Claire and Collin were thrown backward onto the pavement. Ron's scream rebounded about them, echoing in ever rising, oscillating pitch. The ground beneath them seemed to heave and ripple. In a flash of violet and mauve, lightning struck a large pine tree and with a deafening crack, it toppled across the roadway directly behind them. Ron crumpled down onto the wet pavement once again, his body glowing in the spectrum of the lightning.

"What the hell!" Collin scrambled to his feet.

"Get him up!" Claire commanded, diving back onto the roadway.

The two jerked Ron to his feet.

"We need to get him home." Claire's tone invited no debate. "Now!"

"Ron!" Collin grabbed his friend about the waist. "You have to come with us. We'll take you home."

Ron stumbled along with them, numb and expressionless.

"Claire?" Collin looked at her questioning. "What's wrong with him—and what was all that shit?"

"I don't know, Collin," Claire responded, tightening Ron's arm about her neck. "We just need to get him home. Mab will know what to do."

"Ron!" Collin stopped, shaking Ron, trying to get his attention. "Dude, you're acting crazy man! What's up with you? And don't you think as a friend, you might of thought it important to tell me . . ." He released his hold on Ron and stood back angrily. "Tell me you were . . . a . . . you know . . ."

"The word is gay, Collin!" Claire interrupted harshly. "You better help me Collin O'Quinn. Ron's been going through a lot. He's just begun to realize these things." She glared at Collin. "Ron was there for you for your shit behavior last year when your father left."

Collin's anger ebbed slightly and he looked at his feet.

"Oh, so you remember that little problem you had with your mother's prescriptions?" Claire pressed. "Ron got you through that. You were a total shit and only someone who really cared about you would've put up with all that. Briana almost broke up with you, you might recall!"

"I'm gonna help, I'm gonna help!" Collin protested weakly. He took hold of Ron's arm and helped pull him along the road. "I'm just sayin' . . . he could have told me."

Claire rolled her eyes.

"Looks like he just did, if you ask me." Claire reached up to pat Ron's cheek. "Stay with us, hon," she said quietly. Then to Collin, "Looks like he told everyone!" She laughed lightly.

They guided Ron to the gravel cut-off that led to Ron's house.

"Almost there, baby," Claire cooed. "Ron? . . . Ron!" She shook him.

Ron's face returned to life for a second.

"Yeah?" Ron's voice trembled.

"Almost home," Claire said. "Collin, I've got him. Get the gate please."

"Sure." Collin sprinted the short distance to get the black, iron gate opened. He returned quickly to hold up his side of Ron. "If he's drunk, Mab's gonna hit the ceiling."

"He's not drunk, Collin," Claire said. "He's just . . . really upset."

"Okay." Collin sighed. "If you say so."

"Do you need reminding about how upset and depressed you were when Briana threatened to break up with you?"

"Yeah, but—"

"But nothing! Ron's in love, too," Claire said. "With Finn. There's no difference."

"That's not what I meant," Collin protested. "I don't care what you say, but there's more than love going on here. Love doesn't make a person glow strange colors or cause earthquakes and lightning strikes."

Claire nodded. "It was strange, I'll give you that, but there could be a perfectly logical reason for that . . . coincidence."

"Riiiight!" Collin moved in front to help guide Ron through the gate. "Ron is different—and not because of this gay thing—and there's nothing logical about any of it."

"And that bothers you?"

"Hell no," Collin said, pulling a limp Ron through the gate. "It's part of his cool-vibe."

Ron's palm brushed against the crusty gate.

"Ow!" Ron yelled out, jerking his hand back.

"Shit!" Collin stopped. "What happened?"

"Let me see," Claire said gently, taking Ron's hand.

Claire lifted the hand and coaxed Ron's fingers open. A streak of angry red, steaming skin crossed his palm.

"Jesus!" Claire stared down at the sizzling imprint of the ornate ironwork on Ron's palm.

"Case in point," Collin said, smirking.

"Let's get him inside," Claire commanded, "and keep him clear of the gate!"

They eased Ron through the opening.

"Knock on the door," Claire said. "I'll hold him here."

Collin leapt up the front steps and pounded on the door.

The locks rattled as a prelude to the door swinging inward. The formidable Mab Maguire filled the dark portal. She took in the scene quickly.

"Get him inside," Mab said sharply, stepping back and holding the door.

Claire and Collin struggled through the doorway, dragging Ron's almost limp form into the house.

Mab swooped over to the bright yellow and gold sofa, tossing throw pillows onto the floor except for one she positioned on the far end. "Put him here," she said, pointing to the sofa.

Claire and Collin did as they were told. Ron fell back onto the sofa.

"What happened to him?" Mab asked, already searching her mental catalogue of potions and incantations.

"We're not sure, exactly," Claire responded. She sat on the sofa beside Ron, stroking his hair. "We found him drenched and sitting in the roadway by the mountain trail."

"And Finn?" Mab's eyebrow went up.

"I think they had a fight," Collin offered from the foot of the sofa.

"Why?" Mab's eyes cut into Claire's.

"Well . . ." Claire thought quickly. "I think it was just a misunderstanding of some sort." She grasped for words. "Finn was . . . well, he was . . ." she stuttered. "Ron was having trouble . . . It's . . ."

"A lover's quarrel?" Mab's voice echoed in the resulting silence.

"You know?" Claire said, finally.

"Oh, please! Some things are too obvious." Mab waved a hand. "Let me at him."

Claire changed places with her. Mab looked into Ron's eyes.

"Ron!" Mab patted her son's cheek.

Ron's eyes opened a slit. He didn't seem to see her.

"What's this?" Mab said, sitting up sharply.

Mab centered herself and engaged her other eyes to study her son's aura more closely. Her face collapsed into a frown. Ron's aura was imploded to nothing more than a dark, almost indistinguishable halo. She leaned in to examine his skin. It was paper thin, and underneath . . . Mab sat back sharply.

"Hell's bells!" Mab said, shaking her head. She jumped up. "I'll be right back," and she disappeared down the long hall to the kitchen.

"What's up with that?" Collin asked, craning his neck around to watch Mab's sudden recessional.

"Who knows," Claire responded, regaining her seat beside Ron. She stroked his hair again. "She'll know what to do. She has to." She patted Ron's cheek. "Ron, baby, hang in there, sweetheart. Mab will fix it." She tried to sound confident, more so to convince herself.

Mab barreled back into the room bearing a white marble mortar and pestle.

"This'll do it!" Mab announced, kneeling beside the sofa. "It'll clear whatever poison it was that fairy demon gave him!"

"You mean, Finn?" Claire asked. "I can't imagine that. You must not have noticed the way he would look at Ron. It wasn't the look of someone who would poison him."

"Then," Mab asked, imperiously, "how do you explain these symptoms? Obvious poisoning. Who else would have done it?"

"Well, I don't know," Claire wailed. "I thought he was lovesick, or—"

"Lovesick!" Mag laughed. "A lovesick teenager doesn't get physically sick to the point of death!"

"Death!" Claire looked at Ron.

"What about the burns?" Collin piped up.

Mab looked at him.

Tears had struck Claire silent.

"What burns?" Mab's eyes cut into her son's friend.

"Here!" Collin lifted Ron's hand. "Where his hand touched the iron gate outside."

Now it was Mab's turn to be speechless. She took hold

of her son's hand and examined it closely.

"But?" Mab turned the hand from one vantage point to another. "How?"

Collin only shrugged.

"You say the iron fencing did this?" Mab croaked.

Collin nodded. "Right, Claire?"

Claire nodded, brushing away tears.

"Oh dear goddess!" Mab stood slowly. She looked down at the mortar and pestle containing her crushed concoction of herbs and essences. "I . . ." She threw the marble bowel and its contents across the room. "I could have killed him!"

"What?" Claire lifted her head.

Mab's face dropped into her hands. "Goddess help me!" She sobbed, her shoulders heaving.

"Mab!" Claire stood. "Mab! What does it mean?"

Mab continued to sob.

"Mab!" Claire shook the older woman by the shoulders. "You know what's going on?"

Mab suppressed her sobs long enough to nod.

"Well, do something!" Claire shouted. "Help him!"

Mab returned to Ron's side and knelt down.

"My boy," Mab said, embracing her adopted son. "I'm so sorry!"

"Do something, Mab!" Claire grabbed the woman's arm and pulled her up. "Tell him you're sorry after you've fixed . . . this!"

Mab wiped her face on her sleeve.

"Right," she said, forcing her powerful emotions into submission. "Right!" She raced back down the hall as fast as her old knees would carry her.

Collin and Claire stood at opposite ends of the sofa.

"Collin," Claire said softly. "Thanks for remembering

that burn."

"Huh?"

"I should have," Claire continued, "but I was more worried about the big picture. You've probably saved his life!"

"He's my best friend." Collin swallowed hard and looked down at the trembling sickness stretched out on the sofa. "He always will be."

"I know," Claire responded managing a slight smile.

"Thanks . . ." Collin turned his face. "For helping me remember that."

Mab blew back into the room with hurricane force. She carried her ceramic honey pot like one of the crown jewels.

"If this doesn't work," Mab said gravely, "then it's beyond me. We'll have to take him to the hospital!"

"What is that?" Collin asked, pointing to the small pot cradled in Mab's hands.

"Honey?" Claire's eyes widened. "Are you serious? What else is in it?"

"Just honey," Mab said, once more kneeling beside her son. "If I'm right . . . if this works . . ." She shook her head.

Mab drew the honey dipper from the pot and let the excess organic liquid return in ribbons into the small glazed pot.

"Ron," she said soothing. "Take this." She touched the honey-laden dipper to her son's parched and pale lips.

At first there was no reaction. Slowly, some of the thick nectar oozed its way between Ron's lips. Suddenly, the tip of Ron's tongue darted to the surface and scooped the honey into his mouth.

"Take some more, boy," Mab encouraged. She refilled

the honey dipper and held it over Ron's mouth.

With lightning speed, Ron's hand shot up and grabbed Mab's hand, pulling the whole of the honey dipper into his mouth.

"Whoa!" Mab's eyes widened to saucer size.

"He wants him some honey, that's for sure!" Collin said, cracking a wide smile.

"Give it back to me, boy," Mab said with a chuckle, "and I'll give you some more." She tried to extract the honey dipper from Ron's clenched teeth. "Ron!" she said. "Oberon Maguire!" Her voice boomed.

Ron released the honey dipper. His eyes opened and stared at Mab, pleading—his mouth open like a baby bird's.

"Okay, okay." Mab drew a ball of honey about the honey dipper and quickly held it up over Ron's open mouth.

The honey streamed into the gaping hole and Ron licked the small, wooden dipper clean.

"More!" Ron managed, his lips trembling.

Over and over, Mab fed him scoop after scoop of the sweet liquid. Ron swallowed hungrily and with each feeding, his color returned.

"Give me!" Ron said, suddenly sitting up.

Ron grabbed the honey pot from Mab's hands and upturned it over his open mouth, draining it of the reserves. When it was empty, he sat on the edge of the sofa, breathing heavily.

"Shiiiiiiiit!" Ron screamed at the top of his lungs.

Mab grabbed her son's face in her hands and turned him to face her.

"Ron!" Mab said sternly. "Look at me!"

Ron blinked as if staring into the dark.

"It's me, boy! Ron!" Mab shook his head. "It's mom!"

Slowly Ron's pupils receded and his mother's face came into focus.

"Mab?" Ron said weakly.

Mab pulled the boy into her arms. "Here I am, my boy!" She hugged him roughly.

Ron stared over her shoulder at the other two figures that had quickly moved up behind his mom.

"Claire?" Ron said. "Collin?"

"It's us, Ron." Claire bent over and kissed Ron lightly on the lips. "We love you sweetheart!"

"It's about time you woke up!" Collin said, slapping his friend on the shoulder.

"How did I . . .where . . . Ron looked about the room, trying to get his bearings. "Finn," he said, his voice trailing off.

"It's going to be okay, Ron," Claire said, taking Ron's face in her hands.

"Yeah, don't worry, bud," Collin agreed. "He can't have gotten too far. There aren't any trains or buses out till later."

"Oh, dear," Mab said with a deep sigh. "I'm afraid it's more complicated than that."

"What do you mean?" asked Claire.

"Finn," Ron repeated. "I've got to find him. I've got . . ." He tried to stand but fell back onto the sofa. "What's wrong with me?"

"You're just upset," Claire said.

"I'm not upset," Ron said. His skin seemed to darken slightly. "I'm . . . I'm . . ." He could find no words to match his feelings.

"Take it easy, boy," Mab said. "You and I need to talk."

"What's to talk about," Ron said sharply. "Finn's gone! I fucked up! I can't . . ." His fists clenched at his chest. "He's not on a bus. He's not on a train!"

Ron looked up into Claire's eyes.

"He's nowhere I can find him." Ron's eyes shut against threatening tears. "He's gone back . . . there!"

"Where's he gone that we can't find him?" Claire asked. "You're not thinking clearly, Ron. "You need to—"

"He . . . is . . . gone!" Ron insisted. "Where he's gone I can't go. I can't find him!"

"Ron," Mab intoned, bopping the boy on the head. "That's enough!"

"But, Mab," Ron said in desperation. "Oh, what does it matter."

"What's he talking about, Mab?" Claire stood, arms crossed. "Where is Finn that Ron can't go?"

"The boy's just upset, Claire," Mab responded. "He needs—"

"Finn is *Fey!*" Ron shouted between them. "Don't you understand? He's not human!"

An uneasy silence settled over the room. Mab turned away, eyes shut. Collin shuffled from foot to foot, wringing his hands hyperactively.

Claire recovered from Ron's announcement. "What the *fuck* is going on here?" she asked.

"Jeez, Claire," Collin piped.

"What?"

"Language," Collin said, looking at the floor.

"Screw it!" Claire dropped to her knees in front of Ron. "Ron, you can't be . . ."

Ron met her eyes evenly. "What's so hard to believe?" he asked softly. "You think Mab's the only supernatural occurrence around here? What about the park the other night?"

"Well," Claire began. "The park . . . a freak storm . . .
a—"

"Freak storm!" Ron laughed harshly. "Your memory
is very selective."

"Ron . . . I . . ." Claire thought back, recalling the terror
she had felt in the park that night. Most of what she
remembered she had discounted as hysteria.

"What about the earthquake and lightning." Collin
took a deep breath. "What about Ron's light show?"

Claire cocked her head at the older woman. "Mab?"
She reached out. "Mab, what's going on?"

Mab sighed and turned back to the group. She only
shook her head.

"It's okay, Mab," Ron said, wiping his eyes. "These are
my friends. I'm not gonna hide anymore. I'm out . . . why
not Finn?"

"Dude!" Collin grinned at Ron.

Ron forced himself to meet Collin's gaze and shrugged.

"It's okay," Collin said. "But you could have told me—"

"Collin!" Claire interrupted.

Collin threw his hands up at her.

"Okay." Claire put her hands on Ron's knees.
"Sweetie, the gay thing is old hat, so let's talk about Finn.
You have to admit that his being . . . *Fey*, is a bit . . . far-
fetched, unless of course that's just a euphemism for—"

"It's true." Ron's voice was tired. "He is *Fey* . . . and
he's . . . in danger . . . and I drove him away. I can't protect
him now. I . . ." He met Claire's gaze once more.

"You love him," Claire said, smiling. "That much is
obvious—but, Ron . . . *Fey*? That's just—"

"Tell her, Mab!" Ron slumped back onto the quilted
sofa. "It's okay that they know."

"It doesn't matter what I say," Mab said, shaking her head. "Your friends have a modern world view. There's no room for *otherness*."

"If they can accept me, they can accept Finn." Ron took Claire's hand. "What'll it take to convince you?"

"I . . ." Claire shrugged. "I don't know what to say."

"Do some of your voodoo tricks," Collin said excitedly.

"Voodoo tricks!" Mab could not hide her disgust.

"You know," Collin said, backing away from Mab to the foot of the sofa. "Earthquake? Lightning? Something!"

"Boy!"

"Can it Mab!" Ron sat up. He squeezed Claire's hand. "I don't know if I can do anything without Finn."

"Bullshit!" Collin said. "Finn wasn't there when you knocked those trees down with lightning back on the road."

"What are you . . ." Ron looked at Claire. "What's he on about with this lightning crap?"

"I can't help you there, Ron," Claire said, sighing heavily.

"Okay!" Mab stood, hands on hips. "If you're gonna do it, then do it!"

"Mab?" Ron questioned.

"Use the ring, boy! It's your birthright."

"My ring?" Ron had all but forgotten the circle of silver about his thumb. He toyed with it. "Well . . ." He stood and pushed Claire away to the center of the room.

"What are you gonna do?" Claire asked, smoothing her dress nervously.

"What?" Ron returned to his perch on the sofa. "Now you think I can do something?"

"No." Claire tried to smile. "I'm just . . . Oh, whatever!" She stiffened her posture and stood her ground.

"All right then." Ron took several deep breaths, centering himself as Mab had taught him. "Everyone just relax."

"Relax, my ass!" Collin said, almost giggling with excitement. "Shit's gonna hit the fan now!"

"Chill out, Collin!" Claire commanded. She gave Ron her most skeptical look. "How long is this gonna take?"

Ron did not respond. He had shut down his physical senses and was already studying the spectrum of Claire's aura. He sensed it trying to reach out to him and he experienced the concern—the love . . . and the doubt she projected at him. He could feel Mab's presence as she joined him, watching with her own spirit eyes. He considered the ring on his finger.

"*Ta me i gcruachais anois,*" Ron said invoking the ring's aide.

The outside observers could feel the air about them begin to swirl.

"Oh, shit!" Collin chanted, nervously. "Oh shit!"

"Hush!" Claire ordered, not taking her eyes off Ron. She squinted at her surroundings, trying to discern the source of the lavender filter that had dropped like a curtain over the room.

Ron could feel the waves of psychic energy that his body suctioned in from the ground below, connected to him by the floorboards, connected to the foundation stones, and then to the great Mother Earth. He experienced the hum of vibration as the primal forces coursed over the surface of his skin.

"*Oh mu anim,* from my heart," Ron said with his spirit lips. "*Ardú suas!*"

Ron willed his aura to expand and observed with his own amazement as the swirling, vibrant lavender light extended from him like another set of arms and hands. The rays of colored light arced and bent about Claire, melding with her own azure halo.

The limpid, silken hair on Claire's arms and neck rose in alarm. Her long auburn mane seemed to lift from her shoulder. She could not pull her eyes from Ron's beatific face. His eyes were shut, but the orbits still appeared filled with a pulsing, faceted amethyst glow.

Ron stood with arms and hands extended like the aura tendrils that only he and Mab could see. He experienced the sensation that Claire was actually in his arms and not standing some six feet away. He took a deep breath and raised his arms as if to lift her.

"Jesus, Mary and . . ." Claire's voice caught in her throat.

Claire felt her feet leave the floor below, and she could feel nothing about her but the undulating air. Yet, there she was, floating, a good foot and a half off the floor, her head almost touching the ceiling above. She tried to see Collin through the pulsating, muted light. He stared at her, mouth hanging open, confirming for her that she wasn't having a personal moment of hysterical non-reality.

Claire returned her panicked gaze to Ron. What was she afraid of? Ron wouldn't do anything to hurt her. She forced herself to relax, matching her breathing to Ron's, and calm returned . . . and then Claire heard him.

"*Creidim*, Claire," she heard.

Ron's lips did not move—no sound reached her ears—but she heard him just the same. Why would he ask her to believe him?

"*Creidim*," she heard again.

An unfamiliar euphoria gripped Claire. This was real. This was happening. She started to laugh.

"Of course I believe you, Ron," Claire said without speaking. "I believe you!"

The forces of gravity returned and Claire felt it pulling her back to the floor. Whether she could trust her eyes or not, when she looked up from her earthbound feet to Ron, there was no sign of the previous changes she had witnessed. His eyes were open. The simple sunlight had returned, streaming in from the window behind him as he sat on the sofa smiling at her.

"Mab," Claire said, testing the floor beneath her. "You wouldn't have any . . . strong drink on hand, would you?"

"Depends," Mab answered with a knowing twinkle in her eye. "How strong?"

"Distilled," Claire said. "Whiskey would be nice."

"Claire!" Collin said, recovering from his own shock.

""Whiskey it is!" Mab boomed, heading back to the kitchen. "Wondrous medicinal properties!"

Claire returned to the sofa and sat by Ron. "That was interesting," she said, motioning for Collin to join them on the sofa. She took Ron's hand. "Why is it always the gay guys who are the most interesting?"

"Hey!" Collin said, plopping down on the other side of Ron. "I haven't gotten any complaints!"

"Unfortunately," Ron said softly looking at his feet, "I guess I have."

"I can't believe that someone with your extraordinary abilities would give up so easily." Claire squeezed his hand.

"Claire." Ron's face contorted into pain. "You don't understand. Finn's gone—left this dimension. I can't—"

"Bulls balls!" Mab shouted from the hallway as she returned bearing two glasses of amber fluid.

"What?" Ron asked, annoyed that no one would listen to him.

"Boy, you're being awful slow on the uptake today." Mab deposited one of the glasses into Claire's free hand. "You're so busy levitating your friends and whining, you can't put two and two together."

"Where's mine?" Collin asked, ignoring the conversation and pointing to Claire's glass.

"This is for the women." Mab gave him the eye and took a substantial swig of the fragrant liquor. "You X chromosomes aren't mature enough to handle it."

"*Sláinte!*" Claire said, laughing and clinking her glass against Mab's. "Now what do you mean, Mab? Obviously you think Ron's overlooked something important."

"What?" Ron asked with growing irritation.

Claire lifted the glass to her lips and nodded to Mab.

"Yes, well," Mab said, swallowing another portion. "Let me ask you, boy. How is it you're able to perform these miraculous tricks of yours—earthquake, lightning, levitation, and the like?"

Ron blinked at her.

"Can *you* do it?" Mab asked of Collin.

Collin shrugged, still eyeing Claire's glass of whiskey.

"Can you?" Mab asked Claire.

Claire merely smiled and sipped her drink.

"Well, I can't either," Mab continued, gesturing with her highball, "and I'm a card-carrying witch!"

"Obviously it's the ring," Ron said, toying with the silver he wore on his thumb. "It's charmed. You said so yourself."

"The ring is a . . . catalyst," Mab retorted. "It has no power in and of itself or I could use it—anyone could use it. It only sparks what's already in you."

"But . . ."

"But nothing, boy." Mab drained her glass. "What about the iron burn on your hand?"

"I . . ." Ron shook his head. "A fluke, I guess. It's never happened before—hell, I've painted that damn fence before!"

"Before what?" Mab said with a mix of amused triumph.

"Well," Ron answered. "Before . . . Finn!" The name exploded from his lips. "Before Finn!"

"Exactly," Mab said, looking at her empty glass with dismay. "That young *Fey* set something in motion with you—awoke something in you. *Fey* and human—it's obviously a volatile mix!"

"That makes no sense," Ron objected. "How can—"

"Get off it already!" Mab was almost laughing. "We've already had the birds and the bees talk. Of course, the *bees* and the bees might have been more helpful."

Ron blushed at the laughter around him.

"So," Claire said, draining her own glass. "They do say sex changes a person."

"Dude!" Collin said. "Did you really—"

"Shut up, Collin!" Ron put his head in his hands. "Don't ask, don't tell."

"That's not fair," Claire said, nudging Ron with her elbow. "I'm sure Collin's regaled you with all sorts of tall tales about his sexual escapades with—"

"No, I haven't," Collin piped.

"Yes, you have," Ron responded, sitting up. "But, Mab, that's all just conjecture. You need more . . ."

"What about the honey?" Mab offered.

"What honey?" Ron's brow furrowed.

"Dude," Collin said. "You ate the stuff like . . . like . . . man, you couldn't get enough of it!"

Claire smiled. "That's what brought you back out of . . . wherever it was your mind went. We thought you had been poisoned."

"Don't remind me," Mab said, setting her empty glass on the coffee table. "Anyway, boy, who else craves honey?"

"Well," Ron answered. "Finn, of course."

"Why?"

"He's *Fey*. *Fey* love honey. It's . . ." Ron froze. "Wait a minute! Are you trying to say . . ."

"Facts are facts, boy."

"That's impossible!"

"*Fei*-like powers!" Mab shouted. "*Fei*-like cravings, and . . ." She waved her arm at Ron's face. "*Fei*-like auras! Your aura is almost imperceptible. It's . . . imploded almost . . . The color's all wrong."

"But, I'm human!" Ron insisted. "I weigh 170 pounds— I eat meat!"

"Made you sick this morning," Mab reminded him.

"I bleed!" Ron insisted. "I—"

"Burn when iron touches you," Claire said, matter-of-fact.

"And, dude," Collin interrupted. "You're gay!"

Ron shook his head. "What's that got to—"

"Gay . . . *Fey* . . ." Collin grinned at him. "Fairy!"

"Really?" Ron glared at his friend. "That's the kind of logic you bring to the table?"

Claire reached around Ron to punch Collin on the arm. "He can't help it, hon! He's a straight boy, and . . ." She looked at Mab. "Their auras don't burn very brightly!"

Mab threw her head back, laughing.

"Hey!" Collin answered. "That's straight bashing!"

"Take it like a man," Ron said, feeling lighter. "Mab, how's this possible?"

"Good question." Mab stood and took Claire's empty glass from her. "I have an idea, but I need to research my journals. But . . ." Mab looked down at her son. "You and Finn are joined in some . . . some otherworldly kind of bond. His absence affects you as much as his presence did. That means you're joined on this plane and the next. If *Fey* can cross over to this world, I think there's every good chance the *Fey* that's now in you can cross over to that plane."

Ron pondered this. "Mab?" he said, as if seeking direction.

"Boy!" Mab waved the empty glasses in the air. "Well . . . *man* now. You're eighteen. I've taught you everything I know. I can't make these decisions for you. Act like a man! Think like a man!" She disappeared down the hall.

The three teens sat quietly. Ron's breathing calmed, belying his clenched fists resting on his knees.

"Well?" Claire asked. "What's it gonna be?"

"Why are you even asking?" Collin said, eyeing Claire over Ron's shoulder. "He's going after Finn!"

"Damn right!" Ron smiled, drawing in his breath.

"Okay," Claire said, hugging her friend, "but just get it through your head that you're not alone in this. We're helping."

"Shit, yeah!" Collin piped.

Ron looked from one to the other. "You sure?"

"How can you ask that?" Claire poked Ron's chest with a fingernail. She tried to refocus her eyes against the rising buzz from the alcohol. "*Fey* . . .or screwed-up gay boy . . .we're your friends!"

Ron smiled at her atypical choice of words. "And if I'm now, somehow both?" he asked.

"You'll definitely need us." Claire stood. "Now where's Mab . . . we need to make a toast!"

Chapter 9

The first front of warm air had rolled into the valley, resulting in a heavy downpour that, by morning, had ebbed to a shower of fine, almost misty rain. As the small group of purposeful, new graduates reached the higher elevations of the mountain, the mist morphed into a fog, until it abated altogether as they reached the familiar campground just below the summit.

"It's gotten a little warm," Ron said, shedding the hood of his green poncho to survey the expansive opening in the tree line.

The others plodded into the clearing, panting and pulling off their own plastic rainwear.

"It's . . . freakin' . . . hot!" Collin said, bending over, gasping for air.

"Doesn't seem to bother Ron," Briana said, checking the integrity of her pony tail before rubbing Collins back.

"Yeah," Nolan said. He daubed the sweat from his forehead. "What's with that?"

"We talked about this, Nolan," Claire said sharply. She caught up to Ron. "You climbed that mountain trail like it was a morning stroll." She put a hand to Ron's chin to better see his face. "I swear, your skin is getting thinner. You're streaked with bluish veins. Do you feel okay?"

"I'm fine," Ron responded, pulling his face away. "Better check on your boyfriend—looks like he's about to faint." He grinned at her.

"He'll be fine," Claire said. She looked back at Nolan and shrugged. "It's you I'm worried about."

"I'm good," Ron responded. "Collin?"

Collin stumbled up to him.

"Did you bring them?" Ron asked.

"Yes, oh *Fei* one." Collin rolled his eyes and let his back pack drop to the ground. "I brought them."

"Collin!" Claire glared.

"It's okay," Ron said. He thumped Collin on the chest. "Hand 'em out. Did you get enough?"

Collin dropped to his knees, breathing hard. "I got all my dad had in the hardware store." He rifled through his backpack. "I've got a dozen, I think."

"Great!" Ron motioned to the others to gather round. "Okay, everyone, there's enough for everyone to have three."

"Three what?" Nolan took one of the small metal tubes. "What the hell are we gonna do with all the flashlights. Hell, I could've brought a spotlight."

"They're not flashlights," Ron said. "They're little, ultraviolet laser pointers."

"Laser pointers?" Nolin turned the small device over in his hand. "Are we doing a slide show?"

Ron stared at Nolan until the boy backed away. "You remember the other night what happened up here?" he asked.

"Yeah, what about it?" Nolan shuffled his feet.

"If it happens again," Ron said with a smirk, "you'll want to use one of these."

"Some sort of witchy thing?" Nolan asked, holding one up.

"No, shit-for-brains!" Collin said. "It's good ol' fashioned, twenty-first century technology." He turned it on to be sure it worked. "If the *Phooka* fuck with us, we fuck the *Phooka*!"

"God, Collin." Claire rolled her eyes. "You're so poetic.

"As Ms. Pettis would say, good use of alliteration, sweetie!" Briana put her hand on Collin's head.

Even Ron chuckled at the joke, but quickly grew serious again.

"Okay," Ron began, "first on the agenda is to find the door . . . Gateway . . . or whatever it is that Finn took to cross over."

"What makes you think it's up here?" Claire asked.

"The last I saw of him was when he disappeared into that aspen grove over there." Ron pointed at the line of glittering aspens on the other side of the clearing. The memory almost overwhelmed him.

"Ron?" Claire put a hand on his arm.

"There's nothing behind there but granite." Ron shrugged away the sadness. "A whole wall of it."

"Could be some sort of a secret passage or something," Collin offered.

"I searched back there for hours," Ron said. "Nothing."

"Well," Nolan began with a sarcastic edge. "Maybe your little . . . *friend* can walk through granite."

"Nolan!" Claire cut him a glance.

"I'm sorry," Nolan said, putting his hands on his hips. "This all sounds to me like a load of crap? *Fey . . . Phooka . . .* Fuck! How's that for alliteration?"

"Dammit, Nolan!" Claire began.

"It's okay, Claire," Ron said, pulling her back. He circled the group to stand face to face with Nolan. "What's crap about it?"

"Out of my face, Maguire!" Nolan took a step backwards. "You may have the rest of these patsies fooled, but—"

"Really?" Ron closed the space between them. "So . . . I can't fool you. You're too smart for me, is that it?"

"I know shit when I smell it!" Nolan crept another step back.

"Do I make you nervous or something?" Ron laughed and stepped back up into Nolan's face.

"Look!" Nolan pushed Ron back. "I get it! You're quee . . . ." He looked at Claire glaring at him. "Gay and whatever, but I'm *not*, and I don't appreciate your crowding me with all your fag . . . gay vibes and all?"

Ron turned his back on the blustering teen.

"Come on, Claire," Ron said, shaking his head at the angry girl. "Really?"

"The only shit I smell up here," Collin said, rising to his friend's defense, "is your breath, so I doubt you have anything to worry about." Collin pointed at Nolan. "Basically, no gay guy's ever gonna give you the time of day, and that's a fact."

Nolan looked down his nose at Collin. "What are you—"

"Turn around!" Collin snapped his fingers. "I'll prove it."

"There, dipshit," Nolan said, turning full circle, "What's your point?"

"That's what I thought," Collin said, giving Ron a wink. "You could lay down naked in a dark room full of horny gay guys and be absolutely safe."

Nolan stared at Collin. "Maybe *you* could," he retorted, "but this . . ." He gestured up and down at his own muscular physique, "would drive gay guys crazy, right Ronnie?" Nolan batted his eyelashes at Ron.

The group broke into laughter. Ron covered his mouth and shrugged, trying not to join in.

"I'm serious!" Nolan said, annoyed at the laughter. "Gays always want what they can't have!"

"Total crap, dumbass!" Collin wiggled his index finger at Nolan. "I mean . . ." He gave Ron a meaningful look. "Am I right? He ain't got no ass!"

Ron almost went to the ground with laughter.

"Seriously, dude!" Collin continued pointing to Nolan. "No ass—all muscle, but no ass . . . well, except for above the neck!"

The girls were holding each other, snorting with laughter as Nolan grew redder with embarrassment and anger.

"But, double seriously, dude," Collin said, mentally preparing his *coup de gras*. "There's also that other problem." He held up his thumb and forefinger as if measuring a minute quantity. "That other . . . little problem." Collin pointed down to Nolan's crotch. "So chill! You're completely safe, dude. Consider yourself lucky. You have nothing any self-respecting gay guy wants. Now me on the other hand . . ." He puffed up proudly adjusting his nether regions. "Be on the alert, baby doll," Collin said to Briana. "You'll probably have to beat those *Fey* off me!"

"You should be so lucky!" Ron winked at him.

"Okay, okay!" Claire said, rolling her eyes. "Back to business."

"Right." Ron faced his friends. "I'm really not sure what you all will be able to do, but I'm glad you're here. So . . . the ancient Celts believed that there were many different planes of existence . . . other worlds, other dimensions . . . spirit, physical . . . other. I believe that. I've experienced that."

"As have I," Claire said, putting a hand on Ron's arm.

"As have we all," Ron continued, smiling down at his friend. "Some of you may not realize it, I understand that, but it doesn't change the reality of it. What happened up here the night we camped out was not a natural phenomenon. It wasn't something of this world."

"Here we go," Nolan began.

"Then what do you think it was, Nolan?" Ron held up his hands. "The smallest tornado on record? Your imagination."

Nolan remained silent.

"It was a creature not of this plane of reality.," Ron continued. "Yes, a *Phooka*! An evil presence—a light absorbing being—Mab says we would probably say it's a being of dark matter!"

"If it absorbs light, are we really safe in the daylight?" Briana asked.

"The ultraviolet spectrum in sunlight is fatal to *Phooka*," Ron responded.

"Ah!" Collin said, brandishing his laser pointer.

"But not all light contains a strong component of ultraviolet," Ron continued. "Ultraviolet light can be filtered out so some areas of shade may be accessible by the *Phooka*."

"Why don't the fairies just blow them away?" asked Nolan with a smirk. "I thought you said they were made of light."

"They are," Ron said gravely, "but not the ultraviolet spectrum. They're formed from light that the *Phooka* absorb—crave."

"*Phooka* eat *Fey*!" Collin announced.

That's about the gist of it," Ron said, nodding.

"But, Ron," Briana said. "Claire said that you had . . . that you were sorta *Fey* yourself. Doesn't that put you in extra danger?"

"Well," Ron said. "Not really. You see, I'm human. I'm not made of photons—just regular ol' atoms and molecules. My special abilities apparently stem from my . . . connection with Finn."

"Ha!" Nolan said, pointing at Ron. "By connection you mean the homo stuff!"

Ron couldn't stop the hot blush of embarrassment.

"Well," Claire began, getting in Nolan's face, hands on hips, "at least Ron's been getting some, which is more than can be said for some of the people standing here."

"Jeez, Claire," Nolan said, contrite. "I was just playin' with him."

"Okay," Ron said, drawing out the word. "Let's get to it."

Ron led the group into the aspen grove and then to the wall of rock and granite beyond.

"Everyone take a section," Ron said. "See if there's any hidden door or other way through."

The teens fanned out along the towering rock face. They each searched a section of the rock wall, tapping, scratching, and kicking to no avail.

"This is stupid!" Nolan said, kicking up a cloud of dust. "There's no way anyone got through this."

"Look, Nolan," Claire said. "Ron last saw Finn go into the trees. He had to have a way out." She turned to Ron. "Maybe it has nothing to do with the rock wall. Maybe the doorway is in the grove, or a particular tree."

"You people are wacked," Nolan said and spit into the dust at his feet.

"Claire's right, Ron," said Collin, ignoring Nolan's whining. "We need to think about what we're looking for. What kind of door? How does it work? You know, shit like that."

"I haven't a clue!" Ron shrugged.

"Whatever it is," Briana said, "It has to be invisible or we would have seen it by now."

"That's the point!" Nolan waved his arms dramatically. "If it's invisible, there's no way we'll find it!"

"Shit!" Ron backed against the granite wall, rubbing his tired eyes. "I hate to say it, but Nolan's right. This is a waste of time."

"Finally!" Nolan said. "We can't see it—we can't find it!"

"Just a minute." Claire pushed Ron against the wall by the shoulders. "You have got to start thinking differently."

"What?" Ron objected.

"Just because we can't see it, doesn't mean you can't see it. Do I have to spell it out?" Claire's hands went to her hips. "Bitch-slap some sense into you?"

Ron stared at her, then a broad grin broke across his face. He took Claire's hand and returned to the edge of the aspen grove, sitting down in the dirt facing the wall of granite.

"Everyone back away," Claire ordered. "Give the man some room."

"What's this about?" Nolan said, rolling his eyes.

"Just do it, Nolan!" Claire's tone did not invite debate.

The teens grouped behind Ron, and watched. He sat quietly, breathing deeply, his eyes closed.

"What's he gonna do now?" Nolan said in a whisper. "Levitate?" He tried not to laugh at his own joke.

Claire gave him a tight smile. "He might," she whispered back. "Now shut up!"

The banter had no effect on Ron. His physical senses were redirected. All his inner attention was focused on seeking—seeing with his other eyes. If people had auras, maybe the rocks had some spiritual component that he had missed. Mab said that everything was connected.

Slowly, he opened his physical eyes, but what he saw was not the physical world he was accustomed to. The rock in front of him seemed almost phosphorescent in the filtered sunlight. He could make out every ant, beetle, and strip of moss inhabiting the rock face. It glowed with life. The granite itself seemed to be possessed of a teeming, almost imperceptible motion of swirling energy. Ron sat dazzled, enjoying the unexpected vitality of the previously dull, unyielding rock.

"Ron," a voice whispered.

Ron became aware of Claire, kneeling beside him.

"Ron," she said more insistently.

"I'm here," Ron answered, amazed that the inter-action with physical reality was not interfering with his other-worldly perceptions. He had never been able to do this before.

"Ron," Claire whispered. "What's going on?"

"I'm . . . I'm seeing things . . . differently," Ron replied.
"Like you said."

"Ron."

Ron could feel her breath against his ear.

"You've been sitting here for almost thirty minutes," Claire said.

"Wow," was all Ron could manage.

"The door," Claire reminded him. "Do you see the doorway?"

"Sorry, Clare," Ron said. "I . . . Everything is so different. I wasn't expecting this."

"Remember Finn," Claire said softly.

The wave of guilt and longing threatened to break Ron's concentration, but Mab had taught her son well. Ron forced himself back into the moment. This was about Finn. He stood easily, as if the air itself was lifting him. He turned his gaze down one side of the rock face. Even the air currents were visible to him. He could feel pulsing atmosphere rippling about him. The sunlight streaming through the twinkling leaves of the aspen trees possessed substance, direction and a seemingly infinite gradation of colors—all distinguishable to Ron's sensitive vision. He scoured the rock face for some evidence of a way through to Finn's world, but there was nothing. He turned his gaze down the other side—again, nothing—just the ever undulating liquidity of the supposedly solid granite matter.

"Holy Shit!" Ron whispered into the air.

"What?" Claire asked. "What?"

"Maybe . . ." Even Ron couldn't believe what he was thinking.

Ron walked . . . no, the ground no longer possessed any attribute of solid matter and he couldn't feel his physical feet anyway. On an impulse he kicked off his Vans and socks. Regaining his footing, he realized he could now sense . . . feel . . . know the current of matter that was Mother Earth below him. He couldn't specifically feel any particular part of his body, but he could . . . experience the shape—the form of light and matter about him. Ron knew his own form and shape by how he occupied his own space in the midst of the swirling ether that surrounded him.

The chatter of excited disbelief crescendoed from his friends in the space behind him. He stood . . . he occupied the space directly in front of the rock and marveled at the apparent fluid nature of it. He thought for an instant that if he pushed against it, he could . . . no that was impossible.

"Ron," Claire said close to him. "What do you see?"

"Claire," Ron felt his whole being smile. "I think . . ."

"What?"

Ron could also sense Claire's anxiety, wonder, and excitement.

"Would you go with me?" Ron asked.

"How? Ron . . ." Claire stopped. She wanted to know the truth—whatever it was. "Yes," she said, drawing in her breath.

Claire reached out her hand, but was immediately aware that Ron had already enfolded her in whatever it was he had levitated her with back at Mab's.

"Take me with you, Ron."

"Are you sure?" Ron waited.

"Hurry!" Claire responded with urgency. "Before something makes me change my mind."

Ron held her tightly in the arms of his extended aura. He extended his hand into the wall. It felt cool and rushing like a stream of glacial water from up in the mountains. He dove into the swirling pool of grey-green granite, pulling Claire in with him.

The other teens stood at the tree-line.

"What the hell's going on?" Nolan said, still unable to believe that he had actually seen Ron float over the ground toward the rock face.

"Stay still," Collin ordered, not taking his eyes off Ron.

"Claire!" Briana called out as her friend left them to pursue Ron's path to the granite.

Collin held his girlfriend back. "Stay by me," he said. "Ron won't let anything happen—"

It was a flash—like a blink in nature's vision. One moment Claire and Ron were there—the next—they were gone.

"Shit!" Collin managed, an octave higher than usual.

"Shit!" Nolan echoed. He stared at the rock wall where Claire and Ron had just stood.

Briana stood speechless, wringing her hands.

"It's okay, baby," Collin said, throwing an arm about her.

Briana was to shocked to answer.

"Let's get down off this mountain," Collin said, poking Nolan's arm.

"Wha . . ." Nolan jerked his eyes off the rock wall to face Collin. "What do we do?"

"We need to let Mab know what's happened!" Collin bolted ahead, pulling Briana behind him.

Bolcán observed the scene from the top of a soaring loblolly pine that towered above the grove of aspen trees below. Rare it was for him to leave the confines of the *Caillech*'s temple, but his *Phooka* were useless in the world of men during the solar day. However, he was more than curious about this human boy, this child of the *Wicca* who had destroyed his warrior *Phooka* with a power not natural in men—but it was for more than curiosity that he had undertaken the tortuous journey from his blessed *Álfheimr* to the inconstant human world and its confused duality of light and dark. Knowledge was power and one required power to serve The Great Lord Salach.

The tribulations of his journey had been more than repaid. How clever of the *Fey* to conceal the entrance to their world in the domain of men—ignorant men. He closed his eyes remembering the sweet taste of *solas bán sídhe* flesh. With this new knowledge, he could assure his people of that holy sustenance required by his people for fertility and reproduction. The elven race would once again flourish and overflow from *Álfheimr* into *Tír na nÓg* itself— the *Fei* world . . . paradise. The leathery skin of his wings danced with pleasure.

Still, he would have to solve the riddle of how this human boy had forded the Gateway. The *Fey* held great power with the indigenous spirits of this world. Men were ignorant of the mystical forces that inhabited the substance of their world.

Bolcán unfolded his wings and left his perch in the pine to begin the long and arduous journey back to the ancient Gateway, forged in eons past, that connected this world to his own. Yes, this boy was a problem, but Bolcán was a seeker of knowledge. The idea of learning something new pleased him—pleased him almost as much as knowing that after achieving this knowledge, he would annihilate the problem.

Chapter 10

The veil of inorganic matter dissipated like a wisp of vapor, replaced by the sharpest, cleanest, most vivid light Ron had ever experienced. He looked down from atop the escarpment where he had stepped out of the wall of rock behind him. He appreciated the wide expanse of rolling hills carpeted with a vibrant green sod that trailed up the mountain to the small mesa that he stood upon. Looking closer at the soft, fleecy strands of grass under his feet, he realized there was not just one shade of green, but a myriad of hues, all visible to him in each individual blade—like dancing pixels on a retina display. He laughed unconsciously at the marvel.

He could also feel the coolness of the grass beneath his feet—he could feel his feet! His bare feet—the sight slightly unnerved him. His feet didn't look good, what with the snaking purple veins right at the surface. His skin was speckled like an ink splatter. Still, he didn't feel sick or anything. In fact, the lightly sweetened air filled him with energy. He took a tentative step, but something seemed to pull at him. He turned.

"Claire!" Ron felt the panic rise in his throat.

Claire stood behind him, frozen, eyes opened, but completely still, unmoving.

"Claire?" Ron said, studying her face from different angles.

Nothing. Something was definitely wrong. She seemed faded, almost spectral. He reached out to touch her cheek. As if causing a ripple in a pool of still water, the point where he touched her developed a brighter hue and expanded out in a circle flowing through and down her body until she stood—an improved version of herself. She moved.

"Damn it to hell, Ron!" Claire hugged herself as if to make sure she was all there.

"Sorry, Claire," Ron said apologetically. "For a second, I forgot you were there."

"You forgo . . ." Claire gave him one of those looks reserved for the certifiably insane. "It was more than a minute, mister! I have been aware the whole time, I just couldn't move or speak."

"Well, sorry, I mean . . ." Ron thought quickly. "Look at this place. I was in shock!"

"Yeah, yeah, whatever." Claire looked about. "It *is* beautiful. Looks like home."

"Are you kidding?"

"That was some trip" Claire said, laughing. "How did you know you could pass through the granite like that?"

"I could see it, Claire. Not as it appeared, but . . . as it was. I'm not sure . . . like . . . its molecules and the spaces between. It was as if I were looking through a waterfall."

"Okay . . ." Claire gave him another strange look. "I hope you're done freakin' me out. I'm not sure I can handle much more." She saw Ron's eyes widen as he stared out into the field.

"Well," Ron said tentatively. "I think you'd best get used to it—the freaky is about to become the status quo."

Claire followed his gaze. "What do you see?"

"Grazing below us there," Ron said, pointing down to the valley below. "You can't see that?"

"Not without binoculars," Claire responded.

She could barely make out movement. Something there, but all Claire could make out was a mass of bobbing motion, like ants in the grass.

"Oh, I see it now!" Claire cried excitedly. "Horses! It's a herd of horses!"

"Yes," Ron said haltingly. "But not exactly."

"Let's go down," Claire started out on the narrow footpath that snaked its way in a series of cutbacks down the side of the mountain.

"Be careful where you step," Ron said pushing ahead of her. "Not sayin' there are snakes here or anything, but . . ." He smiled back at her. "You never know."

Claire stopped in her tracks.

"You'd just better be joking," Claire said, eyeing a good sized throwing rock at her feet. She thought better of it. "And slow down!"

She couldn't tell if Ron was running down the path or leaping. Before she could even get halfway down, he was already at the bottom. It took her several minutes to reach the end of the path.

"Don't go any farther, Claire!" Ron bellowed up at her.

"You got to be kidding!" Claire froze, staring down where the footpath suddenly ended in a twenty foot drop to the valley floor below.

"Problem?" Ron looked up at her.

"That does it!" She picked up one of the gravely rocks and held it threateningly. "You better tell me how you got down there!"

"I jumped."

"You . . . You're lying to me, Ron Maguire!"

"No, seriously," Ron called up to her. He was still trying to believe it himself. "I don't know. I just feel so light—and I didn't jump. I fell . . . sorta . . . I may have . . . kinda floated down."

"And you're still freakin' me out." Claire stood, hands on hips. "How am I supposed to get down?"

"Jump. I'll catch you."

"Jump? You'll . . ." Claire gave him that look again. "That's not funny, Ron."

"No, I'm serious." Ron held out his hands. "Jump. I'm pretty sure I can catch you wi—"

"Pretty sure?" Claire threw the rock, just missing Ron. "Pretty sure?"

"Okay, okay. I'm certain," Ron said, then mumbled to himself, "well, pretty certain."

"What was that?"

"Nothing." Ron bent his knees and, as if going for a rim-shot, pushed off the ground and into the air.

In an effortless arc, Ron sailed up and landed lightly on his feet beside Claire. He smiled at her gaping expression and then jumped back into the air to land gracefully on the grass below.

"There," Ron said, holding out his hands once more. "Jump."

Claire closed her eyes and shook her head. "I must be crazy," she muttered.

Claire looked down at Ron and without another word, jumped off the edge of the cliff. She fell downward like a rock, and just as she was about to scream,

Ron stepped forward and caught her in his arms.

"Now, that wasn't so bad, huh?" Ron sat her feet back on the ground.

Claire stood shakily. "Excuse me?" she said, smoothing out her jeans. "Were you the one dropping to your death from up there?"

"Claire, you were—"

"I've had enough of you." Claire held up a hand. "I'm going to see the horses now." She walked around him.

The herd of about twenty, four-footed and hooved animals slowed their grazing progress as they scented the two people in their path. They were close enough for Claire to make out white, iridescent coats and golden manes.

"They're beautiful!" Claire said. "Look, they've seen us."

A larger, probably male, animal held up his head and loped closer to Claire and Ron, sniffing the air.

"They're certainly different from the horses I'm used to," Claire said, watching the stallion admiringly. "They look like they've been powdered with glitter—and those manes! I should have hair like that."

"They're different alright," Ron said, catching the large stallion's eye.

"Oh, they're not that different," Claire said, taking a step forward. "I'd just love—"

"Claire!" Ron pulled her back.

"What?"

"You're overlooking something very important."

"What?" Claire looked back at him. "What are you on about?"

"Look at him," Ron said, pointing. "Claire. I mean, really look at him for Christ's sake!"

Claire rolled her eyes. She smiled at the muscled, Clydesdale-sized animal, slowly walking toward her. He was magnificent. He shook his massive head, splaying his sparkling, gold mane like a peacock.

"He's as proud as a . . ." Claire froze. "What the . . ."

As the stallion threw his head upward, Claire could see the spiraling, pointed horn protruding upward from the animals brow.

"You've got to be kidding me!" Claire retreated behind Ron. She looked at the animal over Ron's shoulder. "This is not funny!"

Ron was laughing. "Yeah. I'd say that's a unicorn—or at least a good impression of one."

"He's looking at us," Claire said, no longer confident. "Do you think he'll charge?"

"Just stay calm," Ron said, "and don't show fear."

"Yeah. Right."

The unicorn was close now. It stopped not twenty feet from them and cocked its head to the side, snorting.

"Hello, unicorn!" Ron called out, holding up a hand making the Vulcan sign of greeting.

"Christ, Ron!" Claire poked him in the back. "This isn't an alien encounter."

They watched the large animal, trying to read its intention. The stallion concentrated its gaze on Ron. Lowering its head, it stretched out a foreleg and, bending the other, seemed to bow to Ron.

"I'd say that's friendly," Ron whispered. He returned the bow.

"Do you think I could pet him?" Claire whispered back.

Before Ron could respond, the resplendent stallion spun back toward his herd at full gallop. The herd joined him obediently and they thundered off across the hills and out of sight.

"Oh, no," Claire wailed.

"That was something," Ron said. He took Claire's arm. "I don't think we're in Kansas anymore."

"What?"

"Never mind." Ron smiled. "We'd better get moving."

"Where to?"

"Over there." Ron pointed to the line of trees at the horizon." From the escarpment, I think I saw what looked like man . . .uh, *Fey*-made structures in among the trees. If I'm wrong, I guess we'll just keep walking until we find some sign of civilization."

"Why didn't you talk to the freakin' unicorn?" Claire asked, distraught. "Maybe he could have given us a ride."

"Come on lazy girl," Ron said, pulling her along next to him. "Better see what else this place has to offer."

"That's what worries me," Claire said. She trekked along beside Ron. "If you see any dragons overhead, I'm outta here!"

Ron laughed. "I'll be right behind you."

"No you won't." Claire took Ron's arm and raised an eyebrow at him. "You'd just do something brave—and stupid. You're not going anywhere without Finn."

"No comment." Ron returned her smile and shrugged.

Claire struggled to keep up with Ron who seemed untiring. After the first three minutes of trekking across the rolling hills she was panting heavily—but not Ron. Occasionally he would take in a deep breath of the sweet atmosphere, but this only invigorated him further. What were supposed to be gently rolling hills were more like small mountains to scale as far as Claire's aching thighs and calves were concerned. Finally, she grabbed Ron and pulled him to a stop.

"Please, Ron," Claire begged, gasping. "Can we take a rest stop for God's sake!"

Ron saw her reddened face and labored breathing.

"I'm sorry, Claire." Ron said, taking both her hands. "Let's sit here a little." He helped her to the ground.

"Well," Claire said, gratefully stretching out on the carpet of blooming clover. "I must say this place seems to agree with you."

"I don't know what it is," Ron said, stretching his arms out, "but I feel lighter . . . stronger."

"Duh!" Claire said, continuing her stretch.

"Let's not take too long, okay?" Ron said, looking up in the sky. "I'm not sure if the light will hold. Hell, I can't even see where it's coming from."

"I hadn't noticed," Claire said, following his gaze, "but you're right." She looked at the increased streaking in her friend's face. "Are you sure you feel okay?"

"I feel fine," Ron answered. He arched his back, pulling his shoulders forward. "Except for my back." He manipulated his upper back again. "I must've injured my shoulders when I jumped back there. It feels at times like someone is stabbing me in the shoulder blades with a knife!"

"Your shoulders . . . my legs." Claire snorted. "I tell you what . . . you carry me and I'll massage your back as we go."

"Oh, right!" Ron laughed. "You'd think a cheerleader would have a bit more stamina."

Claire sat up. "I have more than most, thank you very much!"

"Come on, woman." Ron held his hand out to her. "Time to follow your man."

He pulled Claire to her feet where upon she draped her arms about his neck.

"So," Claire said, seductively. "You're my man now."

"You're a woman, I'm a man . . ." Ron smirked.

"And?"

"I'm a man—"

"Who likes men."

"Bingo!" Ron hugged her. "Now can we get going? My man needs me!"

"I'm sorry," Claire said, rolling her eyes, "but your Finn doesn't look that manly to me."

"Well," Ron said with a knowing smile. "I've seen a side of him you haven't."

"What's that . . ." Claire punched Ron on the arm. "You nasty boy!"

"Ow!"

"I'm gonna slap that nasty right out of you!"

"You have to catch me first!" Ron started up a nearby hill.

They ran a short distance before Claire had to stop and catch her breath.

"Damn you, Ron!"

"Hush!" Ron said quickly, putting a finger to his ear. "Listen!"

Claire strained her hearing. All she could make out was the breeze cutting through the grasses. Then she heard it— the light, tinkling sound of bells.

"Where's it coming from?" Claire asked.

"From somewhere over that rise, I think," Ron said, pointing.

They crossed the remaining distance, staying alert. As they breached the summit of the rise, they encountered the source.

"Sheep," Claire said excitedly at first. Then she stopped. "Tie-dyed sheep?"

They stared out over the large flock of pastel colored sheep, for lack of a better genus.

"Well," Ron said. "At least this is a sign that we're a little closer to civilization."

"Do you see anyone looking after the flock?" Claire asked, scanning the terrain around them. "It's customary for sheep to have a shepherd—or at least that's what my grandfather used to say. He tended sheep in Ontario at one time."

"I don't see anyone," Ron answered. "They may be hiding somewhere, watching." He started down the hill for the flock. "Let's get down there and see if we can stir up someone."

Claire followed him close behind. As they got closer, Claire could make out subtle differences between the sheep she was familiar with, and this flock.

"These aren't the sheep of my grandfather." Claire pointed to one of the nearby animals. "The snout is longer . . . and the tail . . . and is it my imagination or are the eyes green?"

Ron reached out to try and touch one of the skittish beasts. "Take it easy, fella," he said as the animal's coat shuddered. "We won't hurt you."

"I was just wondering," Claire said nervously, "if it might be the other way round. Just because they look like sheep, doesn't mean these are meek like sheep."

"I still don't see anyone," Ron said, sighing. "Maybe these sheep don't need someone to look after them."

"What next?"

"You can see the trail the herd made on their way here." Ron eyed the hills head. "Let's follow it."

"We still may not find anything!" Claire held up her hands. "Do some of your fairy stuff."

"Jeez, Claire!" Ron laughed. "I don't come equipped with google maps or GPS directions for . . . *Faerie*."

"*Faerie?*"

"Fairy Land."

"How do you know you don't?"

"Don't be—"

"Whatever," Claire said, "but I'm not walking miles in the wrong direction."

A sound that was not even close to the bleat of a sheep rose up from inside the flock. Ron pointed to a large animal in the midst of the flock from which light seemed to prism upward causing nearby sheep to back away in a circle about it. The animal itself stretched upward and, in an instant, the two watching teens were confronted by a tall figure covered in a brown, hooded cloak, holding a thick shepherd's crook in one hand. The figure's face was hidden in the shadow of the over-sized cowl.

"Uh, oh," Ron whispered.

Claire took his arm and drew in close. In the next instant, the figure was in front of them. Ron and Claire looked up at the strange robed figure, trying to discern its features cloaked by the dark cowl. Ron started to speak, but the statuesque creature interrupted.

"Humankind!" The figure threw back its cowl. "Why are you here? How did you cross into this sanctuary?"

The thin but muscular shepherd held his golden crook in front of him as if to bar the way. Ron marveled at the points on the man's ears and smiled to himself, wondering if Finn had the same mark of distinction in his true form.

"Speak!" the *Fey* thundered.

Claire poked Ron in the ribs with her elbow, startling him from his private thoughts.

"Oh," Ron said, returning to the problem at hand. "Hello," he said to the shepherd. "I'm Ron and this," he pointed to Claire, "is my friend Claire."

"Irrelevant!" the *Fey* said, narrowing his eyes on the two teens.

Claire leaned into Ron's ear.

"Okay," she whispered, "not a very good impression of Mr. Spock, so we're obviously not on Vulcan."

Ron rolled his eyes and tried not to laugh.

"We are looking for Finn," Ron said, looking the shepherd in his startling metallic yellow eyes. "Finn of the *Fey*."

"How dare you say that name," the *Fey* said in disgust.

"Whatever dude," Ron replied, holding up his hands as if in surrender. "But, that's why we're here. Where do we find him?"

The *Fey* glared at Ron in momentary silence. Ron and Claire exchanged glances. The tall *Fey* backed away slowly. In a crackling flash of golden light, the *Fey*'s robe and staff were gone, along with any other clothing.

"Okay," Claire whispered looking down at the ground embarrassed.

Behind another rippling wave of gold light, the *Fey*'s butterfly-like wings unfolded, stretching out a good six feet on either side. The wings were a shimmering, almost transparent golden hue. Two great eyes seemed to peer from the upper corners of the wings. The *Fey*'s head went back and a powerful but practically inaudible sound pierced the surrounding air in a shock wave that was palpable.

"That doesn't sound very friendly," Claire whispered to Ron.

"I think he's calling for reinforcements."

"That's not good."

"Depends." Ron put an arm about his friend.

The *Fey* hovered in the air just above the ground—his massive, delicate wings undulating about him. Claire and Ron could feel air swirling about them.

The response to the *Fey*'s alarm was almost immediate. The airspace about the two teens was suddenly crowded with one winged *Fey* after another in a pastiche of individual colors, each bearing a spear or sword tipped with iron—all pointed at Claire and Ron.

"Let's all chill!" Ron stepped in front of Claire to shield her. "A bit of an overreaction, don't you think?"

"What now?" Claire whispered.

"Let me handle it," Ron mumbled over his shoulder.

The sight of the iron-tipped weapons caused the skin over Ron's shoulder blades to tingle painfully. Despite the wisdom of his fight-or-flight instinct—the dominate urge being to run like hell back where he came from—Ron stood his ground.

"I said chill out, guys!" Ron said, forcing confidence into his tone. "We're not here to cause any trouble. I just need to talk to Finn."

"Heretic!" shouted the *Fei* soldier fronting the host of winged men who hovered above like an umbrella.

For the first time, Ron was aware that there were no shadows—no evidence anywhere that anything was blocking or even filtering the light that seemed to infuse everything in this world.

"Look," Ron continued, holding the palm of his hands up to show he had no weapons. "We're from the human world. Finn visited us. We just want to be sure that he's okay."

The fiery, red-headed *Fey* who seemed to command the soldiers sailed through the air and alit directly in front of the two human teens. He stood, legs apart, the blunt end of his spear resting on the grass. His skin, though not as pale as Finn's, appeared transparent nonetheless. He was much larger than Finn, more muscled, and much, much less gentle in his demeanor.

"The White Wing is sacred," the general *Fey* stated in a bass voice that invited no debate. "No human may lay eyes on him. No human may talk to him. No human may stand in the White Wing's presence!"

"Really?" Ron's hands went to his hips. "Well, I hate to tell you, but I've already seen him. I've already spoken to him—at length, and I've already embraced him as my friend, and—"

"Enough!" The general commanded. "Your fate will be determined by the *Ardsagart*. The penalty for the crimes you have described is death!"

The swords and spears rattled like thunder above Ron and Claire's heads.

Then general gestured to the humans. "You will come with us now."

Ron pulled Claire up next to him, his arm about her shoulder.

"I will be happy to accompany you," Ron said to the general. "But I would ask that you let the female return to the human world unharmed. She's not—"

"Impossible!" The general said. "You will both be questioned."

"The female?" Claire said into Ron's ear. "Really?"

"Shhh!" Ron kept his eye contact with the general. "She knows nothing that would benefit your—"

"She knows the Gateway into this sanctuary!" the general thundered. "That alone threatens this world's very existence."

"But—"

"Enough!" The general straightened to his full height. "You are my prisoner."

At the general's signal, the other airborne *Fey* surrounded Ron and Claire. A bright light engulfed them all and in the blink of an eye, the two teens found themselves in the center of a wide circle of standing stones as tall as houses. Enormous capstones connected each standing stone to the next, completing the circle. Claire and Ron faced a smaller, flattened stone that lay prone in the grass like a large table, off center of the circle. Behind the table on a seat carved out of more stone, sat a *Fey* resplendent in a sparkling silver robe. He pushed back the cowl of his robe revealing an ancient, weathered face, mirroring the surrounding stone in strength and impassivity.

"What is the meaning of this?" the silver *Fey* demanded. "Who are these creatures you have brought into this Holy of Holies?"

"Lord Carrig," the general began. "These are human intruders who have bridged a Gateway from their world to our sanctuary. They have knowledge of the White Wing and they have inquired of him by name. I believe them to be assassins—"

"Assassins, my ass!" Ron interrupted. "You are so full of shit. All I've asked is to speak to my friend, Finn."

The *Fey Ardsagart* held up a hand for silence, his face calm and unmoved. His steely gaze settled on Ron.

"You are human?" the *Ardsagart* inquired evenly.

"Guilty," Ron responded, stepping forward. The sarcasm was not lost on the *Fey* High Priest.

"Are you dying?" the priest arched one eyebrow.

"Wha . . ." Ron felt Claire's hand on his back. "What's that supposed to mean. Are you threatening—"

The High Priest's hand went up again.

"It is a simple question." The priest said. His face still betrayed no sign of intent. "Your aura is almost non-existent. A human whose aura is departing is dying."

Ron stood silent. Was the High Priest just employing some sort of psychological warfare?

"Your body betrays you as well," The priest continued. "I can see the physical components breaking down rapidly—decomposing. Of course, that is the fate of all humans—creatures of matter—you have no inherent permanence. Pity in one so young."

"Whatever," Ron responded, trying not to reveal his new anxiety.

"Ron," Claire whispered behind him. "We need to get you back to Mab."

The *Ardsagart*'s other eyebrow went up.

"I'm not leaving without Finn," Ron said, not taking his gaze off the priest.

"You are right about one thing," the *Ardsagart* said, the side of his mouth barely hinting at a smile. "You will not be leaving." He waved his hand dismissively.

Ron pointed a finger at him. "Wait just a—"

A flash of silvered light engulfed them.

Ron blinked his eyes clear to find himself in a small stone cell. A dim light shone from the heavy stone walls and ceiling that blocked out the sky overhead. Ron turned sharply, looking about, but there was no sign of his friend.

"Claire!" he called out in a panic. "Claire!"

"I'm here!"

"Where?" Ron tried to triangulate the source of her voice.

"Next door," Claire called back. "I think."

Ron sighed with relief. "Are you okay?"

"Well . . ."

Ron could hear the tremor in her voice.

"I'm not hurt," Claire said. "Just a little scared."

"Give me a sec."

Ron looked over the stone wall separating them. He had walked through rock before. A thin smile was all that betrayed his thoughts. He closed his eyes, breathing deeply. Slowly his eyes opened to his other sight, revealing the liquid, subatomic flow of matter in the stones. But there was something different. Strands of blackened brown wove its way through the other minerals, blocking Ron's vision to the other side. He moved steadily toward the wall. It was still lacking the solidity it projected onto the real world.

Ron reached out his hands, thrusting them at the swirling matter. The pain was agonizing. Ron fell backwards, crying out and pulling his throbbing hands to his chest. He shook himself out of his trance and stared at the ugly blisters bubbling on the palms of his hands. He became aware of his name.

"Ron!" Claire's muffled voice echoed off the outside walls and through the small barred window over the door in Ron's cell.

"I'm okay!" Ron called back, shakily. The blisters on his hands had healed to angry red patches. "The walls of this damn cell are full of iron. I tried to get through to you but . . . it's impossible!"

"Are you really okay?" Claire shouted.

"I'm fine," Ron said, pushing up off the floor back onto his two feet. "I wish I knew how they built this place. Iron is poison to *Fey!*"

"And to you, apparently," Claire responded.

"Apparently," Ron muttered to himself. He checked his hands again to find them completely healed except for the overall sickly changes in his skin which was now cracked, appearing ready to slough off.

"What the fu . . ." Ron shook his head, no longer able to deny the obvious. "Dammit," he said sharply, staring at the heavy, rusting iron door to his cell.

The bars on the transom window were also iron. Ron sighed heavily, wondering how he could know that without even getting close enough to examine the bars.

"Ron?"

"Still here," Ron responded. "How's your cell?" he called out.

"Empty, hard, and cold," Claire shouted.

Ron smiled at the annoyance in her voice. She never whined, but she certainly called it as she saw it. If he could have been physically attracted to a girl, she would have been it. He had tried. It had really bothered him that, even though he loved her, there was never any component of physical desire. Since his encounter with Finn, loving Claire was a little more comfortable. He understood that love now, and hoped that she did as well.

"Claire?" Ron called out. "Sit down and close your eyes. I want to see if I can reach out to you."

"Good idea," Claire shouted back. "Just don't make me float off the floor. It'd make for one hard landing."

"Okay." Ron laughed. "No levitation! I promise."

Ron lay down on the cold marble floor, instantly knowing that it separated him from the iron bearing rock below. He slowed his breathing and opened himself to his extra senses, letting his mind breach the space between the iron bars. He could see the vaulting hall beyond the cell, veneered with iron bearing rock like his cell. He sailed through the window above the door to Claire's cell and watched her sitting, cross-legged on the floor, eyes closed. She looked well . . . calm . . . unharmed. He could feel the silver ring on his thumb tingling and growing warm. He extended his astral arms, entwining Claire in an invisible embrace. He sensed her smile.

"Hi, sweetie," Claire thought, aware of Ron's closeness.

"How's my girlfriend?" Ron said into her mind.

"Probably not doing as well as your boyfriend." Claire giggled.

The reference to Finn gave Ron pause. He wondered if he could reach out to him.

"Are you sure you're okay?" Ron thought.

"I'm fine," Claire thought back. "Right now, anyway."

"I won't let anything happen to you!" Ron let his love for her fill the space about her.

Claire was silent for a moment. Finally she sighed.

"I love you too, Ron," Claire thourht. "Now get us the hell out of here!"

Satisfied, Ron withdrew. He sent his mind down the outside hall, trying to sense Finn's presence. He decided to trust his own connection to Finn and let his mind follow the path of least resistance. His thoughts traveled to the farthest end of the wide hall where it terminated at another massive, blank wall of iron ore. His whole being became anxious and agitated and he felt the desperate urge to somehow get through—get through to Finn—Finn was beyond that impenetrable wall. The ubiquitous presence of iron repelled his mind like opposite poles of a magnet. There was no way through.

A dim light at the edge of the wall caught his attention. A small sprig of tenacious ivy clung to the wall, its life force sparkling about it. Ron approached it with his mind, tracing the plant's spiraling, tender trunk up the wall. It seemed to disappear into an impossible small fissure in the rock—a way in.

Ron tried to focus his mind into the space, but could feel the fatigue in his physical self, all the more weakened by the iron surrounding it. He sensed his material self, tugging for his return, but he resisted, marshalling his concentration, focusing his aching love for Finn into the small plant. The tug on his mind became too great and he felt himself begin to be pulled back into his physical form. If his mind couldn't make the journey along the twig of ivy. . .

"Finn!" Ron's soul all but screamed into the plant's essence.

ℭhapⱦⱸℛ 11

Finn stretched out on the thick, upper limb of the giant *sceach gheal* tree that dominated the center of the expansive, walled garden where he spent his days—his life. He stared up at the pale, blue dome of bright, silver light that protected him from the taint of the *Fei* world beyond. At least that's what the moon priest taught about the impenetrable dome to which all *Fey* lent an iota of their inner powers.

He rolled over and embraced the sturdy limb. He had practiced hard to master his fractured emotions, but a memory—a feeling from the human world invariably would break through and tease another tear from his eye. For an instant, the security imparted by the strength of the limb he hugged sparked the memory of the human boy he had embraced—embraced with all his heart—much to his pleasure—his wholeness—and now, much to his shame.

A shimmering tear broke from his ivory lashes and dropped to the garden's grassy floor. As expected, a brilliant, white blossom immediately germinated up from the ground. It was one among many that carpeted the ground beneath the tree. Their delicious scent wafted up to Finn, seeking to cheer him and relieve his suffering. Finn stared at the miraculous floral display as if not even seeing it—as if it was a normal development—and it was.

For those select young *Fey* chosen to commit to years' of service to the Royal household, the spread of milky white blossoms was heightening their already stressful duties. The flowers themselves were holy and inviolate and it was becoming increasingly difficult to ford a safe path through them to minister to the White Wing. The massive *sceach gheal* tree that commanded the garden was now virtually unapproachable.

Kian, the senior page, stood stiffly at the perimeter of white. He weighed the urge to take to the air, but it was forbidden in the Cloister. Instead, he stood quietly waiting for the White Wing to acknowledge him. His throat was sore from the litany of subtle coughs he made, hoping to call attention to himself without success. The iris cup he held, brimming with honey and nectar, was becoming an almost irresistible temptation—but he dared not soothe his dry throat with its contents. The nectar from this protected plant, and the honey from the sacred hive of specially bred bees, was nourishment only for the White Wing. The penalty for broaching royal protocol was unthinkable.

Kian and his fellow pages had been imprisoned in the iron citadel the entire time that the White Wing had gone missing. They had been starved and interrogated incessantly, but to have confessed to aiding and abetting the White Wing's escape would have violated their consecrated oath to obey the White Wing. This oath, Kian had assured his confederates, was a higher and more holy pledge than fealty to the greater family of *Fey*. Besides, everyone who served the White Wing, loved him. He was the most beautiful of the *Fey*—the most desirable. The pages would have done anything for the White Wing, including the most difficult, letting him go. His suffering in isolation broke their hearts.

Kian had not expected the wrathful indignation of the Elders. The earth spirits were the only beings that moved freely between the human world and the extension of that reality inhabited by the *Fey*. Following the White Wing's return, the Elders had summoned an unheard-of, ancient binding. In response to that spell, the earth spirits had caused walls of iron to encircle the Royal mews. The Elders themselves had bound the air above in light—an impenetrable fortress of protection, and at the same time, an inescapable prison.

Kian could not stand the silence anymore. He fanned his wings forcefully, stirring the air about him, and focused the resultant breeze up into the *sceach gheal* tree. The White Wing's silken hair fell back from his face at the wind's behest, and his shimmering pale wings, caught up in the breeze, rolled his body back and forth on the limb beneath him. The White Wing turned his head slightly, aware of the figure standing in the grass.

Kian fought the urge to speak. It was forbidden to speak to the White Wing unless first spoken to. Kian remembered a ploy of his predecessor and the edges of his mouth curled up.

"Did you say something, My Lord?" Kian asked, feigning innocence should any snoopy eyes be observing. "I can't get any closer, so I'm not sure if I heard you right."

Finn couldn't help but smile at his page and friend. He saw the iris cup in Kian's hand.

"Take it away, Kian! I won't have any."

"But, My Lord, you haven't had food since you returned," said the young page. "Please, sir."

"No!" Finn turned away.

"As you wish, sir." Kian tried another ploy. "They will beat me again, but I will serve your will."

"Beat you?" Finn said, turning his head back sharply.

"Not to worry, sir." Kian backed away slowly, bowing. "They're just still angry about your being away so, naturally, they blame us that you languish, unhappy and starving." He turned away as if to leave.

Wait!" Finn called out. He sat up on the tree limb. "Wait."

Kian smiled to himself. Just as quickly his expression blanked as he turned back to the White Wing.

"My Lord?" Kian asked with another bow.

"You little pile of sheep dung!" Finn yelled at the boy.

"Yes, My Lord."

"You're lying!"

"Yes, My Lord."

"But you know I won't take the chance."

"Yes, My Lord." Kian's wings quivered with self-satisfaction. "Please do not worry yourself, sir."

"Shut up and bring me the damn cup!"

"I am unable to approach, sir." Kian looked about. "You're tears block my way."

"Have your wings been clipped?"

"No sir," Kian responded, smiling.

That was all the young page needed. He rose up in the light and soared up to the tree limb where he hovered, offering the cup of nectar to the White Wing.

"Sit beside me," Finn said, patting the tree limb.

"Sit, sir?" Kian eyed the branch.

"Yes, sit!" Finn's voice rose in exasperation. "It's a perfectly good use of your buttocks."

Kian swallowed. A new twist on an old insult.

"Yes, sir," Kian said, settling on the limb beside Finn. "I suppose I should use them for sitting as I am denied any other . . . use."

"Oh, pitiful you!"

The White Wing wanted to pat the young *Fey*'s cheek but he was forbidden bodily contact for which his page, and not himself, would be harshly punished.

"You'll leave me at the next full face of the goddess." Finn closed his eyes, and marveled again that the goddess shone in the human night sky as brightly as she did in the perpetual light of *Faerie*. "Then," he continued. "You'll be free to fall in love, to mate, to birth your young . . ." Finn looked into Kian's eyes. "And I will remain here, alone, untouched, barren, and unloved."

"No, My Lord." Kian's own eyes filled. "You will never be unloved. I and all of your servants worship you."

"Worship is not the kind of love I'm talking about, and you know it."

Kian lowered his gaze.

"But I have been loved," Finn said, trembling. "I have made love. At least I won't end my days never having known . . . love."

"Still, My Lord," Kian said. "You are the Blessed and Holy One. Promised to the Great Purple Wing. Have hope, sir. One day he will come for you."

"I have no hope, Kian!" Finn covered his face. "There is no Purple Wing. He doesn't exist and hasn't for longer than most *Fey* can remember. I'm not betrothed—I'm sacrificed—sacrificed to a legend."

"My Lord." Kina offered up the iris cup, trying to change the subject. "Take nourishment, sir, and I will hope for you."

"Why?" Finn eyed the chalice of clear nectar.

"Because, sir." Kian held the cup to Finn's lips. "We have no Purple Wing, but we have you. You hold the light that binds us all as *Clann*. If we have no other hope, we have you."

Finn refused the nectar with a shrug.

"If I am consumed, the light will inhabit another," Finn said. "The light doesn't need me like you seem to think."

Kian caught his breath, but the repressed sob broke through anyway.

"My Lord," Kian managed as his ordinary tears streamed down his cheeks. "We need you, sir, not just the light you hold." His shoulders heaved in anguish. "I need you, sir."

Finn's fists clenched. The need to encircle his page in a forbidden embrace was almost overwhelming.

"Give me the ambrosia then," Finn said, resigned to his fate. "Let me drink it."

Kian held the cup up shakily, still fighting the sobs. "May the Goddess bless you," he croaked hoarsely.

"And you." Finn smiled at Kian. No one could stop him from extending his feelings out to embrace the light inside his servant.

The meeting of their light calmed Kian and a smile returned to his face. He watched his Lord sip the nourishment from the cup, noting for the first time, the unnatural hue, a sallowness to the White Wing's usually creamy complexion.

"Sir!" He could make out the streaks of dark violet that traced the capillary pathways of light beneath the White Wing's skin. "You aren't well!"

"What do you mean?"

"You look awful, sir," Kian responded without thinking. "Sickly."

"Well," Finn said with a sigh. "Thank you for that."

"No, sir, I'm serious." Kian tossed the empty cup to the ground. "As soon as the Elders and the generals have finished their meetings, I'll—"

"What meetings?" Finn stiffened. "What generals? What's going on?"

"Oh," Kian responded. "I thought you had heard. Intruders were captured. They are believed to be spies of the Great Elven Lord." Kian shuddered at the reference. "They will probably be consigned to fire and iron."

"Intruders?" Finn's brow knotted. "Have you seen them?"

"Oh, no, My Lord." Kian shook his head vigorously. "Such evil terrifies me!"

"See what you can find . . ."

Finn suddenly clutched his ears. A sound vibration thundered through his being, knocking him off the tree branch. He tumbled down into the carpet of flowers below. A name—a memory caused the light in him to prism outward, engulfing the whole of the Cloister in a blinding flash.

Kian dove off the tree branch and knelt beside the White Wing. A mighty seizure had gripped his master— some evil attacked his Lord's very soul.

Just as suddenly, all went quiet. Finn stirred, crushing the flowers beneath him. He sat up slowly, hands shaking involuntarily—his eyes saucer round—his head bowed.

"Lord White Wing!" Kian reached out to steady his Lord, unmindful of the statutes forbidding such encroachment on the person of the Holy One. "My Lord, what's happened? What has done this to you?"

Slowly, Finn's head lifted. Kian could see the White Wing's open eyes, but they were blind to the sights about them. The White Wing's eyes were focused on some unseen plane—perhaps on the evil one who held him in this unholy grasp. Finn's mouth opened, silent at first, then . . .

"Ron!" Finn whispered breathily. "Ron!" His voice ripped the leaves off the tree above. "Ron!"

Chapter 12

Ron Maguire felt his body slump to the floor, drained of physical energy. The psychic effort had completely drained him. He tried to pull strength up from the earth into his body, but the expanding distance from his mind to his body and the iron-bearing rock below the flooring prevented his life force from making a connection. He turned his attention up to the arched stone ceiling above the high, unbroken walls of stone that surrounded him. He thought for a second that he could feel Finn's presence, but it was a fleeting impression—and probably just a wish fulfillment interrupted. A mood of hopelessness descended, a further drain on his energy reserves. Where before he had felt so close to his goal, now he felt even farther apart.

Ron looked down at his hands and arms, mottled with a spidery web of blackened veins. The skin covering was all but transparent. He felt feverish, achy, and licked his leathery lips. His shoulder blades throbbed with a stabbing pain as if the bones themselves were trying to slice their way to the surface. Ron closed his eyes, admitting to himself for the first time that he was in bad shape.

"Ron?"

Ron started at the sound of his name.

"Ron!"

"Claire?" Ron called out, breathless.

"Ron, are you okay." Claire's voice was panicked. "What happened? I heard you scream! Are you hurt?"

"I'm fine, Claire." Ron willed strength into his own voice. "Nothing to worry about."

"Bullshit!" Claire yelled back. "What happened?"

Ron drew in a shallow breath against the pain that clamped about his chest from his shoulder blades.

"It's . . ." He took another deeper breath. "I . . . I felt I was so close to him, Claire—like he was within reach!" Ron's fists clenched against the stone beneath him. "I couldn't get through, though." Ron closed his eyes and lay back onto the hard floor. "I'm too weak."

Claire remained silent. She could almost feel Ron's despair. She rose and went to her cell door. Standing on tiptoe, she peered out into the emptiness beyond. What she saw sent her quickly crouching back onto the floor.

The clanging of metal against metal echoed out in the hall. The heavy, metal door to Ron's cell swung inward. Ron struggled to his elbows as the *Fei* general swaggered into the Spartan cell flanked by two soldiers armed with the requisite spear and shield. The general stood over Ron like a conquering hero, hands on hips. A thin, gloating smile curled like an angry scar across an otherwise perfect face.

"You will be shortly consigned to fire and oblivion, human!" the general said, almost gleefully. "Your kind will not invade this—"

"Go fuck yourself!" Ron said sharply, spitting at the floor at the general's feet. "I haven't invaded anything. I'm here to see Finn!"

"You matter-tainted animal!" the general thundered. "You will have no concourse with the White Wing."

"I've already had *concourse* with the White Wing!" Ron shouted back. "And if you harm me or my friend, you can bet your little bat ears the White Wing will be mucho pissed with you!"

The general arched an eyebrow at Ron. "You strange creature," he said without pity. "You are deluded beyond comprehension."

The general signaled to the solders at the door and they moved quickly to positions at Ron's head and feet.

"No, human," the general said, sneering. "Before you are redacted to your base elements, you will tell me how you came here. Tell me and I will make sure your destruction is quick and sure, and—"

"What about *go fuck yourself* did you not understand?" Ron sat up haughtily. "The only fairy I'll talk to is Finn, so you're wasting your time and mine!"

The *Fei* general drew himself to his full height, glaring down at his defiant prisoner.

"I hear humans ooze out their life force in puddles of red slime," the general said, nodding to the two soldiers. "Let us see if this human bleeds!"

The young soldiers thrust their spears at Ron. The silver ring on Ron's thumb hummed and the air about him cracked as a bubble of amaranthine energy encircled him, repelling the spear thrusts violently. The young soldiers stood back, stunned.

"Again!" the general ordered.

The soldiers snapped to and tried once more to pierce the bubble of light surrounding their target. Both were thrown back, slamming against the high stone walls of the cell.

The *Fei* general snatched up one of the fallen spears and stood over Ron, aiming it at Ron's head. Ron could feel his own body weakening as his energy flooded into the light shield protecting him. He winced as the general flexed heavily muscled arms, preparing to thrust the heavy spear.

With a cry of exertion, the general threw his weight into the spear.

Ron fell back to the floor as the spear tip pierced the infinitely thin membrane of light about him. With a sound like a gunshot, the sheltering light pushed back with explosive force, knocking the general to his knees and repelling the heavy spear so violently it flew against the opposing wall. The iron point pierced the stone up to the spear's wooden shaft which splintered like broken glass at the force.

The young *Fei* soldiers had recovered enough to witness their general's humiliation. They rushed to try and help him to his feet, but the general shook them off angrily. He stood fuming above Ron, eyes blazing red.

"Your magic weakens you, you sniveling *Phooka*!" the general said in a low, anger-laden voice. "But I can assure you that the Great Council is more powerful and you will most surely burn!"

Ron, too, had recovered his confidence despite the weakening effects of the protective canopy of light about him.

"Blah, blah, and blah," Ron said, throwing sarcasm like his own spear. "You're a coward! You and your little minions."

The general straightened. He nodded to the two young soldiers and stormed out of the cell. The soldiers scrambled to follow and the heavy door slammed shut by some unseen force. Just as quickly as it had appeared, the shell of light dissolved in the space about Ron.

"Ron." Claire called out.

"I'm here," Ron called back, his voice echoing off the stone walls about him.

"We've got to get out of here," Claire said, hearing the weakness in her friend's voice. "You have to get back to Mab. You've done nothing but get sicker and sicker since we arrived."

"There's no way, Claire," Ron said, shaking his head, despairing. "We're surrounded by iron—the walls, the subfloor, the door. I'm too weakened."

Claire bounced her back against the cold, metal door, thinking. Ron was right. Iron surrounded them.

"Damn . . ." Claire froze.

The polished, metal behind her captured her attention.

"Ron!" Claire yelled suddenly, spinning to face the door to her cell. "Everything's not iron!"

"Don't let the stone tiles fool you, Claire." Ron turned over on his side. "Iron is all around us."

"You're wrong!" Claire rushed about her cell, touching the walls excitedly. "There's iron in the walls, but the walls are not iron!" She turned back to the steel door. "There's iron in the door, but it's steel—an alloy of carbon and iron! The carbon is its weakness, just like the rock and minerals that hold the iron in the walls."

"Yes, but . . ." Ron looked about his cell, seeing things with a fresh perspective. "Give me a minute!" he yelled through the wall separating his cell from Claire's.

Ron pushed up to his knees. He focused his mind on the wall. In an instant his other sight took over. Ron smiled to himself at how easy engaging his other eyesight was becoming. What had been a stone wall was now the

familiar swirl of physical matter—the energy trails of molecular, atomic, and subatomic structures and their tenuous connections. He could recognize the dense, black mask of iron superimposed over and behind the ephemeral smoke of the surrounding mineral structure.

Then Ron looked at the heavy, steel door to his cell. This was a different picture. The carbon trails formed a complex, interdependent crystalline structure about the iron. A house of cards was the best description that came to Ron's mind—a picture that brought a smile to his face. If he could interrupt one component of the stable complex . . .

Ron took in his breath, trying to open his other sight to some source of power he could draw on, but there was no familiar spell for him to invoke. Mab had taught him to see, but not how to use what he saw. He thought back to the granite cliff he had passed through earlier. He still didn't understand how he had accomplished this—still, he had accomplished it.

Ron rubbed his hands together and was instantly aware of the silver ring on his thumb. He had almost forgotten it as it had become almost a part of his physical self, having no sensation of being a foreign object attached to his hand. Perhaps it was the source of his recent new powers—or maybe just a conduit for them. The powerful light that had defeated the *Phooka* in the park had not emanated from the ring, but from his own hands.

Ron turned his second sight on the ring itself. It almost caused him to lose his concentration. The appearance of silver was deceptive. In the reality of Ron's preternatural vision, the ring that encircled his thumb was a photic band, a dense, wave of light. There were no energy traces of matter, no hint of directionality or flow—it just was—not solid, but solid—not liquid, but undulating about his thumb—not gas, but tightly encircling his thumb without really touching it.

"Ron!" Claire's voice broke through Ron's fascination.

"Working on it!" Ron yelled back.

Ron lay back on the stone floor, his physical weakening was now very real as well. His ability to envision the other reality was unimpeded, and seemed to be independent of his physical resources and immune to his body's debilitation. He gave himself over to the weakness and felt an unfamiliar, independence of his mind from his body. The previous tug his body had exerted on his out of body mind was now only a faint, string of connection. It was an exhilarating, but at the same time scary feeling.

Ron was suddenly aware that he was seeing the room about him as if from a standing position. He looked down, wanting to gasp, but had no physical connection to do it. His eyes focused on his own, prone body, stretched out on the swirling floor below. Mab had talked about out of body experiences, but this was Ron's first real experience of being full-on, out of body.

For a moment Ron was slightly unnerved, but it didn't take long for the freedom from his physical body's weakness to turn his attention back to the heavy steel door. There was more clarity in his vision and the elemental structures stood out with greater detail. Even so it looked like it would involve a significant amount of energy to take apart the door. Instinctively, he knew the weakest point of the door was the three, heavy hinges that attached it onto the stone walls—that, and the simple deadbolt lock assembly opposite the hinges.

Ron turned his disembodied vision back to the silver ring on his physical body. It was actually gleaming with energy, as if poised to act. Again Ron looked to the door and concentrated on hinges and lock. He marveled that, though he could see the whole door, the energy trails of the four weak points stood out. He considered the problem iron and steel—the big problem was rust. He couldn't remember anything from last year's chemistry class. Claire, on the other hand, had an almost eidetic memory as well as a natural grasp of science.

Ron had no trouble sensing Claire's mind. In his hyper-energized state, the walls had no effect on him. It was his physical body that they harmed. He sent his thoughts to Claire.

"What do I need to make steel rust?" Ron called out. He could feel Claire's excitement and her almost immediate response.

"Carbon dioxide for an electrolyte," Claire called back, "and oxygen and hydrogen."

If Ron could have laughed he would have. He had no idea what an electrolyte was but at least he recognized the two elements and the main component of human expiration. His body was exhaling carbon dioxide and so was Claire. Oxygen was in the surrounding air, but what about hydrogen. H_2O—at last a useful memory. Now, what to do with it?

Ron called up his training under Mab.

"Name it, invoke it, send it out to do something."

He focused his mind, named the physical elements he needed, called on the Mother Goddess to gather them from the earth, and commanded them to . . . what?

"Rust the damn hinges and locks on both doors!"

Light flashed about Ron as the elements invoked were gathered. If must have been visible to Claire as well because he could hear her calling to him, terrified. Ron sent her a sense of well-being and the yelling in his mind stopped. He could see the once dense and black iron in the hinges and lock begin to wave and glow a sickly orange. He watched as the carbon energies were released along with the other trace element. The hinges dissolved into crystalline dust along with the dead bolt that locked the other side of the door to the wall.

Ron watched as the shiny, metal door succumbed to the pull of gravity, its bottom dropping an almost imperceptible distance to the floor and then, like a slow motion movie reel, the top of the door began to arc inward accelerating to a tremendous crash, shattering the floor tiles it struck, coming to rest inches from the feet of Ron's physical self. Another crash next door kicked up more dust as the door of Claire's cell fell out into the hall.

Ron smiled at the billowing cloud of iron oxide slowly clearing from the now open doorway. He could just make out a figure in the hall just outside the door. Panic filled his being. Had soldiers responded so quickly? An instinctual halo of ultraviolet light surrounded Ron's physical body as he prepared a different kind of spell for the intruder.

"Ron!"

Ron heard his name—but a different voice—not Claire's. The stranger at the door waved a hand and obediently, the dust retreated to the floor. Ron glimpsed the mop of platinum hair rise up from the settling cloud.

"Ron!" Finn's voice cried again as he stared into the cell at Ron's still, physical body and the threatening specter of violet that pulsed above it.

"Finn!" Ron's mind shrieked, sending Finn to his knees holding his head.

Chapter 13

Quickly recovering, Finn jumped to his feet. He stepped over the fallen steel door, his feet protected by thin sandals woven out of tree bark—his only clothing.

"Ron," Finn whispered to the still figure stretched out before him on the hard stone floor.

The purple haze above his friend's body dissipated. The body stirred.

"Ron, how . . ."

"Ron!" screamed another voice from the doorway.

Claire bolted into the cell. She stopped short.

"Finn!" Claire said in surprise. "You're here. Thank God!"

Claire hugged the white-haired *Fey*, ignoring his nudity. She dropped to her knees beside Ron.

"Dammit, Ron!" Claire expelled her breath as she saw Ron's eyes open. "You look like shit!" She held his face in her hands. "We have got to get you home!"

"What is wrong?" Finn also knelt beside Ron, restraining the urge to embrace his love. "Ron, what's happened to you?"

Ron stared at the vision that was Finn, marveling at the young *Fey*'s beauty, unable to quell the rising emotion roiling to the surface.

"Finn, you're really here." Bloody tears began their slow descent down Ron's cheeks. "I found you." He reached out and touched Finn's face.

"Ron!" Finn responded, staring in shock at the dark veins running through Ron's face. "What has happened to you?"

"I had to find you, Finn." Ron grabbed Finn's hands.

"I am here," Finn said. "How are you here?"

"I needed to explain." Ron sat up, clenching Finn's hand to his chest. "I'm sorry for what I did. I was a coward. I—"

"Ron . . ."

"Please!" Ron took Finn's face in his hands. "You have to forgive me, Finn. I was an idiot."

Finn looked to Claire questioning.

"These changes started when you left, Finn," Claire said with a shrug. "I don't know what's going on. We just have to get him back to Mab."

"Ron," Finn began, trying to help Ron to his feet. "Are you able—"

"I'm fine," Ron persisted, weakly. He looked into Finn's eyes. "I just needed to find you," he said. "I needed you to know—"

"Listen to me!" Finn shook Ron by the shoulders. "You are not well. Some sickness has possessed you. We—"

"I don't give a damn about how I look!" Ron shouted. He caught himself. "I love you," he said softly. "I need you to know that." Ron focused his inner voice.

Finn caught his breath. For a moment he was over-whelmed by the emotions flooding over him from Ron's mind. He gave himself over to the newness of it, feelings that had never been directed to him. Love. After a moment he spoke to Ron in his own mind. The light between them became a swirl of prisming radiance, finally settling as they equally shared an understanding, an assurance of each other's truth.

"Jesus, guys!" Claire said, breaking the spell. "I'd say get a room, but we've got more important things to worry about."

"The female is right," Finn responded with a nod.

"The female is Claire," the female said curtly.

"Of course," Finn said, batting his eyes at her. "I'm sorry . . . Claire. While I can negotiate the language, I do not always grasp all the social requirements that go with it."

"The female accepts your apology," Claire responded, grinning. "And would appreciate it if you were . . . Oh, I don't know . . . clothed?"

Finn cocked his head at her.

"Of course," he said, and was instantly clad in a white, silken tunic. "Human modesty is very . . . human," he added, adjusting the sash tied about his waist.

"Much better," Claire said, breathing a sigh of relief.

"Ron, Claire thinks your . . . Mab can heal you." Finn wrapped his arms about Ron, steadying him. "You need to go back to the human world."

"Like hell!" Ron struggled to stay on his feet. "I'm not going anywhere without you. I'm not letting you go again."

"But, Ron . . ." Claire began.

"I just need some aspirin or something. I'll be fine."

"Dammit, Ron!" Claire's arms crossed. "You're being ridiculous and stubborn—and I doubt the *Fey* have any aspirin."

"What is this aspirin?" Finn asked.

"It's a human medicine," Claire said, glaring at Ron.

"We have no . . . medicine here," Finn said, his face clouded with concern. "We have no need . . ." Finn caught himself. "Wait . . . Kian!" He called over his shoulder.

Finn's young page instantly appeared in the doorway.

"My Lord . . ." Kian's mouth hung open. "My Lord, you are beautiful again."

"What is that supposed to mean?" Finn frowned at the boy.

"Your face, My Lord," Kian replied. "Your skin . . . your sickness has left you."

"Have you my iris cup?" Finn said with a sigh.

"Yes, My Lord," Kian replied. The flower chalice appeared in his hands. "Do you need nourishment, my Lord?"

"I do not, but my friend here does." Finn pressed close to Ron.

"But Lord White Wing, it is forbidden!" Kian shrank backwards.

"It is forbidden to any other *Fey*, except the extinct Purple Wing. Do you see any other *Fey* in this room?"

Kian shifted nervously.

"No, My Lord . . . but . . ." He looked from Claire to Ron, sniffing the air. "What are they?"

Finn took the cup of nectar and held it to Ron's lips.

"Drink, my love. It will give you strength."

Ron inhaled at the sweet nectar's aroma and took a tentative sip.

"Tastes like peaches," Ron said, before taking a huge gulp. "Not bad."

"It is Royal Nectar," Finn said, licking a drop from the edge of Ron's lips. "Do you like the honey, too?" he asked with a seductive smile.

"Well . . ." Ron swallowed hard. "Yes, but I don't think I'm in any shape to deal with the . . . side effects."

Finn giggled, squeezing Ron tightly. Ron drank deeply from the chalice.

"This isn't bad," Ron said, licking his lips. "I feel . . ."

Ron's eyes bugged like headlights and then rolled back in his head. He sank to his knees with a groan.

"Dammit, Ron!" Claire sank to Ron's other side. "We've got to . . ." She stopped.

Ron's skin had gone blue. The tips of his ears curled to a point. His hair went raven black.

"My God, Ron," Claire whispered.

"I . . ." Ron struggled to regain his conscious awareness.

"My love," Finn managed against the fear that clouded his face. "What is happening to you?"

Ron shook his head vigorously, trying to clear the fog in his mind.

"I . . . I got woozy there for a second," Ron managed against the waning dizziness.

"That ain't all, boyfriend!" Claire said, reaching out to touch the glistening, thick sable hair that now crowned Ron's head. "Your hair's gone black!"

Ron frowned and tried to pull a strand of his hair into his sight line.

"What do you mean?" Ron said. "I—"

"And your ears have gone pointy!" Claire said, aiming a finger at Ron's ear, too afraid to touch the new pointed tip.

"Wha . . ." Ron's hands went to his ears.

"And you're Smurf-blue!" Claire added, before covering her mouth with her hands.

"No," Finn said, eyeing Ron with a mixture of horror and fascination. "Well . . . bluish."

"Maybe dusty rose?" Claire said.

"Blackish," Finn said with finality.

"Well," Ron said, back on his feet. "I do feel stronger. That nectar seems to have done the trick."

"Fascinating!" Finn said.

"Yeah, yeah, Spock," Claire said, cutting Finn one of her best you're-not-helping looks.

Finn blinked at her.

"Look, Ron." Claire squeezed Ron's shoulders. "You may feel a little better, but you look worse. We need to get you back to Mab before this progresses so far that she can't reverse it."

"My Lord," Kian said, leaning into Finn's ear. "I thought you said he was humankind."

"He is," Finn responded. "It must be an effect of the Royal Nectar. It is causing some confusion in his physical matter."

"Crap!" Claire insisted. "His physical matter has been . . . was confused long before we got here."

Finn stared at her wide-eyed. "Ron," he said, nodding his agreement. "You must go back to Mab."

"I don't care what I look like," Ron said with a dismissive wave. "I'm not going back, so . . ." He turned to Claire. "That's all there is to it."

Claire sighed, throwing her hands up in exasperation.

"Then I need to get home to Mab," Claire insisted, "and try to bring back to you whatever Mab whips up to counteract this . . . these changes."

"That's a better idea." Ron nodded. "Let's get you back to the mountain."

Kian darted to the open doorway.

"Soldiers are coming, My Lord," Kian called back to Finn. "A lot of them."

"Back against the wall," Finn commanded. "All of you!"

Claire obeyed instantly, but Finn had to shove Ron behind him.

"You!" Finn said sharply to his young page. "Back to the cloister, this instant!"

The young page disappeared in a blink, just as a cadre of soldiers bearing their requisite spears crowded into the narrow door. Finn held up a hand at the soldiers. His shimmering, white wings unfolded instantly shielding his friends. A silvered light radiated about him and a low crackling hum filled the small cell. Instantly the soldiers fell to one knee.

"How dare you approach me with weapons!" Finn's voice bounded off the polished, stone walls, filled with overtones that gave his voice an otherworldly reverberation. "What is the meaning of this intrusion into my cloister?" Finn stood his ground confidently.

The *Fei* general stepped through his guards. He stopped short at the sight of the radiant figure in the center of the room.

"Lord White Wing!" The stunned general froze.

"Explain yourself," Finn demanded. "On your knee, General Darragh!"

Without further argument, Darragh dropped quickly to one knee. His face reddened.

"My Lord," Darragh began, now aware of the humans hiding behind his *Fei* Lord's translucent wings. "We ahave been ordered by the *Ardsagart* to secure these prisoners for sentencing. They have invaded our sanctuary. We . . ." He stopped. "How are you outside your cloister—"

"Enough!" Finn's high authoritative voice cut through like a bolt of lightning. Electromagnetic forces snapped in the air swirling about him. "These humans are under my protection!"

"My Lord," Darragh said, stung with the humiliation. "The Council has decreed—"

"My council has erred!" Finn stated with a finality that, coupled with the rising levels of ozone in the air, invited no debate. "I will take my human friends to the Council and explain their error. Now stand aside!"

Darragh stood slowly, his jaw tightly clamped by barely restrained anger.

"We will escort you there in safety," Darragh said, forcing his eyes to lower before his Lord.

"Unnecessary!" Finn said with a dismissive wave.

"It is our duty, My Lord," Darragh insisted. The edge of his mouth curved upward. "Your safety is our sacred charge." He knew the White Wing must agree.

Finn took a deep breath and cut a glance over his shoulder to his friends.

"Very well, Darragh," Finn said.

His omission of Darragh's title brought a gasp from the surrounding young soldiers and wiped the half-smile from Darragh's face like a sharp sword.

"But stay at a distance," Finn said with cold aloofness. "And dispense with those weapons!"

The general nodded to his soldiers and the spears dissolved into light. The young *Fey* retreated to the walls, opening a path for Finn.

"Stay close to me," Finn cautioned over his shoulder to his friends. His glistening wings instantly reabsorbed back into his shoulder blades.

Claire and Ron followed Finn out of the cell into the high-walled hall beyond. Finn tucked a hand behind him which Ron quickly took into his own. With his other hand,

Ron took Claire's arm and pulled her to him. Closely knit, they proceeded down the hall flanked by *Fei* soldiers, who exchanged furtive glances that betrayed their awe and fascination, more in Finn than the captive humans.

"Jesus, Finn," Claire said in a low voice she hoped no one could hear. "You'd think these guys had never seen the White Wing before."

"They haven't," Finn responded, aloof to the buzzing interest from the guards. "A White Wing has not . . . How shall I put it, *officially* left this compound in over twenty thousand moons."

"But you escaped?" Ron asked.

"No." Finn stopped momentarily and turned his head in an arc, eyeing the soldiers who quickly dropped their eyes to the floor as if, to look on the White Wing was forbidden. "The White Wing is cocooned in this . . . these walls to protect his light from outside taint. It's the way things are. I . . ." Finn smiled to Ron. "I just got tired of being alone."

"So you just left?" Ron asked, returning the smile.

"It's unheard of," Finn said. "But the *Clann* light I hold provided me a way. It was either that or die of despair like so many before me."

"Then why did you come back?" Ron squeezed Finn's hand.

"Despair." Finn brought Ron's hand to his lips and kissed it.

The ensuing agitation among the young soldiers clearly indicated that the gesture had not gone unnoticed.

"Ow!" Ron cried out, rubbing his shoulder where Claire had just punched him. "What was that for?"

"Because you're the *taint!*" Claire said, trying to project her most offended demeanor. "That was for Finn!"

"You're supposed to be my friend," Ron objected weakly.

"Finn is my friend, too," Claire said. "So take it like a man!"

"Thank you, Claire," Finn said, trying not to laugh.

"Don't mention it," Claire responded. "If he gives you any more trouble, just let me know." She glared at Ron. "I'll take care of it."

"I promise to behave," Ron said, smiling down at Finn.

"We'll see about that," Finn said. His eyes delivered a clear message to Ron's pleasure centers.

"Lord White Wing," the *Fei* general said from behind the assembly. "You must relent. You cannot . . . must not leave the protection of these walls. It is forbidden. The Lord *Ardsagart* and the elders have placed power bindings to keep you safe."

"To keep us prisoner is more like it!" Finn sniffed in derision.

"Lord White Wing," the Darragh continued. "It is ill-advised. Your presence outside these walls will cause much unrest, confusion, and anxiety among the people. The elders will not allow . . ."

Finn gave Darragh a look that caused even the self-possessed, older *Fey* to avert his eyes.

"*Oscail!*" he commanded the wall before him.

Obediently, the stones appeared to reassemble themselves into an arched and pillared doorway. The young soldiers gasped.

"So much for the elders' bindings," Finn said, straightening his shoulders.

The guards looked one to another, awed by the display of power.

Light streamed into the once dim hall and Ron looked out onto the lush, alive landscape beyond. He became instantly disoriented. His eyesight was overwhelmed by the strange, shifting colors—colors that were disconcertingly different. Everything in front of him was now bathed in an iridescent overlay of amplified brightness that blurred the boundaries of what were supposed to be discrete, individual trees, plants, and . . . people.

"What's wrong, Ron?" Claire asked, leaning into him.

"I . . ." Ron squinted into the kaleidoscope world expanding before him. "I'm not sure. Things look different . . . brighter . . . I can't seem to focus. I can't distinguish where one color ends and another begins."

"You're like a *nuabheirthe* . . . a newborn," Finn said, laughing. "Obviously an effect of the nectar. Don't worry." He pulled Ron out onto the greenish . . . bluish grass. "Your eyes will adjust."

"I think there was a little LSD in that nectar." Ron winked at Claire.

"And how would you know?" Claire tried to see if his eyes were dilated.

"Well . . . Mab . . . you know."

"I can only imagine." Claire sighed.

As they walked across the grassy field, strewn with blooming wildflowers, Ron felt weightless, as if his bare feet only grazed the tips of the grass blades. He felt stronger than before—more alive.

"I like your place," Ron said, suddenly wanting to take Finn in his arms and kiss him . . . and . . . Ron took a deep breath and closed his eyes.

"Ron!" Finn shook Ron lightly. "Are you okay? Perhaps you should—"

"I'm fine." Ron opened his eyes to meet Finn's. An unfamiliar emotion gripped him. He felt his spirit-self reach out . . . envelope Finn with his aura.

"I love you, too, Ron," Finn said softly, succumbing to Ron's aura.

They became aware of Claire's laughter.

"When I think," Claire said between eruptions of laughter, "of the number of times I tried to get you . . . this excited about me!" She covered her mouth to stifle another burst of laughter.

"What are you going on about?" Ron asked, confused.

"You're horny, honey!" Claire burst out.

"What?"

"You're horny! Admit it!"

"You . . ." Ron blustered. "I . . ."

"Boy are you horny." Claire nodded to Finn. "He's got it bad for you, hon."

"Geez, Claire!" Ron took a deep breath. "Can't a guy have a moment without—"

"Any more of this moment," Claire said, nodding to the front of Ron's jeans, "and we'll have to reinforce that zipper."

Ron looked down and flushed blue. He jerked his t-shirt out of his jeans and pulled the hem down over his pants as far as it would go.

"That can't be comfortable," Claire added, dissolving into laughter again.

Finn sidled up to Ron. "I can make you more comfortable," he said, draping himself around Ron's neck.

Ron felt helpless against the desire that swept through him.

"Finn." Ron swallowed hard.

Finn pulled Ron's face to his and pressed his lips hard against Ron's. In response, Ron's arms enveloped the smaller *Fey* and drew him so close even light couldn't pass between them.

"Okay boys!" Claire said, turning to the stunned general and his soldiers. "Maybe we'd better give these two lovebirds a little privacy?"

"My Lord!" General Darragh regained his voice. "This is an abomination! You are betrothed to the *Sciathán Corcra*!

Finn released his kiss.

"And where is he?" Finn poured his love into Ron's eyes. "Do you see him?" He turned on the general. "If the Purple Wing wants me, where is he? Let him show himself now." He looked about for effect. "What? Nothing?" The air pulsed with his growing anger. "There is no *Sciathán Corcra* . . . no Purple Wing, General. He and his White Wing died before the dawn of this world. Died childless! Out of whose imagination is this new savior to be born?"

"My Lord—"

"Shut up, you . . ." Finn searched Ron's mind for a word.

"I've got one for you," Claire said.

Finn took her thought with a smile. "You, asshole!" he thundered at the general.

General Darragh dithered at the unfamiliar insult.

"We'll continue this later," Finn said, taking another kiss from Ron for emphasis. He pulled Ron along as he started back across the field toward the mammoth stone circle that capped the high knoll ahead of them.

"Damn," Claire said, skipping along behind them. "I never new this man-on-man action would be so hot!"

"Finn's not a man, per se," Ron said with a sigh. "He's *Fey*."

"*Fey*, schmey!" Claire grabbed Ron's shoulders and pulled up to his ear. "He's got a dick hasn't he?"

"Wha . . ." Ron stuttered. "Well . . ."

"Too late, I've already seen it!" She giggled into his ear. "Lucky boy. Man-on-Man action!" She poked at Finn's shoulder. "I wonder what else he's got?"

"Claire!" Ron glared at her. "What's that supposed to mean?"

"Well, I mean . . . Jesus, Ron, catch up. Where do all the little *Fey* come from?" She gasped dramatically. "He's not pregnant is he?"

Ron stopped short. "Wha . . . You . . . I . . ."

"*Fey* do not get . . . pregnant," Finn said lightly, smiling at Ron. "That is strictly human biology," he added quickly, heading off Claire's next comment. "It's very simple, really." He smiled at the two humans. "I'll explain later." He gave Ron a knowing look and started out again.

"Oooo, baby!" Claire almost shrieked. She pushed Ron forward beside Finn. "Probably has something to do with fairy dust."

"Claire!" Ron sighed audibly.

Even Finn laughed at Claire's joke.

Ron became aware of new interest in their group as nearby *Fei* persons took notice. It was not long before a crowd of brightly arrayed *Fey* had gathered, following the growing procession across the field. Young and old alike clamored for a view, but keeping a respectful distance. Though they had never laid eyes on the White Wing, it was clear that Finn's identity was quickly sensed in some form of group consciousness. Ron could palpably sense the shock and surprise from the adults, excitement and thrill from the young, and anxious foreboding among the aged.

Finn made no eye contact with the throngs about him, deeply aware of his role in *Fei* society. When his eyes did stray to either side, the eyes of the onlookers immediately dropped to the grass. They could not meet Finn's eyes and he could not meet theirs, but the tension of mutual interest on many levels was acutely evident.

By the time they reached the temple grounds, a host of *Fey* had surrounded the circle of mammoth standing stones. On a sign from the general, some of the young soldiers left the procession and paired off to stand guard in the spaces between the stones, more out of ceremony than necessity. No *Fey* attempted to break the perimeter of the temple circle and the path Finn and his entourage followed was unimpeded up to what appeared to be the prescribed entrance.

"Looks like we're expected," Ron whispered to Claire.

Claire nodded, wide-eyed at the assembly of at least a hundred *Fei* elders in unrepeated pastel colored, cowled robes, standing on either side of the stone paved aisle that bisected the interior of the temple circle up to a raised black marble platform on which sat two immense white marble chairs, one with distinct veins of purple, mauve and violet, and a smaller, unveined chair of brilliant alabaster.

The *Ardsagart* stood at the base of the platform, blocking them from further progress.

"Lord *Ardsagart*," Finn addressed the *Fei* elder. "I have come to remind this council who my friends are."

"Lord White Wing," the elder said with a slight bow. "Your council is assembled here to remind you who your enemies are."

"Bring my friends a place to sit." Finn commanded. He gave a dismissive wave and the *Ardsagart* stood aside.

With that, Finn took both Ron and Claire by the hand and brought them up the platform where, by hands unseen, appeared a small stone bench to the right of what Ron had surmised to be thrones of some sort.

Finn motioned for his two friends to take their seats facing the assembly. Without further preamble, he swept up to the alabaster throne and sat, aloof and seemingly unmoved by the spectacle of *Fey*dom before him that now dropped, *en masse*, to one knee. Still, Ron was aware of the tightness by which Finn clasped his hands in his lap, and Finn's nervous tendency to slightly bite his lower lip. Finn made the slightest gesture with his hand and the entire assembly, including the masses outside the temple, rose to their feet and returned to rapt attention.

"Lord *Ardsagart*," Finn said evenly. "You have illegally imprisoned my friends from the world of people. Why would you also seek to keep their presence from me, much less imprison them under sentence of dissolution?"

"But Lord White Wing, this is not true. Dissolution? Does a human dissolve into light?" The *Ardsagart* smiled at the nods from the other elders. "No, Lord White Wing. The humans have no proper place in this sanctuary. We only wished to . . . set their souls free of their material prisons."

"Really?" Finn considered this concept that was totally foreign to the other *Fey*. He too smiled. "You forget, Lord *Ardsagart*, that I have spent time in the human world. I have gleaned much of their essence. You are right that they do not dissolve into light at their end. But their physical bodies and their souls are intimately joined. That part of them that has life, will dissolve to dust when you burn them, thus ending their existence even in this world of light." Finn raised an eyebrow. "I'm sorry, was that not your plan?"

The crowd buzzed at this revelation.

"The White Wing is well-schooled." The *Ardsagart*'s eyes narrowed.

"Indeed, Lord *Ardsagart*," Finn continued. "Your plan to . . . how did you put it . . . set their souls free was nothing more than a conspiracy to kill them!"

The *Ardsagart* stood silent. His face had all but lost its previous stoicism as he considered his next words very carefully.

"The safety of the White Wing is our obligation . . . our over-riding responsibility," The *Ardsagart* began, measuring his argument. "You say these are your . . . friends, but you have no assurance to offer your people other than your own belief. I have already received reports the Great elven Lord's *Phooka* have—"

"You are correct about the *Phooka*, Lord *Ardsagart*," Finn said interrupting. "And you want proof that my friends are not in league with the elven lord. I appreciate that. I can assure the Council that these are indeed my friends. While among the humans, a powerful *Phooka* attacked the three of us. I was not strong enough to defeat the demon, but my friend, Ron," Finn nodded to Ron with a smile, "easily destroyed the attacker."

"Impossible!" The *Ardsagart* said, turning to the other members of the Council for validation.

"Whether you think it impossible or not," Finn continued, glaring at the *Ardsagart* for the interruption, "is irrelevant. The fact remains that Ron Maguire, human though he is, is a powerful warlock! See how his appearance has matched out own? He defeated the *Phooka*, not once but twice. I was present on both occasions, and on the first one, Ron was not yet aware of my presence in his world."

The *Ardsagart* shook his head vehemently as the muttering among the Council indicated that the changes in the human warlock's appearance elicited a sense of sympathy on their part.

The *Ardsagart* raised a hand for silence. "The White Wing is only trying—"

"Are you saying that I am lying?" Finn's voice assumed its other-worldly pall of echoing overtones.

The *Ardsagart* stared at the White Wing, now aware of his egregious error and lapse in protocol.

"I am not," the *Ardsagart* said against the angry stirrings of the surrounding *Fey*. "I only wish to say that you could be mistaken—"

"I am not!"

"You are yet young and unfamiliar with the devious machinations of the Evil Lord."

"You are the one who is mistaken, Lord *Ardsagart*," Finn said, "if you think the White Wing is so ignorant of reality and truth. You will undo your Order of Dissolution immediately!"

The *Ardsagart* stood fuming inwardly. He knew he had lost this skirmish and looked for some honorable way to extract himself.

"Lord White Wing knows that I have only his well-being as my motivation," the ancient *Fey* priest said. "I would stand against a hundred *Phooka* to keep you safe."

Finn rose from his white marble throne, looking over the assembly without acknowledging the *Ardsagart*'s words.

"The Order, Lord *Ardsagart*," commanded the White Wing.

The *Ardsagart* took a deep breath. He stared daggers into the paving stones at his feet.

"The Order of Dissolution," the priest began.

"Louder!" Finn commanded. "For all to hear."

The *Ardsagart* threw back his head. "The Order of Dissolution is revoked!" he said in sonorous, even tones.

The assembled elders nodded their agreement.

Ron caught sight of General Darragh, lingering at the stone circle's entry. His face was a blank mask, exhibiting no reaction.

"Good," Finn said, holding out a hand for Ron. "We're done here."

Ron rose and took Finn's hand. "I knew you were special," he said where only Finn could hear, "but . . . damn, dude!"

"We have to get Ron back to Mab," Claire said, wasting no time.

"I'm not leaving," Ron insisted, clasping Finn's hand tightly. "You go and see what she can do."

"Dammit, Ron!" Claire faced him, hands on hips.

"That's the deal," Ron said, wrapping his free arm about her for a hug.

"And how will I get back?" Claire asked.

"Any ideas?" Ron looked to Finn.

"Not a problem," Finn said. "*Tearmann Solais!*"

In an instant, the three stood in an expansive, enclosed garden, strewn with white blooms, anchored by an immense hawthorn tree at its center.

"Welcome to my prison," Finn said lightly, leading his friends to a natural gazebo, constructed of heavy, flowering vines about a smaller tree.

"You've never left this place before?" Claire asked.

"I wouldn't say that," Finn replied with a twinkle in his eye. He sat on a wooden bench and motioned for Ron to join him.

"Well," Ron said, taking a seat. "It's a cool place, but I can't imagine staying cooped up here . . . forever!"

"Being the White Wing has never been a choice," Finn explained. "White Wings are born and fiercely protected and isolated."

"Okay," Claire said, sitting opposite them on a facing bench. "You boys have a lot to talk about. I've got to get back to Mab. You may be feeling better, Ron, but you still look a mess."

"Thanks," Ron said with a grimace.

"I think the ears are very cute," Finn said, giving one a kiss.

"Whatever!" Claire rolled her eyes. "How do I get home?"

"Kian!" Finn called out.

Immediately, the young, spritely page appeared out of the surrounding flora.

"My Lord?" He stood obediently at the edge of the gazebo, studying the humans with undisguised interest.

"This is Ron." Finn squeezed Ron's hand. "And this is Claire," he added, gesturing in her direction.

Kian bowed shyly to each.

"Claire needs to get back to the human world," Finn continued. "You remember where we found the forbidden Gateway?"

"Yes, My Lord," Kian responded with a nod.

"See her safely back to her world."

"Yes, My Lord."

"And no messing about!"

"No, My Lord." Kian grinned broadly.

Screams sounded from nearby. Finn and Ron jumped up in unison, looking about for the source. From across the garden, four young *Fey* flew chaotically toward the gazebo, terror in their faces.

"What is the meaning of this?" Finn demanded, stepping out on to the grass.

"Flee!" screamed one of the young *Fey* pages, falling to the grassy floor.

"Hide!" another screamed, landing at a run and falling at Finn's feet.

"Stop this at once!" Finn ordered. He pulled the one at his feet up to face him. "Ailín, what has made you act this way?"

The other young pages began talking at once.

"Silence!" Finn ordered, exasperated. "Now, Ailín, what has happened?"

"The *Phooka*, My Lord!" The boy brushed a tangle of sky-blue hair from his face. "The Demon Elf has invaded!"

"What?" Finn looked at Ron. "*Phooka?*"

"Yes, Lord White Wing! The soldiers war with them now! They attacked the Council, just as you left!" His eyes narrowed at Ron and Claire. "With them."

"That is neither here nor there," Finn said, releasing his grip on the boy. "*Phooka!* How is this possible?"

"The Gateway, My Lord," Ailín said in a wail. "They found the Gateway!"

"Claire!" Ron said. "The others—we left them on the other side. What if . . ."

"I have to get back—now!" Claire said, grabbing for Kian. "Show me the way."

"But . . . but . . ." Kian looked pleading to Finn. "The *Phooka*, My Lord."

"I'll take care of them," Ron said without hesitation. "Finn, how do we get out?"

"I transport us," Finn answered.

"My Lord," one of the young pages said. "Please, My Lord!"

"Okay," Finn said, sighing. "The rest of you can stay here. Claire, I'll show you the way to the Gateway."

"No, My Lord," Kian said, defiantly regaining his courage. "You must stay here with your human love. He will protect you." He grabbed Claire's hand. "I will show this . . . Lord Claire the way."

"Thank you, my little Kian, but please take care." Finn put a hand on his page's cheek. "Use all of our hidden routes."

"Yes, My Lord."

Without thinking, Kian embraced the White Wing to the gasps of the other pages.

Finn hugged him tightly. "Now, off with you!"

"Don't worry, Kian," Claire said. "I've still got this." She held up the small ultraviolet pointer she had in her jeans pocket.

"I forgot about those," Ron said. "Good girl!"

"What is it?" Finn studied the object.

"Death to a *Phooka*!" Ron said. "And Claire can bring a lot more back with her."

"I'm on it!" Claire said. "Which way, Kian?"

"Take my hand." The young *Fey* said, smiling up at her.

The instant Claire touched him, they were both gone.

"All right," Ron said, taking Finn's hand. "Now it's our turn."

"Yes, My Lord," Finn said, pressing his body to Ron's. His lips touched Ron's in a lingering kiss. "To war!"

And they, too, disappeared.

Chapter 14

"There's another one!" shouted Collin as he ducked behind one of the boulders that covered the base of the granite escarpment. "Somebody get it! I have to change a battery!"

Nolan spun around to face the swirling dark menace that had appeared within the aspen grove behind the besieged group of teens.

"I got it!" Nolan shouted in response, whipping his laser pointer up.

He fired on the *Phooka* as it bore down on the group, accompanied by the now rumbling bear-like growl of aggression. The beam of invisible light struck the attacking demon dead center and the goblin dissolved into nothingness with a screeching protest.

"How many of these damn things are there?" Kane yelled from his position midst a collection of boulders stacked at the base of the granite wall.

"I count forty so far," Dylan responded from a gnarled canopy of stunted loblolly pin tree roots further down the rock face.

Nolan studied the aspen grove, looking for any sign that another of the creatures might be waiting to strike.

"I'm glad you sent Briana back for more batteries and shit," Nolan said, nodding in Collin's direction.

"Just in time," Collin said, screwing the cap back on his laser pointer. "Before all this hell broke loose!"

"I hope she's back soon, though," Kane said, standing up to stretch a moment. "We don't have any batteries left."

Dylan stood as well, taking advantage of the momentary lull to work the kinks out of his neck.

"I think a couple of the SOB's got through though," Dylan said, looking over his shoulder.

"Yeah," Nolan spat on the ground. "I saw a couple disappear through the granite before we really knew what was going on."

"Don't worry," Collin said, also studying the tree perimeter. "Ron can handle them."

"How long's it been?" Nolan checked his watch.

"About three hours," Collin responded.

"I'm getting' hungry!" Kane said.

"Me, too." Nolan knelt to dig in what was left of his back pack after one of the demons had ripped it off his shoulders. "I got about eight or nine energy bars," he said, triumphantly. Lunch's served!"

He tossed one of the small granola bars to each of his friends.

"I've got some packs of cheese and crackers in my bag," Kane said.

"Anyone want to go get them." Kane eyed his backpack laying at the base of the aspens.

"You get them!" Nolan said, daring.

"I'm not going near those trees," Kane responded, crouching back behind his rock.

"Screw this!" Collin stuffed the empty energy bar wrapper in his jeans pocket. "I'll get them." He sidled toward the tree line brandishing his laser pointer.

"Cover him!" shouted Nolan, and all laser pointers came up to the ready.

Collin crept along, his eyes darting in all directions for any sign of attack. He reached the backpack where Kane had abandoned it, and went down on one knee to retrieve it, all the while alert and vigilant. He grabbed the shoulder strap and pulled the bag into his arms.

"Got it!" Collin said, relieved.

"Don't turn your back!" Nolan shouted.

"No chance of that," Collin said, edging backwards toward his position of safety. "Kane, you are such a pu . . ."

A loud crack was followed by a small aspen breaking at the trunk and topping over. Four mottled pockets of black barreled out of the grove like cannon balls. The concussion effect knocked Collin on his back.

"Star Line!" shouted Nolan, calling out one of their modified soccer plays. He ripped off the rest of his tattered t-shirt.

Unperceivable beams of light shot out toward the attacking demons in tandem.

"Left down!" shouted Kane as the evil entity on his side dissolved in the familiar shrieks.

"Dammit!" Dylan fired his laser a second time, but the *Phooka* darted from left to right faster than Dylan's human eyes could discern.

"Hah!" Dylan said as his human mind anticipated the demon's next move and caught the thing as it tried a vertical trajectory.

The *Phooka* dissolved violently.

"Right is down!" Dylan shouted triumphantly.

Kane held the other two demons at bay as they circled in all directions looking for a way through. One goblin dove straight for Collin, keeping low behind the rows of boulders.

"Collin!" shouted Nolan, standing directly in front of the Cliff face.

In the moment's distraction the other *Phooka* shot down the center toward the granite rock face, gleaming talons protecting from the formless mass.

"Got it!" shouted Nolan, diving over the boulders and nailing the demon before it could get through the mysterious doorway.

"Help!" Collin cried out, seeing the dagger pointed talons bearing down on him.

He scrambled across the gravel on his back, trying to feel for the laser pointer he had dropped.

"Collin!" screamed Nolan, realizing he couldn't get his arm up in time.

A stream of ultraviolet shot out from the rock face, ending the taloned demons flight instantly. Collin rolled onto his stomach to find the source. The other boys froze.

"Claire!" shouted Nolan, popping up from behind the boulder field.

"Claire!" echoed Collin.

"Looks like you boys have been playing war." Claire lowered her makeshift weapon.

"Ain't no playing about it," Collin said with gasping relief. He jumped up and ran for Claire, but stopped suddenly, suddenly aware of the small, pale creature beside her. "What the hell?"

The other boys slowly surrounded Claire.

"Please tell me that's not Ron," Collin piped.

"This is not Ron," Claire responded, rolling her eyes. "Guys, this is Kian."

The strange youth clung to Claire's jeans, trembling.

"It's okay, Kian," Claire said, pulling him in front of her. "These are my friends."

Kian looked up at the tall men surrounding him. He straightened a little, trying to smile.

"*Tá mé* Kian," the boy said, taking special note of the taller, shirtless and muscled human male.

"They won't understand you, Kian," Claire said, "unless you imprint on their minds."

Kian giggled. He sent out his aura to the group, but not before sidling up to Nolan and attaching himself about the human's waist.

"I am Kian," the young *Fey* said, batting golden eyelashes up at Nolan.

Nolan froze, staring down at the slight, pointy-eared fledgling clinging to his waist. "What the hell is this?"

"I am Kian," the young *Fey* said, patting his human's chest. "Honored page to the sacred White Wing."

"The hell you say," Nolan quipped, trying to peel the youth's hands from about him. "Well I'm Nolan, honored boyfriend to the lovely Claire."

Kian released his hold on Nolan and embraced Claire.

"I am her honored boyfriend, too," Kian said. "Claire is a mighty warrior."

"What's he talking about," Nolan asked, hands on hips.

He's a boy," Claire said laughing. "Well, a *Fei* boy . . . and he's my friend."

Kian immediately returned to Nolan, once again wrapping his arms about the tall human.

"I am your boyfriend, too!" he said, hugging Nolan tightly.

"Jesus!" Nolan sighed and tried to extricate himself from the young *Fey*'s grasp. "Are all *Fey* gay?"

Claire rolled her eyes again. "*Fey* are not gay," she said, heading for Collin. "*Fey* are just . . . *Fey*." She looked about. "Collin, where's Briana?"

"I sent her down to dad's store to get more batteries." Collin responded, holding up his laser pointer. "These apparently have a very short life span."

Claire nodded. "What's it been like out here?"

"Rough!" Collin brushed dirt off his clothes. "These damn *Phooka* things have been hitting us pretty hard. I think a couple got through the . . . door or whatever you call the thing you came through."

"You're right," Claire said nodding. "A couple got through, but Ron's gonna handle it."

"How's Ron doing?" Collin gave her a worried look.

"Good and not so good," Claire responded. "His body's changed and he looks like hell, but when I left, he was feeling stronger."

Collin nodded to the exasperated Nolan who was still trying to delicately escape the amorous clutches of the young *Fey*.

"Is Ron still gay?" Collin asked.

"Yes, Collin, he's still gay." Claire glared at the shorter redhead. "He's always been gay. He always will be gay!"

"Okay, okay!" Collin held up his hands in surrender. "I get it . . . just checking." He laughed, nodding at Nolan. "Better be careful Claire, or you may be losing another boyfriend to the *Fei* side."

"Good grief!" Claire shook her head. She couldn't help but laugh. "Kian! Kian, come here please."

"But . . ." The young *Fey* looked from her to Nolan and back again.

"Just come here, dear. The big strong human's not going anywhere."

Reluctantly, Kian released his hold on Nolan.

"Yes, Lord Claire." Kian approached her wringing his hands. "Are you angry?"

"Heavens, no!" Claire laughed and embraced the boy. "But, honey, you just don't go up and grab a man. You have to seduce him . . . tease him . . . make him want you."

"Oh, thanks a lot, Claire," Nolan said. "A little help here."

"Like I said, you're a big strong human." Claire released the boy and sashayed over to Nolan. "You can handle a little puppy love."

"Dammit, Claire!"

"You be nice to Kian!" Claire's eyes narrowed at him.

"Yes, Lord Claire," Nolan said, throwing his hands up.

"That's more like it." Claire surveyed the scene. "We need to seal this Gateway until I can get to Mab."

Collin shrugged. "How?"

"Silver," Claire said, reviewing the relevant parts of Father Hugh's lessons in her head.

"Silver?" Nolan asked. "What do we do, rob a jewelry store?"

"Don't be ridiculous!" Claire thought a moment. "Kane? Your dad's paint store . . . doesn't he have a paint with silver in it . . . to inhibit mildew?"

"Yeah," Kane said. "He's got an indoor latex that fills the bill."

"How much can we get?"

"I have a key to the storage container," Kane said with a conspiratorial smile.

"Excellent." Claire clapped her hands.

"Hello!" Briana's voice filtered through the aspen grove. "You guys still up here?"

Briana ducked through the low hanging aspen branches, toting a bulging plastic bag.

"I've got the batteries."

"Briana!" Collin shouted. "Get down!"

Before he could finish, a rush of dark forms descended upon Briana, striking her from behind, knocking her to the ground. A set of sharp talons took hold of the plastic bag and arched upward.

Nolan hit the creature with his laser light and it dissolved overhead. A hoard of AAA batteries showered down on the grassy clearing. The other teens fired off their laser pointers. *Phooka* cries echoed into oblivion.

One goblin held his position over Briana, talons poised to rip her to shreds. Briana lay on her back whimpering, staring up at the swirling dark form over her, talons sparkling like wet knives.

"Stay still, Briana," shouted Collin, fighting panic. "Don't move!"

"Keep your positions!" Nolan ordered the other boys who had quickly scrambled back into their respective holes in the boulder field. "Watch the woods for any new visitors!"

Nolan approached the demon slowly.

"Okay, dude," Nolan said, fingering his laser pointer. "Chill out!"

The creature did not budge.

Nolan could almost make out the goblin's hunched, ape-like features in the black miasma that surrounded it.

"Kian!" Nolan shouted over his shoulder to where Claire and the young *Fey* were hiding behind a stack of boulders. "Does this thing understand English?"

"Kian says, no!" Claire responded, cradling the very terrified young page in her arms.

"I need a distraction," Nolan said over his shoulder.

Claire nodded began making distorted faces at the creature.

"Hey, dumbass!" Claire yelled at the creature. "Look what I've got." She pulled Kian up into view. "Look at the nice, tasty *Fey*!"

Kian fought to drop back out of site. The dark matter poised over Briana seemed to freeze. The sight of the *Fey* dissolved its concentration into unbridled hunger.

"Claire!" yelled Collin. "What the hell. . ."

Nolan drew up his laser weapon in a flash and fired.

"Eat laser, you mo . . ." Nolan's words were obscured by the violent, cries of the creature's dissolution.

Collin rushed over to his girlfriend, pulled her up from the gravel, and dragged her to the safety behind the cover of the other laser pointer positions.

"Good shootin', dude!" whooped Kane accompanied by applause from him and Dylan and as they stood up from their respective positions of cover.

Claire eased Kian to his feet. "It's okay, hon," she said, stroking the boy's face. "The big bad wolf is dead!"

Kian blinked at her, not fully comprehending her metaphor.

"No more *Phooka*!" Claire assured him. "You helped Nolan kill it!"

Kian's trembling from fear changed to trembling with excitement. He rushed to reattach himself to Nolan's waist.

"Not again!" Nolan rolled his eyes.

"You saved us from the *Phooka*," Kian said, hugging tightly to Nolan.

He raised his worshipful eyes up to Nolan.

"I must kiss you in thanks!" Kian pulled at Nolan's arm.

"The hell you wi—"

"Nolan!" Claire said sternly, shutting him up. "Kian, you may kiss him on the cheek."

"But, Claire . . ." Nolan protested.

Claire snapped her eyes at him.

"Okay," Nolan said. "But then you own me one."

Nolan bent down and turned his cheek to the young *Fey*. Kian wrapped his arms about Nolan's neck and bussed the giant human's cheek with gusto. He did not release his hold.

"Okay, okay!" Nolan said, prying the boy's arms from his neck. "You're welcome."

"There, see?" Claire patted Nolan's cheek. "That wasn't so bad."

Without warning Nolan grabbed Claire into his arms and kissed her passionately.

"Nolan!" Claire sputtered, finally breaking free. "That's not fair. Kian only kissed you on the cheek!"

"Tough!" Nolan replied, laughing. "That was payback with interest."

"I can kiss you like that, too?" Kian, said, pulling on Nolan's arm again.

"Uhhh." Nolan's eyebrows went up. He looked to Claire.

"Now, Kian," Claire said gently. "You're not ready for a kiss like that, yet."

She tousled the boy's gold curls, smiling at the young *Fey*'s crestfallen expressions.

"But," she added, pursing her lips at Nolan "you can kiss him on the other cheek."

"Claire!" Nolan protested.

"On the other cheek, Nolan," Claire said sharply. "Bend over and take it like a man!" She suppressed a grin.

Kian brightened expectantly.

"Yeah, Nolan!" Dylan called out from a safe distance. "Bend over and take it like a man."

The other teen males laughed from a safe distance.

Nolan glared at his girlfriend, but she wouldn't budge. He leaned down within Kian's reach.

Kian took hold of the tall man's face. Quivering with excitement, he kissed Nolan's other cheek, unhurried.

"Okay," Nolan said, straightening out of Kian's grasp. "That's eno . . . that's good."

Kian's grin cut his face in half. He clasped his hands to his chest with glee.

"Calm down, honey," Claire said to the ecstatic young *Fey*, nodding her approval to Nolan.

"I better not see you sucking face with a *Fey!*" Briana said lightly, elbowing Collin in the ribs.

Kian's rapturous smile left as quickly as it had formed. He looked up to Claire, fretting.

"She just means that Collin belongs to her," Claire said. "They're an exclusive couple."

"They are bond-mates?" Kian asked.

"That's right, dear." Claire patted the boy on the head. "Bond-mates."

"And what are we?" Nolan asked, arms folded across his chest.

"That's yet to be decided," Claire said lightly.

"Claire!"

"Not until you can get along better with Ron," Claire said, turning her back on him to wave at Briana. "Love me, love my friends."

"Shit," Nolan said under his breath.

"I heard that!" Claire led Kian to the others. "These are my friends Briana and Collin," she said. "And over there are Kane, and Dylan."

Kian gave each of them a deep bow.

"Right!" Claire said, grabbing Kian's hand. "You come with me—Kane, you too. You'll need to get us some paint. Briana, you can help him. I'll head for Mab's to see what she can do."

"Again?" Briana rolled her eyes. "I just climbed this mountain once."

"You wanna stay here and fight the *Phooka*?" Claire asked.

"You convinced me," Briana replied, grinning. "Lead the way."

"Are you guys okay without my firepower?" Kane said, climbing over the rocks to join the girls.

"Don't be scared," Collin said. "You go ahead. Briana will protect you. She's a better shot than you. Her dad takes her to the firing range regularly."

Kane raised an eyebrow at Briana. She gave him a Cheshire grin.

"All right," Kane said to Claire, rolling his eyes. "Let's get going."

"I think we'll go around the aspen grove," Claire responded, pulling Briana and Kian along beside her.

Kian took Kane's hand as well.

"Whoa, little dude," Kane said, reaching down to pull the *Fey*'s hand from his.

"Leave it!" Claire snapped.

"But . . ."

"Leave it alone!" Claire glared at him.

Kane sighed.

"Yeah, Kane," Nolan called out. "Don't be such a *Fey*-aphobe!"

The others laughed with him.

Kian interpreted Kane's actions differently.

"Do not worry," Kian said, smiling up at Kane. "We will not take you from your bond-mate for very long."

"My . . . what?"

Claire and Briana giggled.

"What bond-mate?" Kane said, looking back to where the other boys were securing their position to do battle. "What's he talking about, Claire."

"You know," Claire said, trying without success to suppress her laughter. "Your bond-mate . . . Dylan?"

"What!"

Claire and Briana embraced each other laughing.

"I'm not . . ." Kane stuttered. "He's not . . ."

He pushed ahead of Claire and Briana, dragging Kian with him.

"Dammit it to hell!" Kane shouted, shaking his head.

Chapter 15

Ron held his head in his hands, trying to overcome the dizzying disorientation that followed crossing time and space in an instant. Finn steadied him before pulling him to the marble floor on the platform behind the large stone throne they had left not long before.

"What the hell?" Ron could hear screams about him.

"*Phooka* attack!" Finn whispered, shivering with fear.

Ron pulled free of Finn and stood up to survey the situation. Dark forms descended on the *Fei* population, engulfing the helpless populace. Ron could sense the light explode from the devoured *Fey* immediately absorbed by the demonic black holes that were the *Phooka*.

A roiling anger quickly overcame Ron's horror.

"Stay here," Ron ordered, standing over Finn. He bent down and kissed Finn lightly on the lips. "Don't worry," Ron said gently. "I won't let anything or anyone hurt you."

Finn tried his best to smile up at Ron, but every ensuing scream from the battlefield beyond cut through him like a razor.

Ron stepped out from behind the purple throne. He focused his concentration on the nearest demon.

"Hey, Asshole!" Ron shouted above the din of battle.

Ron felt more than saw the *Phooka*'s attention turn to him. He strode to the center of the platform.

"Coward!" Ron shouted, giving the demon a one finger salute.

The dark goblin shot toward Ron, its enormous talons protruding from its dark shape.

Ron refused to acknowledge the pang of fear that clamped onto his gut. He raised his hands, palms toward the creature bearing down on him.

"No!" Ron cried out, and the ring on his thumb vibrated and hummed. "No!" he shouted again.

He felt the rush of energy from below his feet course through him, pushing past the fear at his core. A burst of magenta light pulsed outward from his palms.

The *Phooka* was stopped in mid-flight, violet lightening erupted at its center, shattering its structure into atoms of dark matter. But not just the one—in the same instant, the other two demons suffered a similar fate. The thunderous clap of their ultimate dissolution sent a compression wave in motion like a tidal wave radiating from the center of a pond. One of the sacred circle capstones toppled from its high perch, crashing and shattering onto the stone pavers below. Those *Fey* who did not have time to drop face down on the ground, were knocked into submission by the forceful wave.

Finn dashed from his hiding place to wrap his arms about Ron, just as Ron's knees buckled beneath him. They both sank slowly to the marble platform.

The *Fei* populace recovered quickly. They slowly stood, searching the skies above them for any sign of *Phooka* presence. Shouts went up, becoming a roar of exultation. The thousands assailed the stone circle, breaking the thread of tradition and entering the sacred premises of the circle. The remaining elders began to gather at the foot of the throne platform, their eyes wide with wonder at the human victor who knelt in exhaustion on the marble platform.

The *Fei Ardsagart*, who had found refuge behind the platform, had come out to the sounds of the crowd. He climbed the platform steps and stood to the side. He raised a hand calling for quiet which slowly rippled through the crowd.

"How?" The *Ardsagart* asked of Ron. "How is this possible that you have such power over the dark forces?"

Ron struggled to his feet with Finn's help.

"I told you before," Finn cried out where all could hear. "This man is an ally of our people. The Goddess has given him power over the dark demons."

Ron struggled to get a breath. An excruciating pain radiated from his shoulder blades through his chest. His voice had no breath to form.

"How can a human do this?" The *Ardsagart* said. "He is matter. He has no light!"

"You are a fool then," Finn responded above the murmuring of the crowd. "All here saw the light expel from him, destroying the *Phooka* in one strike! Have you no eyes to see with?"

The *Ardsagart* stood silent. He had no argument against the eyewitness testimony of the *Fei* populace whose displeasure with its high priest's doubt rose in combined voice.

The *Ardsagart* once again raised a hand for silence, but no one obeyed.

In contrast, Finn raised his hand for silence and silence immediately ensued. He turned to the crowd.

"Our human friends on the other side of the world portal will fight to prevent further attacks from getting through." Without another word, Finn transported Ron back to his garden cloister.

"Óisín!" Finn called out as they materialized beneath the giant *sceach gheal* tree.

The pages who had remained, in fear dropped down from the boughs of the giant tree.

"My Lord," said Óisín. "We heard the people's mind . . . that the *Phooka* were destroyed.

"For now," Finn said, leaning Ron up against the tree. "Fetch my chalice, quickly!"

In a blink, the young *Fey* went and came, chalice in hand.

"Give it!" Finn ordered, taking the iris cup from his page. "Ron . . . Ron!" he said, shaking Ron by the shoulders.

Ron stirred weakly, opening his eyes.

"What happened," he whispered.

"You destroyed the demons," Finn said, cupping a hand behind Ron's head. "Now drink. You need your strength back."

Ron sipped the nectar, gratefully. The dark violet veins behind his skin became more prominent.

"Whatever this stuff is," Ron said between sips. "It sure as hell works." He could feel his strength return with each gulp of the sweet liquid.

Finn ran a hand over the cracking skin covering Ron's arms. "You do look ghastly," he said, frowning.

"But I feel great!" Ron straightened. "Hopefully, Claire will get back with one of Mab's special concoctions that'll straighten all this out." He returned the empty cup to the page. "But until that time . . . I feel fine."

Finn pulled Ron's face to his and kissed him, long and hard. Ron circled his arms about the smaller *Fey*, drawing their bodies together. The heat of their shared passion shimmered about them as their aura's intertwined. Finally they became aware of the giggling pages surrounding them.

"Pages!" Finn said, not taking his eyes from Ron's. "Go and fill my chalice."

"Yes, My Lord," the pages said in unison.

"And don't come back until I call you!" Finn added.

"Yes, Lord White Wing!" In an instant the pages were gone.

Ron brushed his lips over Finn's forehead. "Good," he said. "I could use a little nap."

"Nap?"

Finn's hands traced a path down Ron's chest, quickly covering squeezing the rising hardness in Ron's jeans.

"You still have work to do," Finn whispered, his eyes burning.

Ron caught his breath as Finn's massage grew more insistent. He felt a rush of heat through his body as the nectar

"But, I've already taken care of the *Phooka*," Ron said, his voice shaking with sexual need.

He pulled Finn to him for another long kiss, sliding his own hands down to Finn's buttocks, pulling his love tightly to him, suddenly aware that Finn was in his natural, unclothed state.

Finn nipped at Ron's lower lip and pushed away slightly.

"Now," Finn said, as Ron's jeans dropped, as if on command, down to human's feet, "it's time for you to take care of me."

Ron stepped out of his jeans and tugged his t-shirt over his head. He pulled Finn down onto the soft bed of white flowers.

I want to take care of you forever," Ron said hoarsely, and ran his tongue over Finn's hardened nipples.

"And I will let you," Finn said groaning at Ron's ministrations. "I have no intention of dying a virgin."

"But . . ." Ron lifted up on his hands, looking down at Finn's sparkling violet eyes. "If you recall, we kinda took care of that back at my house."

"No," Finn said, taking hold of Ron's hard engorged member and guiding it between his butt cheeks. "That was just foreplay."

⬡⬡⬡⬡⬡

"What kind of charges?" Mab asked, taking a seat across from Claire at the kitchen table. "Be very specific." She eyed the small *Fey* sitting at Claire's side.

Claire took a deep breath.

"His skin," she said. "His skin is so thin, you can see all the veins . . . dark purple veins. He looks like he's covered in spider webs."

"I see." Mab wrung her hands. "Anything else."

"Well . . . his ears . . ."

"What about his ears?"

"They're . . . sort of pointy.

"Pointy?" Mab shut her eyes.

Claire tried to read the older woman's expression. "Is this bad?" she asked.

Mab stared first at the strange young creature sitting quietly beside Claire.

"Depends," Mab said returning her gaze to Claire. "What else?"

"Well, that's pretty much the physical—oh, except that he gets very, very weak . . . till he almost can't even stand."

"Is that how you left him?" Alarm filled Mab's voice.

"No, no." Claire shook her head." Finn has this cup."

"It is one of my duties," Kian piped up suddenly.

"Well," Claire continued smiling at the boy. "It's some sort of honey. When Ron drinks it he gets stronger."

"Stronger?" Mab sat forward.

"A lot stronger," Claire responded.

"Royal Nectar." Mab sat back again.

Kian cupped his hands to whisper in Claire's ear. "The witch woman is very wise," he whispered

"Yeah," Claire said, excited that Mab knew about it. "Royal Nectar. That's what Finn called it."

"It is a nectar from the sacred *seamair báhn*." Kian said excitedly. A special hive of bees makes it."

"The white clover." Mab nodded. "And this gives Ron strength." Mab drummed her fingers on the wooden table. "What else?"

"Well," Claire began, hesitating. "You already know about his ability to extend his aura and physically move . . . things."

"You mean when he lifted you up?"

"Yes, but one thing you don't know about . . ."

Mab raised an eyebrow.

"He . . . he can emit an energy . . . a light from his hands that . . . well . . . that can destroy *Phooka*."

"That is *Fei* power!" Kian interjected meekly.

Mab sucked in a deep breath.

"And . . ." Claire began."

"There's more?" Mab expelled her breath heavily.

"When the *Fei* soldiers came for Ron," Claire said, "tried to hurt him, Ron covered himself with some sort of energy shield that protected him."

"This too is *Fei* power," Kian said.

"Ron is not *Fey*," Mab said gruffly. "He's human."

Kian looked at Claire, too cowed to say more.

"How do you explain the changes, then, Mab?" Claire asked. "And these *Fey*-like abilities he has?"

"It's impossible!" The drumming of Mab's fingers grew louder.

"Well," Claire said. "Yes, but . . ."

"It must be the ring."

"Ring?" Claire asked, confused.

"Ron wears a ring that was with him when he was left on my porch as a baby."

"I don't know about a ring," Claire said, shaking her head. "Are you saying some sort of . . . I don't know . . . magic ring is doing this to him?"

"It could explain the special powers," Mab said, stirred from her thoughts.

"And the physical changes?"

"I don't know," Mab said, finally, pushing away from the table. "I mean, it sounds like . . . " She stood, still in thought. "But that's impossible as well," Mab said, refusing what her intuition was saying.

"What?"

"No," Mab said, shaking her head. She turned to look out the window above her sink.

"Mab," Claire said, rounding the table to stand insistently next to the older woman. "Tell me! What do you think is going on?"

Mab looked at Claire, studying the girls aura. Finally, she took a deep breath, hoping her intuition about Ron's friend was true.

"I've been going through the family journals for references to *fey* matters," Mab said. "It seems that my predecessors have had many encounters. There was a case reported by an ancestor in the Old Country . . . sometime around the four-teen fifties, I think." She went quiet again.

"And?" Claire asked.

Mab pushed away from the sink. "I have to prepare you a potion for Ron," she said, embracing her plan. "It'll take a couple of hours."

"I'll help!" Claire said, following Mab to a narrow door by the kitchen hearth.

Mab stopped. "This isn't something a good, catholic girl needs to get involved with."

"Well, Mab," Claire said, smiling. "I'm not such a good, catholic girl . . . Kian's a fricken fairy . . . you're a fricken witch . . . Ron's a . . . I don't know what, so don't talk to me about being a good, catholic girl. I think, at this point, we've overshot the entire catechism. I want in. I want to learn. You can teach me."

"You want to be Wiccan?"

"Mab, these things you know shouldn't die with you."

"Who said I'm gonna die?" Mab chuckled.

"Well," Claire stuttered. "You know . . . eventually."

"Okay, girl," Mab said, roaring with laughter. "You're right. I don't want my family's accumulated knowledge to end with me. If you want to learn, I'll teach you. Ron was never that interested and, besides, this is woman's work!"

"Woman's work!"

"Honey," Mab said with a wave. "The only good man is a naked man in the bedroom . . . and even, then there's nothing to guarantee the good part."

"I'm ready to learn?" Claire responded, laughing.

"You!" Mab almost shouted at Kian.

The boy was sniffing in the small ceramic honey pot on the table.

"Put that honey pot down," Mab ordered. "You're too young! Now get over here! I'm gonna need you for this."

Kian dropped the lid on the small container and shot up from the table.

"Me?" Kian asked nervously.

"You," Mab said, pointing at the floor beside her.

The anxious boy sidled up to her.

"Okay." Mab put a hand on Claire's shoulder. "We're going down to my cellar workroom."

"Ahh," Claire said excitedly. "A secret room."

"No, dear," Mab said, opening the small door. "Just my cellar."

She turned and smiled, dragging the young *Fey* in ahead of her. "But it's where all the magic happens."

Chapter 16

Ron squeezed the slumbering Finn tightly in his arms. The *Fey*'s head fit perfectly under his chin and the herbaceous scent of his love's platinum locks gave to Ron a sense of completeness, joy, and calm. He ran his fingers down the smooth, pale skin of Finn's back, marveling at the tingly, photic sensation and reaction that the touch of his fingers excited in Finn's skin.

The squeeze was protective, too. If he failed to adequately protect his lover, Ron knew full well the fate that would befall Finn. Considering the violence that had filled the morning prior, Ron felt deeply the trust that allowed Finn to sleep undisturbed in his arms.

The young *Fei* pages had appeared on pallets of flower blossoms, once the lovemaking under the *sceach gheal* tree had climaxed. Though appearing to sleep quietly at a respectful distance from Ron and the White Wing, their eyes watched their Lord and his partner, occasionally eliciting a melodic chuckle from their midst.

Ron smiled to himself, feeling no inhibition due to the lack of privacy. He understood the curiosity that poured over him from the young pages, who stared at the hair growing in adult areas about Ron's naked body—hair that was peculiarly absent from the *Fey*—at least the bodies Ron had seen, Finn included.

Ron heard soft footsteps in the lush ground cover behind him. The older page, Óisín, crept softly up beside the two lovers. Ron looked up at the boy expectantly.

"Lord Ron," Óisín said softly, not wanting to disturb the White Wing. "The council is waiting."

"So?"

"The *Ardsagart* is very impatient," the page said, suppressing a smile.

Ron took a deep breath. "You go tell him to kiss my ass!"

Óisín giggled through the fingers he had clamped over his mouth.

"What's so important?" Ron whispered.

Óisín knelt in the grass.

"There is still much fear in the people," Óisín said, betraying his own inner anxiety. "The world portal . . . the Gateway remains open. All fear another incursion from the elven lord."

Ron returned his gaze to Finn. He kissed the white, silky locks nestled beneath his chin. Carefully, he slid out from under the slumbering *Fey* and lay Finn's head gently on the carpet of grass and flowers. He stood, stretching, only peripherally aware of his own nakedness. He sensed the young page's undisguised fascination with his human body, mottled though it was.

"I guess I'd better find my clothes," Ron said, startling the page from his stare.

"My Lord?"

"Clothes," Ron repeated. "Where are my clothes?"

The page shrugged. "Confined to the fire, My Lord."

"Fire?"

Ron covered his groin, thinking about the more public venues he might have to face.

"You burnt my clothes?"

"They smelled bad," the page responded, showing little concern.

"What am I supposed to wear?"

"Coverings are ceremonial," Óisín responded. "I wear no cover here." He looked down at his own smooth nudity, shrugging.

"Yes," Ron said with a smirk, "But I don't stare at you."

"That is true, My Lord." Óisín giggled. "But you are very different."

"So," Ron said, "don't you think it's best I don't draw attention to it?"

The page nodded, understanding. "You must weave a covering then," he said.

"And how long will that take?" Ron asked, rolling his eyes. "I need . . ."

Laughing, Óisín stood clothed in a silken, white tunic, a tunic that only seconds before had not been there.

"See, My Lord?" Óisín said. "I have woven my covering."

"Obviously you mean something different by weaving that I do." Ron looked down at his annoying nakedness. "How do I do it?"

Óisín cocked his head to one side. "How?" he asked, not understanding.

"Okay." Ron sighed. "It's a *Fei* thing. Well, I've had luck with that up 'til now." He closed his eyes. "Visualize and believe . . . that's what Mab would say." His face drew up in concentration.

"No, Lord Ron!" Óisín cried out.

The urgent horror in the page's voice pulled Ron's eyes back open. He was wearing a tunic similar to the page's. It was thin to the point of ephemeral—silky and weightless.

"You mustn't!" Óisín continued, averting his eyes.

"Mustn't what?" Ron smoothed the rippling, amethyst-colored fabric over his thighs.

"That color is forbidden, My Lord," Óisín said, pointing without looking. "It is a blasphemy to wear it."

"Okay," Ron said, shrugging.

Ron visualized a color more closely akin to what the page was wearing. The cloth covering him faded to a cottony white.

"Better?"

"Much better, My Lord." The poor page relaxed.

"So tell me, Óisín," Ron said, looking about. "What do you guys do around here all day?"

"Oh, many, many things, My Lord," Óisín responded. "There are many, many ceremonial duties."

"Really." Ron surveyed the immense walled garden. "I imagine it takes a day or two to mow the lawn, but then . . ." He shrugged.

"Mow, My Lord?"

"Keep up the grounds!" Ron said, laughing. "You know, cut the grass so it doesn't get too high, prune the trees, deadhead all the flowers . . . the usual."

The pages eyes widened with confusion.

"The garden tends itself, My Lord," Óisín responded, trying to understand the concept. "Our duties, My Lord, are to tend the people's treasures, including the White Wing."

"Treasures?" Ron snorted. "What, is there a leprechaun nearby with a pot of gold?"

"No, Lord Ron!" The Óisín's eyes widened in horror. The other pages sat up, eyes wide.

"Those filthy creatures are not permitted in this world any more than *Phooka*!" Óisín said. "The people's treasure is a treasure of great power!"

"Power?" Ron's hands went to his hips. "Why isn't this power used against the invaders?"

"It is the sacred treasure of the *Sciathán Corcra*, My Lord."

"The Purple Wing?"

"Yes, My Lord. Power that only the great Purple Wing can use."

"I hear a lot about this Purple Wing," Ron said, feeling an unaccustomed green emotion. "Where is this so-called *Sciathán Corcra*, anyway?"

"Unknown, My Lord." Óisín's face clouded with doubt and guilt. "Many await his return, and then many believe he is dead—killed by the Demon Elf in those forgotten past ages before the people fled to this world—dead without progeny to assume his place. Many believe he is myth."

"Many don't care anymore," Finn spoke up suddenly.

Ron looked down at the face that stirred so much in him.

"Hello," Ron said, smiling.

Finn stood, clothed in his own shinning, white tunic.

"I have found my bond-mate," Finn said, encircling Ron's waist with his arms. "I need only Ron." He lay his head on Ron's shoulders. "The *Sciathán Corcra* is no longer necessary."

"My Lord!" Óisín covered his mouth. "That is blasphemy!"

The other pages leapt from their Feigned slumber to Óisín's side, their faces wide with shock.

"It is truth." Finn narrowed his eyes at his page. "Would all of you have me die unbonded like those who came before me?"

The pages shook their heads.

"No, My Lord," Óisín whispered, leading to the other pages to their knees. "We serve you."

Finn gestured for Óisín to come to him, and embraced the shocked boy affectionately.

"Speaking of treasure, don't you have something that needs polishing?" Finn asked lightly.

"Of course, My Lord." Óisín said with a grin, understanding more than he should.

"Where is this treasure?" Ron asked.

"Would you like to see it?" Finn beamed a smile at Ron.

"Why not," Ron replied.

"The Council, My Lord," Óisín reminded.

"Let 'em shake in their booties a while longer," Ron said with a shrug. "Let's see this so-called treasure."

Finn took Ron's hand and let him across the expansive of deep green grass. The procession of young pages followed, watching every intimate gesture between the two Lords. When Finn slipped an arm into Ron's, several of the younger pages followed suit with each other and then giggled among themselves.

Ron followed Finn's example and simply ignored the pages' voyeuristic play-acting. He blinked into the bright array of light and colors ahead. He had begun to adapt to the heightening of his senses, a new way of perceiving that seemed to blend his physical vision with his astral vision. The flood of scents that filled the air were somehow fresher, sweeter, and stronger. The surrounding flora had become almost fluorescent and he was suddenly aware of the rapid fluttering of Finn's heartbeat next to him.

Finn sensed Ron's thoughts turning inward.

"Is everything all right, my love?" Finn asked. "Are you feeling weak again?"

"Just more changes," Ron responded, shaking his head, "hearing, sight, smell . . . all my senses like nothing much about me is the same."

"Do these changes hurt?" Finn stopped their journey across the garden and studied Ron's face.

"No," Ron said. "It's just something to get used to." Ron saw the arched opening into the high stone wall and nodded. "I guess that's where the treasure waits."

With that, Ron took Finn's arm and they closed the distance remaining, not stopping until they had reached the doorway.

"Doesn't look like a very secure place to keep a great treasure," Ron said, gesturing to the open, unprotected portal.

"Looks can be deceiving," Finn replied. "Powerful bindings protect this entrance. Not just anyone can get through."

"Do tell."

"It is true," Óisín said from behind. "We wear the *bríocht draighean*." He pointed to the runed band of silver, studded with black, wooden inlays about his neck.

"The blackthorn amulet allows these pages to pass unmolested," explained Finn.

Ron stared at the doorway, trying to focus his spirit eyes to see the magical strands of the protection spells. There was nothing.

"I can't see any bindings in place here," Ron said.

"You would not," Finn responded. "They have no light to see them. They are dark light and will destroy all matter and light that pass through them."

"How do I get in then?"

"You need only take my hand," Finn said, offering up his hand.

"I don't see an amulet around your neck." Ron ran his fingers about Finn's delicate neckline.

"The *Sciathán Bán* is immune to the bindings," Finn replied, cocking his head to one side.

"Maybe the White Wing is," Ron said, "but what about me?"

"My touch is all you need," Finn said, pursing his lips seductively.

"All right, then!" Ron grabbed hold of Finn's hand tightly. "Here's hoping you're right."

Ron started through the door, when he was unexpectedly overcome with a dizzying pain erupting at his shoulders. He fell forward into the door, pulling free of Finn's grip on his hand.

"No!" Finn screamed as he lost his hold and Ron fell into the dark bindings that now pulsed ominously about and within the portal.

The pages surrounded Finn, holding him back as he struggled to reach Ron.

"My Lord," Óisín cried out. "Even you cannot do battle with the dark bindings!"

Finn and the frightened pages stood frozen, awaiting Ron's inevitable dissolution. Finn sobbed uncontrollably.

'I'm okay," Ron called out, trying to sit up on the stone tile beneath him. "Sorry! No damage done!" He turned and froze at the sight of Finn's anguished tears and the pages huddled together. "What's wrong?"

Ron reached out to Finn.

"Why's everyone looking like I've fallen off a cliff?" Ron got back on his feet, hands on hips. "Hello?" he called out, waving his hands. "Finn?" He reached out a hand.

"You're . . ." Finn managed, taking Ron's hand, in both of his, staring at it as if it weren't real. "You're alive."

"Of course I'm alive," Ron said, pulling Finn's hands to his lips. "Why wouldn't . . .

The full import of what had occurred finally dawned.

"Oh," Ron said, seeing the dark bindings swirling about him for the first time. "I guess I am still alive . . . wow!" He fingered the ring humming about his thumb. "Once again this thing—"

His voice muffled as Finn suddenly wrapped him in a suffocating embrace.

"I'm okay, Finn," Ron managed in spite of the constricting embrace. Finn's hug loosened.

Finally able to take in sufficient air to speak, Ron added, "I'm not hurt, okay?"

"How?" Finn stared wide-eyed. "How can you not have been . . . affected by these most powerful of bindings?"

"Good question." Ron shrugged. "Maybe, they don't affect humans."

"They destroy all light and matter!" Finn said, not letting go of Ron. "Living or dead, sentient or soulless—everything!"

"Well," Ron responded, tilting Finn's face up to his own by the chin. "Everything but you and these little guys."

Finn nodded confused.

"And now," Ron added, "me."

"But . . ."

"There are no buts." Ron kissed Finn lightly on the lips. "I wasn't harmed. We can stew about that all day and never understand it."

Finn sniffed and pressed his forehead into Ron's neck.

"Okay." Ron looked from Finn to the pages, still frozen in shock. "Come on, boys. I want to see this treasure."

With that, Ron threw his arm about Finn and started down the long, dark corridor. The magical protections swarmed about them chaotically, as if confused or angered at their own impotence against the human intruder. The pages followed at a respectful distance.

"Only the sacred White Wing can pass this way without a *bríocht draighean*," Óisín whispered to the others.

The youths murmured their agreement with this fact.

"Lord Ron must be of the sacred elements," Óisín said, pointing at Ron's back.

Again the other pages chattered excitedly.

Ron's wondrously enhanced hearing had picked up this conversation He cast a glance over his shoulder at Óisín.

"I'm just your everyday, ordinary human being," Ron said insistently.

The pages laughed in unison. Ron started to respond.

"It's fruitless to argue with their logic," Finn said, winking at his pages. He held up his hand in the Vulcan greeting.

"Yes, Mr. Spock!" Ron said, laughing. 'What? Do you *Fey* get TV programs from my world here? How did you get that hand sign?"

"From Claire's mind," Finn replied. "And from yours." He smiled suggestively. "And from when we bond-mated. We shared much in those moments of joining."

Sounds of muffled giggles assailed Ron's ears and he raised an eyebrow back at the pages. He could feel Finn's delicate fingers caressing the nape of his neck.

"Treasure!" Ron said quickly, taking Finn's hand into his. "Let's go treasure hunting!"

"Are you sure?" Finn asked.

"I'm fine, okay?

"But you weren't!" Finn pressed. "Something made you fall. I saw the pain in your face."

"Okay," Ron admitted. "You're right, but it only lasted a moment. I thought some of your royal bees had stung me on the back."

"It still feels sore," Ron said arching his back. "My shoulders." Ron stretched his neck from side to side. "The shoulder blades on both sides."

Finn started to speak.

"But, I'm okay," Ron interrupted. "Now let's go."

"All right, then," Finn said with a sigh, hesitating. "But if that pain strikes again, we are leaving."

"You're the mighty White Wing." Ron kissed Finn reassuring. "Whatever you say."

"And don't you forget it!" Finn's face brightened. He pulled Ron down the snaking corridor.

Ron followed obediently, trying to keep an easy smile on his face in spite of the nagging, sharp pains that continued to plague his shoulder blades. The small group approached an imposing arched door of heavy, black metal. Ron surmised it was probably iron, like all the other doors in this world that barred passage.

Finn signaled to Óisín who darted ahead.

Raising his hands to face the door, Óisín's soft cambiata intoned, "*Bealtaine an Claíomh Solais fáilte dúinn!*"

Accompanied by the creaking of ancient metal, the door slowly swung outward. For a moment the intense, glaring light flooding out the door blinded Ron. He allowed himself to be guided into the ensuing chamber where he was allowed to pause and acclimate his excruciatingly sensitive vision.

"Well," Ron said, rubbing his aching eyes. "It's not as big a room as I'd thought."

Ron studied the ceiling overhead.

"Where the hell does all this light come from?"

Ron watched the *Fey* bow deeply toward a large, amethyst incrusted crèche in the opposing wall. The gleaming container was set into the white, marblesque stone of the wall like a giant amethyst geode that had been halved.

"Is that the treasure?" Ron asked, skeptical. "Looks like a big hunk of semi-precious rock."

"That is only the treasure's resting place," Finn said, signaling once more to Óisín and another page.

The young *Fey* approached the jewel studded shelf with great deference, bowing repeatedly. As Óisín reached into the crèche, the gemstone covering seemed to melt away, exposing a long scabbard of gold and silver, studded with amethyst cabochons. The hilt, which Ron assumed was of an immense claymore or gallowglass, protruded from the scabbard. The tip of the hilt was crowned with avian talons of gold gripping a ball of amethyst that pulsed with a strobing violet light.

"That's quite a sword," Ron said through teeth clenched against the worsening pain in his shoulders.

Óisín and the other young Fey carefully hoisted the scabbard from its magical coffer. It took both of them to negotiate the sword's weight until, one on each end, they bore the glittering, ancient artifact toward Finn and Ron.

The closer they came, the more excruciating the pain was for Ron.

"Wait," Ron cried out when it became too much. "That thing . . ." He collapsed to his knees. "Take it back. Don't bring it any closer!"

"Ron!" Finn shouted. He waved the sword bearers back. "What is it?"

"I can't . . ." Ron's shoulders spasmed against another wave of stabbing pain. "Just keep that thing away!"

"Return the sword!" Finn commanded.

The pages scurried to return the sword and scabbard to its purple niche on the wall.

Ron fought to control his breathing.

"I don't know what it is about that sword," Ron said, panting as the pain ebbed to a more bearable level. "But I don't think it likes me!"

"We must get you back to the Cloister." Finn helped Ron back to his feet. "Put your arm around my shoulders," Finn ordered, looping his other arm about Ron's waist.

They made their way slowly back along the serpentine corridor. Ron felt the pain lessen even more as the light from the treasure room extinguished behind the heavy metal door which closed at the behest of Óisín's reverse spell.

"Well, that was fun," Ron said weakly as he and Finn stepped out of the menacing bindings and back into the flower-carpeted garden. "What was that about?"

They stood for a moment until the pages joined them. Finn cast a worried eye over Ron's furrowed face, the spidering violet veins throbbed visibly under the thin, cracking covering of tissue-like skin. The young pages fixed themselves to Ron's other side to help Finn bear the weakened Lord back to the protection of the *sceach gheal* tree's umbrella of leafy branches.

"Tell me more about that sword," Ron said, as Finn and the pages settled him down in a grassy inlet of the tree's exposed roots. "Whose sword is it?"

"It is the *Claíomh Solais*," Finn said, sitting beside Ron. "The Sword of Light, forged by the god *Núada* from the light of the goddess—the light which is the very source of *Fey*.

"I know it now," Ron said, nodding remembering his Mab's lessons on Celtic history. "It is one of the four treasures of the *Tuatha Dé Dannan*, the god-ancestors of the *Fei* peoples."

"It is the *Sciathán Corcra* sword," whispered Óisín from his perch on a low hanging limb. "I don't think the Purple Wing likes, Lord Ron."

"Don't be stupid!" Finn said sharply, cowering the young page. "The sword is the sword. There is no Purple Wing. And I'll hear no more of it!"

Óisín reclined on his limb, mewing softly.

"If the truth be told," Ron said, feeling a little sorry for the young page, "I'd be inclined to agree with you, Óisín."

The page flashed Ron a quick grin out of Finn's line of sight.

"So," Ron continued quickly before Finn could respond. "What's so special about the sword anyhow?"

"It is the Sword of Power!" Finn said reverently. "No force can stand against it. Its wielder is invincible, as was the Purple Wing before the treachery of his *Ardsagart*!"

"Treachery?"

"The great shame of my tribe," Finn said, shaking his head sadly. "It allowed the elven lord a way into the Purple Wing's inner circle. The Purple Wing's light was poisoned by a mighty elven curse. Still he was the most powerful of the *Fey*. His dissolution was slow and painful, but it gave him time to seal his tribe into this paradise with his great sword. It is ours to protect, and it is highly coveted by the dark one . . . Lord Salach! Finn spat the name. "If he were to dissolve the powerful bindings on the sword placed by the *Sciathán Corcra* . . ." Finn fell silent.

"Was that the binding that I felt?"

Finn shrugged. "The binding is an ancient, powerful and impenetrable binding forged of the Purple Wing's own essence. The sword can be unsheathed by no one but the Purple Wing or his heir."

"Could the Demon Elf dissolve that binding?" Ron asked, stroking Finn's silver hair.

"His dark light is powerful," Finn responded, leaning into Ron's caress. "We would not like to find out."

"No shit, Sherlock!" Ron said.

Finn cocked an eyebrow at him.

"Just a saying." Ron brushed Finn's lips with his own.

"In any event," Finn said, eyes still closed from the kiss, "the sword is now just a pretty relic that we polish— a pretty and useless relic that we cannot use."

"Has anyone actually attempted to take the sword out?" Ron laughed. "It could all just be a load of—"

"Only once!" Óisín said, sitting up on his branch and forgetting his previous dressing down. "Our history says that one of the council lords tried to take the sword from its scabbard to protect our tribes as they fled to this other world."

"He couldn't do it?" Ron asked.

"As the story goes," said Finn, taking over. "The elder managed to unsheathe the sword a wee bit when the force of the sword's bindings instantly resulted in his dissolution."

"Looks like the sword can take care of itself," Ron said. "Why all the dark bindings at the entrance to the treasure room?"

"To protect it from the world," Finn responded, "and the world from it."

"Bummer."

Two other pages rocketed through the air to a crash landing in the nearby grass. Without a seconds delay, they were kneeling in front of Finn.

"What has happened now?" Finn asked, alarmed at the frantic, pale and shaking pages.

"Great Lord," one of the glittering fairy's managed to croak.

The other page's hands went to his face in horror.

"The Demon Elf comes!"

Chapter 17

"Keep up, Kian," Claire called over her shoulder.

"Yes, Lord Claire," the youthful *Fey* said, adjusting the pack on his back. "Is it much farther?"

"Another few minutes," Claire responded, feeling sorry for the boy. "I know it's heavy."

Still, the boy had volunteered.

"You sure I can't take a turn carrying that?" Claire asked.

The page looked as if she had slapped his face.

"I serve the Lord Claire!" he said, flexing his preadolescent muscles under the load. He smiled. "Or should I say, the Witch Claire."

"Claire will do just fine."

Claire felt the burn in her own legs, unaccustomed to the sharp incline. She gripped the straps of her backpack tightly in her hands. Already she doubted her own ability to accomplish what Mab had instructed. If only Mab could have come but, she had a more important task of her own to perform. Claire still didn't know what it all meant but, she was determined perform her assigned role, she pushed up over the trail edge to the camp ground.

"Stay back," she whispered sharply to Kian.

Kian froze in place.

Through the trees, Claire could see her friends stretched out on the ground or kneeling, surrounded by armed, armored and unusually tall beings, grey-skinned, white-haired, and snarling. She could feel the tangible evil infecting the air.

"Elves!" Kian almost shouted from between Claire's legs. His hand clamped quickly over his mouth.

"Get out of sight!" Claire snapped.

Kian obeyed instantly, dropping to a lower section of the path below the campground line of sight. His outcry, however, had caught the attention of the elves.

Claire took the offensive.

"What the hell is going on here?" she yelled and started forward aggressively.

Momentarily startled, the elves recovered quickly. At a sign from the particularly angry elf standing over a prone Nolan, three of the elves brought their lances forward and bore down on Claire. Claire let her own back pack drop to the ground. From her waist band, she pulled up an eight-shot, nine millimeter pistol and quickly went into firing position.

"Suck some silver, you ass . . ." Claire began to fire.

The first iron bullet struck the fastest of the three elves. Its hollow point, packed with Mab's special philter, exploded in the creature. She picked off the next two without waiting on the outcome of the first.

One by one, the tall elves stopped in their tracks to stare in shock at the black, oozing holes that opened up respectively in their chest, stomach or neck. In turn, their bodies dilated slightly before seeming to crack along a spider web of blackened fissures that expanded quickly through their lanky bodies. In another series of instants, their bodies imploded to a puddle of black, vomitus goo on the ground where once they had stood.

"Three for three!" Claire trumpeted triumphantly.

She held a steady aim at the other three elves, concentrating her attention of the apparent leader who stood over Nolan.

"Freeze assholes!" she ordered. "Or I'll turn you into a pile of poop, too!"

One of the elves on the perimeter of the camp sight, hoisted his lance up to throw at Claire. She quickly caught him in the front and rear sights of her pistol and fired. The bullet was faster than the elf's throwing arm. It made a path through the elves solar plexus and within seconds the elf collapsed into black slime.

"What?" Claire yelled, pulling her sights down on the leader. "Are you people that stupid? I said freeze! You move, you die!"

She bore down on them.

"Drop your weapons!" she commanded.

The elves stared at her.

"*Buail do airm!*" Kian cried out, peeking around Claire's back.

The elves let their lances fall to the ground.

"You must speak their language, Lord Claire," Kian said. "It is not exactly our own." He held onto Claire's blouse trying to glare fiercely at the tall, grey creatures.

The nostrils of the elf commander flared. The other elves sniffed the air in turn. An ominous hunger overcame them and their agitation magnified as fangs were bared and cat-like pupils dilated.

"*Fey!*" one of the elves hissed.

"Settle down there, dumbass," Claire ordered, sensing the change in the creatures. "You move one step and you're ground snot!"

"*Múcasacha talún!*" Kian shouted from behind his protector.

"Really?" Claire glanced down at Kian's head, pressed against her side. "They have a word for ground snot?"

"They want to eat me," Kian whispered, hugging Claire tightly. "Make them all ground snot!"

Claire resisted the urge to comply.

"Nolan?" she called out. "Are you okay?"

"I'm good!" Nolan shouted back weakly.

He did not stand, and lay holding his shoulder with the opposite hand.

"We're a little worse for wear!" Collin shouted back.

He moved to help Nolan up.

"Dylan!" Collin glanced over at the other two boys who remained face down in the dirt. "Kane?"

The two prone teens stirred.

"We're okay," Kane said, sitting up.

"That son-of-a-bitch!" Dylan scrambled to his feet looking down at his tattered shoes. "He tore up my Nike's! Let's see how you like it!"

Dylan grabbed up one of the heavy spears.

"Stop it, Dylan!" shouted Collin above the fray. "Nolan's hurt!"

"What?" Claire started for her friends but stopped to take aim at the elven commander who had started to reach for his spear. She waved the pistol, signaling the creature to back up. "How bad is he hurt?" Claire's asked, her voice shaking. "What's wrong?"

Collin had dropped to his knees to examine Nolan and the other two boys surrounded them.

"Shit!" Collin said.

"What?" Claire responded, trying to keep her eyes on the enemy.

"He took a spear jab in the shoulder," Collin said. "He's losing a lot of blood."

"I'll be fine," Nolan's weakened voice said.

"Who did it?" Claire's anger blossomed. "Which one of you bastards is next?" She bore down on the elven leader.

As if on signal, the remaining three elves moved in concert, grabbing for their spears. Claire reacted instantly, taking out their leader with a head shot. As she spun her weapon to take out the elf at the camp perimeter, Dylan fell back to the ground, preventing the creature from regaining the spear, by grabbing it up first. Dylan shoved the heavy spear between the elf's grasping hands and was rewarded with the pop of thick skin as the sharply honed spearhead sliced its way deep into the elf's abdomen.

The clearing became quiet except for the bubbling of elven slag on the dirt.

"Nolan!" Claire pushed the pistol back into her waistband and knelt beside him. "Oh, my God, Nolan!"

The muscular teens t-shirt was soaked with red on one side.

"We have to get him back down the mountain!" Claire said, urgently.

Kane shook his head. "How?"

"What the hell do you mean, how?" Claire responded angrily. "Just get him—"

"Lord Claire?" Kian piped up.

Startled, Claire turned to him.

"If I may?" The diminutive *Fey* knelt beside her. "I will help him."

"Help him?" Claire shook her head not understanding. "How?"

"Humans are matter," Kian said, grimacing at the blood still soaking into Nolan's short. "We of the Light can affect matter at will."

The air she had been holding in escaped Claire's lips. "Do it!"

The boy pressed a hand against Nolan's brow, pushing him back.

"Rest, Lord Nolan," Kian said gently.

Nolan eyed the young *Fey* suspiciously.

"What are you gonna do?"

"Make you feel better," Kian responded smiling broadly.

"Right." Nolan tried to relax back onto the ground, but kept a protective hand over his groin. "And by make me feel better, you mean . . ."

"Oh for God's sake, Nolan!" Claire said. "He's not going to rape you. He's just a boy."

"I will heal you, Lord Nolan," Kian said, tugging at Nolan's shirt. "Then you will want to thank me."

"Look, kid . . ."

"Shut up, Nolan," Claire ordered. "And be still."

Kian exposed the ugly wound just below Nolan's shoulders.

"Oh Jesus, Nolan!" Claire said, covering her mouth.

"Does it look really bad?" Nolan tried to pull his head up for a look.

"Dude," Kane said from over Claire's shoulder. "It looks pretty damn bad!"

"I can run down and get Father Brian," Dylan said, pointing back to the path. "You know . . ." He bent down to whisper in Claire's ear. "For last rights."

"Dylan!" Claire pushed the boy away. "There will be no need for a priest. Kian will make him better." She threw the young page a pleading look.

Kian touched a finger to Nolan's forehead. Instantly, Nolan was out.

"Oh, dear God!" Claire said, gasping.

"He only sleeps, Lord Claire," Kian said.

He held his hands out about six inches apart, finger tips facing.

"*Mo rún,*" Kian said softly. "*Ni neart go cur le cheile.*" His voice echoed with an unfamiliar hollowness. "*A bheith ina iomláine.*"

A pulsing ball of brilliant, white light formed between his hands.

Dylan and Collin took a few steps back.

Kian turned his hands and they hovered over Nolan's wound, not quite touching it. The attending light intensified, bathing the wound in a brightness that forced the humans to shield their eyes. Suddenly, the light retreated back into Kian's fingertips as quickly as it had appeared.

"Oh . . . my . . . God!" Claire whispered. She stared at the undamaged shoulder, previously assaulted by gaping wound.

The skin still glowed iridescently in the filtered sunlight peeking through the pine needles over-head.

"It's completely healed!" Claire managed in her astonishment.

The other boys bent over her to examine the evidence.

"Shit!" Dylan said, pointing to where the wound had been. "You can't see anything—not even a scar!"

"Thank you, Kian!" Claire hugged the boy. "You saved his life!"

"Holes in humans are easy to fix," Kian said, snuggling up against Claire.

"Can you wake him up now?" Claire asked.

"Of course." Kian crawled back to Nolan's side. "I must kiss him."

"Beg your pardon?" "Claire's eyebrows went up.

"I . . . I must kiss him," Kian repeated. "To wake him up as you asked."

"Dude!" Collin howled.

"Let the kid kiss him, Claire," Dylan said with a sheepish grin. "You want him to wake up, don't you?"

"Dylan!" Claire tried not to laugh.

"I don't understand," Kian said, flushing with embarrassment. "Perhaps," Kian said, unable to hide his disappointment, "Lord Dylan wishes to kiss him awake?"

"Ha!" Collin said, slamming Dylan on the back with his hand. "The kid catches on fast. Go ahead, Dude," he said, pushing Dylan forward. "Slip him some tongue!"

Dylan pushed back. "Kiss my ass, Collin," he said laughing. "And no, Kian, I do not want to kiss Nolan's ugly puss. He's all yours."

"I will kiss him awake!" Kian's face lit up like a flashbulb.

The human teens watched as the trembling young *Fey* leaned over Nolan's face and planted his lips squarely against the giant human's.

"This is too good!" Collin said, sputtering with laughter. "Where's a camera when you need one. Nolan's Kian's bitch now!"

Nolan shot up to a sitting position, dazed and disoriented. Kian clung to him, arms wrapped about Nolan's chest.

"What the . . ."

Nolan took in his surroundings, trying to get his bearings. "What happened?" He flexed his shoulder. "I don't . . . Claire?"

"It's okay, baby," Claire said, soothing. "Kian healed you. You're good as new."

"Yeah," Collin said, laughing. "It was way cool—especially when he woke you up."

"Collin!" Claire warned.

"I want tell him," Dylan shouted, leaping around Claire to Nolan's side.

Claire sighed. "Dylan!"

"How did it feel?" Dylan asked, face to face with Nolan.

"What?" Nolan asked.

"How did it feel?"

"What the hell are you talking about?" Nolan shook his head. "Claire, what's he talking about?"

"You know," Dylan persisted. "When the kid turned you . . . *Fey*."

"What?" Nolan's face clouded.

"Dylan!" Claire warned.

"When the kid turned you *Fey*. You know . . ." Dylan batted his lashes at Nolan. "When he kissed you!"

"What?"

"Dylan!"

Dylan turned to Claire. "What?"

"It was magical," Collin said, sighing dramatically.

Nolan pushed Dylan hard, sending the teen tumbling backwards.

"Claire?" Nolan looked at Claire, pleading. "What the hell is this dumbass yapping about?"

"Nolan Reid!" Dylan lay on his back, laughing. "Sucked face with a *Fey*."

"What's he talking about, kid?" Nolan pulled Kian's face from his neck.

"I kissed you awake, Lord Nolan," Kian said, breathily. "I made you all better."

"You kissed . . . what!" Nolan jumped to his feet shakily, dropping the boy to the ground. "You kissed . . . me?"

"Nolan!" Claire yelled, holding her arms out and the frightened young *Fey* scrambled into them. "Just chill out!"

"Goddammit, Claire!" Nolan ranted. "You just sat there and let this . . . horny little . . . dude do whatever he wanted with me?"

"Oh," Claire said, becoming extremely annoyed. "He hardly did whatever—"

"It's not right, Claire!" Nolan shouted back. "Just because your ex-boyfriend's a—"

"Nolan!"

Kian began to sob against Claire's chest.

"It's okay, Kian. Dylan!" Claire ordered. "Get over here!"

Dylan obeyed without thinking.

"Here!" Claire said, pushing Kian into Dylan's arms. "Take care of him a second."

"But Claire . . .'

"You have a little brother at home." Claire shot the teen a look that bucked no argument. "Now, take care of Kian."

Dylan sighed and patted the sobbing little *Fey* on the head."

Claire turned her look of death to Nolan.

"I don't care what you say, Claire," Nolan began, "it's not—"

"You . . . stupid . . . boy!" Claire said, pointing a bright red fingernail at him. "You insensitive, ungrateful, shit!"

"Gee, Claire, I . . ."

"Don't even try!" Claire continued with chilling anger. "This child saved your miserable, hateful ass! You should be dead on the ground right now. But this boy . . . yes, he has a big crush on you. Why, I don't understand, because you haven't done anything but treat him like . . . like leprosy. Oh, I see you so clearly right now!"

"Claire, I'm not—"

"Once!" Claire bellowed. "Just once, I'd like to see you act like a man—not some insecure, overcompensating, adolescent . . . shit who thinks those . . . pine nuts you call balls'll fall off if someone . . . different gets too close."

"Claire, if you just—"

"Don't," Claire said, jabbing her pointed finger at him. "Don't even think about talking to me."

She turned her back on him and went back to retrieve the grieving young *Fey* from Dylan.

"Okay, Kian," Claire said, stroking the boy's hair. "It's you and me. I need you to stop crying. We have to get back and help Finn and Ron."

"Fuck!" Nolan dropped to his knees, defeated.

"I will serve you, Lord Claire," Kian said, sniffing. He turned his teary, trusting eyes up to her. "I will do whatever you say."

"Good." Claire stood. "The sooner we leave this . . . little boys' club the better!" She took Kian's hand. "Let's get back to our friends."

"Claire!" Nolan's roaring shout caused the surrounding aspen leaves to rustle. He stood hands on hips. "Now you're acting childish!"

Claire turned to finish him off.

"Save it!" Nolan yelled. "Enough!"

Claire stood silent, glaring at him, but somewhat taken aback by Nolan's surprising tone.

"You two!" Nolan said, pointing to Kane and Dylan. "Get our things packed up."

They looked at him.

"Now!"

The two teens stumbled over the glacial rock field to recover their backpacks.

Nolan closed his eyes and took a deep breath. He released it slowly, opening his eyes back at Kian.

"Come here, Kian," Nolan said, calm returning to his voice.

Claire's hands went to her hips. "Don't you talk—"

"I'm not talking to you, woman!" Nolan's basso echoed off the granite cliff face.

"Come here." He motioned to the young *Fey*.

Kian froze against Claire.

"It's okay, kid. Just come here." Nolan repeated, again motioning for the boy.

Kian looked up at Claire. She looked at Nolan for a moment and then nodded for Kian to go. He hesitated.

"It's fine, honey," Claire said. "Go ahead. He won't hurt you," she said, cutting her eyes at Nolan again, "or I'll kill him."

Slowly Kian shuffled the short distance, wringing his hands nervously. Dry sobs wracked his small body as he went. He stood at Nolan's feet, too afraid to look up from the ground. Nolan put his hands on Kian's shoulders and bent over him.

"I'm sorry I freaked out, kid," Nolan said.

Nolan closed his eyes again, suddenly feeling like the asshole Claire had labeled him as he felt the boy trembling beneath his hands.

"Sometimes," Nolan said. "We humans go crazy in situations we're not used to. I've never thought I was dying before. It messed with my head. My yelling at you was just me yelling at me 'cause . . ."

He looked at Claire and then back at Kian.

"I couldn't deal with it like a man." Nolan pulled Kian to him in a tight hug. "You didn't do anything wrong. You saved my life."

Kian's arms looped about Nolan's neck. After a moment, Nolan pulled back and held the boy at arm's length.

"You forgive me?" Nolan asked.

Kian blushed, smiled and nodded.

"Okay." Nolan sighed. "Now, look at me."

Kian met the man's gaze shyly.

"So." Nolan said, tapping the boy on the chest. "You have this big crush on me."

"I love you, Lord Nolan." The boy's voice carried the weight of sincerity.

"Right." Nolan sighed again. "Got it. That's okay." Nolan sat on the ground. "Sit here."

Nolan motioned to the spot beside him and Kian obeyed, hugging himself.

"Kian," Nolan began. "Humans are very confusing when we talk about love."

Kian blinked at him.

"You see," Nolan continued. "We love our parents. Parents love their kids. We love our friends . . ." Nolan looked at Kian for some sign of understanding. "And then there's that very special kind of love . . ." Nolan paused, looking for the right words. "That special kind of love just for that very special one and only one person in your life."

"Bond-mates," Kian said, nodding. "The love that makes you . . ." He blushed gold. ". . . join as one. We learned about that from our elder."

"Bond-mates," Nolan repeated for lack of a clearer reference. "Exactly."

"Like you and Lord Claire," Kian said, smiling toward the human female.

"Well," Nolan said, trying not to look at Claire. "Sort of . . . well, not yet . . . but, anyway, you see how I love Claire and how . . ." He hesitated again.

"How you love me is different," Kian said, finishing for the older male.

"Well." Nolan shrugged. "Yes."

Kian gasped and broke free of Nolan to dance his way across the camp ground to Claire.

"Lord Nolan does love me," Kian said embracing Claire once again.

"Does he now?" Claire said, trying not to let Nolan see her smile.

"Yes, he does!"

Kian's green and gold wings billowed into the air as his tunic dissolved in a wisp. He darted through the air from tree to tree, giggling with naked excitement.

"Kian!" Nolan called out. "Get back down here and put your clothes back on! We have to get back to Finn and Ron."

In a blur, Kian was back on the ground, his tunic back in place. He danced about, circling everyone in turn.

"Grab the kid!" Nolan said to Dylan.

"Slow down there, kid!" Dylan caught Kian by the arm.

"Hey everyone!" A female voice called from across the clearing.

"Briana!" Claire ran to her friend. "We had almost given up on you."

She reached for two of the four paint cans, Briana was carrying.

Briana shifted the weight of one of the other two cans she was carrying to her free hand.

"Whew!" she said with relief. "Those handles were cutting through my fingers."

"Where's . . ." Claire looked about.

"I'm down here!" Kane called out as he appeared over the path horizon. "Can I get a hand here?"

He dropped the eight cans of paint he was carrying and wiped the sweat from his brow.

Dylan and Collin came to the rescue and each grabbed up four of the cans.

"Dude," Dylan said. "You sure took long enough. We were attacked by these giant elves. They killed Nolan, and—"

"Whoa, whoa, whoa!" Kane said. He squinted his eyes across the clearing to Nolan. "What do you mean, they killed Nolan? He's . . ."

"Yeah," Kane jumped in. "Kian healed him. But not before Claire, gunned down the whole damn—"

"Hold on!" Kane said, adjusting the load on his back. "What do you mean, Claire . . ."

"Briana's father taught her how to shoot," Claire said, "and Briana taught me. Simple."

Kane bore his load across the campground toward Nolan.

"Dude! They killed you?" He asked, squinting at Nolan, looking for some sign of injury.

"No, no," Nolan said, laughing. "I just took a spear in the shoulder."

"Dude!"

"I'm all better now, thanks to Kian.

Kian was on him like a flash.

"Okay, kid," Nolan said, patting the boy on the head. "Keep your feet on the ground."

"Shit!" Kane yelled out. "What the hell am I standing in?" He looked down at the black goo beneath his shoes.

"That, dude, is what's left of one of the elves Claire blasted," Collin said, setting the paint cans down. "Forgot to warn you. Watch out for elf crap."

Kane stepped out of the ooze to scrape his feet over the surrounding untainted rocks.

"Thanks a lot, man," Kane said, setting down the paint cans and orange, plastic gasoline can.

"What the hell is that contraption?" Nolan asked, eyeing the heavy tank and its collection of hoses that Kane unstrapped from his back.

"It's a gas-powered paint sprayer," Kane replied, stretching his aching back. "Ought to make the job go quicker."

"Excellent," Claire said, joining them. "Do you think we have enough silver-laced paint?"

Kane nodded. "With the sprayer we can get a thinner, more even coat over the rock and any nooks and crannies," he said. "We can paint the whole face with this. "

"It gets awful high up," Claire said eyeing the granite rock face.

"No problem." Kane said, motioning to Briana. "Come her, girl. I'll help you off with that bag."

"You keep your shirt on," Collin said, pushing in front of Kane. "I'll help her off with the bag."

Briana had a long bag, like an arrow quiver, slung across her back. She pulled the strap over her head and handed the bag off to Collin.

"It's a telescoping extension pole," Collin said, with business-like efficiency. "We can reach as high as we need. When do we get started?"

"Kane and Briana can handle that," Claire said. "I need you with me."

"What about me?" Nolan asked, almost pouting.

"And me!" Dylan said.

"You're coming too," Claire said, only a hint of a smile showing. "What's our status on laser pointers?"

"We're good," Kane responded. "Got plenty of batteries still."

"Perfect." Claire unzipped her backpack. "Kane," she said, all business. "You worked in the paint store last summer with Collin's Dad?"

"Yep," Kane said.

"You still remember how to use this paint equipment?"

"Sure," Kane responded. "I had to show customers what to do."

"Okay." Claire nodded. "You take care of the paint. After we go through, cover over and around the doorway in particular."

"No problem." Kane knelt down to assemble the paint sprayer.

"How many of those pointers should we take with us," Nolan asked, looking about for the pointer he had dropped in the earlier skirmish.

"None."

"You'll use these instead." Claire pulled a plastic, space gun-like toy out of her pack.

"What the hell!" Nolan, said, jumping over a pile of rocks to take the plastic gun from Claire. "What are we supposed to do with this?"

"It's a laser tag gun," Claire said, pulling out another and handing it to Collin. "I was able to get two pair at Goodall's. They had them left over from Christmas."

"Cool!" Collin turned the compact pistol over in his hands. "What's the battery life?"

"Uses these nine-volts," Claire said, pulling open her pack to show it half-full of the small, square batteries. "We're good to go."

"Who's the extra one for?" Nolan asked. "Ron?"

"Ron doesn't need it," Claire said with a dismissive wave. "This one's for Kian."

The boy *Fey* accepted the gun from Claire with eyes wide as twin full moons.

"You can kill a lot of *Phooka* with that," said Claire.

"What about elves?" the boy asked, grinning down at the toy.

"You and the other guys kill *Phooka*." Claire popped out the ammo clip from her nine millimeter and began to replace the spent rounds. "The elves are mine."

"Why don't we all have guns?" Nolan said, looking from his toy gun to Claire's real one. "Then we can kill everything!"

"Mab only had time to prepare a hundred rounds for me," Claire said. "And I have to make each one of these count."

"Let's face it, hon . . ." She expertly snapped new rounds into the ammo clip. "You can kick a ball into a goal, but I'm a hell of a better shot!"

Nolan rolled his eyes. "I can—"

"Dude!" Collin nudged Nolan with his elbow. "Give it up. She's a better shot."

Nolan stared at the shorter redhead. "Whatever, dude," he said, drawling out the appellation. "How do we get through the door?"

"Kian will take us," Claire said, stroking the boy *Fey*'s hair. "Won't you, baby."

Kian looked up at Nolan and then Collin.

"The men people are a lot of matter for me to transport," the boy *Fey* said. "I don't know if I can do it and walk through myself."

"No problem," Claire replied. "Nolan will carry you."

"What?" Nolan said, giving his girlfriend a pleading look.

Kian hopped on his toes excitedly.

"You are strong, Lord Nolan," Kian said, batting his silken lashes up at the muscular human. "I am very light."

"I'm not . . ." Nolan stopped, seeing the ominous twitch of Claire's lips. "I have to keep my hands free, baby," he said pleading, "in case I have to shoot something."

"He can ride on your back," Claire replied flatly. "Or you can stay here."

"Damn it to . . ." Nolan caught himself again in Claire's unbending gaze. "Shit!" He said, looking down at the fawning young *Fey*. "Okay, kid, get up—"

Before Nolan could finish, humming bird wings beat, lifting Kian up like a shot onto Nolan's back. The boy's slender arms wrapped about Nolan's neck.

"Jesus H . . ." Nolan stiffened with surprise. "Hey! He's right. He doesn't weigh anything."

"It's your great strength, Lord Nolan," Kian said, clinging tightly to Nolan. He pressed his cheek against the side of Nolan's neck. "I'm ready."

"That's good, hon." Claire suppressed a chuckle and took one of Nolan's free hands. "Okay, we need to be connected. Grab a hand, Collin."

Collin looked down at Nolan's other free hand. He shook his head and moved quickly to Claire's other side.

"Okay," Collin said, taking Claire's hand. "We're connected. Let's do this!"

"Dylan," Claire said. "Take Nolan's other hand."

Dylan rolled his eyes. "Why do I—"

"Dylan!"

"Okay, okay." Dylan sidled up beside Nolan. "Your woman sure is bossy."

"Take my hand dick-wad and shut up." Nolan grabbed Dylan by the wrist.

The three teens, with Kian tight about Nolan's neck, made their way over the rocks to the cliff face.

"You gotta let me breathe a little kid," Nolan gasped, twisting his neck.

"Yes, Lord Nolan," Kian responded.

"That's better." Nolan reached out and touched the cold, solid granite in front of him. "Now what?" he asked. "You said you can get us through this, kid?"

"Absolutely, my lord," Kian answered fervently. "You're my bitch!"

Before Nolan could respond, the world flashed as Claire and Dylan yanked him into an abyss of blackness.

Chapter 18

"What the hell!"

The surrounding chaos hit Ron like a wall as he once again materialized into the center of the great stone circle.

"*O amháin ársa, cad atá ag tarlú?*" Finn called out to one of the elder's shouting orders.

The elder spun around, fear etched across his face.

"Lord White Wing!" the elder sputtered. "The elven lord comes with his soldiers! They will be upon us in moments!"

"How soon before the people are sealed in Sanctuary?"

"These are the last," the elder said with a sweeping gesture. "The Council, the generals, and our remaining soldiers will barricade in the Great Temple."

"Barricade?" Ron asked. He surveyed the open circle of standing stones. "With what . . . and where?"

"Powerful bindings," Finn responded. "But there is little hope. The Demon Elf is very powerful and the Sanctuary itself will fall if the elders cannot hold the evil ones at bay."

"And if they can't?"

"The only hope will be to transport the people to another hidden plane."

"Is that possible?"

"It is very dangerous," Finn said, shaking his head. "We have found few if any alternate planes, hidden enough and hospitable enough for the people."

"Well," Ron said. "We'll just have to kick some elf ass." He pointed to the temple. "Pop us up to the platform so we can take stock of what we have."

In an instant the two were standing on the throne platform, facing the gathering elders. From a distance, Ron could make out a line of foot soldiers bearing down on the temple. As they came closer, the *Fei* elders raised their hands in unison releasing a laser bright light which pooled above the temple circle and slowly spilled out into a dome of transparent, but solid protection that bent the exterior light like a convex lens. The elders turned to face the invading hoards who had begun to encircle the temple.

The elven soldiers were freakishly tall, but unwinged and suited out in an iron-age style of armor. Ron could see their hairless, but wolf-like features with slanted orange eyes glaring out from their helmets. Their sharp teeth dripped a thick saliva at the sight of so many *Fey*, standing in the bowl of the temple circle like tasty morsels ready for the taking. The soldiers pounded to no avail against the dome of protection with their heavy lances.

High above the Dome of Bindings, a giant bat-like creature hovered, its taloned fingers flexed impatiently.

"*Fei Ardsagart!*" thundered the winged elf, baring his teeth. "Show yourself and properly welcome your *sídhe* brothers!"

The *Fei* high priest stepped out onto the center of the temple surrounded by the other elders who were surround in turn by an outer circle of *Fei* Soldiers.

"Bolcán!" The *Ardsagart*'s said, his voice rising strong and without fear. "You will leave this sanctuary immediately or face your dissolution!"

Bolcán threw his head back with laughter.

"You ancient fool!" Bolcán bellowed down at the high priest. "You lost this battle a thousand moons ago. It was only a matter of persistence until we found you. Surrender and face a merciful death!"

The *Ardsagart* nodded to General Darragh. In an instant, the outer circle of *Fei* Soldiers were armed with golden crossbows, seated with silver tipped arrows. The barrage of slender missiles were released in unison and passed through the Dome of Bindings unimpeded to take down any elf unfortunate enough to be on the domes peri-meter. A great black pool of elf remains simmered about the rim of the *fey* Temple.

"Good shots!" Ron shouted, pleased with the result of the attack.

"There are hundreds more," Finn said, his voice strained with worry. "If the elven priest disrupts our bindings, we will not stand a chance.

Ron looped a protective arm about Finn.

"It's not over till it's over," Ron said reassuring. "What are they made of? How do I destroy them?"

"Our light will be useless against them," Finn replied. "They are part matter, part light, and part dark matter. Silver is all that will put an end to them. Iron will hurt them."

Bolcán circled about overhead, chanting a spell of dissolution. The sky overhead darkened as the elven priest bombarded the upper dome bindings with discrete spheres of dark matter from his hands.

"See?" Finn said in alarm. "It has begun!"

"Is he powerful enough to get through the bindings?" Ron asked.

"No," Finn responded. "But he can certainly weaken them. If another elf as powerful as he joins the attack, we will surely fall."

"Not if I can shore them up!"

Ron ran down the steps of the throne platform. He lay on his back at the feet of the *Ardsagart*, staring up at the Dome of Bindings. The *Ardsagart* stepped back, unsure of Ron's intention.

Immediately Ron released himself from his body's limitations. His spirit eyes marveled at the impenetrable depth of the *fey* bindings that sparkled like an aurora above and about the temple. He could also make out a measurable thinning of the powerful magic at the points where Bolcán's relentless dark matter bombardment attacked the dome.

Already Ron could feel the ring of light about his thumb vibrating. This time, there was no impediment between himself and the Earth Mother. He drew deep from her, allowing the binding forces to build in him. He opened his mind and raised his hands, palms to the roof of the dome. He spoke through his mouth a simple invocation to the goddess, taught to him as a child at Mab's knee.

"O bandia Dhiaga, a chosaint do dhaoine."

The sound and substance of the plea for protection of the goddess achieved a sum greater than its parts. It was Ron's voice, and then it wasn't—a sonority that came from the depths of Mother Earth took possession of the vibrations of Ron's voice. The floor of the temple and out beyond the Dome of Bindings to the earth beneath the elven hordes trembled as the spirits indwelling the rocks, the streams, the flora, and all earth-bound elements shook with such quaking force, that all standing found it difficult to stay on their feet.

From the palms of Ron's hands, a dark light went out with such force and intensity that all eyes were averted. The air crackled as its elemental bonds broke and reformed. The space about Ron's physical self, folded and expanded forcing the *Ardsagart* and all the nearby elders back a good fifty feet. The Dome of Bindings absorbed Ron's photic strength hungrily. Its depth tripled and the front cadre of surrounding elven soldiers were pushed back even farther from the temple.

An amazed cheer went up from the hundred elders, overpowering the cries of anger that accompanied the repulsion of the elven army. Bolcán hovered overhead, stunned into silence by the unexpected manifestation. Ron regained his sense of the present and stood looking up at the blustering winged elf. He gave Bolcán a one-finger salute.

The *Ardsagart* wasted no time. He signaled again to his general and another volley of silver-tipped arrows struck down another line of elf minions. Ron climbed back up the throne platform to join Finn.

"How do you do these things, Ron?" Finn asked in amazement.

"Hell if I know." Ron stumbled on the last step and went to his knees.

"The exertion has weakened you again," Finn said, dropping to his knees as well to steady Ron. "Page!" he shouted into the air.

"My Lord?" a high voice called from behind the stone thrones.

"Kian!" Finn smiled at his head page and Claire who was holding the boy's hand. "Ron, they are back!" he said with relief.

"Claire!" Ron turned his head up to smile weakly at his friend. "How did the two of you get into this fortress when the elves can't?"

"Through a secret tunnel, of course," Claire said rushing to Ron's side. "There's always a secret tunnel."

She helped Finn lift Ron to his feet.

"Finn, let's get him to that chair." Claire nodded to the purple veined marble throne and heard Kian gasp. "What?"

"Let's put him in my . . . chair," Finn said with a chuckle as they guided Ron to the smaller white throne. "Kian, my chalice, please!"

In a blink, Kian left and returned bearing the iris cup. Finn took it and tipped the edge into Ron's waiting lips.

"Drink, my love, and grow strong again," he said.

Ron drank hungrily.

"I'm gonna have to bottle this stuff," he said between gulps. "Talk about your energy drinks!"

"Shut up and drink!" Claire stroked her friend's hair. "Catch me up on what's been happening, Finn."

Claire nodded to the angry legion of elven soldiers, pounding in vain on the outside of the Dome of Bindings.

"Ron has defeated the efforts of the elven priest to pierce through our defenses!" Finn said proudly.

"Good!" Claire patted Ron's cheek. "And where is this son-of-a-bitch?"

Ron pointed upwards. Claire's eyes followed and widened at the sight of the winged elf wringing his hands and screeching angrily overhead.

"The others didn't have wings," Claire commented, cocking her head to one side.

Ron pushed the cup of nectar away. "What others?" he asked, sounding more himself.

"They attacked the boys while I was down the mountain to confer with Mab. When I got back, these assholes had apparently gotten through the Gateway and a few were left behind to guard my guys."

"Are they okay?"

"We're just fine," Nolan said, popping up from behind the thrones.

Collin and Dylan followed behind.

Claire's hands went to her hips. "I thought I told you to stay—"

"Who you talkin' to woman!" Nolan said sharply.

"Woman?" Claire glared him down. "Let me—"

"Just kidding," Nolan interrupted. "Just kidding.

"How's Ron?" Collin pushed between them. "Dude!" he said, seeing the physical changes in Ron. "You look like a Vulcan with plague!"

"Collin!" Claire snapped.

"Good to see you too," Ron said, laughing. "But I feel fine. Finn's taking good care of me."

"Thank you for coming back." Finn said, smiling at the small group of humans. "You are truly Ron's friends.

"And mine as well," Kian said, latching on to Nolan's side. "This is Lord Nolan."

Nolan rolled his eyes.

"He is my bitch!" Kian added, batting his eyelashes at the tall human looking down at him.

"Dammit, kid!" Nolan bent down face to face with the young *Fey*. "I ain't your bitch. You're the only bitch I see around here."

"Wheeeee!" Kian danced about the towering human. "I am Lord Nolan's bitch!"

"No!" Nolan pressed his hands against his temples. "That's not what I meant."

"Okay, okay," Claire said with a sigh. "That's enough of that." She turned to Ron and Finn. "The Gateway's being painted with silver-bearing paint even as we speak."

"That will keep us safe from further incursions," Finn said, relieved. "Thank you, Claire. That is good news."

"Well," Claire added with a shrug. "There's a little bad news as well." She smiled sheepishly at Finn. "From the escarpment where you come out of the Gateway, we could see a huge . . . I'm talking huge encampment of elves. They're circled about an enormous black tent. Looks important."

"Lord Salach!" Finn almost spat the name. "The Great Dark One. If he is here, we are already doomed."

"Not so fast, sweetheart," Ron said. "We've done a good job keeping bat boy up there are bay." He nodded at Bolcán overhead.

"Who," said Nolan, "or should I say, what is that thing?"

Dylan nudged him. "Did Ron call Finn *sweetheart?*" he whispered.

"Catch up, Dylan for Christ's sake!" Collin watched the elven priest dart to and fro over the dome.

"I remember seeing that asshole when we were attacked on the mountain," Dylan whispered.

"We need a plan," Ron said standing. "Finn, what's this Lord Salach's weakness? How do we get to him?"

"He has no weakness," Finn said, shaking his head. "He is an ancient and all-powerful foe. Even your amazing powers will not deter the Dark Demon."

"That's not good," Collin said, still watching the winged elf overhead.

"But there must be something," Ron said. "There was a time when the *Fey* ruled the other worlds."

"Yes." Finn nodded. "But that was in the time of the Purple Wing. His power was ordained and anointed by the goddess and the *Tuatha*. He wielded the Sword of Light. He who holds the light cannot be usurped."

"But he was usurped!" Claire said. "The elves defeated him. How?"

"Betrayal," Finn responded. "Treachery! The Purple Wing was persuaded to give the Sword to the Council as a symbol of unity. A great temple was built and the Sword enshrined there. Once separate from the Sword, agents of the Dark Demon, including the *Ardsagart* at that time, were able to poison and curse the Purple Wing. He was so weakened that the elves rose up to seize power. The Purple Wing sacrificed himself to allow the *Fey* to escape to this hidden sanctuary where we have been for lo these many ages. The Purple Wing's consort, my ancestor, smuggled the Sword to safety with the people and it remains with us today . . . a symbol and nothing more."

"But if it is that powerful . . ." Ron began.

"It is," Finn replied. "But its power cannot be harnessed. The bindings upon it are greater than any magic other than what the goddess can create."

"And where does one find the goddess!" Ron's voice betrayed his frustration.

"Can one locate a goddess?" Finn said with a weak smile. "We have nothing but her symbol in the sky."

"Shit!" Ron muttered. "He eyed the orb overhead that was somehow visible even in the pervasive light.

"What about escape?" Nolan asked. "The *Fey* escaped once before."

"But to where?" Ron slumped back into the white marble throne.

"Besides," Finn added. "There is one way in to this sanctuary and so only one way out. We could never get the people past the Dark One without great loss if not total annihilation.

"Shit, shit, shit!" Ron slammed a fist against the marble armrest.

"Kian," Finn said, motioning for the young page.

"My Lord," Kian replied.

Reluctantly he disengaged himself from Nolan to wait on the White Wing.

"The other pages are in Sanctuary," Finn said sternly. "You need to join them now as well. You will be safer there."

"Please, my Lord," Kian said, going to his knees. "I serve you, *Sciathán Bán*, wherever you are. Let me stay. I have a weapon to fight with!" He brandished the plastic laser tag gun Claire had given him.

"Kian," Finn began.

"I can fight, my Lord," Kian said. "And I can bring the Royal Nectar to Lord Ron whenever he requires it. My Lords needs me!"

"Let the kid stay," Nolan said. "From what you say, I can't see he's any better off in hiding than here with us."

"Fine," Finn said, relenting.

"Salach!"

The name echoed off the Dome of Bindings like a sonic boom. The elven lord, Bolcán, hovered directly overhead, his massive grey-skinned wings beat the atmosphere like a dark cloud.

"*Tar chugainn*, Salach!" Bolcán invoked.

"He calls for the Dark Demon!" Finn whispered, visibly trembling. "We are doomed!"

Chapter 19

The rising full moon seemed stripped of its usual grandeur and Mab stared up into a night sky, darkened not only by the strange veiled appearance of its moon, but also bereft of all but a few of the brightest stars, now mere pinpoints in the pervasive greyness. Mab was also aware of the cooling air and she adjusted her woolen shawl against the goose bumps rising on her arms. Everything was as wrong as the old journals had warned. This same sky had been witnessed once before, journaled by the farthest ancestor she would trace. Mab considered what else the night might bring. She had read the account over and over, but could not glean even the smallest atom of under-standing about the events. She had unwavering faith in the truth of the account, but even the ancestor seemed to have no understanding of the purposes involved. The ancestral coven had been charged with the impending tasks by a powerful *Fey*, at the time of the great uprising of the elf nation and the ensuing disappearance of *fey* presence from the Old Country.

"Mab!" The raspy voice returned Mab to the present. "Are you still waiting for the mother ship or do you plan to help your poor sisters get this circle prepared?"

Mab glanced over with a smirk at the thin, weathered old face sneering at her.

"What's this?" Mab asked in mock surprise. "Bea Barrett is asking my help?"

"Get over yourself!" Bea said with a dismissive wave.

"I'm not expecting any alien landings tonight," Mab said, chuckling. "The sight of your wrinkled old asses sent them off to another galaxy entirely."

"Well, if that ain't the pig calling the goose fat!" Another half-naked old woman cackled into her hand, dropping some of the firewood she had gleaned.

"Dorothy Bate!" Mab struck a pose. "At least this old pig has kept some shape about her. I can't tell where those sticks you're holding begin and your saggy old tits end!"

The air shivered with the vibrating laughter that engulfed the whole coven of nine. They continued to arrange the field stones into a large and intricate labyrinth. At its center, Edith Kent, the coven's youngest at fifty-seven, tossed her load of kindling onto the pile of wood that had been carefully assembled.

"That's done," Edith announced, brushing the bits of bark from the folds of skin that draped her ample bosom. "Hope I'll have the strength to type out Father's sermon in the morning."

Again, the ladies cackled with laughter.

"Wear something low-cut," said a swarthy, gypsy-like woman, cupping her own bountiful breasts. "That always keeps the priests attention."

"You always were a slut, Agatha Dury!" Mab cried, popping the cork on a large jug of her elixir.

"That," Agatha said unashamed, "is because I happen to like a man in my bed."

"Yeah," Edith responded with a wagging finger. "But what does your husband think about that?"

The group laughter echoed off the surrounding oak trees a little too long, betraying and at the same time assuaging the frayed nerves and rising anxiety that permeated the women's efforts.

"Coven!" Mab finally intoned in her throaty contralto.

The other eight witches immediately formed a circle about Mab who held up a heavy cup carved out of jasper.

"We'll need this tonight, ladies." Mab said, nodding. She took the first draft of her home-distilled whiskey. "That's a true gift of the goddess, blessed be!"

She passed the cup to her left. Each coven member took their turn.

"That's a bloody good brew," Agatha said, wheezing from the effects of the whiskey. "You did good, Mab."

"That one's been aging for almost forty years," Mab said with undisguised pride. "This was the night for it."

"How much longer?" Edith asked, daintily daubing the edges of her mouth before imbibing another sip of Mab's brew.

Mab studied the sky again.

"Not much longer," Mab said with a shrug. "We can go ahead with the usual thanksgiving rubrics."

"Are we expecting any trouble in this?" Dorothy swayed her bulk from side to side for warmth.

"Why do you ask that?" Mab asked cocking one eyebrow. "You ever done this before?"

"Mab Maguire!" Dorothy laughed. "You think I didn't see the pile of bindings you've got lined up at the altar?" Dorothy nodded to the small, rustic table at the circle axis facing the rising moon. "You'd think we were going to war?"

Mab drained the last of the jug in silence.

"Come on, Mab," urged Agatha. "Out with it!" You got something special planned?"

"I'll need one of you at each of the other eleven axis of the circle." Mab eyed each of the women. "I'll man the altar as usual."

"But what are we doing?" piped the oldest, a thrice widowed eighty-year old named Frieda.

The other coven members began to talk at once.

"I'll explain as we go along!" Mab boomed, holding up a hand.

The women grew silent.

"Those are not bindings one the altar," Mab continued. "Tonight we will be releasing a bind—a very powerful binding!"

"Well, Jesus and Methusala, Mab!" said Agatha. "From the looks of all that bottled craft over there, I'd guess we'll be releasing the devil out of hell!"

That caused another flurry of cackling laughter from the group.

"To be quite honest, girls . . ." Mab sighed. "I'm not really sure what we're going to be releasing. I just know it's gonna take everything we've got. Each of you will need to hold fast at your axis and protect the cone of power we'll be raising from . . ."

"From what?" Edith said, crossing her arms. "Spill it Mab."

"It's for Ron." Mab pulled all their eyes into her own. "My Ron."

"Mab," Dorothy said. "What could that sweet boy possibly—"

"Not a boy anymore, Deedee." Mab left the group for the altar. "A young man, with a big problem."

"We're listening," Agatha said, moving to her place in the circle.

"*Fey*, Mab said, her face dead serious. "Elves and *Phooka*!"

"*Phooka?*" Dorothy almost laughed, but Mab's demeanor made her think better of it. "You're not kidding!"

"The journals describe a powerful binding, invoked by the ancestors on a night such as this. It was a binding given them by the fairy king, and it was a life and death situation. Several of the Wiccan ancestors died in the ritual."

"Died!" several coven voices whispered.

"But we have an advantage," Mab said quickly.

"And that would be?" asked Frieda.

Mab gestured to full moon's light breaking over the surrounding treetops.

"Okay," began Dorothy, "the Mother Goddess, I get it, but that's a given where we're concerned." She eyed the altar. "But those bindings . . . that's overkill . . . unless . . ." Dorothy stopped, noting Mab's impassivity.

"Mab?" asked Agatha, more a demand than an inquiry.

Mab signed. "It is what it is, ladies," she said solemnly. "The old demons have already visited this plane and, based on what we're about to do, I would not be surprised if they attempt to stop us!"

The witches stood in silence, studying each other for any sign of defection.

"*Phooka*!" rattled Frieda with a wrinkled sneer.

"*Go hIfreann leo!*" Agnus said, invoking an ancient curse.

"We must do this to maintain the balance," Mab said. "To ensure survival of the *Fei* world." She returned to her preparations of the herbal smudge. "We will at once be binding the dark elf prince," Mab said, "and then releasing the powerful binding that was placed on *Fei* power by the fairy king."

'Mab, are you mad?"

"If we fail, there will be retribution against this plane!" Dorothy moved to her spot on the circle and drew her athame from her pocket.

"If we don't try," Mab said, looking up from her ritual tasks, "there will be nothing to stop an attack on this plane that would be inevitable from the elf prince's dreams of conquest."

The others nodded their understanding.

"Let's begin." Mab said solemnly.

Mab raised the stone paten of smoldering herbs and slowly made her way around the circle, bowing in turn at each compass point outward from the circle, and to each of her sisters inward.

"Blessed be!" Mab exchanged with each witch in turn.

The air had grown very still and the lunar orb's light had begun to peek over the surrounding pines and bathe the sacred circle in an amber light. As Mab completed the circle back to the altar, even the chirping of crickets had stopped.

"Mother goddess!" Mab cried out. "Your circle is complete. Your faithful daughters stand before you!"

The witches bowed to the center of the circle. Naked they raised their small athame daggers to the sky. Then with arms outstretched, they formed another circle in the air above the circle of stones in the earth.

"O goddess, divine!" Mab continued. "We call your power to the sacred circle within this sacred grove!" She tossed another dash of herbs into the burning crucible.

"Come, goddess," Mab continued, "in whose being all is sustained. Give aid to your daughters gathered here. Indwell this circle of life with your presence and power. As your iconic moon gleams in the night sky, cast your favor and protection over us!"

"Come, goddess," the coven echoed and repeated in a crescendoing chant.

A slight breeze began to waft from outside the circle inward as if pulled by a vacuum. For a moment, the breeze became a gale and the women shifted their center mass closer to the ground to keep from being pulled inward. The wind suddenly stilled as quickly as it had arisen. The moon's light reflected off the faces surrounding the circle such that the surrounding grove was in darkness, the pale light being contained with the circumference of the circle.

Agatha's broken laughter filled all ears. The goddess' presence always reduced the old woman to ecstatic utterance.

The other witches exchanged nods and smiles. Invoking the goddess was common place to them, but never failed to fill them with an expectation and excitement unlike any other.

"We are in the goddess!" Mab announced solemnly.

"Blessed be!" the witches chanted in unison.

"May the goddess defend us!" Mab continued.

"Blessed be!" came the response.

"May Mother Earth defend us!"

"Blessed be!"

"May Sister Fire defend us!"

"Blessed be!"

"May Sister Water defend us!"

"Blessed Be!"

"So mote it be!"

"So mote it be"

Mab extracted the small, leafy fetish from the basket she had brought. She placed it carefully on to the altar between the chalice and the paten of burning herbs.

"What is that plant?" Bea whispered.

"Nightwort!" Agatha responded. "The elven plant. Mab means to do this up right!"

Mab looked up, eyes blazing.

"Ladies," Mab said, pulling out a long braided cord of hemp. "Let's begin with the binding!"

Chapter 20

The cold and roiling dark clouds that moved in to cover the skies and block the full moon's light were the first signs that something, or someone with great power and command of the elements, was approaching the Temple circle. As the last reflected lunar light was blocked out and a great, still darkness had fallen, Ron became aware that Finn was no longer beside him. He turned to find Finn regaining his white throne. Finn sat and lifted his face, impassive and regal.

"Finn, what are you doing?" Ron asked, leaving his friends for the white throne. "We have to fight!"

Finn cast Ron an empty look. A great sadness cloaked him.

"We cannot win, Ron," Finn said, his voice steady and still, unlike his quivering body. "It is over for the *Fey*. You and your human friends must get out the same way they came in. The Great Lord Salach approaches. His camp will be empty. You should be able to get by."

"Finn!" Ron shook his head. "I'm not going anywhere. "I will protect you."

"You cannot protect me." Finn reached out to caress Ron's cheek.

"I am the one the demon elf desires. His power exceeds that of the combined power of the *Fey*."

"Finn!"

"It is hopeless." Finn said with soft finality. "You and your friends should make it back to the safety of your world."

Ron turned to his friends. "You all need to get out now!" he ordered. "Kian, see to it they make it back to the portal and get through!"

Powerful claps of thunder accompanied the roiling, black clouds. The feral, fanged countenances of innumerable *Phooka* could be seen in the swirling blackness and the small group of humans became aware that the clouds were, in fact, not clouds at all.

Overhead, the elf high priest, Bolcán, had ceased his growling charges and hovered at the side of the Dome of Bindings, scowling down at the *Fey* and human inhabitants. The angry cloud of *Phooka* parted and the Great Lord came into view. He was larger than even the impressive Bolcán, clothed in gleaming, gold armor like a Caesar. His enormous grey-skinned wings beat slowly in the air and he glided down to the apex of the protective dome.

Silence fell over the hordes of elves that surrounded the dome and they dropped to one knee in obeisance. Their evil Great Lord fastened his eyes on the white throne below him.

"*Bán Corcra!*" The Great Lord Salach's voice thundered overhead. "I have found you at last!"

"Kian!" Finn looked for his page. "Kian!"

"He's gone," Claire said, looking about. "And Nolan seems to be gone as well."

"That son-of-a—"

"Collin!" Claire said, stopping him with a look.

"Well," Collin said. "Are you telling me that his leaving just before the fight is all right with you?"

"We don't know that," Claire said, calmly.

"Right!" Collin threw his hands up.

"Let it go, Collin," Ron said, staring up at the giant elf who was slowly circumnavigating the outside of the Dome of Bindings. "Finn, what's that guy think he's doing?"

Finn, too, had been watching Salach's progress about the dome.

"He's looking for a weakness in the bindings," Finn said, closing his eyes to the inevitable.

"Is there a weakness?" Ron asked.

Finn nodded. "And he will find it."

"But there's got to be a way to shore things up," Ron said.

"No," Finn replied, shaking his head. "Magic has a beginning and an end. The protection above us is a web of individual bindings—very complicated, very intricate." He drew in a breath as he saw Salach change directions. "The Great Demon Lord is looking for just that one weakness in the web. That's all it will take for a creature of his power and experience to break through."

Ron took Finn into his own aura. He felt the terror . . . and something else . . . resignation.

"No!" Ron said, pulling Finn from the white throne into his arms. "There's no way! I will not let you be harmed!" he said, feeling Finn press against him.

"Ron," Finn whispered, looking up into the face of his human love. "He is too powerful. We cannot win a battle with him."

"Baby?" Ron sat Finn back onto the hard, white marble throne. "It ain't over 'till it's over!"

Suddenly the air around them was filled with a blazing

crimson light as if an inferno had descended on them. All eyes went to the dome as a tremendous clap of thunder followed. The dome above seemed to shimmer in response, but it quickly recovered its form, unharmed.

"See?" Ron cried. "No luck. He can't get through!"

"He is just testing the strength," Finn said softly. "Looking for any small hesitation in the dome's recovery that would signal weakness."

"So what do we do," asked Claire. "Just stand here and wait?"

Finn shrugged.

Another clap of thunder shook the ground beneath their feet. Above them, the Great Lord's growling concentration had morphed to a fanged grin of exultation.

"It's done!" Finn cried out, covering his face.

Again, the dome shimmered through the spectrum. A small circle of clarity unwarped by the convexity of the dome, began to form at the apex.

"There!" Ron shouted, pointing to the widening hole in the bindings.

"Weapons up, boys!" Claire ordered, pulling her own pistol from her waistband.

The demon lord's wings fanned the air, and he backed away from the dome, hovering at a great height above the temple.

"Go, my pets!" the Great Lord Salach commanded. He signaled to the dark, misshapen creatures of blackness that swirled about him. "Bring me the white wing!"

The High Priest Bolcán clapped his hands excitedly, saliva dripping from his mouth.

The *Phooka* dove for the ever widening breach in the bindings, streaking through it. One, or at least it seemed to be one of the creatures, inadvertently brushed against the activated and now highly agitated bindings surrounding the new portal. It was instantly dissolved in the familiar screech of pain.

The first two to approach the temple platform were dispatched in a beam of ultraviolet light from Collin and Kane's laser guns. The remaining *Phooka* halted their advance and hovered at a distance in apparent surprise and, by their occasionally visible bared fangs, great anger.

"Good shot, guys!" Ron said, stepping in front of them. 'How it's my turn!"

Ron straightened, raising his hands, palms facing the creatures. His mottled skin darkened and a surge of primal energy rose up from the earth below, through the natural stone platform, and into Ron's body as if he were a lightning rod. The air crackled with electromagnetic force until the energy released itself from Ron's hands in a blinding flash. The beam of energy rocketed like a shock wave across the intervening space, slamming the startled *Phooka* against the dome of binding's unaffected sides. Deafening *Phooka* screams echoed off the bindings as the demon creatures met their explosive dissolution.

Ron looked up at the glowering demon lord whose feral visage slowly lost its triumphant glow. Ron's middle finger pointed upward.

"Fuck you, asshole!" Ron shouted to the applause of his friends.

The Great Lord Salach snarled and growled, his angered cries cowered his elf minions surrounding the dome.

"Bolcán!" The Salach almost screamed. "Bring him! Bring me the White Wing!"

Bolcán glared at the small group of defenders within the dome. He rose over the sides of the dome to the portal his master had created.

"Ron!" Claire said. "Distract him."

Bolcán breached the dome and hovered over their heads snarling.

"I'll do more than that," Ron said.

"He is very powerful!" Finn cried in alarm.

Paying no heed, Ron again invoked the power of Mother Earth. The energy beams from his hands formed a concentrated stream of energy aimed at the elf descending on him.

Bolcán was ready and raised his own shield of bindings that blocked and appeared to absorb the stream of light from Ron. The battling forces of opposing energy roared in a stalemate.

"Let him come closer," Claire said, stepping up beside Ron.

"Closer?" Ron arched an eyebrow, not taking his eyes off the demon above him.

"Closer," Claire responded with a thin smile.

Ron backed away lightly on the strength of the energy he was releasing. With a cry of triumph from Bolcán, his own bindings inched closer to Ron as the human's energy was absorbed into the elf's shield. Bolcán descended lower and lower, snarling excitedly at his apparent success.

"Close enough!" Claire shouted raising her pistol.

She fired.

The silvered missile disappeared into Bolcán's midsection. For a moment, he appeared unaffected, but then a different look—a look of disbelief dropped like a curtain over his features. Bolcán's substance imploded and rained down onto the stone floor of the temple in steaming globules of brackish slime.

"Whoa, girl!" Ron shouted, giving Claire a high-five. "Hope you brought some heavy artillery with you!"

Claire nodded up at Salach, who had dropped almost on top of the dome, having momentarily forgotten to beat his wings, such was his state of stunned disbelief. She turned away where hopefully only Ron could hear her.

"No heavy artillery," Claire said. "Mab made some special silvered bullets for me. We've a very limited supply—not enough for that horde out there."

"Silver bullets?" Ron said, pursing his lips. "Elves and werewolves."

"Well," Claire said with a chuckle. "Mab hinted at the former being the source of the latter's legend."

"My God," Ron replied. "Now you're starting to sound like Mab."

"Someone's pissed off!" Collin piped up.

All eyes went to the demon lord.

"You dare challenge me!" The Great Lord Salach thundered.

His army of elves silenced their frightened chatter caused by the unexpected death of their powerful high priest. Their feral snarls returned, bolstered by their great lord's anger.

"What now?" Kane said, nervously eyeing the agitated horde.

"I will have what I came for!" Salach boomed, rising above the hole he had created in the Dome of Bindings— a whole that was now a good two meters in circumference.

"If he comes through that hole," Claire began. "I've got him for sure!"

Claire was silenced by a deafening explosion of thunder accompanied by another flash of blinding, blood-colored light.

"Again!" the Great Lord's voice echoed like a sonic boom.

Again the thunder and fiery light struck the Dome of Bindings, causing the temple defenders to stumble in the ensuing earthquake. The dome lost its transparent, lens-like quality and the undulating ropes of magic became visible, straining to hold their waning connections.

"Again!" Lord Salach's entire being became a conduit for his demonic power.

The burning red, almost liquid light exploded from Salach's body and poured over the Dome of Bindings, consuming the strands of *Fey* magic.

Ron and his friends watched as the sides of the dome dissolved downward until there was nothing standing between them and the elven hordes, much less the elf lord's seemingly inexhaustible power.

"It's over!" wailed Finn, collapsing into the marble throne.

Ron made himself a shield in front of Finn. He stood at his full height. A flood of adrenaline flexed his muscles against the paper thin jigsaw puzzle that was his fragmented skin. Claire was down on one knee, her pistol aimed, for now, at the Great Lord Salach, who hovered out of her range, cachinnating in vain mirth at his own sense of invincibility.

"Kill the humans!" Salach commanded to his troops. "And bring me the White Wing!"

"Shit!" Collin said at a pitch that made his voice crack.

"Shit!" Ron echoed, as the horde of bestial elves poured into the temple of standing stones, screeching and slathering.

The witches danced in slow processional about the

circle, pausing as each covenant reached one of the four directional nodes in the circle. Like a game of musical chairs, the odd witch who did not end up on one of the major or minor nodes, danced along the inner labyrinth, spiraling and spinning round and round, until reaching the center, where they served as a conduit for Mother Earth to raise the Cone of Power that was a witch's stock and trade. The others, in turn, addressed the earth spirit particular to their node or direction, invoking its power and protection.

With each pass, the powerful bindings multiplied about the circle, climbing higher into the night sky before meeting at a point, a lens that would focus the power of the Goddess into the circle's center just as a magnifying glass focuses sunlight. As the moon rose higher, the witches' ecstatic dance became less ordered. Their hands waved in a chaos of sacred, magical gestures. The monotone pitch of their voices rose and fell randomly.

"Frieda!" Mab called out, sensing a weakness in the balance of power. "Dear, you're not keeping up."

The ancient witch sucked in her breath.

"It's my arthritis," Frieda responded, rubbing her leathered bony hip with gnarled fingers. "I'll take over the center if that's okay."

"It that wise?" Agatha asked from her position at the Northern Node.

"I can handle it!" Frieda rasped defensively.

"You're eighty-eight, dear," Agatha said.

"The circle needs an agile body," Frieda said. "The center needs an agile spirit." She waved away the other witch currently manning the labyrinth's center. "You may be younger, Agatha, but my spirit is the strongest here. In the world of the Goddess, the experience of age trumps a good dance any day."

The other witches cackled with laughter. Agatha joined in without any sign of slight.

"When she's right, she's right," Agatha said.

"Okay then," Mab said. "Back to work!"

The witches' circumambulation proceeded at the same feverish pitch as when it had left off. Frieda stretched her body out over Mother Earth, embracing both the earth and the Cone of Power in her aura. In turn, Mother Earth embraced her elder child and the ensuing flood of energy doubled the depth and height of the witches' Cone of Power.

"Blessed be, Frieda!" shouted Mab in amazement.

"Blessed be, Frieda!' echoed the other witches, acknowledging the old witch's power.

Frieda laughed in gratitude, more for Mother Earth's easing of the pain in her hip, than the accolades of her sisters.

"Goddess hear us!" May intoned, returning to the altar.

"Goddess hear us!" the coven echoed.

Mab took up the sacred chalice, a silver cup inset in a bowl of jasper.

"Mother Earth!" Mab continued in her powerful contralto. "Join with us!"

"Join with us, Mother Earth!" the circle of witches responded.

"We call upon you Brigit, and upon you, Danu," Mab continued. "We call upon you, Banda, Fodla, and Eriu! Lend your mighty power to our cause!"

"Brighid, Danu, Banda, Fodla, Eriu!" the witches cried out. "We call upon you!"

Mab walked the inside of the circle, pouring out a libation of herbs at each node. The Cone of Power rising from the center of the circle, now entered the visible spectrum. The sounds of the surrounding forest and meadow were silent except for the cold wind that spiraled about the outside of the circle—a physical manifestation of the surrounding, protective bindings.

The full moon approached its zenith. Its size was like that of a harvest or super moon, commanding a cloudless and starless black sky.

"Come Goddess!" Mab shouted raising her left hand in the sacred sign.

In her right hand she pointed her athame to the rising moon.

"Come Goddess!" the coven echoed, raising their hands and athames in kind. "Come Goddess!" They repeated over and over in a building crescendo as the moon drew immediately overhead. "Come Goddess!" The shout went up.

A cacophony of shrieks split the night air. An inky swirl of animated shadows blotted out the view of the surrounding countryside.

"*Phooka*!" shouted Edith, interrupting the sacred litany.

"Keep at it, sisters!" Mab shouted back. "The bindings will hold as long as we don't get distracted!"

The dark cloud of elven demons pounded against the powerful magic that protected the Wiccan circle.

"Come Goddess!" The coven continued the chant. "Come Caillech! Come Morrighan! Send your power and protection!"

The frustrated *Phooka* swirled about the circle boundaries. Their angry screams and hissing failed to deter the experienced Wiccans. The swirling Cone of Power intensified, becoming a tornado like vortex of gleaming energy.

The chanting stopped. The witches' arms lowered—

outstretched to their sides. The Cone of Power began to ascend above the circle.

"Is it strong enough, Mab?" Agatha called out!"

"We need more!" Mab shouted back above the annoying screeching of the *Phooka*. "We'll have to send everything!"

"Including the bindings?" Dorothy said in alarm.

Mab nodded.

"But the *Phooka*!"

"First things first!" Mab shouted, kneeling on the earth.

The other witches followed suit.

"Goddess!" Mab invoked. "Send forth your Cone of Power. Undo what was done. Free what was imprisoned. Restore the balance!"

Again her arms went up.

"We send you forth!" Mab cried out.

The witches' arms raised skyward in turn.

"We send you forth!" they shouted in unison.

The earth itself seemed to groan. The Cone of Power erupted in flashes of lightning and thunder, disappearing into another plane—and with it the bindings protecting the circle and its inhabitants. The circle of witches collapsed to the ground, drained of power.

The swarming Phooka had backed away, frightened by the Cone of Power's explosive release. They recovered quickly and their attack began. A laser-like beam of dark energy targeted the coven leader and Mab tried weakly to cast a binding spell of protection. It only succeeded in bending the destructive beam which struck her hard in the shoulder rather than the true target, her heart. Mab screamed in pain causing the other witches collapsed about the circle to rally.

"Stay down sisters!"

The shout startled the circle of fallen witches. All attention went to the center of the circle where the old witch, Frieda, stood, bathed in a bubble of silver light.

"Stay down, girls."

Frida raised her athame, sweeping it in a circle as the cloud of *Phooka* descended on her.

"*An bandia ceangal tú,*" Frieda cried out, fearless. "*Domhain a mháthair dhíbirt agat, agus solas scrios tú!*"

The bubble of light about her exploded outward like a band saw, cutting through the roiling, screeching *Phooka*. In an instant, the air cleared. The surrounding landscape returned into view. The sound of crickets chirping broke through the momentary silence.

"Frieda!" Agatha shouted in surprise.

Frieda only shrugged. "The flesh is weak," she said, "but the spirit still packs a hell of a wallop!"

"Frieda, you're one major bitchy witch!" Even through her pain, Mab's laughter was strong.

Dorothy joined the others in laughter even as she applied an improvised poultice to the angry burn still steaming from Mab's shoulder.

Mab sat up, nodding her admiration for her coven sisters.

"We did it!" Mab said, grimacing at her shoulder. "We did what we set out to do."

"Well!" Agatha said, moving to support Mab from behind. "Do you think it was enough?"

"Whatever the Goddess wills," Mab responded. "Now the last thing," she said. "Give me an aura boost, girls."

The coven surrounded Mab laying hands on her. Mab closed her eyes, pulling all her concentration to bear.

"Claire," Mab whispered into the night. "It's time, Claire. Blessed be!"

Chapter 21

"I can't shoot them all!" Claire shouted above the din as the army of elves surrounding the Temple circle began to breach the standing stones, spears raised.

"Lord *Ardsagart!*" Ron yelled out. "Order the elders behind the platform for protection!"

The *Fei* high priest signaled and the elders blinked in and out of time and space to a position behind the stone platform.

"The rest of you," Ron ordered. "Behind the thrones."

Claire, Kane and Collin obeyed without question. Claire kept her gun at the ready, wishing that haughty Salach would drop down a little closer.

"Finn!" Ron called over his shoulder. "Please get back with the others!"

"It is no use," Finn said with flat resignation. "Let the Demon Lord have me, Ron. Perhaps he will allow all of you to return to your world unharmed."

Finn's words only strengthened Ron's resolve.

"There is no way," Ron said. "General Darragh!"

The *Fei* general turned. "Lord Ron?"

"Move your men to both sides of the platform. Don't let any of those scumbags through to attack our flank!"

"And the center?" the general asked, eyeing the slow, deliberate march of the elves into the sanctuary.

"I've got that," Ron said, staring up at the Dark Lord, hovering beyond reach overhead.

As the *Fei* soldiers took their positions, Ron, once again, joined his aura with the earth below.

"Any sign of Kian?" Ron asked, now focusing his concentration at the invaders ahead.

"He and Nolan are still MIA!" Collin called out from behind the marble thrones.

Ron took a deep breath. He had weakened since his last use of power and his craving for the royal nectar was overwhelming. Still the ring on his thumb hummed and vibrated.

"Ron, "Finn said from behind. "You're too weak to defeat him. I can feel your need for my cup."

Ron nodded to himself, not to agree with Finn, but to acknowledge the ring as the source of his power and not any reliance on his own physical strength.

"I'll show you weak!" Ron said with grim determination. His voice was drowned out by the growling shouts of the elves as they began their attack on the run.

Ron pulled energy from the earth like an infant at its mother's breast. He let it fill him until he wondered if his splintering, physical self would rip apart. His palms went up, aimed out at the war-frenzied elves bearing down on the platform.

"*Ní gá duit a mbaineann anseo!*" Ron thundered over the war shrieks of the elves.

The earth accepted Ron, not as a vessel, but as a conduit. Power erupted up, into, and out of Ron in a volcanic blast. The shock wave of elemental energy decimated the elf attack. Elf bodies littered the Temple floor in pieces that slowly dissolved into dark globules that seeped through the seams on the stone floor. The legion of elves was reduced to less than a hundred, including those elves at both sides of the Temple who were not spared the earth's wrath.

A recoil wave of the blast threw Ron backwards into Finn's lap.

"Jesus Freakin' Christ, Ron!" Collin said, peeking out from behind the larger purple throne. "That was awesome!"

Finn sat back in shock, arms wrapped about Ron.

"What the hell just happened?" Kane said, standing to survey the damage.

"Better stay down," cautioned Claire. "Batman's still up there, and he looks super pissed!"

The Great Lord Salach hovered in stunned silence. The rage he exuded was almost palpable.

"Impossible!" Salach shrieked from the heavens. "What weapon does a puny human have to decimate my troops?" He descended at lightning speed.

As Claire raised her pistol, the elf lord made a sweeping gesture.

"Dammit!" Claire screamed, letting the pistol drop to the stone floor of the throne platform.

The small weapon glowed orange and melted into the seams between the stone pavers till there was nothing.

"Claire!" Ron jumped to his feet.

"I'm okay," Claire responded, shaking her scorched hand. "That son-of-a-bitch!"

Ron shifted his weight shakily. He felt as if his body was fighting to leave him, to melt into the stones like Claire's pistol. He felt Finn's hands on his back. Finn's aura caused a wave of physical strength from the earth into

Ron's disintegrating body, pulling the atoms back into their molecular structures. Ron steadied himself.

"Thanks, baby," Ron said over his shoulder.

"Retreat to sanctuary!" Finn ordered the troops. "See to the people!"

Reluctantly the general and his men disappeared in a blink.

Lord Salach alit in the center of the standing stone circle. His cat-like eyes fastened on Ron. He grunted to himself in satisfaction as Ron's physical weakness and the instability of the human's bodily integrity became apparent. Salach strutted slowly across the distance toward the throne platform.

"I got this!" Kane said popping up from behind the larger, empty throne.

He aimed his laser gun and a bolt of invisible ultraviolet light struck Lord Salach in the abdomen.

With his more evolved sight, Salach eyed the impotent beam of ultraviolet light with interest. He reached his taloned hand up and turned it over, back and forth in the beam. Of course, it had no effect on him.

"Fool!" Lord Salach boomed.

His laughter was a mixture of snarling growls and head shakes.

"That only works on *Phooka*, Kane," Claire said, pulling Kane back behind the darker marble throne with her and Collin.

"Oh, yeah!" Kane whispered, ducking his head down.

"Not another step!" Ron shouted, feeling a little stronger.

"How will you stop me?" the Great Lord Salach responded. "I shall disintegrate your already miserable body, and then I will eat your friends' hearts before I take my final prize!" Dark saliva slathered from his fangs as his eyes feasted on Finn. "I will have the White Wing!"

"Blah, blah, blah!" Ron said, straightening and firming his stance. "You might wanna take a second look at the piles of shit that were once your wimp-ass army, big guy!"

Salach's features darkened.

"Your powers were remarkable for a human," Salach said without any evidence of concern. "But I am the Great Lord Salach of the elven nation. Even your unusual power is no match for my own." Salach straightened to his full height with megalomaniacal pride. "It was I who defeated and killed the Purple Wing that these remnant *Fey* have barely a memory of!"

"You lie!" Finn countered, pushing Ron to the side. "The Great Purple Wing was poisoned by the traitor *Ardsagart*! You defeated no one! You would not have dared to face the *Sciathán Corcra*!"

Finn's anger took Ron by surprise. His attention left the demon elf to try and pull Finn behind him. At the sight of the White Wing suddenly exposed, Lord Salach took full advantage. He gestured a spell and the surrounding darkness coalesced into a streaming blast of furnace-like heat that billowed in a wave toward Ron.

The only warning Ron had was the buzzing vibration of the charmed ring about his thumb. Even before he could turn, the glassine bubble of energy surrounded him and the vulnerable *Fey* he had pulled into his arms.

The inky fire swallowed Ron and Finn, scorching the marble thrones behind. When the air cleared, Ron and Finn stood untouched.

"Impossible!" Lord Salach screeched.

"The cavalry has arrived!" The voice yelled out from below.

Out of the safety of the stone platform, Nolan and Kian emerged from the doorway, lugging a heavy, sparkling object between them.

"Let's get this over with!" Nolan said, bearing the weight of the object at the rear as Kian climbed the step ahead of him.

"Kian!" Finn cried. "By the goddess, what have you done?"

Kian knelt before the White Wing, signaling to Nolan to lay the object at Finn's feet.

"My Lord," Kian pleaded. "This defeated the demon lord before. It is the only hope to do it again."

"It cannot be drawn from the scabbard, much less used," Finn said in despair. "To do so, means certain death to whoever tries."

"Jeez, Nolan!" Ron said dropping to his knees. The object was having a debilitating effect on Ron. "That's the last thing we need here."

The darkness of Ron's cracked skin paled in the presence of the object. The fissures, running like the lines of a jigsaw puzzle over his body, seemed to glow with an ominous emphasis.

Finn grabbed Ron up and helped him down the stairs for some distance from the object.

"*Claíomh Solais!*" thundered Lord Salach, his eyes flashing at the sight of the fabled sword and its jewel encrusted scabbard. "*Núada* has truly blessed my victory."

"Bullshit!" Nolan yelled at the elf lord. "Ron, you're the only one who might be able to use the thing!" He pulled the sword and Kian down the steps. "You're the one with all the weird powers. If you can't work the thing, then we're all fucked!"

"Nolan!" Finn cried. "Can't you see what the Sword

of Light does to him?

"It's okay," Ron said with a grimace of pain. He released his hold on Finn. "Nolan's right. It's our only hope."

"It's killing you!" Finn said, desperately grabbing Ron's arm.

"But if I can last long enough . . ."

"I will not allow you to defile the Sword of Light, human!" Lord Salach boomed, raising his clawed hands in magical gesture.

A pulse of flaming energy exploded from the demon elf's palms. Nolan was too busy trying to pull the heavy sword the rest of the way down the steps. He didn't see the deadly energy bearing down on him.

"Nolan!" Claire screamed, realizing the intended target was not Ron.

"Wha . . ." Nolan stopped and looked up. He stumbled as the other end of the sword's scabbard clattered to the stone steps.

"Lord Nolan!" Kian cried.

The deadly missile of energy exploded in a sulfurous, intense orange light.

"Nolan!" Claire screamed again, shielding her eyes from the blast.

As the fiery light subsided, Claire looked to find Nolan, still standing.

"Ha!" Nolan straightened. "Missed me, you son-of-a-bitch!"

"Kian . . ." Finn's voice caught in his throat.

"Oh God!" Claire whispered, covering her eyes again.

"What?" Collin asked, looking about. His eyes went to the step below his feet.

The small *Fei* form lay in a fetal position, quivering. Kian's physical being began to fissure like Ron as light seemed to leak from the cracks."

"Kian!" Nolan jumped down a step and went to his knees beside Kian. "You okay little guy?"

Kian could not speak. His eyes fixed on Nolan.

"Kian?" Nolan said, pulling the boy into his arms. "Kid, what . . ." Nolan realized what had occurred. "Kid, you shouldn't have done that! You shouldn't . . ." Nolan's voice cracked into silence.

"Human fool!" Lord Salach shouted. "You have robbed me of part of my meal!" Salach's wings unfolded and he began to rise into the air. "But no matter. You will all meet the same fate as that puny *Fey*. I will feast on the White Wing over the fire of your burning carcasses!"

"No!" Ron broke free of Finn.

He pounced on the heavy gold sword and scabbard, pulling the sacred object out into the midst of the standing stones to a safe distance from the others. He screamed in agony as the polarization of his physical self and the opposing force of the *Claíomh Solais* approached critical.

"Finn!" Claire ran down the steps to the White Wing, pulling Collin with her. "Come with us," she said urgently, taking Finn by the shoulders.

Suddenly, she froze. A familiar voice spoke to her mind.

"Now, Claire," the soothing voice urged. "It's time."

Claire glanced up into the dark sky. The full moon had begun to break through the dark curtain the demon elf had evoked.

"Collin," Claire said, pushing Finn into Collin's arms. "Take him into the tunnels beneath the platform!"

"No!" Finn protested. "I will not leave Ron!"

"Take him!" Claire ordered and Collin began to wrestle the *Fei* prince across the platform.

"Pathetic humans!" Lord Salach thundered. "I will make an end of this."

"Eat shit!" Ron cried out in agony. He had the hilt of the Sword of Light firmly in his hands. "If it's the last thing I do . . ."

The sword slid from the hilt.

"Got it!" Ron shouted.

The *Claíomh Solais* flared like a sun gone nova. Ron's scream ricocheted from one giant standing stone to another. Claire could see the fissures in Ron's body expand as her friend's physical form evaporated in the flames. She pulled out the small bag of charmed herbs Mab had sent with her.

"*Saor in Aisce méid a bhí i bhfolach uair amháin!*" Claire called out to the brightening goddess overhead. "Blessed be!" She lobbed the small herbal philter at Ron.

The small charm fell into the flames that engulfed Ron. She watched her friend's form explode and then dissolve into the resulting shock wave that caused even the demon elf lord to drop from the sky.

Where Ron had been, there was now nothing except the empty scabbard that had cradled the infamous sword. It, too, was no more.

Ron!" Claire managed in a croaking whisper. Her head dropped into her hands. She had acted too late.

Finn's screams filled the temple grounds. He pushed Collin to the ground and ran for the spot Ron had last inhabited. He stood anguishing over the empty scabbard that had held Ron's destruction. Finn's face clouded into a blistering fury. He glared across the temple nave to where Lord Salach pulled himself up from the ground.

Finn could not speak, so great was his anger, grief, and despair, but those things fed the building wall of laser bright light that grew before him. Finn threw his hands out and screamed through his tears. The light exploded from him, striking the elf lord like a giant hammer. Lord Salach was knocked once more to his knees and the surrounding darkness was broken.

The demon slowly looked up. A scant smile broke over his exposed fangs.

"*Sciathán Bán!*" Salach called out, snarling. "Prepare yourself!"

Salach stood to his full height and bore down on Finn, claws outstretched to grasp his prize.

"Finn!" Claire cried out.

Nolan had picked up the enfeebled Kian and Claire was pulling them across the throne platform, hoping to make it to the room beneath and the catacomb of tunnels that ended there.

"Run!" Claire shouted as Salach closed in on his prey. "Finn!"

Chapter 22

A discrete ray of reflected moonlight opened like a dim spotlight on the place where Finn stood, the very spot where Ron had been consumed. The air swirled violently about the empty scabbard of the *Claíomh Solais*. Its amethyst inlays radiated color in the moonlight, tinting every-thing with their royal purple essence.

The Great Lord Salach was stopped in his tracks.

"What is this sorcery?" Salach demanded.

The elf lord gestured his own spell without effect.

Ah!" Salach said, assuming the obvious. "The White Wing still fights!" Salach's laughter shook the very ground beneath. "How delicious you will be!"

Finn uncovered his eyes, not understanding why Salach had not already attacked him. He stared into the swirling purple air that kept the demon elf at bay. Finn turned to Claire, but she only shrugged through her tears.

In a blink, the temple grounds were filled with the remnants of the *Fei* population, cowering as if surprised to find themselves back in dangers path. General Darragh and his soldiers were quick to dispose of the few elven drones that had escaped the human Ron's previous assault.

"General Darragh!" Finn called out. "What have you

done? I ordered the people to safety!"

"*Sciathán Bán!*" The *Ardsagart* climbed the steps and knelt before Finn, his face a mask of fear and confusion. "This was not our doing."

"*Núada* has given me a sweeter triumph!" shouted Salach, swollen with pleasure at the site of so many *Fei* morsels surrounding him. "I shall be sated with *Fei* light before the day is over."

Salach directed his magical gestures to the sky, invoking blackness to blot out the moonlight and stop the escalating hum of the ever strengthening, tornado of purple light that barred his way to the White Wing.

"I blot you out, you whore of the gods!" Salach shouted at the moon. "*Núada* commands you!"

In rebellion, the moon's intensity and size blossomed, consuming the surrounding darkness.

Salach turned on the swirling air and purple light. "Be gone!" he commanded, gesturing.

Blazing beams of Salach's orange fire exploded into the vortex of violet.

The wind subsided suddenly and Salach's derisive laughter could once again be heard.

"Fools!" The demon lord trumpeted. "I am invincible!"

As the roiling dust settled, Salach prepared to make his meal. A hovering ball of amethyst light continued to block his way. The ball coalesced into a hominid form.

"What demonic trick . . ." Salach began.

The light formed a distinct, recognizable shape.

"Ron!" a wide-eyed Claire screamed at the form of her friend . . . and yet . . . different. "Ron!" she cried out again.

Ron stood between Salach and Finn, bathed in a violet aura, his eyes a blaze of amethyst radiance.

"Impossible!" Salach said, snarling.

Ron's hands outstretched. In the same moment his back arched and enormous, monarch-like wings unfurled into the surrounding space—ephemeral, transparent, purple wings.

Finn sank to the platform in a faint. A roar went up from the assembled *Fey* who dropped to their knees in stunned obeisance.

Mutterings of "*Sciathán Corcra*" rumbled through the crowd, firing the demon lord's anger.

"You abomination!" the Great Lord Salach roared, pointing a glistening talon at the figure bathed in purple light. "The *Sciathán Corcra* is no more. I destroyed him ages ago." He bared his fangs. "Do you think I am fooled, impressed, or in fear of this counterfeit?"

"Do you presume that the *Sciathán Corcra* is but one *Fey*?" the violet phantom said in a hollow, otherworldly voice.

The Ron-like entity walked unhurried across the temple grounds toward the elf Lord.

"Is that really Ron?" Collin whispered.

Claire had dropped to Finn's side and was trying to rouse him.

"It's the real Ron." Claire lifted Finn's head, patting the White Wing's face. "The true Ron."

"I am heir to *Sciathán Corcra*," Ron pronounced evenly. "Just as surely as the *Sciathán Bán* is renewed from generation to generation." He turned his head to gaze at Finn. "Wake up, my love."

Finn's eyes blinked, focusing on Claire looking down at him.

"Claire," Finn said shakily.

"Get up Finn," Claire urged. "Your future husband wants you up!"

"Puny human heretic!" Salach shouted, spitting saliva. "Because you can conjure the Purple Wing's light means nothing." He turned on the cowering *Fei Ardsagart*. "Who has conjured this empty apparition of one I have already destroyed?"

Claire had pulled Finn to his feet.

"Ron?" Finn said, staring at the inconceivable in front of him.

"This is not our doing!" the *Ardsagart* said, shaking his head at the apparition. "This is not *Fei* magic."

Ron turned again to smile at his beloved Finn.

"I am the one you love," Ron said with soothing calm. "The one you've been promised to."

"But . . ." Finn leaned back against Claire. "How? You are physical . . . human. I saw your body incinerated—I saw you die!"

"No, love," Ron said. "That was only a covering . . . a shroud of physical substance that needed to be shed—to release my light!"

"Ron," Claire interjected. "I hope that is you, but . . . you seem so different."

"I have regained most of my *Clann* memories," Ron responded. His mauve and periwinkle wings undulated in the surrounding violet haze. "The goddess . . ." He gazed up at the moon ". . .and your Wiccan craft have released me."

"Glad to be of help," Claire said, giving Finn a tight hug.

"It hurt," Ron said, cocking his head to one side with a sardonic smile.

"Blame Mab," Claire responded with a shrug and a smile.

"Enough!" Salach snarled. "It is clear, now, that the

witch has invoked this . . . this thing!" He raised his claws. "Revoke your spell, witch, or I will consign you to the flames!"

"I don't think so!" Ron raised a quicker hand and the purple field of protection left him and enveloped the entirety of the throne platform.

Salach released a barrage of powerful spells that exploded against the protective bubble without effect. This continued for several minutes until even the Great Lord Salach was convinced he could not penetrate the powerful binding surrounding the witch.

Salach turned on Ron.

"Whatever you are," the Demon Lord said, "you have sacrificed your own safety to save these worthless *Fey*!" Streams of sweat dropped from the elf lord's brow. "Whatever this witch has done, I can and will undo!"

The demonic elf's wings extended into the air and he pounced through the air at Ron. Space seemed to blink and Ron was then behind Salach. The elf turned his attack, but once again, in some instantaneous warpping of space, Ron was suddenly beyond Salach's attack. The repeated elusive-ness of his prey inflamed the elf lord into a savage fury. Ron met each attack with alert impassivity, anticipating each assault and changing location like a quantum particle.

Still, in his own way, Lord Salach had also been observant and had sensed a pattern in Ron's evasive maneuvers. Salach Feigned an attack, then turned suddenly to the spot where Ron reappeared. Talons extended, Salach sought to sever the human's head from its body.

Ron ducked with a speed that belied the sight of the onlookers. He countered Salach's swing with a right hook of his own. The sound of cracking bone still echoed, even after the elf lord had landed in a heap, knocked some thirty feet from the fist that had hammered him.

A cheer went up from human and *Fey* alike.

Salach pulled himself up from his disgrace. He stared wide-eyed at the impossible that had accomplished the equally impossible.

Ron closed the distance between them.

"That was for Claire," Ron said.

Salach straightened. He unhinged his broken jaw and roared. Once again his leathery wings opened and pushed against the air with a thunderclap. He circled Ron at blinding speed.

"I will have the White Wing!" Salach screamed. "I will have the Sword of Light!"

From a great height, Salach began his supersonic descent, claws slashing the air in front of him.

"I am the *Claíomh Solais*!" Ron shouted back.

The Purple Wing raised his hand and there arose an enormous humming sound, not unlike the sound made by the now absent thumb ring Ron had once worn. A projection of solid light prismed from Ron's hand. The surrounding inhabitants gasped at the sight of the familiar gold and jewel encrusted hilt clasped firmly in Ron's raised hand.

Even the Great Lord Salach could not defy Newton's first law of motion. Ron swung the sacred sword of the *Tuatha Dè Danann* at the rocketing elven lord whose own downward momentum the demon could not reverse quick enough, Lightening broke from the light blade in all directions as it sliced through the blur that was Salach.

The demon lord's head went in a different direction than the trajectory taken by his body. The ancient, dark forces released from the headless corpse detonated into the atmosphere, being just as quickly washed into nothingness by the shimmering moonlight that bathed the temple grounds.

The remnants of the *Fei* people stood stunned. The ensuing silence was broken only by the continued humming of the *Claíomh Solais*, raised high into the air in the steely hand of the violet winged victor.

In another instant, the light sword retracted, absorbed back into its new scabbard—the new and powerful prince—the youth that still held a striking resemblance to the human, Ron Maguire. This luminescent creature stood with its back to the stunned crowd of *Fey* and human alike.

Gradually and with great calm, Ron turned to face the confused onlookers. His majestic wings slowly fanned against the air.

Claire slowly descended the steps of the throne platform, staring at her friend, noting the familiar shape and face and smile, but also marveling at the tapestry of changes; the muted mauve skin, the pointed ears, and the all-encompassing halo of purple, pied wings. More importantly, with her new Wiccan skills she could see that Ron's once, very human aura was now decidedly unhuman, dense, powerful.

"Ron?" Claire asked, approaching the haunting figure cautiously. "Ron, is that still you?"

Ron arched his back and the broad, gauzy wings folded and withdrew into his shoulder blades. His surrounding shield of amaranthine light dissipated. He looked at his friends, smiling, but was distracted by Collin's not-so-subtle gesturing. Ron looked down at the terminal point of Collin's line of sight and gesturing. He shrugged at his own overt, now hairless nudity. With a chuckle, he nodded a spell and was immediately clothed in a royal purple tunic, hemmed with gold thread at the arms and thighs.

"Sorry about that," Ron said with a sheepish grin.

He went straight for Finn, enfolding the White Wing in a tight embrace.

"It's over," Ron said softly into Finn's ear.

Finn returned the clinging embrace.

"Ron, I . . ." A frown broke over Finn's face and he pushed Ron away. "You!" he said sharply. "How?"

"Finn." Ron reached out for slender, young *Fey*. "It's okay. Everyone is safe. You're safe."

"But, you . . ." Finn continued, backing away. "You are human, but . . ."

Finn looked to Claire and then to Collin as if for help. He turned back to Ron.

"Your tunic . . . your . . . wings!" Finn said. "Purple!"

"Check that," Ron replied with a wink.

"How can you now be *Fey*? How . . ." Finn backed up another few steps. "How can you call yourself . . . *Sciathán Corcra*!"

"A little help over here!" A voice cried out from the platform steps below.

"Nolan!" Claire gasped. "Kian!" She ran down the steps.

Finn followed her, nervously side-stepping Ron.

"Somebody do something!" Nolan said, his voice cracking in despair.

"Kian," Claire said softly, kneeling beside the little *Fey*.

Kian's eyes blinked barely open as he mewed softly. His body was faded like a blurry photo. Light continued to pulse from the wound in his chest.

"Ron!" Nolan shouted. "Do something. The kid's dying!"

Ron descended the steps slowly to stand behind Finn who was stroking the boy's pale hair.

"Kian," Finn said bending over the boy. "My little Kian." His tears showered over the boy.

"Ron, you gotta help him!" Nolan was too overcome with his own feelings to notice the streams down his own cheeks. "Please, Ron. You're the one with all the mojo!"

Ron shrugged.

"There must be something," Nolan demanded, unconsciously rocking the young *Fey* in his lap. "We have to do something!"

Finn put a hand gently on Nolan's shoulder.

"He is hurt too badly," Finn said, shaking his head. "There is nothing we can do but stay with him until he is no more."

"No!" Nolan almost shouted, trembling with anger and despair. "That's not good enough!" He shook Kian. "Don't you dare die, kid! Don't you . . ." He pulled the boy to his chest as helplessness overcame his anger.

"It should've been me," Nolan managed through clenched teeth. "He jumped in front of me—that lightning bolt was meant for me!"

"Sweetheart," Claire said, taking Nolan's face in her hands. "He loved you."

"But . . . he knew I couldn't . . . he knew I loved you and that . . ." He met Claire's gaze unable to continue.

"It doesn't matter, baby," Claire said, still holding his face. "That doesn't mean he couldn't still love you . . . or that you couldn't still love him." She put a hand on Kian's shoulder. "Immature love though it was, it was still love."

"Ron!" Nolan croaked. "Please! Try something!"

"Nolan," Finn said through tears. "Nothing can be done. I have his light, but only . . ." He stopped.

"Only what?" Nolan asked sharply. "What?"

Ron knelt beside Finn. "He means that only the joining of the *Sciathán Bán* and the *Sciathán Corcra* can change the course of Kian's end."

"How do you know this?" Finn stammered, looking at Ron in disbelief. "That . . . that is just a legend. "Not in a thousand moons—"

"Until now," Ron said softly. "What is the formula? How will you heal him?"

"I . . ." Finn searched his *Clann* memory. "With the people's light. I must reconceive his being and pour that light back into him."

"Do it!" Nolan said, pleading.

"I . . ." Finn looked at his dying page. "I cannot," he said, unable to look at Nolan. "Only the Purple Wing can gather the people's light."

"And then?" Ron asked.

"The Purple Wing would give it to me. I am the conduit. The people are the source—the Purple Wing the reservoir. Only the *Sciathán Corcra* is strong enough to take the power into himself and focus it to his will."

"How?" Ron asked, standing.

"The *Bailiú Mór*," Finn replied, shaking his head. "The Great Gathering . . . but it has never—"

"*Ardsagart!*" Ron shouted for the *Fei* priest. "Assemble the people for the *Bailiú Mór!*"

The *Ardsagart* rushed forward, still unable to accept what his eyes had seen.

"That is a sacrilege without the *Sciathán Corcra*," the *Ardsagart* protested. "The gathering of power will destroy a human!"

"Do I look human to you?" Ron asked. He raised an eyebrow to emphasize his sarcasm.

"Consider what you ask," The *Ardsagart* replied, straightening. "If you are not what you now claim, the power will also destroy the *Sciathán Bán!*"

Ron sensed Finn's fear. He turned to the White Wing,

embracing him in his aura.

"Finn," Ron's mind spoke in love. "Know me and trust me."

"But . . ." Finn's mouth quivered. "I love you, Ron."

"Then?"

"We haven't been properly joined?"

"Haven't we?" Ron caressed his love's thoughts and felt Finn surrender to him.

"*Ardsagart!*" Ron commanded, turning to face the priest and the remnant of *Fey* gathering into the temple about the platform. "*Bailiú Mór!*"

Ron released his wings in an explosion of purples.

The *Ardsagart* fell to his knees in fear. "*Bailiú Mór!*" he cried out to the gathering *Fey*.

The multitude of the *Fey Clann* fanned out. Taking to their wings they rose into the air and hovered just above the stone floor. As from a single mind, an audible and tactile chant rose up from them in a contrapuntal unison.

"Ron," Finn whispered, trembling noticeably. "I have never done this."

Ron smiled at him. "That's what you said those few nights ago in my bed."

Finn looked at Ron without understanding.

"As I recall," Ron continued, "you were pretty damn good!"

Finn giggled and stilled. He bent over Kian, kissing the boy lightly on the cheek, resting a hand over Kian's wound.

"*Sciathán Corcra!*" Finn shouted, releasing his own white, gossamer wings. "Witness your *Sciathán Bán!*" He held up the palm of his other hand to Ron.

"*Sciathán Bán!*" Ron responded, raising his own palm at Kian. "Your love is mine and my love is yours!"

The hum of wings accompanied the *Clann*'s rising chant.

"Let's have it!" Ron shouted. "*Tabhair dom do éadrom!*"

The assembly's palms rose as one and a kaleidoscope of light prismed forth striking Ron with a force that echoed off the standing stones like a cannon barrage.

Ron cried out and his body was pulled up into the air. His amethyst skin glowed, fighting to absorb the blinding luminescence assaulting him.

"*Páirt a ghlacadh dom!*" Ron chanted, his voice undercut with unfamiliar, other-worldly overtones.

"*Tá mé i duit!*" Finn cried out in response.

In a crack of electromagnetic excitation, a focused beam of purple light emitted from Ron's palm to Finn's. Finn's eyes widened preternaturally as the immense and focused power funneled into him. He looked to Kian as a brilliant purple aurora engulfed the boy's frail body.

Nolan did not release his hold on Kian and the excess energy engulfed him like a lightning strike. He gritted his teeth against the pain, refusing to let Kian's body fall.

"He's healing!" Claire shouted above the din as the rip in Kian's chest began to meld. "Hold on Nolan!"

Just as quickly as it had begun, the influx of *Fei* power to Ron stopped. Ron's feet settled back to the platform and his wings again retracted. Finn, too, pulled his wings in and sat back, studying the effect of the rebirthing. Kian remained still and silent, cradled in Nolan's arms.

"Okay!" Nolan shook off the prickly sensations in his skin. "That was different." He squeezed Kian in his arms. "Kid? Hey . . . kid?"

Kian remained motionless, his head resting under Nolan's chin.

"What's wrong?" Nolan shook Kian. "Wake up, kid?"

The previous hope he had harbored left him. "Claire?" he said, his face clouding with the rising dread.

Claire reached out to him, but couldn't speak. Tears once more traversed her cheeks.

Nolan patted the *Fei* boy's cheek.

"Come on, kid, wake up!" he pled. "Wake up!"

Finn looked up to Ron and shook his head sadly. Ron stepped down and wrapped his arms about Finn.

"We tried, Finn," Ron said, kissing Finn's ear as he hugged him. "We . . ." He paused, closing his eyes. "What the . . . the little shit!"

A slight smile broke the edges of Ron's mouth.

"What?" Finn asked in confusion.

"Nothing," Ron replied. "Nolan," he began. "You'll have to kiss him."

"Wha . . ." Nolan stared at Ron. "What are you talking about?"

"Kiss him," Ron repeated. "Like Prince Charming and Sleeping Beauty."

"What the hell do you—"

"Just do it, Nolan," Claire said, slapping Nolan on the arm. "Kiss the boy. If it breaks this curse, kiss him!"

"But . . ." Nolan looked from one of his friends to the other. "You gotta be kidding!"

"You want him to wake up?" Ron asked. "Then finish the rebirthing and kiss the kid."

Nolan stared at them. Finally, he looked down at the motionless boy in his arms who had sacrificed himself to save Nolan.

"Nolan," Claire said gently. "Even a father will kiss his child. Do that for Kian."

"Okay." Nolan sighed, resigned to his duty. "Everyone turn around."

"Bullshit!" Collin said. "This is something I gotta see."

"Collin!" Claire's glare brooked no argument.

"Okay, okay," Collin said and turned away.

Nolan nodded to Claire. "Turn a—"

"Do it!" Claire ordered, pointing her finger at him. "Now!"

Nolan shook his head, trying to prepare himself.

"What's a kiss going to accomplish?" Finn whispered to Ron. "There's nothing in the *Bailiú Mór* about—"

"It will wake Kian up," Ron responded quickly, trying to hide his smile.

"But . . ."

Ron pressed his lips against Finn's, silencing him.

"Now, Nolan!" Claire insisted.

"Okay, okay!"

Nolan gently turned the boy's face up to his and lightly pecked Kian on the cheek.

"Dammit, Nolan!" Claire pounded a fist on Nolan's knee. "On the lips, dumbass!"

"All right!" Nolan gritted his teeth. He held his breath and clenched his eyes shut. He leaned in, kissing Kian firmly on the lips.

Nothing.

"Well?" Nolan shot his eyes at Ron. "What's up? You said this would bring him to."

"Oh, I assure you, Kian's okay now." Ron tried unsuccessfully not to laugh.

"But . . ."

"Kian," Ron chided the boy. "Open your eyes this instant!"

"I don't understand!" Nolan stared at Ron and then down at the boy in his arms. "What's . . ."

Kian's eyes fluttered and the boy grinned up at Nolan.

"He's okay!" Claire shouted out in relief.

"You . . ." Nolan sat the boy up in his lap.

Something about the look behind Kian's broad smile told the whole story.

"You little fucker!" Nolan shook the boy by the shoulders. "You were okay even before I . . . I . . ."

"Kissed me!" Kian said in swooning triumph.

"Kian!" Claire shook her finger at the boy, but was unable to stop giggling.

"You knew, didn't you?" Nolan glared at Ron.

Ron laughed, pulling Finn up like a shield between himself and Nolan.

"He deserved a kiss," Ron said, "after what he did for you."

"What the hell are you doing?" Nolan spotted Collin with his cellphone at the ready. "You son-of-a—"

"Relax," Collin said, quickly pocketing his cellphone. "I was just videoing a little keepsake of our adventures."

'Dammit!" Nolan shoved Kian into Claire's arms. "You give me that cellphone now!" He jumped to his feet.

"Chill out, big guy, I've already uploaded it," Collin protested, laughing.

"What?" Nolan's fists clenched

"You know," Collin said. "Facebook, YouTube, Instagram . . ."

"I'll kill you, asshole!" Nolan started for the smaller teen.

"Hold on, Nolan," Claire said, stepping in between them.

"But, Claire . . ."

"Think about it, Nolan," Claire said, holding him back. "There's no cellphone signal here."

Nolan stopped struggling with her.

"She is right, Lord Nolan," Finn said. "And *Fey* cannot be photographed."

Nolan straightened. "Asshole!" he said to Collin.

Nolan started to turn, but found Kian's arms suddenly wrapped about his waist.

Kian looked up at him, starry-eyed with juvenile love.

"Now, Lord Nolan," Kian said. "We can be together."

"Shit." Nolan sighed. "Look, kid—"

"That's right," Claire interjected, stroking the young boy's hair. "You and Nolan will be friends forever."

She leaned in to kiss Nolan.

Kian gasped, wide-eyed.

"Hey!" Claire said with a chuckle. "You stole a kiss. Now it's my turn."

"Lord Nolan is much loved." Kian grinned up at her.

"That he is," Claire agreed.

"Jesus H. Christ!" Nolan said, staring up at the crystal blue sky.

"And you, Lord White Wing," Kian said. "You have your Purple Wing."

Finn leaned back into Ron's arms.

"It is true," he said, accepting the caresses of Ron's lips on his neck. "I do not know how, but it is true."

"I can help with that," Claire said.

"Mab?" Ron asked.

"Who else?" Claire laughed. "After I described all your . . . shall we say, symptoms, she got rather hyperactive. Have you ever heard of a changeling?"

Finn broke the ensuing silence.

"At the time of the great war and exodus from our homeland," Finn said, "the noble families secreted their seed in human form, and placed them in the care of unsuspecting humans. This was to protect the child from discovery by agents of the Demon Lord."

"That's right," Claire said. "But, of course, human mythology took that reality and couched it in negative terms with stories of fairies switching human children for fairy children.

"So," Ron said. "Mab's conclusion was that I was a changeling?"

"Of course!" Finn reacted, throwing his arm about Ron. "Now this makes sense."

"So," Ron said, tickling Finn's sides, "you're now okay with the fact that I've been unconsciously *Fey* all along?"

"Hidden in human form," Claire said. "Mab believed the *Fei* light was locked in a material matrix."

"My body, you mean?"

"Your . . . how shall I put it . . . messing around with Finn . . ." Claire paused until the laughter of the others settled. "Anyway, that created a conflict between your *Fei* essence and your human body."

"So, I was gonna *come out* as *Fey* eventually in any event?"

"Not exactly." Claire felt another arm encircle her as Nolan stood by her. "You were in danger of dissolution."

"Well," Ron said, "Love do make a guy crazy."

"Obviously," Claire said, batting her eyebrows at him.

"Sorry guys," Collin said. "But there's still a problem with all this."

The group stared at Collin.

"Come on!" Collin persisted. "If the Purple Wing was killed centuries ago, how could Ron possibly be his . . . heir, or whatever."

"Legend was that the Purple Wing and the White Wing had birthed before the exodus," Finn said softly, looking into Ron's eyes. "They must have hidden the child's light in human form. The light cannot die. It would pass down from generation to generation until released." He touched Ron's cheek. "Or it would die with a childless host."

"So," Ron said with a chuckle, "I'm actually the Purple Wing's great-great-great-etc. grandson."

"Yes," Finn said, tucking his head under Ron's chin. "You are very great."

"It took a special, powerful spell to break the hold that matter had over your *Fei* self," Claire reminded him.

"Ah," Ron said, nodding. "Spells. Mab's specialty."

"Lucky was the changeling given into the care of a human practicing the Old Religion," Claire said.

"It was luck in many respects to have Mab for a mom." Ron winked at Claire. "And to have a good friend like you to stand by me."

"Hey!" Collin said, waving his plastic laser gun. "What about the rest of us?"

"All of you!" Ron gestured to the group. "The *Fei* people owe you all a debt of gratitude."

Ron turned to face the assembled *Fey*. Again his wings rose up in a regal display—violet, periwinkle, pomegranate, mauve, and lilac—significantly larger than any of the other *Fey* whose wings expanded in response. The Sword of Light once again was held out in Ron's hand, blazing and sparkling as only the legendary *Claíomh Solais* could.

"The threat is over!" Ron said to the people in a voice confident and consoling. "The Demon Lord of the elves is no more. We will celebrate our victory and mourn our noble dead."

A great stir went up from the crowd.

"The time of fear is over!" Ron announced, letting his powerful aura envelope the thousands gathered at his feet.

"I am Oberon," he said firmly, glancing briefly back at his human friends. "Your *Sciathán Corcra*!"

He motioned to Finn to join him.

"And my *Sciathán Bán* is with me!"

A joyous cry, like none ever heard by humans before, went up from the *Fei* people. Wings of every color beat the air, sparkling like iridescent sequins across the horizon.

Oberon's wings withdrew and he took Finn's hand, returning to his human friends.

"So," Collin said, grinning. "It's Oberon now?"

"Yep," Oberon responded with a shrug.

"I don't have to remind you . . . that's the name you used to almost kill anyone for using."

"Yep," Oberon repeated, laughing.

"Means, King of the Fairies," Nolan said, pointing and smirking.

"Nolan," Claire cautioned.

"Not a problem, Claire," Oberon interjected. He gave Finn a quick kiss. "It's a name I plan to own up to now."

"What's a king?" Kian piped.

"The Purple Wing," Finn said.

"King of the Fairies." Oberon shrugged. "I kinda like that."

"Well, honey," Claire said. "You don't really have any choice in the matter now."

"Touché!" Oberon reached to take her hand. "I love you, you know that." He pulled Claire into his arms.

"Hey!" Nolan protested.

Oberon released Claire, laughing, and sidled over to Nolan.

"You don't have anything to worry about, big guy," he said, opening his arms for a hug.

"I ain't gonna kiss you!" Nolan said, holding up a

hand.

"Aw come on, big guy!" Oberon said above the ensuing sniggering. "Just wanna hug."

"Hell!"

"Take it like a man, Nolan," Oberon said, pushing aside the protesting arm.

He pulled Nolan into a bear hug and released him just as quickly.

"Damn you, Maguire!" Nolan began.

"That's Lord Maguire to you!" Oberon said, grinning. His face grew serious. "You'd better take good care of my girl," he added, nodding to Claire.

"I don't need to be told that," Nolan said with a sigh.

"Good." Oberon slapped Collin on the back. "Time to get you guys back home."

"Yeah," Kane said with a sigh. "Guess we missed graduation . . . and all the parties!"

"Oh, shit!" Collin slapped himself on the head. "Briana! She's gonna kill me!"

"Nah," Oberon said. "You'll make it. Time is a little disjointed between this world and yours. You'll find you've probably only been gone a couple of hours."

"Cool!"

"Are you coming to graduation?" Claire asked.

"Of course," Oberon responded. "I worked my ass off for that diploma."

"Will you be back soon?" Finn asked. He stood off from the group of teens, holding Kian's hand. "We will miss you."

"Miss me?" Oberon smiled at his bond-mate. "You're my date to the after graduation party."

"I will be honored." Finn's eyes went limpid.

"I want to come! I want to come!" Kian mewed. He

rushed to grab Nolan's hand. "I will be your . . . date."

Nolan began to sputter.

"Only if you're my date as well," Claire said quickly, jabbing Nolan in the side.

"Kid," Nolan began. "Those pointy ears aren't—"

Before he could finish Kian had transformed himself to human form.

"I can go now?"

"But . . ." Nolan turned to Claire for help. "Nobody knows him. It'll be too—"

"Don't be silly, Nolan," Claire said, pulling Kian into her arms. "He's Ron's other cousin . . . Finn's little brother."

"But . . ."

"That's settled." Claire gave Nolan her case-closed look. "Besides, Johnny Brogan's little brother will be there."

"You mean . . ."

"Exactly," Claire said with a nod.

"Claire!" Oberon whooped. "Don't you think Kian and Teddy Brogan are a little young to be—"

"Pipe down, Maguire," Nolan said, nodding to Claire in agreement. "Teddy Brogan's perfect. He's definitely . . ." He rocked his open hand back and forth to make the point. "You know . . ."

"Teddy Brogan's gay?" Collin cocked his head to one side.

"I don't care if he's a freakin' alien," Nolan said. "He's more Kian's age and . . ."

"I care nothing for this . . . this Teddy human," Kian said, eyes blazing with disdain. "I love Lord Nolan, and I will be true—"

"Sweetheart," Claire interrupted. "Teddy Brogan's a gorgeous boy . . ."

"He's into gymnastics." Nolan said as if that statement

alone was enough.

"Muscular," Claire continued, "dark-haired, sweet . . ."

"Sweet?" Kian asked.

"Like honey," Claire said with a seductive smile.

"Oooooo!" Kian trembled with excitement. "I will meet him then."

"Kian!" Finn snapped.

The boy *Fey*'s eyes went down and his hands clasped in front of him.

"My Lord," Kian whispered, chastised.

"Finn!" Oberon spun the White Wing around to face him. "Leave the boy alone."

Finn's eyes widened. "But . . ."

"He's old enough. The boy has acted like a man." Oberon took Finn's face in his hands. "He deserves love." Oberon's amethyst eyes looked deeply into Finn's silver ones. Now tell me you love me."

Finn's face softened to a smile.

"I love you, my *Sciathán Corcra*," Finn whispered, closing his eyes.

Oberon's lips settled on Finn's. Still holding Finn's lips to his, Ron glanced over to his friends. He winked at Kian.

Kian screeched, clapping his hands with joy. His silvery wings unfurled and his tunic melted into light. With youthful abandon, he darted in a joyous, naked dance about the platform.

"Aw, crap," Nolan said, sighing.

"What, sweetheart," Claire asked, taking Nolan's hand in hers.

Nolan shook his head at the naked boy swirling about them.

"I hope he doesn't do this at the party."

Epilogue

It's me, Oberon . . . Ron Maguire. I am the *Sciathán Corcra*, the *Fei* Purple Wing. I mean that literally. I live between two worlds—mine and yours. My adopted mother is a witch. I mean that literally, too. My real parents were the noblest of the fairy people. I love both my families. My essence is *Fey*, the goddess light. My mind is decidedly human, because that is how I was raised. My soul . . . well, who really knows what the soul is and who can say if mine is different from yours.

I will tell you that there was a great war on another plane in another dimension of space and time. By a great treachery, the father of my light was murdered, and my people were hunted down—forced to flee their homeland into exile. Many of our seed were placed under a powerful spell and became changelings—*Fei* essence imprisoned in a human body—placed in the care of human families to hide them from the hunters and to keep them safe. They walk among you, look like you, think like you, but love a little differently.

I've written my story as a message—a call to self-examination. Perhaps you have sensed that you do not belong where you are—that you are out of place in some way. Perhaps you are drawn to others like you—those who think, feel, and have the same physical attraction as you. There are aspects of your life that you do not understand— things that set you apart, that put you in danger, or that drive a wedge between you and your human family.

I have sent out emissaries from *Faerie*, the *Fei* nation, into your world, seeking out our lost children. I have decreed that this supernatural and painful diaspora must end. I will put an end to their suffering. I will restore these lost descendants to their birthright of light and love.

Perhaps you are one of the beloved changelings we are searching for. If so, take heart. There will come a time when one of my *Fey* may recognize you, spot you in a crowd, meet you at a party, or come up to you on a street.

Be open. Be aware. Be in hope.

Stay your course and don't despair.

I will bring you home.

Bealtaine Grá fhaigheann tú.

May love find you.

"Faeries, come take me out of this dull world,
For I would ride with you upon the wind,
Run on the top of the disheveled tide,
And dance upon the mountains like a flame."

W.B. Yeats, *The Land of Heart's Desire*